THE MODERN LIBRARY
OF THE WORLD'S BEST BOOKS

SELECTED SHORT STORIES OF
Isaac Bashevis Singer

SELECTED SHORT STORIES OF *Isaac Bashevis Singer*

Edited and Introduced by

IRVING HOWE

Professor of English at

Hunter College of the City University of New York

THE MODERN LIBRARY

New York

FIRST MODERN LIBRARY EDITION, *February, 1966*

 Published in New York by Random House, Inc., and simultaneously in Toronto, Canada, by Random House of Canada Limited.

Library of Congress Catalog Card Number: 66-13012

Reprinted by arrangement with Farrar, Straus and Giroux, Inc.

MANUFACTURED IN THE UNITED STATES OF AMERICA

THE MODERN LIBRARY

is published by

RANDOM HOUSE, INC.

BENNETT CERF DONALD S. KLOPFER

Introduction

The Stories of I. B. Singer

INTERVIEWERS: Would it be fair to say that you are actually writing in a somewhat artificial or illusory context, as if none of the terrible things that have happened to the Jewish people during the last two decades really did occur?

SINGER: Yes, very fair. There was a famous philosopher, Vaihinger, who wrote a book called *The Philosophy of "As If,"* in which he showed that we all behave "as if." The "as if" is so much a part of our life that it really isn't artificial. . . . Every man assumes he will go on living. He behaves *as if* he will never die. So I wouldn't call my attitude artificial. It's very natural and healthy. We have to go on living and writing.

INTERVIEWERS: But do you agree that at the heart of your attitude there is an illusion which is consciously sustained?

SINGER: Yes.*

* This and the following direct statements by Isaac Bashevis Singer are from an interview that appeared in *Commentary,* November, 1963.

No other living writer has yielded himself so completely and recklessly as has Isaac Bashevis Singer to the claims of the human imagination. Singer writes in Yiddish, a language that no amount of energy or affection seems likely to save from extinction. He writes about a world that is gone, destroyed with a brutality beyond historical comparison. He writes within a culture, the remnant of Yiddish in the Western world, that is more than a little dubious about his purpose and stress. He seems to take entirely for granted his role as a traditional storyteller speaking to an audience attuned to his every hint and nuance, an audience that values storytelling both in its own right and as a binding communal action—but also, as it happens, an audience that keeps fading week by week, shrinking day by day. And he does all this without a sigh or apology, without so much as a Jewish groan. It strikes one as a kind of inspired madness: here is a man living in New York City, a sophisticated and clever writer, who composes stories about Frampol, Bilgoray, Kreshev *as if they were still there*. His work is shot through with the bravado of a performer who enjoys making his listeners gasp, weep, laugh and yearn for more. Above and beyond everything else he is a great performer, in ways that remind one of Twain, Dickens, Sholom Aleichem.

Singer writes Yiddish prose with a verbal and rhythmic brilliance that, to my knowledge, can hardly be matched. When Eliezer Greenberg and I were working on our *Treasury of Yiddish Stories*, he said to me: "Singer has to be heard, to be believed." Behind the prose there is always a spoken voice, tense, ironic, complex in tonalities, leaping past connectives. Greenberg then read to me, with a fluency and pith I could never capture in my own reading of Yiddish, Singer's masterpiece "Gimpel the Fool," and I knew at once—it took no great powers of judgment—that here was the work of a master. The story came as a stroke of revelation, like a fiction by Babel or Kleist encountered for the first time.

Singer's stories claim attention through their vivacity and strangeness of surface. He is devoted to the grotesque, the demonic, the erotic, the quasi-mystical. He populates his alien subworld with imps, devils, whores, fanatics, charlatans, spirits in seizure, disciples of false messiahs. A young girl is captured by the spirit of a dead woman and goes to live with the mourning husband as if she were actually his wife; a town is courted and then shattered by a lavish stranger who turns out to be the devil; an ancient Jew suffering unspeakable deprivations during the First World War, crawls back to his village of Bilgoray and fathers a son whom, with marvelous aplomb, he names Isaac. Sometimes the action in Singer's stories follows the moral curve of traditional folk tales, with a charming, lightly-phrased "lesson" at the end; sometimes, the spiral of a quizzical modern awareness; at best, the complicated motions of the old and the contemporary yoked together, a kind of narrative double-stop.

Orgiastic lapses from the moral order, pacts with the devil, ascetic self-punishments, distraught sexuality occupy the foreground of Singer's stories. Yet behind this expressionist clamor there is glimpsed the world of the *shtetl,* or East European Jewish village, as it stumbled and slept through the last few centuries. Though Singer seldom portrays it full-face, one must always keep this world in mind while reading his stories: it forms the base from which he wanders, the norm from which he deviates but which controls his deviation. And truly to hear these stories one must have at least a splinter of knowledge about the culture from which Singer comes, the world he continues to evoke as if it were still radiantly alive: the Hasidim still dancing, the rabbis still pondering, the children still studying, the poor still hungering, as if it had not all ended in ashes and death.

II

Isaac Bashevis Singer was born in Radzymin, Poland, in 1904. Both his father and grandfather were rabbis, in the tradition of Hasidism, a kind of ecstatic pietism, though on his mother's side the *misnagid* or rationalist strain of Jewish belief was the stronger. "My father," recalls Singer, "always used to say that if you don't believe in the *zaddikim* [the "wonder-rabbis" of Hasidism] today, tomorrow you won't believe in God. My mother would say, it's one thing to believe in God and another to believe in man. My mother's point of view is also my point of view."

Raised in a poor neighborhood of Warsaw, on Krochmalna Street, Singer received a strictly traditional Jewish education. He studied in a rabbinical seminary which "was a kind of college" providing secular as well as religious studies. During his adolescence he spent three or four years in his grandfather's *shtetl,* Bilgoray, which would later show itself as a strong influence upon his work. Bilgoray

> was very old-fashioned. Not much had changed there in many generations. In this town the traditions of hundreds of years ago still lived. There was no railroad nearby. It was stuck in the forest and it was pretty much as it must have been during the time of Chmielnicki. . . . I could have written *The Family Moskat* [a novel set in Warsaw] without having lived in Bilgoray, but I could never have written *Satan in Goray* [a novelette dealing with seventeenth-century false messianism] or some of my short stories without having been there.

A decisive example was set by Singer's older brother, Israel Joshua, who began to write in his youth and would become a leading Yiddish novelist, author of *The Brothers Ashkenazi* and *Yashe Kolb.* Throughout a distinguished career, I. J. Singer would remain pretty much within the main lines of the Yiddish tradition, as to both moral and social attitudes, even though he was strongly influenced by contemporary Western writing, especially the kind of large-scale family novel popular in Europe at the turn of the century. Controlling the older Singer's fiction is the Jewish community, both as social framework and source of values; his style, fluent, relaxed and smooth, can be taken as a model for cultivated modern Yiddish. The older brother represents that which I. B. Singer learned from, struggled with and then mostly left behind. In the Jewish world of Warsaw during the time Singer was growing up, a decision to become a secular writer meant a painful conflict with family and culture, a symbolic break from the paths of tradition:

> It was a great shock to [my parents]. They considered all the secular [Yiddish] writers to be heretics, all unbelievers—they really were too, most of them. To become a *literat* was to them almost as bad as becoming a *meshumed,* one who forsakes the faith. My father used to say that secular writers like Peretz were leading the Jews to heresy. He said everything they wrote was against God. Even though Peretz wrote in a religious vein, my father called his writing "sweetened poison," but poison nevertheless. And from his point of view, he was right. Everybody who read such books sooner or later became a worldly man and forsook the traditions. In my family, of course, my brother had gone first, and I went after him. For my parents, this was a tragedy.

In these early years of the century Warsaw was a lively if troubled city, the main center of Jewish cultural life. The binding tradition of Yiddish literature had already been set by the pioneer generation of writers: Mendele Mocher Sforim, Sholom Aleichem, I. L. Peretz. It was a literature strongly devoted to problems of communal destiny and survival; characterized by a high, sometimes consuming ethical intent; closely tied to folk sources; drawing profoundly upon, even as it kept moving away from, religious tradition; resting upon a culture that might still be described as "organic" and certainly as coherent; and yet displaying many signs of the influence of European, especially Russian, writing. In Warsaw the major social and cultural movements of East European Jewish life found their most sophisticated versions: Yiddishism, the effort to create an autonomous secular culture based on the language of *galut;* Bundism, the organization of a distinctively Jewish socialism; and Zionism, potentially of great importance but at this point still weak. Peretz's home became the gathering place for young writers fresh from the provinces where the majority of Jews still lived; here, in this cosmopolitan haven, they could begin planning their novels and stories about the overwhelming memory of the *shtetl.* And the religious community, though now challenged from several directions and past the high point of its power, remain a major force within the world of the East European Jews.

Growing up in this feverish but immensely stimulating atmosphere, the young Singer carved out a path of his own. He was not drawn to any of the Jewish movements: indeed, he has always been skeptical of the political messianism which, as a partial offshoot of the earlier religious messianism, runs through twentieth-century Jewish life. He edged away from formal piety, yet remained close to the Jewish religious tradition, especially its more esoteric and cabalistic elements. And while a master of the Yiddish language—he is second only to Sholom Aleichem in his command of its idiom—Singer was neither a programmatic Yiddishist nor notably at ease in the world of Yiddish culture, which has in the main been secular and rationalist in stress.

As a youth Singer began to read in forbidden tongues, discovering E. T. A. Hoffmann and Edgar Allan Poe in the libraries of Warsaw. The exotic romanticism of these writers stirred his imagination rather more than did the work of most Yiddish writers, who were then in a realistic or even naturalistic phase, and with whose materials he felt all too familiar. An even stronger alien influence was that of Knut Hamsun, the Norwegian novelist who enjoyed an international vogue during the years before World War II. Hamsun's novels, especially *Pan,* impressed upon the younger Singer the claims of the irrational in human existence, the power of the perverse within seemingly normal behavior. Now, several decades later, it is hard to see much evidence of Hamsun in Singer's work; perhaps it was the kind of influence that does not leave a visible stamp but instead liberates a writer to go his own way.

A still more alien influence—for a young Jewish writer fresh from the yeshiva, an influence downright bizarre—was that curious body of writings known as spiritualism or "psychic research," which Singer somehow came upon in Warsaw and would continue to follow throughout his life. Could anything be more distant from the tradition of Yiddish literature or, for that matter, from the whole body of Jewish religious thought? Fortunately for his career as a writer, Singer has preserved a keen Jewish skepticism—in that department he is entirely traditional! —toward this branch of "knowledge," taking the sophisticated view that belief in the reality of spirits provides his fiction with a kind of compositional shorthand, a "spiritual stenography." As he remarks: "the demons and Satan represent to me, in a sense, the ways of the world. Instead of saying this is the way things happen, I will say, this is the way demons behave." Which is precisely what any cultivated skeptic, totally unconcerned with "psychic research," would also say.

In 1935, convinced that "it was inevitable after Hitler came to power that the Germans would invade Poland," Singer emigrated to the United States. He joined the staff of the *Jewish Daily Forward,* a Yiddish newspaper, in which he printed serious fiction under his own name and a large quantity of journalism under the pen name of Warshofsky. His first major work, the novella *Satan in*

Goray, appeared in Yiddish in 1935. Since then he has written full-scale novels, one of which, *The Family Moskat,* was published in an English translation in 1949, as well as a number of short novels (English titles: *The Magician of Lublin* and *The Slave*) and several collections of stories. His best work has been done in short forms, the novella and the story—exciting bursts and flares of the imagination.

III

Isaac Bashevis Singer is the only living Yiddish writer whose translated work has caught the imagination of the American literary public. Though the settings of his stories are frequently strange, the contemporary reader —for whom the determination not to be shocked has become a point of honor—is likely to feel closer to Singer than to most other Yiddish writers. Offhand this may be surprising, for Singer's subjects are decidedly remote and exotic: in *Satan in Goray* the orgiastic consequences of the false messianism of seventeenth-century East European Jewish life; in *The Magician of Lublin* a portrait of a Jewish magician–Don Juan in late-nineteenth-century Poland who exhausts himself in sensuality and ends as a penitent ascetic; in his stories a range of demonic, apocalyptic and perversely sacred moments of *shtetl* life. Yet one feels that, unlike many of the Yiddish writers who treat more familiar and up-to-date subjects, Singer commands a distinctly "modern" sensibility.

Now this is partly true—in the sense that Singer has cut himself off from some of the traditional styles and assumptions of Yiddish writing. But it is also not true—in the sense that any effort to assimilate Singer to literary "modernism" without fully registering his involvement with Jewish faith and history, is almost certain to distort his meanings.

Those meanings, one might as well admit, are often

enigmatic and hard to come by. It must be a common experience among Singer's readers to find a quick pleasure in the caustic surfaces of his prose, the nervous tokens of his virtuosity, but then to acknowledge themselves baffled as to his point and purpose. That his fiction does have an insistent point and stringent purpose no one can doubt: Singer is too ruthlessly single-minded a writer to content himself with mere slices of representation or displays of the bizarre. His grotesquerie must be taken seriously, perhaps as a recoil from his perception of how ugly—how irremediably and gratuitously ugly—human life can be. He is a writer completely absorbed by the demands of his vision, a vision gnomic and compulsive but with moments of high exaltation; so that while reading his stories one feels as if one were overhearing bits and snatches of monologue, the impact of which is both notable and disturbing, but the meaning withheld.

Now these are precisely the qualities that the sophisticated reader, trained to docility before the exactions of "modernism," has come to applaud. Singer's stories work, or prey, upon the nerves. They leave one unsettled and anxious, the way a rationalist might feel if, waking at night in the woods, he suddenly found himself surrounded by a swarm of bats. Unlike most Yiddish fiction, Singer's stories neither round out the cycle of their intentions nor posit a coherent and ordered universe. They can be seen as paradigms of the arbitrariness, the grating injustice, at the heart of life. They offer instances of pointless suffering, dead-end exhaustion, inexplicable grace. And sometimes, as in Singer's masterpiece, "Gimpel the Fool," they turn about, refusing to rest with the familiar discomforts of the problematic, and drive toward a prospect of salvation on the other side of despair, beyond soiling by error or will. This prospect does not depend on any belief in the comeliness or lawfulness of the universe; whether God is there or not, He is surely no protector. ("He had worked out his own religion," writes Singer about one of his characters. "There was a Creator, but He revealed himself to no one, gave no indications of what was permitted or forbidden.") Things happen, the probable bad and improbable good, both of them subject to the whim of the fortuitous—and the sacred fools like Gimpel, perhaps they alone, learn to roll with the punch, finding the value of their life in a total passivity and credulousness, a complete openness to suffering.

Singer's stories trace the characteristic motions of human destiny: a heavy climb upward ("The Old Man"), a rapid tumble downward ("The Fast"). Life forms a journeying to heaven and hell, mostly hell. What determines the direction a man will take? Sometimes the delicate maneuvers between his will and desire, sometimes the heat of his vanity, sometimes the blessing of innocence. But more often than not, it is all a mystery which Singer chooses to present rather than explain. As his figures move upward and downward, aflame with the passion of their ineluctable destiny, they stop for a moment in the *shtetl* world. Singer is not content with the limitations of materiality, yet not at all indifferent to the charms and powers of the phenomenal universe. In his calculus of destiny, however, the world is a resting-place and what happens within it, even within the social enclave of the Jews, is not of lasting significance. Thick, substantial and attractive as it comes to seem in Singer's representation, the world is finally but lure and appearance, a locale between heaven and hell, the shadow of larger possibilities.

In most Yiddish fiction the stress is quite different. There the central "character" is the collective destiny of the Jews in *galut,* or exile; the central theme, the survival of a nation deprived of nationhood; the central ethic, the humane education of men stripped of worldly power yet sustained by the memory of chosenness and the promise of redemption. In Singer the norm of collective life is still present, but mostly in the background, as a tacit assumption; his central actions break away from the limits of the *shtetl* ethic, what has come to be known as *Yiddishkeit,* and then move either backward to the abandon of false messianism or forward to the doubt of modern sensibility. (There is an interesting exception, the story called "Short Friday," which in its stress upon family affection, ritual proprieties and collective faith, approaches rather closely the tones of traditional Yiddish fiction.)

The historical settings of East European Jewish life are richly presented in Singer's stories, often not as orderly sequences in time but as simultaneous perceptions jumbled together in the consciousness of figures for whom Abraham's sacrifice, Chmielnicki's pogroms, the rise and fall of Hasidism and the stirrings of the modern world are all felt with equal force. Yet Singer's ultimate concern is not with the collective experience of a chosen martyred people but with the enigmas of personal fate. Given the slant of his vision, this leads him to place a heavy reliance upon the grotesque as a mode of narration, even as an avenue toward knowledge. But the grotesque carries with it a number of literary and moral dangers, not the least being the temptation for Singer to make it into an end in itself, which is to say, something facile and sensationalistic. In his second-rank stories he falls back a little too comfortably upon the devices of which he is absolute master, like a magician supremely confident his tricks will continue to work. But mainly the grotesque succeeds in Singer's stories because it comes to symbolize meaningful digressions from a cultural norm. An uninstructed reader may absorb Singer's grotesquerie somewhat too easily into the assumptions of modern literature; the reader who grasps the ambivalence of Singer's relation to Yiddish literature will see the grotesquerie as a cultural sign by means of which Singer defines himself against his own past.

It is hardly a secret that in the Yiddish literary world Singer is regarded with a certain suspicion. His powers of evocation, his resources as a stylist are acknowledged, yet many Yiddish literary people, including the serious ones, seem uneasy about him. One reason is that "modernism"—which, as these people regard Singer, signifies a heavy stress upon sexuality, a concern for the irrational, expressionist distortions of character and a seeming indifference to the humane ethic of Yiddishism—has never won so strong a hold in Jewish culture as it has in the cultures of most Western countries. For Yiddish writers, "modernism" has been at best an adornment of manner upon a subject inescapably traditional.

The truly "modern" writer, however, is not quite trustworthy in relation to his culture. He is a shifty character by choice and need, unable to settle into that solid representativeness which would allow him to act as a cultural "spokesman." And to the extent that Singer does share in the modernist outlook he must be regarded with distrust by Yiddish readers brought up on such literary "spokesmen" as Peretz, Abraham Reisen and H. Leivick. There is no lack of admiration among Yiddish readers for Singer's work: anyone with half an ear for the cadence and idiom of that marvelous language must respond to his prose. Still, it is a qualified, a troubled admiration. Singer's moral outlook, which seems to move with equal readiness toward the sensational and the ascetic, is hardly calculated to put Yiddish readers at their ease. So they continue to read him, with pleasure and anxiety.

And as it seems to me, they are not altogether wrong. Their admiring resistance to Singer's work may constitute a more attentive and serious response to his iconoclasm than the gleeful applause of those who read him in English translation and take him to be another writer of "black comedy," or, heaven help us, a mid-twentieth century "swinger."

IV

The death of Satan was a tragedy for the imagination.

Anyone with even a smattering of Yiddish should try to read Singer's stories in the original. By and large he has been fortunate in his translators, but no translation, not even Saul Bellow's magnificent rendering of "Gimpel the Fool," could possibly suggest the full idiomatic richness and syntactical verve of Singer's Yiddish. Singer has left behind him the oratorical sententiousness to which Yiddish literature is prone, has abandoned its leisurely meandering pace, what might be called the *shtetl* rhythm, and has developed a style that is both swift and dense, nervous and thick. His sentences are short and abrupt; his rhythms coiled, intense, short-breathed. The impression his prose creates is not of a smooth and equable flow of language but rather a series of staccato advances and withdrawals, with sharp breaks between sentences. Singer seldom qualifies, wanders or circles back; his method is to keep darting forward, impression upon impression, through a series of jabbing declarative sentences. His prose is free of "literary" effects, a frequent weakness among Yiddish writers who wish to display their elegance and cultivation. And at the base of his prose is the oral idiom of Yiddish, seeded with ironic proverbs and apothegms ("Shoulders are from God, and burdens too"); but a speech that has been clipped, wrenched, syncopated.

What is most remarkable about Singer's prose is his ability to combine rich detail with fiercely compressed rhythms. For the translator this presents the almost insuperable problem of how to capture both his texture and his pace, his density of specification and his vibrating quickness. More often than not, even the most accomplished translator must choose between one effect and the other, if only because the enormous difficulty of rendering Yiddish idiom into another language forces him either to fill out or slow down Singer's sentences.

By its very nature, pace cannot be illustrated, but the richness of Singer's detail can. As in this characteristic passage from "The Old Man":

His son had died long before, and Reb Moshe Ber said the memorial prayer, *kaddish,* for him. Now alone in the apartment, he had to feed his stove with paper and wood shavings from garbage cans. In the ashes he baked rotten potatoes, which he carried in his scarf, and in an iron pot, he brewed chicory. He kept house, made his own candles by kneading bits of wax and suet around wicks, laundered his shirt beneath the kitchen faucet, and hung it to dry on a piece of string. He set the mousetraps each night and drowned the mice each morning. When he went out he never forgot to fasten the heavy padlock on the door. No one had to pay rent in Warsaw at that time. . . .

The winter was difficult. There was no coal, and since several tiles were missing from the stove, the apartment was filled with thick black smoke each time the old man made a fire. A crust of blue ice and snow covered the window panes by November, making the rooms constantly dark or dusky. Overnight, the water on his night table froze in the pot. No matter how many clothes he piled over him in bed, he never felt warm; his feet remained stiff, and as soon as he began to doze, the entire pile of clothes would fall off, and he would have to climb out naked to make his bed once more. There was no kerosene; even matches were at a premium. Although he recited chapter upon chapter of the Psalms, he could not fall asleep. The wind, freely roaming about the rooms, banged the doors; even the mice left.

Or, in a more colorful vein, from "The Last Demon":

I [the last demon] came here from Lublin. Tishevitz is a God-forsaken village: Adam didn't even stop to pee there.

It's so small that a wagon goes through town and the horse is in the market place just as the rear wheels reach the toll gate. There is mud in Tishevitz from Succoth until Tishe b'Ov. The goats of the town don't need to lift their beards to chew at the thatched roofs of the cottages. Hens roost in the middle of the streets. Birds build nests in the women's bonnets. In the tailor's synagogue a billy goat is the tenth in the quorum.

Or, grotesquely, from "Blood":

Frequently she sang for hours in Yiddish and in Polish. Her voice was harsh and cracked and she invented the songs as she went along, repeating meaningless phrases, uttering sounds that resembled the cackling of fowl, the grunting of pigs, the death-rattles of oxen. . . . At night in her dreams, phantoms tormented her: bulls gored her with their horns; pigs shoved their snouts into her face and bit her; roosters cut her flesh to ribbons with their spurs.

Or, tenderly, from "Gimpel the Fool":

I was an orphan. My grandfather who brought me up was already bent toward the grave. So they turned me over to a baker, and what a time they gave me there! Every woman or girl who came to bake a batch of noodles had to fool me at least once. "Gimpel, there's a fair in heaven; Gimpel, the rabbi gave birth to a calf in the seventh month; Gimpel, a cow flew over the roof and laid brass eggs." A student from the yeshiva came once to buy a roll, and he said, "You, Gimpel, while you stand here scraping with your baker's shovel the Messiah has come. The dead have arisen." "What do you mean?" I said. "I heard no one blowing the ram's horn!" He said, "Are you deaf?" And all began to cry, "We heard it, we heard! . . ."

To tell the truth, I knew very well that nothing of the sort had happened, but all the same, as folks were talking, I threw on my wool vest and went out. Maybe something had happened. What did I stand to lose by looking? Well, what a cat music went up! And then I took a vow to believe nothing more. But that was no go either. They confused me so that I didn't know the big end from the small.

Those of Singer's stories which speed downward into hell are often told by devils and imps, sometimes by Satan himself, marveling at the vanity and paltriness of the human creature. Singer's arch-devil is a figure not so much of evil as of skepticism, a thoroughly modern voice to whose corrosive questions Singer imparts notable force in "A Tale of Two Liars":

Are you stupid enough to still believe in the power of prayer? Remember how the Jews prayed during the Black Plague, and nevertheless, how they perished like flies? And what about the thousands the Cossacks butchered? There was enough prayer, wasn't there, when Chmielnicki came? How were those prayers answered? Children were buried alive, chaste wives raped—and later their bellies ripped open and cats sewed inside. Why should God bother with your prayers? He neither hears nor sees. There is no judge. There is no judgment.

Using demons and imps as narrators proves to be a wonderful device for structural economy: they replace the need to enter the "inner life" of the characters, the whole plaguing business of the psychology of motives, for they serve as symbolic equivalents and co-ordinates to human conduct, what Singer calls a "spiritual stenography." In those stories, however, where Singer celebrates the power of human endurance, as in "The Little Shoemakers" and "The Old Man," he uses third person narrative in the closest he comes to a "high style," so that the rhetorical elevation will help to create an effect of "epical" sweep.

Within his limits Singer is a genius. He has total command of his imagined world; he is original in his use both of traditional Jewish materials and in his modernist attitude toward them; he provides a serious if enigmatic moral perspective; and he is a master of Yiddish prose.

Yet there are times when Singer seems to be mired in his own originality, stories in which he displays a weakness for self-imitation that is disconcerting. Second-rate writers imitate others, first-rate writers themselves, and it is not always clear which is the more dangerous.

v

Having gone this far, we must now turn again. If Singer's work can be grasped only on the assumption that he is crucially a "modernist" writer, one must add that in other ways he remains profoundly subject to the Jewish tradition. And if the Yiddish reader is inclined to slight the "modernist" side of his work, the American reader is likely to underestimate the traditional side.

One of the elements in the Jewish past that has most fascinated Singer is the recurrent tendency to break loose from the burden of the Mosaic law and, through the urging of will and ecstasy, declare an end to the *galut*. Historically, this has taken the form of a series of messianic movements, one led in the seventeenth century by Sabbatai Zevi and another in the eighteenth by Jacob Frank. The movement of Sabbatai Zevi appeared after the East European Jewish community had been shattered by the rebellion-pogrom of the Cossack chieftain, Chmielnicki. Many of the survivors, caught up in a strange ecstasy that derived all too clearly from their total desperation, began to summon apocalytic fantasies and to indulge themselves in long-repressed religious emotions which, perversely, were stimulated by the pressures of cabalistic asceticism. As if in response to their yearnings, Sabbatai, a pretender rising in the Middle East, offered to release them of everything that rabbinical Judaism had confined or suppressed. He spoke for the tempting doctrine that faith is sufficient for salvation; for the wish to evade the limits of mundane life by forcing a religious transcendence; for the union of erotic with mystical appetites; for the lure of a demonism which the very hopelessness of the Jewish situation rendered plausible. In 1665-66 Sabbatianism came to orgiastic climax, whole communities, out of a conviction that the Messiah was in sight, discarding the moral inhibitions of exile. Their hopes were soon brutally disappointed, for Sabbatai, persecuted by the Turkish Sultan, converted to Mohammedanism. His followers were thrown into confusion and despair, and a resurgent rabbinism again took control over Jewish life. Nevertheless, Sabbatianism continued to lead an underground existence among the East European Jews—even, I have been told by *shtetl* survivors, into the late nineteenth and early twentieth century. It became a secret heretical cult celebrating Sabbatai as the apostate savior who had been required to descend to the depths of the world to achieve the heights of salvation.

To this buried strand of Jewish experience Singer has been drawn in fascination and repulsion, portraying its manifestations with great vividness and its consequences with stern judgment. It is a kind of experience that rarely figures in traditional Yiddish writing, yet is a significant aspect of the Jewish past. Bringing this material to contemporary readers, Singer writes *in* Yiddish but often quite apart from the Yiddish tradition; indeed, he is one of the few Yiddish writers whose relation to the Jewish past is not determined or screened by that body of values we call Yiddishism.

Singer is a writer of both the pre-Enlightenment and the post-Enlightenment: he would be equally at home with a congregation of Medieval Jews and a gathering of twentieth-century intellectuals, perhaps more so than at a meeting of the Yiddish P.E.N. club. He has a strong sense of the mystical and antique, but also a cool awareness of psychoanalytic disenchantment. He has evaded both the religious pieties and the humane rationalism of nineteenth-century East European Judaism. He has skipped over the ideas of the historical epoch which gave rise to Yiddishism, for the truth is, I suppose, that Yiddish literature, in both its writers of acceptance and writers of skepticism, is thoroughly caught up with the Enlightenment. Singer is not. He shares very little in the collective sensibility or the *folkstimlichkeit* of the Yiddish masters; he does not unambiguously celebrate *dos kleine menshele* (the common man) as a paragon of goodness; he is impatient with the sensual deprivations implicit in the values of *edelkeit* (refinement, nobility); and above all he moves away from a central assumption of both Yiddish literature in particular and the nineteenth century in general, the assumption of an immanent fate or end in human existence (what in Yiddish is called *tachlis*).

But again qualifications are needed. It is one thing to decide to break from a tradition in which one has been raised, quite another to make the break completely. For Singer has his ties—slender, subterranean but strong—with the very Yiddish writers from whom he has turned away.

At the center of Yiddish fiction stands the archetypal figures of *dos kleine menshele*. It is he, long-suffering, persistent, lovingly ironic, whom the Yiddish writers celebrate. This poor but proud householder trying to maintain his status in the *shtetl* world even as he keeps sinking deeper and deeper into poverty, appeals to the Yiddish imagination far more than mighty figures like Aeneas or Ahab. And from this representative man of the *shtetl* there emerges a number of significant variations. One extreme variation is the ecstatic wanderer, hopeless in this world because profoundly committed to the other. An equally extreme variation is the wise or sainted fool who has given up the struggle for status and thereby acquired the wry perspective of an outsider. Standing somewhere between *dos kleine menshele* and these offshoots is Peretz's Bontsha Schweig, whose intolerable humbleness makes even the angels in heaven feel guilty and embarrassed. Singer's Gimpel is a literary grandson (perhaps only on one side) of Peretz's Bontsha; and as Gimpel, with the piling up of his foolishness, acquires a halo of comic sadness and comes to seem an epitome of pure spirit, one must keep balancing in one's mind the ways in which he is akin to, yet different from, Bontsha.

The Yiddish critic Shlomo Bickel has perceptively remarked that Singer's dominating principle is an "anti-Prometheanism," a disbelief in the efficacy of striving, defiance and pride, a doubt as to the sufficiency of knowledge or even wisdom. This seems true, but only if one remembers that in a good many of Singer's fictions the central action does constitute a kind of Promethean ordeal or striving. Singer makes it abundantly clear that his characters have no choice: they must live out their desires, their orgiastic yearnings, their apocalyptic expectations. "Anti-Prometheanism" thus comes to rest upon a belief in the unavoidable recurrence of the Promethean urge.

What finally concerns Singer most is the possibilities for life that remain after the exhaustion of human effort, after failure and despair have come and gone. Singer watches his stricken figures from a certain distance, with enigmatic intent and no great outpouring of sympathy, almost as if to say that before such collapse neither judgment nor sympathy matters very much. Yet in all of his fictions the Promethean effort recurs, obsessional, churning with new energy and delusion. In the knowledge that it will, that it must recur, there may also lie hidden a kind of pity, for that too we would expect, and learn to find, in the writer who created Gimpel.

IRVING HOWE

Contents

FROM THE SPINOZA OF MARKET STREET

FROM SHORT FRIDAY

SELECTED SHORT STORIES OF

Isaac Bashevis Singer

Gimpel the Fool

I

I am Gimpel the fool. I don't think myself a fool. On the contrary. But that's what folks call me. They gave me the name while I was still in school. I had seven names in all: imbecile, donkey, flax-head, dope, glump, ninny, and fool. The last name stuck. What did my foolishness consist of? I was easy to take in. They said, "Gimpel, you know the rabbi's wife has been brought to childbed?" So I skipped school. Well, it turned out to be a lie. How was I supposed to know? She hadn't had a big belly. But I never looked at her belly. Was that really so foolish? The gang laughed and hee-hawed, stomped and danced and chanted a good-night prayer. And instead of the raisins they give when a woman's lying in, they stuffed my hand full of goat turds. I was no weakling. If I slapped someone he'd see all the way to Cracow. But I'm really not a slugger by nature. I think to myself: Let it pass. So they take advantage of me.

I was coming home from school and heard a dog barking. I'm not afraid of dogs, but of course I never want to start up with them. One of them may be mad, and if he bites there's not a Tartar in the world who can help you. So I made tracks. Then I looked around and saw the whole market place wild with laughter. It was no dog at all but Wolf-Leib the Thief. How was I supposed to know it was he? It sounded like a howling bitch.

When the pranksters and leg-pullers found that I was easy to fool, every one of them tried his luck with me. "Gimpel, the Czar is coming to Frampol; Gimpel, the moon fell down in Turbeen; Gimpel, little Hodel Furpiece found a treasure behind the bathhouse." And I like a golem believed everyone. In the first place, everything is possible, as it is written in the Wisdom of the Fathers, I've forgotten just how. Second, I had to believe when the whole town came down on me! If I ever dared to say, "Ah, you're kidding!" there was trouble. People got angry. "What do you mean! You want to call everyone a liar? " What was I to do? I believed them, and I hope at least that did them some good.

I was an orphan. My grandfather who brought me up was already bent toward the grave. So they turned me over to a baker, and what a time they gave me there! Every woman or girl who came to bake a batch of noodles had to fool me at least once. "Gimpel, there's a fair in heaven; Gimpel, the rabbi gave birth to a calf in the seventh month; Gimpel, a cow flew over the roof and laid brass eggs." A student from the yeshiva came once to buy a roll, and he said, "You, Gimpel, while you stand here scraping with your baker's shovel the Messiah has come. The dead have arisen." "What do you mean? " I said. "I heard no one blowing the ram's horn! " He said, "Are you deaf?" And all began to cry, "We heard it, we heard!" Then in came Rietze the Candle-dipper and called out in her hoarse voice, "Gimpel, your father and mother have stood up from the grave. They're looking for you."

To tell the truth, I knew very well that nothing of the sort had happened, but all the same, as folks were talking, I threw on my wool vest and went out. Maybe something had happened. What did I stand to lose by looking? Well, what a cat music went up! And then I took a vow to believe nothing more. But that was no go either. They confused me so that I didn't know the big end from the small.

I went to the rabbi to get some advice. He said, "It is written, better to be a fool all your days than for one hour to be evil. You are not a fool. They are the fools. For he who causes his neighbor to feel shame loses Paradise himself." Nevertheless the rabbi's daughter took me in. As I left the rabbinical court she said, "Have you kissed the wall yet?" I said, "No; what for?" She answered, "It's the law; you've got to do it after every visit." Well, there didn't seem to be any harm in it. And she burst out laughing. It was a fine trick. She put one over on me, all right.

I wanted to go off to another town, but then everyone got busy matchmaking, and they were after me so they nearly tore my coat tails off. They talked at me and talked until I got water on the ear. She was no chaste maiden, but they told me she was virgin pure. She had a limp, and they said it was deliberate, from coyness. She had a bastard, and they told me the child was her little brother. I cried, "You're wasting your time. I'll never marry that whore." But they said indignantly, "What a way to talk! Aren't you ashamed of yourself? We can take you to the rabbi and have you fined for giving her a bad name." I saw then that I wouldn't escape them so easily and I thought: They're set on making me their butt. But when you're married the husband's the master, and if that's all right with her it's agreeable to me too. Besides, you can't pass through life unscathed, nor expect to.

I went to her clay house, which was built on the sand, and the whole gang, hollering and chorusing, came after me. They acted like bear-baiters. When we came to the well they stopped all the same. They were afraid to start anything with Elka. Her mouth would open as if it were on a hinge, and she had a fierce tongue. I entered the house. Lines were strung from wall to wall and clothes were drying. Barefoot she stood by the tub, doing the wash. She was dressed in a worn hand-me-down gown of plush. She had her hair put up in braids and pinned across her head. It took my breath away, almost, the reek of it all.

Evidently she knew who I was. She took a look at me and said, "Look who's here! He's come, the drip. Grab a seat."

I told her all; I denied nothing. "Tell me the truth," I said, "are you really a virgin, and is that mischievous Yechiel actually your little brother? Don't be deceitful with me, for I'm an orphan."

"I'm an orphan myself," she answered, "and whoever tries to twist you up, may the end of his nose take a twist. But don't let them think they can take advantage of me. I want a dowry of fifty guilders, and let them take up a collection besides. Otherwise they can kiss my you-know-what." She was very plainspoken. I said, "It's the bride and not the groom who gives a dowry." Then she said, "Don't bargain with me. Either a flat 'yes' or a flat 'no'— Go back where you came from."

I thought: No bread will ever be baked from *this* dough. But ours is not a poor town. They consented to everything and proceeded with the wedding. It so happened that there was a dysentery epidemic at the time. The ceremony was held at the cemetery gates, near the little corpse-washing hut. The fellows got drunk. While the marriage contract was being drawn up I heard the most pious high rabbi ask, "Is the bride a widow or a divorced woman?" And the sexton's wife answered for her, "Both a widow and divorced." It was a black moment for me. But what was I to do, run away from under the marriage canopy?

There was singing and dancing. An old granny danced opposite me, hugging a braided white *chalah*. The master of revels made a "God 'a mercy" in memory of the bride's parents. The schoolboys threw burrs, as on Tishe b'Av fast day. There were a lot of gifts after the sermon: a noodle board, a knealing trough, a bucket, brooms, ladles, household articles galore. Then I took a look and saw two strapping young men carrying a crib. "What do we need this for?" I asked. So they said, "Don't rack your brains about it. It's all right, it'll come in handy." I realized I was going to be rooked. Take it another way though, what did I stand to lose? I reflected: I'll see what comes of it. A whole town can't go altogether crazy.

II

At night I came where my wife lay, but she wouldn't let me in. "Say, look here, is this what they married us for?" I said. And she said, "My monthly has come." "But yesterday they took you to the ritual bath, and that's afterward, isn't it supposed to be?" "Today isn't yesterday," said she, "and yesterday's not today. You can beat it if you don't like it." In short, I waited.

Not four months later she was in childbed. The townsfolk hid their laughter with their knuckles. But what could I do? She suffered intolerable pains and clawed at the walls. "Gimpel," she cried, "I'm going. Forgive me." The house filled with women. They were boiling pans of water. The screams rose to the welkin.

The thing to do was to go to the House of Prayer to repeat Psalms, and that was what I did.

The townsfolk liked that, all right. I stood in a corner saying Psalms and prayers, and they shook their heads at me. "Pray, pray!" they told me. "Prayer never made any woman pregnant." One of the congregation put a straw to my mouth and said, "Hay for the cows." There was something to that too, by God!

She gave birth to a boy. Friday at the synagogue the sexton stood up before the Ark, pounded on the reading table, and announced, "The wealthy Reb Gimpel invites the congregation to a feast in honor of the birth of a son." The whole House of Prayer rang with laughter. My face was flaming. But there was nothing I could do. After all, I *was* the one responsible for the circumcision honors and rituals.

Half the town came running. You couldn't wedge another soul in. Women brought peppered chick-peas, and there was a keg of beer from the tavern. I ate and drank as much as anyone, and they all congratulated me. Then there was a circumcision, and I named the boy after my father, may he rest in peace. When all were gone and I was left with my wife alone, she thrust her head through the bed-curtain and called me to her.

"Gimpel," said she, "why are you silent? Has your ship gone and sunk?"

"What shall I say?" I answered. "A fine thing you've done to me! If my mother had known of it she'd have died a second time."

She said, "Are you crazy, or what?"

"How can you make such a fool," I said, "of one who should be the lord and master?"

"What's the matter with you?" she said. "What have you taken it into your head to imagine?"

I saw that I must speak bluntly and openly. "Do you think this is the way to use an orphan?" I said. "You have borne a bastard."

She answered, "Drive this foolishness out of your head. The child is yours."

"How can he be mine?" I argued. "He was born seventeen weeks after the wedding."

She told me then that he was premature. I said, "Isn't

he a little too premature?" She said, she had had a grandmother who carried just as short a time and she resembled this grandmother of hers as one drop of water does another. She swore to it with such oaths that you would have believed a peasant at the fair if he had used them. To tell the plain truth, I didn't believe her; but when I talked it over next day with the schoolmaster he told me that the very same thing had happened to Adam and Eve. Two they went up to bed and four they descended.

"There isn't a woman in the world who is not the granddaughter of Eve," he said.

That was how it was; they argued me dumb. But then, who really knows how such things are?

I began to forget my sorrow. I loved the child madly, and he loved me too. As soon as he saw me he'd wave his little hands and want me to pick him up, and when he was colicky I was the only one who could pacify him. I bought him a little bone teething ring and a little gilded cap. He was forever catching the evil eye from someone, and then I had to run to get one of those abracadabras for him that would get him out of it. I worked like an ox. You know how expenses go up when there's an infant in the house. I don't want to lie about it; I didn't dislike Elka either, for that matter. She swore at me and cursed, and I couldn't get enough of her. What strength she had! One of her looks could rob you of the power of speech. And her orations! Pitch and sulphur, that's what they were full of, and yet somehow also full of charm. I adored her every word. She gave me bloody wounds though.

In the evening I brought her a white loaf as well as a dark one, and also poppyseed rolls I baked myself. I thieved because of her and swiped everything I could lay hands on: macaroons, raisins, almonds, cakes. I hope I may be forgiven for stealing from the Saturday pots the women left to warm in the baker's oven. I would take out scraps of meat, a chunk of pudding, a chicken leg or head, a piece of tripe, whatever I could nip quickly. She ate and became fat and handsome.

I had to sleep away from home all during the week, at the bakery. On Friday nights when I got home she always made an excuse of some sort. Either she had heartburn, or a stitch in the side, or hiccups, or headaches. You know what women's excuses are. I had a bitter time of it. It was rough. To add to it, this little brother of hers, the bastard, was growing bigger. He'd put lumps on me, and when I wanted to hit back she'd open her mouth and curse so powerfully I saw a green haze floating before my eyes. Ten times a day she threatened to divorce me. Another man in my place would have taken French leave and disappeared. But I'm the type that bears it and says nothing. What's one to do? Shoulders are from God, and burdens too.

One night there was a calamity in the bakery; the oven burst, and we almost had a fire. There was nothing to do but go home, so I went home. Let me, I thought, also taste the joy of sleeping in bed in mid-week. I didn't want to wake the sleeping mite and tiptoed into the house. Coming in, it seemed to me that I heard not the snoring of one but, as it were, a double snore, one a thin enough snore and the other like the snoring of a slaughtered ox. Oh, I didn't like that! I didn't like it at all. I went up to the bed, and things suddenly turned black. Next to Elka lay a man's form. Another in my place would have made an uproar, and enough noise to rouse the whole town, but the thought occurred to me that I might wake the child. A little thing like that—why frighten a little swallow, I thought. All right then, I went back to the bakery and stretched out on a sack of flour and till morning I never shut an eye. I shivered as if I had had malaria. "Enough of being a donkey," I said to myself. "Gimpel isn't going to be a sucker all his life. There's a limit even to the foolishness of a fool like Gimpel."

In the morning I went to the rabbi to get advice, and it made a great commotion in the town. They sent the beadle for Elka right away. She came, carrying the child. And what do you think she did? She denied it, denied everything, bone and stone! "He's out of his head," she said. "I know nothing of dreams or divinations." They yelled at her, warned her, hammered on the table, but she stuck to her guns: it was a false accusation, she said.

The butchers and the horse-traders took her part. One of the lads from the slaughterhouse came by and said to me, "We've got our eye on you, you're a marked man." Meanwhile the child started to bear down and soiled itself. In the rabbinical court there was an Ark of the Covenant, and they couldn't allow that, so they sent Elka away.

I said to the rabbi, "What shall I do?"

"You must divorce her at once," said he.

"And what if she refuses? " I asked.

He said, "You must serve the divorce. That's all you'll have to do."

I said, "Well, all right, Rabbi. Let me think about it."

"There's nothing to think about," said he. "You mustn't remain under the same roof with her."

"And what if she refuses?" I asked.

"Let her go, the harlot," said he, "and her brood of bastards with her."

The verdict he gave was that I mustn't even cross her threshold—never again, as long as I should live.

During the day it didn't bother me so much. I thought: It was bound to happen, the abscess had to burst. But at night when I stretched out upon the sacks I felt it all very bitterly. A longing took me, for her and for the child. I wanted to be angry, but that's my misfortune exactly, I don't have it in me to be really angry. In the first place—this was how my thoughts went—there's bound to be a slip sometimes. You can't live without errors. Probably that lad who was with her led her on and gave her presents and what not, and women are often long on hair and short on sense, and so he got around her. And then since she denies it so, maybe I was only seeing things? Hallucinations do happen. You see a figure or a mannikin or something, but when you come up closer it's nothing, there's not a thing there. And if that's so, I'm doing her an injustice. And when I got so far in my thoughts I started to weep. I sobbed so that I wet the flour where I lay. In the morning I went to the rabbi and told him that I had made a mistake. The rabbi wrote on with his quill, and he said that if that were so he would have to reconsider the whole case. Until he had finished I wasn't to go near my wife, but I might send her bread and money by messenger.

III

Nine months passed before all the rabbis could come to an agreement. Letters went back and forth. I hadn't realized that there could be so much erudition about a matter like this.

Meanwhile Elka gave birth to still another child, a girl this time. On the Sabbath I went to the synagogue and invoked a blessing on her. They called me up to the Torah, and I named the child for my mother-in-law—may she rest in peace. The louts and loudmouths of the town who came into the bakery gave me a going over. All Frampol refreshed its spirits because of my trouble and grief. However, I resolved that I would always believe what I was told. What's the good of *not* believing? Today it's your wife you don't believe; tomorrow it's God Himself you won't take stock in.

By an apprentice who was her neighbor I sent her daily a corn or a wheat loaf, or a piece of pastry, rolls or bagels, or, when I got the chance, a slab of pudding, a slice of honeycake, or wedding strudel—whatever came my way.

The apprentice was a goodhearted lad, and more than once he added something on his own. He had formerly annoyed me a lot, plucking my nose and digging me in the ribs, but when he started to be a visitor to my house he became kind and friendly, "Hey, you, Gimpel," he said to me, "you have a very decent little wife and two fine kids. You don't deserve them."

"But the things people say about her," I said.

"Well, they have long tongues," he said, "and nothing to do with them but babble. Ignore it as you ignore the cold of last winter."

One day the rabbi sent for me and said, "Are you certain, Gimpel, that you were wrong about your wife?"

I said, "I'm certain."

"Why, but look here! You yourself saw it."

"It must have been a shadow," I said.

"The shadow of what?"

"Just of one of the beams, I think."

"You can go home then. You owe thanks to the Yanover rabbi. He found an obscure reference in Maimonides that favored you."

I seized the rabbi's hand and kissed it.

I wanted to run home immediately. It's no small thing to be separated for so long a time from wife and child. Then I reflected: I'd better go back to work now, and go home in the evening. I said nothing to anyone, although as far as my heart was concerned it was like one of the Holy Days. The women teased and twitted me as they did every day, but my thought was: Go on, with your loose talk. The truth is out, like the oil upon the water. Maimonides says it's right, and therefore it is right!

At night, when I had covered the dough to let it rise, I took my share of bread and a little sack of flour and started homeward. The moon was full and the stars were glistening, something to terrify the soul. I hurried onward, and before me darted a long shadow. It was winter, and a fresh snow had fallen. I had a mind to sing, but it was growing late and I didn't want to wake the householders. Then I felt like whistling, but I remembered that you don't whistle at night because it brings the demons out. So I was silent and walked as fast as I could.

Dogs in the Christian yards barked at me when I passed, but I thought: Bark your teeth out! What are you but mere dogs? Whereas I am a man, the husband of a fine wife, the father of promising children.

As I approached the house my heart started to pound as though it were the heart of a criminal. I felt no fear, but my heart went thump! thump! Well, no drawing back. I quietly lifted the latch and went in. Elka was asleep. I looked at the infant's cradle. The shutter was closed, but the moon forced its way through the cracks. I saw the newborn child's face and loved it as soon as I saw it—immediately—each tiny bone.

Then I came nearer to the bed. And what did I see but the apprentice lying there beside Elka. The moon went out all at once. It was utterly black, and I trembled. My teeth chattered. The bread fell from my hands, and my wife waked and said, "Who is that, ah?"

I muttered, "It's me."

"Gimpel?" she asked. "How come you're here? I thought it was forbidden."

"The rabbi said," I answered and shook as with a fever.

"Listen to me, Gimpel," she said, "go out to the shed and see if the goat's all right. It seems she's been sick." I have forgotten to say that we had a goat. When I heard she was unwell I went into the yard. The nannygoat was a good little creature. I had a nearly human feeling for her.

With hesitant steps I went up to the shed and opened the door. The goat stood there on her four feet. I felt her everywhere, drew her by the horns, examined her udders, and found nothing wrong. She had probably eaten too much bark. "Good night, little goat," I said. "Keep well." And the little beast answered with a "Maa" as though to thank me for the good will.

I went back. The apprentice had vanished.

"Where," I asked, "is the lad?"

"What lad?" my wife answered.

"What do you mean?" I said. "The apprentice. You were sleeping with him."

"The things I have dreamed this night and the night before," she said, "may they come true and lay you low, body and soul! An evil spirit has taken root in you and dazzles your sight." She screamed out, "You hateful creature! You moon calf! You spook! You uncouth man! Get out, or I'll scream all Frampol out of bed!"

Before I could move, her brother sprang out from behind the oven and struck me a blow on the back of the head. I thought he had broken my neck. I felt that something about me was deeply wrong, and I said, "Don't make a scandal. All that's needed now is that people should accuse me of raising spooks and *dybbuks.*" For that was what she had meant. "No one will touch bread of my baking."

In short, I somehow calmed her.

"Well," she said, "that's enough. Lie down, and be shattered by wheels."

Next morning I called the apprentice aside. "Listen here, brother!" I said. And so on and so forth. "What do you say?" He stared at me as though I had dropped from the roof or something.

"I swear," he said, "you'd better go to an herb doctor or some healer. I'm afraid you have a screw loose, but I'll hush it up for you." And that's how the thing stood.

To make a long story short, I lived twenty years with my wife. She bore me six children, four daughters and two sons. All kinds of things happened, but I neither saw nor heard. I believed, and that's all. The rabbi recently said to me, "Belief in itself is beneficial. It is written that a good man lives by his faith."

Suddenly my wife took sick. It began with a trifle, a little growth upon the breast. But she evidently was not destined to live long; she had no years. I spent a fortune on her. I have forgotten to say that by this time I had a bakery of my own and in Frampol was considered to be something of a rich man. Daily the healer came, and every witch doctor in the neighborhood was brought. They decided to use leeches, and after that to try cupping. They even called a doctor from Lublin, but it was too late. Before she died she called me to her bed and said, "Forgive me, Gimpel."

I said, "What is there to forgive? You have been a good and faithful wife."

"Woe, Gimpel!" she said. "It was ugly how I deceived you all these years. I want to go clean to my Maker, and so I have to tell you that the children are not yours."

If I had been clouted on the head with a piece of wood it couldn't have bewildered me more.

"Whose are they?" I asked.

"I don't know," she said. "There were a lot . . . but they're not yours." And as she spoke she tossed her head to the side, her eyes turned glassy, and it was all up with Elka. On her whitened lips there remained a smile.

I imagined that, dead as she was, she was saying, "I deceived Gimpel. That was the meaning of my brief life."

IV

One night, when the period of mourning was done, as I lay dreaming on the flour sacks, there came the Spirit of Evil himself and said to me, "Gimpel, why do you sleep?"

I said, "What should I be doing? Eating *kreplach?*"

"The whole world deceives you," he said, "and you ought to deceive the world in your turn."

"How can I deceive all the world?" I asked him.

He answered, "You might accumulate a bucket of urine every day and at night pour it into the dough. Let the sages of Frampol eat filth."

"What about the judgment in the world to come?" I said.

"There is no world to come," he said. "They've sold you a bill of goods and talked you into believing you carried a cat in your belly. What nonsense!"

"Well then," I said, "and is there a God?"

He answered, "There is no God either."

"What," I said, "*is* there, then?"

"A thick mire."

He stood before my eyes with a goatish beard and horn, long-toothed, and with a tail. Hearing such words, I wanted to snatch him by the tail, but I tumbled from the flour sacks and nearly broke a rib. Then it happened that I had to answer the call of nature, and, passing, I saw the risen dough, which seemed to say to me, "Do it!" In brief, I let myself be persuaded.

At dawn the apprentice came. We kneaded the bread, scattered caraway seeds on it, and set it to bake. Then the apprentice went away, and I was left sitting in the little trench by the oven, on a pile of rags. Well, Gimpel, I thought, you've revenged yourself on them for all the shame they've put on you. Outside the frost glittered, but it was warm beside the oven. The flames heated my face. I bent my head and fell into a doze.

I saw in a dream, at once, Elka in her shroud. She called to me, "What have you done, Gimpel?"

I said to her, "It's all your fault," and started to cry.

"You fool!" she said. "You fool! Because I was false is everything false too? I never deceived anyone but myself. I'm paying for it all, Gimpel. They spare you nothing here."

I looked at her face. It was black; I was startled and waked, and remained sitting dumb. I sensed that everything hung in the balance. A false step now and I'd lose Eternal Life. But God gave me His help. I seized the long shovel and took out the loaves, carried them into the yard, and started to dig a hole in the frozen earth.

My apprentice came back as I was doing it. "What are you doing boss?" he said, and grew pale as a corpse.

"I know what I'm doing," I said, and I buried it all before his very eyes.

Then I went home, took my hoard from its hiding place, and divided it among the children. "I saw your mother tonight," I said. "She's turning black, poor thing."

They were so astounded they couldn't speak a word.

"Be well," I said, "and forget that such a one as Gimpel ever existed." I put on my short coat, a pair of boots, took the bag that held my prayer shawl in one hand, my stock in the other, and kissed the *mezzuzah*. When people saw me in the street they were greatly surprised.

"Where are you going?" they said.

I answered, "Into the world." And so I departed from Frampol.

I wandered over the land, and good people did not neglect me. After many years I became old and white; I heard a great deal, many lies and falsehoods, but the longer I lived the more I understood that there were really no lies. Whatever doesn't really happen is dreamed at night. It happens to one if it doesn't happen to another, tomorrow if not today, or a century hence if not next year. What difference can it make? Often I heard tales of which I said, "Now this is a thing that cannot happen." But before a year had elapsed I heard that it actually had come to pass somewhere.

Going from place to place, eating at strange tables, it often happens that I spin yarns—improbable things that could never have happened—about devils, magicians, windmills, and the like. The children run after me, calling, "Grandfather, tell us a story." Sometimes they ask for particular stories, and I try to please them. A fat young boy once said to me, "Grandfather, it's the same story you told us before." The little rogue, he was right.

So it is with dreams too. It is many years since I left Frampol, but as soon as I shut my eyes I am there again. And whom do you think I see? Elka. She is standing by the washtub, as at our first encounter, but her face is shining and her eyes are as radiant as the eyes of a saint, and she speaks outlandish words to me, strange things. When I wake I have forgotten it all. But while the dream lasts I am comforted. She answers all my queries, and what comes out is that all is right. I weep and implore, "Let me be with you." And she consoles me and tells me to be patient. The time is nearer than it is far. Sometimes she strokes and kisses me and weeps upon my face. When I awaken I feel her lips and taste the salt of her tears.

No doubt the world is entirely an imaginary world, but it is only once removed from the true world. At the door of the hotel where I lie, there stands the plank on which the dead are taken away. The gravedigger Jew has his spade ready. The grave waits and the worms are hungry; the shrouds are prepared—I carry them in my beggar's sack. Another *shnorrer* is waiting to inherit my bed of straw. When the time comes I will go joyfully. Whatever may be there, it will be real, without complication, without ridicule, without deception. God be praised: there even Gimpel cannot be deceived.

Translated by Saul Bellow

The Gentleman from Cracow

I

Amid thick forests and deep swamps, on the slope of a hill, level at the summit, lay the village of Frampol. Nobody knew who had founded it, or why just there. Goats grazed among the tombstones which were already sunk in the ground of the cemetery. In the community house there was a parchment with a chronicle on it, but the first page was missing and the writing had faded. Legends were current among the people, tales of wicked intrigue concerning a mad nobleman, a lascivious lady, a Jewish scholar, and a wild dog. But their true origin was lost in the past.

Peasants who tilled the surrounding countryside were poor; the land was stubborn. In the village, the Jews were impoverished; their roofs were straw, their floors dirt. In summer many of them wore no shoes, and in cold weather they wrapped their feet in rags or wore sandals made of straw.

Rabbi Ozer, although renowned for his erudition, received a salary of only eighteen groszy a week. The assistant rabbi, besides being ritual slaughterer, was teacher, matchmaker, bath attendant, and poorhouse nurse as well. Even those villagers who were considered wealthy knew little of luxury. They wore cotton gabardines, tied about their waists with string, and tasted meat only on the Sabbath. Gold coin was rarely seen in Frampol.

But the inhabitants of Frampol had been blessed with fine children. The boys grew tall and strong, the girls handsome. It was a mixed blessing, however, for the young men left to marry girls from other towns, while their sisters, who had no dowries, remained unwed. Yet despite everything, inexplicably, though the food was scarce and the water foul, the children continued to thrive.

Then, one summer, there was a drought. Even the oldest peasants could not recall a calamity such as this one. No rain fell. The corn was parched and stunted. There was scarcely anything worth harvesting. Not until the few sheaves of wheat had been cut and gathered did the rain come, and with it hail which destroyed whatever grain the drought had spared. Locusts huge as birds came in the wake of the storm; human voices were said to issue from their throats. They flew at the eyes of the peasants who tried to drive them away. That year there was no fair, for everything had been lost. Neither the peasants nor the Jews of Frampol had food. Although there was grain in the large towns, no one could buy it.

Just when all hope had been abandoned and the entire town was about to go begging, a miracle occurred. A carriage drawn by eight spirited horses, came into Frampol. The villagers expected its occupant to be a Christian gentleman, but it was a Jew, a young man between the ages of twenty and thirty, who alighted. Tall and pale, with a round black beard and fiery dark eyes, he wore a sable hat, silver-buckled shoes, and a beaver-trimmed caftan. Around his waist was a green silk sash. Aroused, the entire town rushed to get a glimpse of the stranger. This is the story he told: He was a doctor, a widower from Cracow. His wife, the daughter of a wealthy merchant, had died with their baby in childbirth.

Overwhelmed, the villagers asked why he had come to Frampol. It was on the advice of a Wonder Rabbi, he told them. The melancholy he had known after his wife's death, would, the rabbi assured him, disappear in Frampol. From the poorhouse the beggers came, crowding about him as he distributed alms—three groszy, six groszy, half-gulden pieces. The stranger was clearly a gift from Heaven, and Frampol was not destined to vanish. The beggars hurried to the baker for bread, and the baker sent to Zamosc for a sack of flour.

"One sack?" the young doctor asked. "Why that won't last a single day. I will order a wagonload, and not only flour, but cornmeal also."

"But we have no money," the village elders explained.

"God willing, you will repay me when times are good," and saying this, the stranger produced a purse crammed with golden ducats. Frampol rejoiced as he counted out the coins.

The next day, wagons filled with flour, buckwheat, barley, millet, and beans, drove into Frampol. News of the village's good fortune reached the ears of the peasants, and they came to the Jews, to buy goods, as the Egyptians had once come to Joseph. Being without money, they paid in kind; as a result, there was meat in town. Now the ovens burned once more; the pots were full. Smoke rose from the chimneys, sending the odors of roast chicken and goose, onion and garlic, fresh bread and pastry, into the evening air. The villagers returned to their occupations; shoemakers mended shoes; tailors picked up their rusted shears and irons.

The evenings were warm and the sky clear, though the Feast of the Tabernacles had already passed. The stars seemed unusually large. Even the birds were awake, and they chirped and warbled as though in midsummer. The stranger from Cracow had taken the best room at the inn, and his dinner consisted of broiled duck, marchpane, and twisted bread. Apricots and Hungarian wine were his dessert. Six candles adorned the table. One evening after dinner, the doctor from Cracow entered the large public room where some of the more inquisitive townspeople had gathered and asked,

"Would anyone care for a game of cards?"

"But it isn't Chanukah yet," they answered in surprise.

"Why wait for Chanukah? I'll put up a gulden for every groszy."

A few of the more frivolous men were willing to try their luck, and it turned out to be good. A groszy meant a gulden, and one gulden became thirty. Anyone played who wished to do so. Everybody won. But the stranger did not seem distressed. Banknotes and coins of silver and gold covered the table. Women and girls crowded into the room, and it seemed as though the gleam of the gold before them was reflected in their eyes. They gasped in wonderment. Never before in Frampol had such things happened. Mothers cautioned their daughters to take pains with their hair, and allowed them to dress in holiday clothes. The girl who found favor in the eyes of the young doctor would be fortunate; he was not one to require a dowry.

II

The next morning, matchmakers called on him, each extolling the virtues of the girl he represented. The doctor invited them to be seated, served them honey cake, macaroons, nuts, and mead, and announced:

"From each of you I get exactly the same story: Your client is beautiful and clever and possesses every possible distinction. But how can I know which of you is telling the truth? I want the finest of them all as my wife. Here is what I suggest: Let there be a ball to which all the eligible young women are invited. By observing their appearance and behavior, I shall be able to choose among them. Then the marriage contract will be drawn and the wedding arranged."

The matchmakers were astounded. Old Mendel was the first to find words. "A ball? That sort of thing is all right for rich Gentiles, but we Jews have not indulged in such festivities since the destruction of the Temple—except when the Law prescribes it for certain holidays."

"Isn't every Jew obliged to marry off his daughters?" asked the doctor.

"But the girls have no appropriate clothes," another matchmaker protested. "Because of the drought they would have to go in rags."

"I will see that they all have clothes. I'll order enough silk, wool, velvet, and linen from Zamosc to outfit every girl. Let the ball take place. Let it be one that Frampol will never forget."

"But where can we hold it?" another matchmaker interjected. "The hall where we used to hold weddings has burned down, and our cottages are too small."

"There's the market place," the gentleman from Cracow suggested.

"But it is already the month of Heshvan. Any day now, it will turn cold."

"We'll choose a warm night when the moon is out. Don't worry about it."

To all the numerous objections of the matchmakers, the stranger had an answer ready. Finally they agreed to consult the elders. The doctor said he was in no hurry, he would await their decision. During the entire discussion, he had been carrying on a game of chess with one of the town's cleverest young men, while munching raisins.

The elders were incredulous when they heard what had been proposed. But the young girls were excited. The young men approved also. The mothers pretended to hesitate, but finally gave their consent. When a delegation of the older men sought out Rabbi Ozer for his approval, he was outraged.

"What kind of charlatan is this?" he shouted. "Frampol is not Cracow. All we need is a ball! Heaven forbid that we bring down a plague, and innocent infants be made to pay for our frivolity!"

But the more practical of the men reasoned with the rabbi, saying, "Our daughters walk around barefoot and in tatters now. He will provide them with shoes and clothing. If one of them should please him he would marry her and settle here. Certainly that is to our advantage. The synagogue needs a new roof. The windowpanes of the house of study are broken, the bathhouse is badly in need of repairs. In the poorhouse the sick lie on bundles of rotting straw."

"All this is true. But suppose we sin?"

"Everything will be done according to the Law, Rabbi. You can trust us."

Taking down the book of the Law, Rabbi Ozer leafed through it. Occasionally he stopped to study a page, and then, finally, after sighing and hesitating, he consented. Was there any choice? He himself had received no salary for six months.

As soon as the rabbi had given his consent there was a great display of activity. The dry goods merchants traveled immediately to Zamosc and Yanev, returning with cloth and leather paid for by the gentleman from Cracow. The tailors and seamstresses worked day and night; the cobblers left their benches only to pray. The young women, all anticipation, were in a feverish state. Vaguely remembered dance steps were tried out. They baked cakes and other pastries, and used up their stores of jams and preserves which they had been keeping in readiness for illness. The Frampol musicians were equally active. Cymbals, fiddles, and bagpipes, long forgotten and neglected, had to be dusted off and tuned. Gaiety infected even the very old, for it was rumored that the elegant doctor planned a banquet for the poor where alms would be distributed.

The eligible girls were wholly concerned with self-improvement. They scrubbed their skin and arranged their hair; a few even visited the ritual bath to bathe among the married women. In the evenings, faces flushed, eyes sparkling, they met at each other's houses, to tell stories and ask riddles. It was difficult for them, and for their mothers as well, to sleep at night. Fathers sighed as they slept. And suddenly the young girls of Frampol seemed so attractive that the young men who had contemplated marrying outside of town fell in love with them. Although the young men still sat in the study-house poring over the Talmud, its wisdom no longer penetrated to them. It was the ball alone that they spoke of now, only the ball that occupied their thoughts.

The doctor from Cracow also enjoyed himself. He changed his clothes several times daily. First it was a silk coat worn with pom-pommed slippers, then a woolen caftan with high boots. At one meal he wore a pelerine trimmed with beaver tails, and at the next a cape embroidered with flowers and leaves. He breakfasted on roast pigeon which he washed down with dry wine. For lunch he ordered egg noodles and blintzes, and he was audacious enough to eat Sabbath pudding on weekdays. He never attended prayer, but instead played all sorts of games: cards, goats and wolves, coin-pitching. Having finished lunch, he would drive through the neighborhood with his coachman. The peasants would lift their hats as he passed, and bow almost to the ground. One day he strolled through Frampol with a gold-headed cane. Women crowded to the windows to observe him, and boys, following after him, picked up the rock candy he tossed them. In the evenings he and his companions, gay young men, drank wine until all hours. Rabbi Ozer constantly warned his flock that they walked a downhill path led by the Evil One, but they paid no attention to him. Their minds and hearts were completely possessed by the ball, which would be held at the market place in the middle of that month, at the time of the full moon.

III

At the edge of town, in a small valley close to a swamp, stood a hut no larger than a chicken coop. Its floor was dirt, its window was boarded; and the roof, because it was covered with green and yellow moss, made one think of a bird's nest that had been forsaken. Heaps of garbage were strewn before the hut, and lime ditches furrowed the soggy earth. Amidst the refuse there was an occasional chair without a seat, a jug missing an ear, a table without legs. Every type of broom, bone, and rag seemed to be rotting there. This was where Lipa the Ragpicker lived with his daughter, Hodle. While his first wife was alive, Lipa had been a respected merchant in Frampol where he occupied a pew at the east wall of the synagogue. But after his wife had drowned herself in the river, his condition declined rapidly. He took to drink, associated with the town's worst element, and soon ended up bankrupt.

His second wife, a beggar woman from Yanev, bore him a daughter whom she left behind when she deserted him for non-support. Unconcerned about his wife's departure, Lipa allowed the child to shift for herself. Each week he spent a few days collecting rags from the garbage. The rest of the time he was in the tavern. Although the innkeeper's wife scolded him, she received only abusive answers in reply. Lipa had his success among the men as a tale-spinner. He attracted business to the place with his fantastic yarns about witches and windmills and devils and goblins. He could also recite Polish and Ukrainian rhymes and had a knack for telling jokes. The innkeeper allowed him to occupy a place near the stove, and from time to time he was given a bowl of soup and a piece of bread. Old friends, remembering Lipa's former affluence, occasionally presented him with a pair of pants, a threadbare coat, or a shirt. He accepted everything ungraciously. He even stuck out his tongue at his benefactors as they turned away from them.

As in the saying, "Like father, like son," Hodle inherited the vices of both parents—her drunken father, her begging mother. By the time she was six, she had won a reputation as a glutton and thief. Barefoot and half naked, she roamed the town, entering houses and raiding the larders of those who were not home. She preyed on chickens and ducks, cut their throats with glass, and ate them. Although the inhabitants of Frampol had often warned her father that he was rearing a wanton, the information did not seem to bother him. He seldom spoke to her and she did not even call him father. When she was twelve, her lasciviousness became a matter for discussion among the women. Gypsies visited her shack, and it was rumored that she devoured the meat of cats and dogs, in fact, every kind of carcass. Tall and lean, with red hair and green eyes, she went barefoot summer and winter, and her skirts were made of colored scraps discarded by the seamstresses. She was feared by mothers who said she wove spells that blighted the young. The village elders who admonished her received brazen answers. She had the shrewdness of a bastard, the quick tongue of an adder, and when attacked by street urchins, did not hesitate to strike back. Particularly skilled in swearing, she had an unlimited repertoire. It was like her to call out, "Pox on your tongue and gangrene in your eyes," or, possibly, "May you rot till the skunks run from your smell."

Occasionally her curses were effective, and the town grew wary of incurring her anger. But as she matured she tended to avoid the town proper, and the time came when she was almost forgotten. But on the day that the Frampol merchants, in preparation for the ball, distributed cloth and leather among the town's young women,

Hodle reappeared. She was now about seventeen, fully grown, though still in short skirts; her face was freckled, and her hair disheveled. Beads, such as those worn by gypsies, encircled her throat, and on her wrists were bracelets made from wolves' teeth. Pushing her way through the crowd, she demanded her share. There was nothing left but a few odds and ends, which were given to her. Furious with her allotment, she hastened home with it. Those who had seen what had happened laughed, "Look who's going to the ball! What a pretty picture she'll make!'

At last the shoemakers and tailors were done; every dress fit, every shoe was right. The days were miraculously warm, and the nights as luminous as the evenings of Pentecost. It was the morning star that, on the day of the ball, woke the entire town. Tables and benches lined one side of the market. The cooks had already roasted calves, sheep, goats, geese, ducks, and chicken, and had baked sponge and raisin cakes, braided bread and rolls, onion biscuits and ginger bread. There were mead and beer and a barrel of Hungarian wine that had been brought by the wine dealer. When the children arrived they brought the bows and arrows with which they were accustomed to play at the Omer feast, as well as their Purim rattles and Torah flags. Even the doctor's horses were decorated with willow branches and autumn flowers, and the coachman paraded them through the town. Apprentices left their work, and yeshiva students their volumes of the Talmud. And despite Rabbi Ozer's injunction against the young matrons' attending the ball, they dressed in their wedding gowns and went, arriving with the young girls, who also came in white, each bearing a candle in her hand as though she were a bridesmaid. The band had already begun to play, and the music was lively. Rabbi Ozer alone was not present, having locked himself in his study. His maidservant had gone to the ball, leaving him to himself. He knew no good could come of such behavior, but there was nothing he could do to prevent it.

By late afternoon all the girls had gathered in the market place, surrounded by the townspeople. Drums were beaten. Jesters performed. The girls danced; first a quadrille, then a scissor dance. Next it was Kozack, and finally the Dance of Anger. Now the moon appeared, although the sun had not yet set. It was time for the gentleman from Cracow. He entered on a white mare, flanked by bodyguards and his best man. He wore a large-plumed hat, and silver buttons flashed on his green coat. A sword hung at his side, and his shiny boots rested in the stirrups. He resembled a gentleman off to war with his entourage. Silently he sat in his saddle, watching the girls as they danced. How graceful they were, how charmingly they moved! But one who did not dance was the daughter of Lipa the Ragpicker. She stood to one side, ignored by them all.

IV

The setting sun, remarkably large, stared down angrily like a heavenly eye upon the Frampol market place. Never before had Frampol seen such a sunset. Like rivers of burning sulphur, fiery clouds streamed across the heavens, assuming the shapes of elephants, lions, snakes, and monsters. They seemed to be waging a battle in the sky, devouring one another, spitting, breathing fire. It almost seemed to be the River of Fire they watched, where demons tortured the evil-doers amidst glowing coals and heaps of ashes. The moon swelled, became vast, blood-red, spotted, scarred, and gave off little light. The evening grew very dark, dissolving even the stars. The young men fetched torches, and a barrel of burning pitch was prepared. Shadows danced back and forth as though attending a ball of their own. Around the market place the houses seemed to vibrate; roofs quivered, chimneys shook. Such gaiety and intoxication had never before been known in Frampol. Everyone, for the first time in months, had eaten and drunk sufficiently. Even the animals participated in the merrymaking. Horses neighed, cows mooed, and the few roosters that had survived the slaughter of the fowl crowed. Flocks of crows and strange birds flew in to pick at the leavings. Fireflies illumined the darkness, and lightning flashed on the horizon. But there was no thunder. A weird circular light glowed in the sky for a few moments and then suddenly plummeted toward the horizon, a crimson tail behind it, resembling a burning rod. Then, as everyone stared in wonder at the sky, the gentleman from Cracow spoke:

"Listen to me. I have wonderful things to tell you, but let no one be overcome by joy. Men, take hold of your wives. Young men, look to your girls. You see in me the wealthiest man in the entire world. Money is sand to me, and diamonds are pebbles. I come from the land of Ophir, where King Solomon found the gold for his temple. I dwell in the palace of the Queen of Sheba. My coach is solid gold, its wheels inlaid with sapphires, with axles of ivory, its lamps studded with rubies and emeralds, opals and amethysts. The Ruler of the Ten Lost Tribes of Israel knows of your miseries, and he has sent me to be your benefactor. But there is one condition. Tonight, every virgin must marry. I will provide a dowry of ten thousand ducats for each maiden, as well as a string of pearls that will hang to her knees. But make haste. Every girl must have a husband before the clocks strike twelve."

The crowd was hushed. It was as quiet as New Year's Day before the blowing of the ram's horn. One could hear the buzzing of a fly.

Then one old man called out, "But that's impossible. The girls are not even engaged!"

"Let them become engaged."

"To whom?"

"We can draw lots," the gentleman from Cracow replied. "Whoever is to be married will have his or her name written on a card. Mine also. And then we shall draw to see who is meant for whom."

"But a girl must wait seven days. She must have the prescribed ablutions."

"Let the sin be on me. She needn't wait."

Despite the protestations of the old men and their wives, a sheet of paper was torn into pieces, and on each piece the name of a young man or young woman was written by a scribe. The town's beadle, now in the service of the gentleman from Cracow, drew from one skullcap the names of the young men, and from another those of the young women, chanting their names to the same tune with which he called up members of the congregation for the reading of the Torah.

"Nahum, son of Katriel, betrothed to Yentel, daughter of Nathan. Solomon, son of Cov Baer, betrothed to Tryna, daughter of Jonah Lieb." The assortment was a strange one, but since in the night all sheep are black, the matches seemed reasonable enough. After each drawing, the newly engaged couple, hand in hand, approached the doctor to collect the dowry and wedding gift. As he had promised, the gentleman from Cracow gave each the stipulated sum of ducats, and on the neck of each bride he hung a strand of pearls. Now the mothers, unable to restrain their joy, began to dance and shout. The fathers stood by, bewildered. When the girls lifted their dresses to catch the gold coins given by the doctor, their legs and underclothing were exposed, which sent the men into paroxysms of lust. Fiddles screeched, drums pounded, trumpets blared. The uproar was deafening. Twelve-year-old boys were mated with "spinsters" of nineteen. The sons of substantial citizens took the daughters of paupers as brides; midgets were coupled with giants, beauties with cripples. On the last two slips appeared the names of the gentleman from Cracow and Hodle, the daughter of Lipa the Ragpicker.

The same old man who had called out previously said, "Woe unto us, the girl is a harlot."

"Come to me, Hodle, come to your bridegroom," the doctor bade.

Hodle, her hair in two long braids, dressed in a calico skirt, and with sandals on her feet, did not wait to be asked twice. As soon as she had been called she walked to where the gentleman from Cracow sat on his mare, and fell to her knees. She prostrated herself seven times before him.

"Is it true, what the old fool says?" her prospective husband asked her.

"Yes, my lord, it is so."

"Have you sinned only with Jews or with Gentiles as well?"

"With both."

"Was it for bread?"

"No. For the sheer pleasure."

"How old were you when you started?"

"Not quite ten."

"Are you sorry for what you have done?"

"No."

"Why not?"

"Why should I be?" she answered shamelessly.

"You don't fear the tortures of hell?"

"I fear nothing—not even God. There is no God."

Once more the old man began to scream, "Woe to us, woe to us, Jews! A fire is upon us, burning, Jews, Satan's fire. Save your souls, Jews. Flee, before it is too late!"

"Gag him," the gentleman from Cracow commanded.

The guards seized the old man and gagged him. The doctor, leading Hodle by the hand, began to dance. Now, as though the powers of darkness had been summoned, the rain and hail began to fall; flashes of lightning were accompanied by mighty thunderclaps. But, heedless of the storm, pious men and women embraced without shame, dancing and shouting as though possessed. Even the old were affected. In the furor, dresses were ripped, shoes shaken off, hats, wigs and skullcaps trampled in the mud. Sashes, slipping to the ground, twisted there like snakes. Suddenly there was a terrific crash. A huge bolt of lightning had simultaneously struck the synagogue, the study house, and the ritual bath. The whole town was on fire.

Now at last the deluded people realized that there was no natural origin to these occurrences. Although the rain continued to fall and even increased in intensity, the fire was not extinguished. An eerie light glowed in the market place. Those few prudent individuals who tried to disengage themselves from the demented crowd were crushed to earth and trampled.

And then the gentleman from Cracow revealed his true identity. He was no longer the young man the villagers had welcomed, but a creature covered with scales, with an eye in his chest, and on his forehead a horn that rotated at great speed. His arms were covered with hair, thorns, and elflocks, and his tail was a mass of live serpents, for he was none other than Ketev Mriri, Chief of the Devils.

Witches, werewolves, imps, demons, and hobgoblins plummeted from the sky, some on brooms, others on hoops, still others on spiders. Osnath, the daughter of Machlath, her fiery hair loosened in the wind, her breasts bare and thighs exposed, leaped from chimney to chimney, and skated along the eaves. Namah, Hurmizah the daughter of Aff, and many other she-devils did all sorts of somersaults. Satan himself gave away the bridegroom, while four evil spirits held the poles of the canopy, which had turned into writhing pythons. Four dogs escorted the groom. Hodle's dress fell from her and she stood naked. Her breasts hung down to her navel and her feet were webbed. Her hair was a wilderness of worms and caterpillars. The groom held out a triangular ring and, instead of saying, "With this ring be thou consecrated to me according to the laws of Moses and Israel," he said, "With this ring, be thou desecrated to me according to the blasphemy of Korah and Ishmael." And instead of wishing the pair good luck, the evil spirits called out, "Bad luck," and they began to chant:

"The curse of Eve, the Mark of Cain,
The cunning of the snake, unite the twain."

Screaming for the last time, the old man clutched at his head and died. Ketev Mriri began his eulogy:

"Devil's dung and Satan's spell
Bring his ghost to roast in hell."

V

In the middle of the night, old Rabbi Ozer awoke. Since he was a holy man, the fire which was consuming the town had no power over his house. Sitting up in bed he looked about, wondering if dawn were already breaking. But it was neither day nor night without. The sky was a fiery red, and from the distance came a clamor of shouts and songs that resembled the howling of wild beasts. At first, recalling nothing, the old man wondered what was going on. "Has the world come to an end? Or have I failed to hear the ram's horn heralding the Messiah? Has He arrived?" Washing his hands, he put on his slippers and overcoat and went out.

The town was unrecognizable. Where houses had been, only chimneys stood. Mounds of coal smoldered here and there. He called the beadle, but there was no answer. With his cane, the rabbi went searching for his flock.

"Where are you, Jews, where are you?" he called piteously.

The earth scorched his feet, but he did not slacken his pace. Mad dogs and strange beings attacked him, but he wielded his cane against them. His sorrow was so great that he felt no fear. Where the market place used to be, a terrible sight met him. There was nothing but one great swamp, full of mud, slime, and ashes. Floundering in mud up to their waists, a crowd of naked people went through the movements of dance. At first, the rabbi mistook the wierdly moving figures for devils, and was about to recite the chapter, "Let there be contentment," and other passages dealing with exorcism, when he recognized the men of his town. Only then did he remember the doctor from Cracow, and the rabbi cried out bitterly, "Jews, for the sake of God, save your souls! You are in the hands of Satan!"

But the townspeople, too entranced to heed his cries, continued their frenzied movements for a long time, jumping like frogs, shaking as though with fever. With hair uncovered and breasts bare, the women laughed, cried, and swayed. Catching a yeshiva boy by his sidelocks, a girl pulled him to her lap. A woman tugged at the beard of a strange man. Old men and women were immersed in slime up to their loins. They scarcely looked alive.

Relentlessly, the rabbi urged the people to resist evil. Reciting the Torah and other holy books, as well as incantations and the several names of God, he succeeded in rousing some of them. Soon others responded. The rabbi had helped the first man from the mire, then that one assisted the next, and so on. Most of them had recovered by the time the morning star appeared. Perhaps the spirits of their forbears had interceded, for although many had sinned, only one man had died this night in the market place square.

Now the men were appalled, realizing that the devil had bewitched them, had dragged them through muck; and they wept.

"Where is our money?" the girls wailed, "And our gold and our jewelry? Where is our clothing? What happened to the wine, the mead, the wedding gifts?"

But everything had turned to mud; the town of Frampol, stripped and ruined, had become a swamp. Its inhabitants were mud-splashed, denuded, monstrous. For a moment, forgetting their grief, they laughed at each other. The hair of the girls had turned into elflocks, and bats were entangled there. The young men had grown gray and wrinkled; the old were yellow as corpses. In their midst lay the old man who had died. Crimson with shame, the sun rose.

"Let us rend our clothes in mourning," one man called, but his words evoked laughter, for all were naked.

"We are doomed, my sisters," lamented a woman.

"Let us drown ourselves in the river," a girl shrieked, "Why go on living?"

One of the yeshiva boys said, "Let us strangle ourselves with our sashes."

"Brothers, we are lost. Let us blaspheme God," said a horse dealer.

"Have you lost your minds, Jews?" cried Rabbi Ozer, "Repent, before it is too late. You have fallen into Satan's snare, but it is my fault, I take the sin upon myself. I am the guilty one. I will be your scapegoat, and you shall remain clean."

"This is madness!" one of the scholars protested, "God forbid that there be so many sins on your holy head!"

"Do not worry about that. My shoulders are broad. I should have had more foresight. I was blind not to realize that the Cracow doctor was the Evil One. And when the shepherd is blind, the flock goes astray. It is I who deserve the punishment, the curses."

"Rabbi, what shall we do? We have no homes, no bed clothes, nothing. Woe to us, to our bodies and to our souls."

"Our babies!" cried the young matrons, "Let us hurry to them!"

But it was the infants who had been the real victims of the passion for gold that had caused the inhabitants of Frampol to transgress. The infants' cribs were burned, their little bones were charred. The mothers stooped to pick up little hands, feet, skulls. The wailing and crying lasted long, but how long can a whole town weep? The gravedigger gathered the bones and carried them to the cemetery. Half the town began the prescribed seven days of mourning. But all fasted, for there was no food anywhere.

But the compassion of the Jews is well known, and when the neighboring town of Yanev learned what had happened, clothing, bed linen, bread, cheese, and dishes were collected and sent to Frampol. Timber merchants brought logs for building. A rich man offered credit. The next day the reconstruction of the town was begun. Although work is forbidden to those in mourning, Rabbi Ozer issued a verdict that this was an exceptional case: the lives of the people were in danger. Miraculously, the weather remained mild; no snow fell. Never before had there been such diligence in Frampol. The inhabitants built and prayed, mixed lime with sand, and recited psalms. The women worked with the men, while girls, forgetting their fastidiousness, helped also. Scholars and men of high position assisted. Peasants from the surrounding villages, hearing of the catastrophe, took the old and infirm into their homes. They also brought wood, potatoes, cabbages, onions and other food. Priests and bishops from Lublin, hearing of events that suggested witchcraft, came to examine witnesses. As the scribe recorded the names of those living in Frampol, Hodle, the daughter of Lipa the Ragpicker, was suddenly remembered. But when the townspeople went to where her hut had been, they found the hill covered with weeds and bramble, silent save for the cries of crows and cats; there was no indication that human beings had ever dwelt there.

Then it was understood that Hodle was in truth Lilith, and that the host of the netherworld had come to Frampol because of her. After their investigations, the clergymen from Lublin, greatly astonished at what they had seen and heard, returned home. A few days later, the day before the Sabbath, Rabbi Ozer died. The entire town attended his funeral, and the town preacher said a eulogy for him.

In time, a new rabbi came to the community, and a new town arose. The old people died, the mounds in the cemetery sifted down, and the monuments slowly sank. But the story, signed by trustworthy witnesses, can still be read in the parchment chronicle.

And the events in the story brought their epilogue: the lust for gold had been stifled in Frampol; it was never rekindled. From generation to generation the people remained paupers. A gold coin became an abomination in Frampol, and even silver was looked at askance. Whenever a shoemaker or tailor asked too high a price for his work he was told, "Go to the gentleman from Cracow and he will give you buckets of gold."

And on the grave of Rabbi Ozer, in the memorial chapel, there burns an eternal light. A white pigeon is often seen on the roof: the sainted spirit of Rabbi Ozer.

Translated by Martha Glicklich
and Elaine Gottlieb

The Wife Killer

A FOLK TALE

I

I am from Turbin, and there we had a wife killer. Pelte was his name, Pelte the Wife Killer. He had four wives and, may it not be held against him, he sent them all off to the other side. What women saw in him, I don't know. He was a little man, thickset, gray, with a scraggly beard and bulging bloodshot eyes. Merely to look at him was frightful. And as for his stinginess—you never saw anything like it. Summer and winter he went about in the same padded caftan and rawhide boots. Yet he was rich. He had a sizeable brick house, a storeroom full of grain, and property in town. He had an oak chest which I remember to this day. It was covered with leather and bound with copper hoops, for protection in case of fire. To keep it safe from thieves, he had it nailed to the floor. It was said that he kept a fortune in it. All the same, I cannot understand how a woman could go to the bridal canopy with such a man. The first two wives at least had the excuse that they came from poor homes. The first one

—poor soul may you live long—was an orphan, and he took her just as she was, without any dowry. The second one, on the other hand—may she rest in peace—was a widow without a cent to her name. She didn't have even an undershirt, if you'll pardon the expression. Today people talk of love. They think that once upon a time men were angels. Nonsense. Clumsy creature that he was, he fell head over heels in love with her, so that all Turbin snickered. He was already a man in his forties and she was a mere child, eighteen years or even less. In short, kind souls intervened, relatives took a hand in the matter, and things came to a head.

Right after the wedding the young wife began to complain that he wasn't acting right. Strange tales were told —may God not punish me for my words. He was spiteful all the time. Before he went to pray in the morning, she would ask him. "What do you want for lunch? Soup or borscht?" "Soup," he might say. So she'd make him soup. He'd return later and complain, "Didn't I tell you to make borscht?" She'd argue, "You said yourself that you wanted soup." And he would say, "So now I am a liar!" And before you could turn around he was already in a rage, and would grab a slice of bread and a head of garlic, and run back to the synagogue to eat there. She would run after him and shout, "I'll cook you a borscht! Don't shame me before people!" But he wouldn't even look back. In the synagogue young men sat studying. "What happened that you eat here?" they would ask him. "My wife chased me out," he would say. To make a long story short, he drove her to the grave with his tantrums. When people advised her to divorce him, he threatened to run off and abandon her. Once he did run away and was caught on the Yanov road, near the turnpike. The woman saw that she was lost, so she simply lay down in bed and died. "I am dying because of him," she said. "May it not be held against him." The entire town was aroused. Some butchers and young bloods wanted to teach him a lesson, because she was of their class, but the community would not allow it—after all, he was a well-to-do man. The dead are buried, as people say, and what the earth swallows is soon forgotten.

Some years passed and he didn't remarry. Perhaps he didn't want to, perhaps there was no suitable opportunity; anyway, he remained a widower. Women gloated over this. He became even stingier than before, and so unkempt that it was positively disgusting. He ate a bit of meat only on Saturday: scraps or derma. All week he ate dry food. He baked his own bread of corn and bran. He didn't buy wood. Instead, he went out at night with a sack, to pick up the chips near the bakery. He had two deep pockets and whatever he saw, he put into them: bones, bark, string, shards. He hid all these in his attic. He piled heaps of stuff as high as the roof. "Every little thing comes in handy," he used to say. He was a scholar in the bargain, and could quote Scripture on every occasion, though as a rule he talked little.

Everybody thought he would remain alone the rest of his life. Suddenly the terrible news spread that he was engaged to Reb Falik's Finkl. How should I describe Finkl to you! She was the most beautiful woman in town, and of the very best family. Her father, Reb Falik, was a magnate. It was said that he bound his books in silk. Whenever a bride was led to the *mikveh,* the musicians would stop before his windows and play a tune. Finkl was his only child. There had been seven and she alone survived. Reb Falik married her off to a rich young man from Brod, one in a million, learned and wise, a real aristocrat. I saw him only once as he went by, with curly *peios* and a flowered caftan and fine shoes and white socks. Blood and milk. But it was fated otherwise. Right after the Seven Blessings he collapsed. Zishe the Healer was called, and he put leeches on him and bled him, but what can you do against fate? Reb Falik rushed a carriage to Lublin to bring a doctor, but Lublin is far, and before you knew it, it was all over with him. The entire town wept, as on Yom Kippur at Kol Nidre. The old rabbi—may he rest in peace—delivered the eulogy. I am only a sinful woman and I don't know much of learned matters, but I remember to this day what the rabbi said. Everybody memorized the eulogy. "He ordered black and got white . . ." the rabbi began. In the Gemorra this is about a man ordering pigeons, but the rabbi—peace be on him—made it mean wedding garments and burial shrouds. Even enemies mourned. We girls soaked our pillows at night. Finkl, delicate pampered Finkl, lost her speech in her great grief. Her mother was no longer living and Reb Falik, too, didn't survive long. Finkl inherited all his wealth, but what use was money? She refused to hear of anyone.

Suddenly we heard that Finkl was going to marry Pelte. The news came on a wintry Thursday evening, and a chill went through everyone. "The man is of the devil!" my mother cried out. "Such a one should be ridden out of town." We youngsters were petrified. I used to sleep by myself but that night I crawled into bed with my sister. I was in a fever. Later we learned that the match had been arranged by a man who was a bit of this and a bit of that and a general nuisance. It was said that he had borrowed a Gemorra from Pelte and found a hundred-ruble note among its pages. Pelte had a habit of hiding paper money in books. What one thing had to do with the other I didn't know—I was still a child then. But what difference does it make? Finkl consented. When God wants to punish someone, He deprives him of reason. People ran to her, they tore their hair trying to dissuade her, but she wouldn't change her mind. The wedding was on the Sabbath after Shevuoth. The canopy was set up before the synagogue, as is the custom when a virgin gets married, but it seemed to all of us that we were attending a funeral. I was in one of the two rows of girls who stand holding candles in their hands. It was a summer evening and the air was still, but when the groom was led past, the flames began to flicker. I shook with fear. The fiddles started to play a wedding tune, but it was a wail, not music that they made. The bass viol mourned. I wouldn't wish anyone ever to hear the like. To tell you the truth, I'd rather not go on with the story. It might give you nightmares, and I myself don't feel up to it. What? You do want to hear more. Very well. You will have to take me home. Tonight I won't walk home alone.

II

Where was I? Yes, Finkl got married. She looked more like a corpse than a bride. The bridesmaids had to support her. Who knows? Maybe she had changed her mind. But was it her fault? It was all from Above. I once heard of a bride who ran away from under the canopy. But not Finkl. She would rather be burned alive than humiliate anyone.

Need I tell you how it all ended? Can't you guess yourselves? May all the enemies of Israel come to such an end. I must say that this time he didn't pull his usual tricks. On the contrary, he tried to comfort her. But he gave off a black melancholy. She tried to lose herself in household duties. And young women came to visit her. There was a constant going back and forth, as with a woman in confinement. They told stories, they knitted, they sewed and asked riddles, anything to distract Finkl. Some even began to hint that perhaps it wasn't such an impossible match. He was rich, and a scholar too. Mightn't he become human living with her? It was reckoned that Finkl would become pregnant and have a baby and get used to her lot. Aren't there many unsuitable marriages in the world! But it wasn't fated that way. Finkl miscarried and had a hemorrhage. They had to bring a doctor from Zamoscz. He advised her to keep herself occupied. She did not become pregnant again, and then her troubles began. He tormented her, everybody knew that. But when she was asked: "What is he doing to you?" she would only say, "Nothing." "If he does nothing to you, why do you have such brown and blue rings around your eyes? And why do you go about like a lost soul?" But she would only say: "I don't know why myself."

How long did this go on? Longer than anyone expected. We all thought she wouldn't last more than a year, but she suffered for three and a half years. She faded like a light. Relatives tried to send her to the hot baths, but she refused to go. Things reached such a pass that people began to pray for her end. One mustn't say it, but death is preferable to such a life. She, too, cursed herself. Before she died, she sent for the rabbi to have him write her will. She probably wanted to leave her wealth for charitable purposes. What else? Leave it to her murderer? But again fate intervened. Some girl suddenly cried "Fire!" and everyone ran to look after his own things. It turned out that there had been no fire. "Why did you cry 'fire'?" the girl was asked. And she explained that it wasn't she who had shouted, but that something inside her had cried out. Meanwhile Finkl died, and Pelte inherited her property. Now he was the richest man in town, but he haggled over the cost of the grave till he got it for half-price.

Until then he hadn't been called Wife Killer. A man is twice widowed—such things happen. But after this he was always called Pelte the Wife Killer. *Cheder* boys pointed at him: "Here comes the Wife Killer." After the Seven Days of Mourning, the rabbi sent for him. "Reb Pelte," he said, "you are now the richest man in Turbin. Half the stores in the market place belong to you. With God's help you have become great. It is time you changed your ways. How long will you live apart from everyone else?" But no words impressed him. Talk of one thing to him, and he answers something entirely different; or he bites his lips and says nothing—you might as well talk to the wall. When the rabbi saw that it was a waste of time, he let him go.

For a time he was silent. He began to bake his own bread again, and to collect chips and cones and dung for fuel. He was shunned like the plague. He seldom came to the synagogue. Everybody was glad not to see him. On Thursdays he went around with his book to collect debts or interest. He had everything written down and never forgot a thing. If a storekeeper said that he hadn't the money to pay him and asked him to come some other time, he wouldn't go but stayed right there, staring with his bulging eyes, till the storekeeper got tired of it and gave him his last cent. The rest of the week he hid away somewhere in his kitchen. At least ten years passed this way, perhaps eleven; I don't remember any more. He must have been in his late fifties, or perhaps in his sixties. Nobody tried to arrange a match for him.

And then something happened, and this is what I want to tell you about. As I live, one could write a book about it; but I will make it short. In Turbin there lived a woman who was called Zlateh the Bitch. Some called her Zlateh the Cossack. From her nicknames you can guess for yourselves what sort of a person she was. It is not right to gossip about the dead, but the truth must be told—she was the lowest and meanest sort. She was a fishwife and her husband had been a fisherman. It's shameful to tell what she did in her youth. She was a slut—everyone knew that. She had a bastard somewhere. Her husband used to work in the poorhouse. There he beat and robbed the sick. How he suddenly got to be a fisherman I don't know, but that makes no difference. Fridays they used to stand in the market place with a basket of fish and curse everyone, whether they bought or not. Curses tumbled from her mouth as from a torn sack. If someone complained that she cheated on the weight, she would grab a fish by the tail and strike out. She tore the wig from the head of more than one woman. Once she was accused of stealing, so she went to the rabbi and falsely swore before black candles and the board on which the dead are washed that she was innocent. Her husband was named Eber, a strange name; he came from far off in Poland. He died and she became a widow. She was so wicked that all through the funeral she howled, "Eber, don't forget to take along all troubles." After the Seven Days of Mourning, she again sold fish in the market place. Since she was a shrew and abused everyone, people taunted her. One woman said to her, "Aren't you going to remarry, Zlateh?" And she answered, "Why not? I'm still a tasty dish." Yet she was already an old hag. "Whom will you marry, Zlateh?" people asked her, and she thought a moment and said, "Pelte."

The women thought she was joking and they laughed. But it was no joke, as you will soon hear.

III

One woman said to her, "But he is a Wife Killer!" And Zlateh answered, "If he is a Wife Killer, I am a worse Husband Killer. Eber wasn't my first husband." Who could tell how many she had before him? She wasn't a native of Turbin—the devil brought her from somewhere on the other side of the Vistula. Nobody paid any attention to what she said, but hardly a week passed before everybody heard that Zlateh hadn't been talking at random. Nobody knew whether she sent a matchmaker or arranged the match herself, but the marriage was going through. The whole town laughed—a fitting pair, falsehood and wickedness. Everybody said the same, "If Finkl were alive and saw who was inheriting her place, she would die of grief." Tailors' apprentices and seamstresses at once began to wager who would outlast whom. The apprentices said that nobody was a match for Pelte the Wife Killer, and the seamstresses argued that Zlateh was younger by some years and that not even Pelte had a chance once she opened her mouth. Anyway, the wedding took place. I wasn't there. You know that when a widower takes a widow, there's little fuss. But others who were there had lots of fun. The bride was all decked out. On Saturday she came to the women's gallery in the synagogue wearing a hat with a feather. She couldn't read. That Saturday I happened to take a new bride to the synagogue, and Zlateh stood right near me. She took Finkl's seat. She talked and jabbered all the time so that I didn't know what to do with myself for shame. And do you know what she said? She abused her husband. "He won't last long with me around," she said; just like that. A bitch—no doubt about it.

For some time nobody talked about them. After all, a whole town can't always bother with such scum. Then suddenly there was an outcry again. Zlateh had hired a maid, a little woman who had been abandoned by her husband. The maid started telling horrible stories. Pelte and Zlateh were at war—not just they, that is, but their stars. All sorts of things happened. Once Zlateh stood in the middle of the room and the chandelier fell down; it missed her by an inch. "The Wife Killer is at his tricks again," she said. "I'll show him something." The next day Pelte was walking in the market place; he slipped and fell into a ditch and nearly broke his neck. Every day something new happened. One time the soot in the chimney caught fire, and the entire house almost burned down; another time the cornice of the wardrobe fell and barely missed Pelte's skull. Everybody could see plainly that one or the other would have to go. It is written somewhere that every man is followed by devils—a thousand on the left and ten thousand on the right. We had a *malamed* in town, a certain Reb Itche the Slaughtered—that's what he was called—a very fine man who knew all about "those" matters. He said that this was a case of war between "them." At first things were fairly quiet; that is, people talked, but the unfortunate couple didn't say a thing. But in the end, Zlateh came running to the rabbi all atremble. "Rabbi," she shouted, "I can't stand it any more. Just think of it: I prepared dough in a trough and covered it with a pillow. I wanted to get up early to bake bread. In the middle of the night I see—the dough is on my bed. It's his work, Rabbi. He's made up his mind to finish me." At that time Reb Eisele Teumim, a true saint, was rabbi in the town. He couldn't believe his own ears. "Why should a man play such tricks?" he asked. "Why? You tell me why!" she answered. "Rabbi, send for him, let him tell it himself." The *shames* was sent and he brought Pelte. Naturally, he denied everything. "She is giving me a bad name," he cried. "She wants to get rid of me and get my money. She cast a spell to make water collect in the cellar. I went down there to get a piece of rope and was nearly drowned. Besides, she brought on a plague of mice." Pelte declared an oath that at night Zlateh whistled in bed, and that as soon as she started whistling there was a squeaking and a rushing of mice from all the holes. He pointed to a scar over his eyebrow and said that a mouse had bitten him there. When the rabbi realized whom he had to deal with, he said, "Take my advice and get divorced. It will be better for both of you." "The rabbi is right," Zlateh said. "I am willing, this very minute, but let him give me a settlement of half the property." "I won't give you the price of a pinch of snuff!" Pelte shouted. "What's more, you will pay me a fine." He grabbed his cane and wanted to strike her. He was held back with difficulty. When the rabbi saw that he would get nowhere in this case, he said, "Go your ways and leave me to my studies." So they went away.

From that time on the town had no rest. It was frightening to pass by their house. The shutters were always closed, even in the day time. Zlateh stopped selling fish, and all they did was fight. Zlateh was a giant of a woman. She used to go to the landowners' ponds and help spread the nets. She would get up in the middle of the night in winter, and in the worst frosts she never used a fire-pot. "The devil won't take me," she'd say. "I'm never cold." And now she suddenly aged. Her face blackened and was wrinkled like that of a woman of seventy. She started coming to strangers' houses to ask for advice. Once she came to my mother—peace be on her—and begged to be allowed to stay overnight. My mother looked at her as one demented. "What happened?" she asked. "I'm afraid of him," Zlateh said. "He wants to get rid of me. He makes winds in the house." She said that though the windows were sealed outside with clay and inside with straw, strong winds blew in her bedroom. She also swore that her bed would rise beneath her, and that Pelte spent half the nights in the outhouse—if you'll pardon the expression. "What does he do there so long?" my mother asked. "He has a mistress there," Zlateh said. I happened to be in the alcove and heard all this. Pelte must have had dealings with the Unclean Ones. My mother shuddered. "Listen to me, Zlateh," she said, "give him the 'dozen lines' and run for your life. If they were to give me my weight in gold, I wouldn't live under the same roof with anyone like that." But a Cossack never changes. "He won't get rid of me just like that," Zlateh said. "Let him give me a settlement." In the end, my mother made up a bed for her on the bench. We didn't shut an eye that night. Before dawn she got up and left. Mother couldn't fall asleep again and lit a taper in the kitchen. "You know," she said to me, "I have a feeling that she won't get out of his hands alive. Well, it won't be a big loss." But Zlateh wasn't Finkl. She didn't give up so easily, as you will soon hear.

IV

What did she do? I don't know. People told all sorts of stories, but you can't believe everything. We had an old peasant woman in town, Cunegunde. She must have been a hundred years old, maybe older. Everybody knew that she was a witch. Her whole face was covered with warts, and she walked almost on all fours. Her hut was at the end of town, on the sand, and it was full of all kinds of animals: rabbits and guinea pigs, cats and dogs, and all kinds of vermin. Birds flew in and out of the windows. The place stank. But Zlateh became a frequent visitor and spent whole days there. The woman knew how to pour wax. If a peasant was sick, he would come to her, and she'd pour molten wax which formed all sorts of strange figures and showed what the sickness came from —though it did little good.

As I was saying, people in town said this Cunegunde taught Zlateh a charm. Anyway, Pelte became a changed man, soft as butter. She wanted him to transfer the house to her name, so he hired a team of horses and went to town to register the transfer. Then she started meddling in his stores. Now it was she who went about on Thursdays with the interest and rent book. She asked for increases right away. The storekeepers cried that they were losing their shirts, so she said, "In that case you can go begging." A meeting was held, and Pelte was called. He was so weak that he could barely walk. He was completely deaf. "There is nothing I can do," he said. "Everything belongs to her. If she wants to, she can drive me out of the house." She would have, too, but he hadn't transferred everything to her yet. He was still bargaining with her. Neighbors said that she was starving him. He used to go into houses and beg for a piece of bread. His hands shook. Everybody saw that Zlateh was having her way. Some were glad—he was being punished for Finkl. Others argued that Zlateh would ruin the town. It's not a small matter when so much property gets into the hands of such a beast. She began to build and to dig. She brought craftsmen from Yanov and they started measuring the streets. She put on a wig, with silver combs, and she carried a purse and a parasol, like a real aristocrat.

She burst into homes early in the morning, before the beds were made, and she pounded on tables and shouted, "I'll throw you out with your junk. I'll have you locked up in the Yanov jail! I'll make beggars out of you!" Poor people tried to fawn on her, but she wouldn't even listen. Then people realized that it isn't wise to wish for a new king.

One afternoon the door of the poorhouse opened, and Pelte came in, dressed like a beggar. The man in charge of the poorhouse turned pale as a ghost. "Reb Pelte," he exclaimed, "what are you doing here?" "I came to stay here," Pelte answered. "My wife has thrown me out." To make a long story short, Pelte had transferred all his possessions to Zlateh, everything, down to the last thread, and then she chased him out. "But how does one do a thing like that?" he was asked. "Don't even ask," he answered. "She fixed me! I barely came out alive." The poorhouse was in an uproar. Some cursed Pelte. "As if the rich don't have enough as it is—now they come to eat the food of the poor," they cried. Others pretended sympathy. In short, Pelte was given a bundle of straw to spread in the corner, and he lay down. The whole town came running to see the sight. I, too, was curious and ran to see. He sat on the floor like a mourner and stared at everybody with his bulging eyes. People asked him, "Why do you sit here, Reb Pelte, what happened to all your power?" At first he didn't answer at all, as if they weren't talking to him, and later he said, "She isn't finished with me yet." "What will you do to her?" the beggars jeered. They made a laughing-stock of him. But don't jump at conclusions. You know the old saying: He laughs best who laughs last.

For several weeks Zlateh was a regular demon. She turned the whole town upside down. Right in the middle of the market place, near the stores, she had a pit dug and hired men to mix lime. Logs were brought and heaps of brick were piled up so that no one could pass. Roofs were torn down and a notary came from Yanov to make a list of all her tenants' belongings. Zlateh bought a carriage and a team of fiery horses, and she went riding every afternoon. She started wearing shoes with pointed tips and let her hair grow. She also began to pal around with the *goyim* of the Christian streets. She bought two vicious dogs, regular killers, so that it was dangerous to pass by her house. She stopped selling fish. What did she need it for? But out of habit, she had to have fish around, so she filled bathtubs in her house and stocked them with carp and pike. She even kept a big tub full of *treif* fish, and lobsters and frogs and eels. It was rumored in town that she would become an apostate any day. Some said that on Pesach the priest had come to her house to sprinkle it with holy water. People feared that she might inform on the community—someone like that is capable of anything.

Suddenly, she came running to the rabbi. "Rabbi," she said, "send for Pelte. I want a divorce." "What do you want a divorce for?" the rabbi asked her. "Do you want to remarry?" "I don't know," she said. "Maybe yes and maybe no. But I don't want to be the wife of a Wife Killer. I'm willing to compensate him with something." The rabbi sent for Pelte and he came crawling. Everybody in town stood outside the rabbi's house. Poor Pelte, he consented to everything. His hands shook as in a fever. Reb Moishe the Scribe sat down to write out the divorce. I remember him as if this happened yesterday. He was a small man and had a tic. He ruled the paper with his penknife, and then he wiped the goose quill on his skull cap. The witnesses were instructed how to sign divorce. My husband, peace be on him, was one of the witnesses because he wrote a good hand. Zlateh sat comfortably on a chair and sucked candy. And, yes, I forgot to mention it, she put down two hundred rubles. Pelte recognized them—he had had a habit of marking his money. The rabbi ordered silence, but Zlateh boasted to the women that she was considering marrying a "possessor," but that "as long as the Wife Killer is my husband, I am not sure of staying alive." When she said this she laughed so that everybody outside heard her.

When everything was ready, the rabbi began questioning the couple. I still remember his words. "Hear me, Paltiel, son of Schneour Zalman"—that was the name by which Pelte was called up to the reading of the Torah—"do you want to divorce your wife?" He said something more, from the *Gemorra,* but I can't say it as he did. "Say 'yes,' he ordered Pelte. "Say 'yes' once, not twice." Pelte said "yes." We could hardly hear him. "Hear me, Zlateh Golde, daughter of Yehuda Treitel, do you want to divorce your husband, Paltiel?" "Yes!" Zlateh shouted, and as she said this she swayed and fell to the floor in a faint. I saw this myself, and I tell you the truth; I felt my brain bursting in my head. I thought I'd collapse too. There was a great outcry and commotion. Everybody rushed to revive her. They poured water on her and stuck pins into her and rubbed her with vinegar and pulled her hair. Azriel the Healer came running and cupped her then and there. She still breathed, but it wasn't the same Zlateh. May God preserve us. Her mouth was twisted to one side and the spittle ran out of it; her eyes were rolled up and her nose was white, like that of a corpse. The women who stood near, heard her mumble, "The Wife Killer! He overcame me!" These were her last words.

At the funeral there was almost a riot. Now Pelte was again on his high horse. Beside his own property he now also had her wealth. Her jewelry alone was worth a fortune. The burial society wanted a big sum, but Pelte wouldn't budge. They shouted, they warned, they abused him. They threatened him with excommunication. Might as well talk to the wall! "I won't give a penny, let her rot," he said. They would have left her lying around, too, but it was summertime and there was a heat wave just then, and people feared an epidemic. In short, some women performed the rites—what other choice was there? The pall-bearers refused to carry her, so a wagon was hired. She was buried right near the fence, among the stillbirths. All the same, Pelte said *kaddish* after her—this he did.

From then on the Wife Killer remained alone. People were so afraid of him, they avoided passing by his house. Mothers of pregnant young women did not allow his name to be mentioned, unless they first put on two aprons. *Cheder* boys fingered their fringes before pronouncing his name. And nothing came of all the construction and remodelling. The bricks were carried off, the lime was stolen. The carriage and its team of horses disappeared—he must have sold them. The water in the bathtubs dried up, and the fish died. There was a cage with a parrot in the house. It squawked, "I'm hungry"—it could talk Yiddish—until at last it starved to death. Pelte had the shutters nailed tight and never opened them again. He didn't even go out to collect the pennies from the storekeepers. All day he lay on his bench and snored, or simply dozed. At night he'd go out to collect chips. Once each week, they sent him two loaves of bread from the bakery, and the baker's wife would buy him some onions, garlic, radishes and, on occasion, a piece of dry cheese. He never ate meat. He never came to the synagogue on Saturdays. There was no broom in his house and the dirt gathered in heaps. Mice ran about even during the day and spider webs hung from the rafters. The roof leaked and wasn't repaired. The walls rotted and caved in. Every few weeks it was rumored that things were not well with the Wife Killer, that he was sick, or dying. The burial society rubbed its hands in anticipation. But nothing happened. He outlived everyone. He lived so long that people in Turbin began to hint that he might live forever. Why not? Maybe he had some special kind of blessing, or the Angel of Death forgot him. Anything can happen.

Rest assured that he was not forgotten by the Angel of Death. But when that happened I was no longer in Turbin. He must have been a hundred years old, maybe older. After the funeral his entire house was turned upside down, but nothing of value was found. The chests had rotted away. The gold and silver were gone. The money and notes turned to dust the minute a breeze touched them. All the digging in the heaps of rubbish was wasted. The Wife Killer had outlived everything: his wives, his enemies, his money, his property, his generation. All that was left after him—may God forgive me for saying so—was a heap of dust.

Translated by Shlomo Katz

The Mirror

I

There is a kind of net that is as old as Methuselah, as soft as a cobweb and as full of holes, yet it has retained its strength to this day. When a demon wearies of chasing after yesterdays or of going round in circles on a windmill, he can install himself inside a mirror. There he waits like a spider in its web, and the fly is certain to be caught. God has bestowed vanity on the female, particularly on the rich, the pretty, the barren, the young, who have much time and little company.

I discovered such a woman in the village of Krashnik. Her father dealt in timber; her husband floated the logs to Danzig; grass was growing on her mother's grave. The daughter lived in an old house, among oaken cupboards, leather-lined coffers, and books bound in silk. She had two servants, an old one that was deaf and a young one who carried on with a fiddler. The other Krashnik housewives wore men's boots, ground buckwheat on millstones, plucked feathers, cooked broths, bore children, and attended funerals. Needless to say, Zirel, beautiful and well-educated—she had been brought up in Cracow—had nothing to talk about with her small-town neighbors. And so she preferred to read her German song book and embroider Moses and Ziporah, David and Bathsheba, Ahasuereus and Queen Esther on canvas. The pretty dresses her husband brought her hung in the closet. Her pearls and diamonds lay in her jewel box. No one ever saw her silk slips, her lace petticoats, nor her red hair which was hidden under her wig, not even her husband. For when could they be seen? Certainly not during the day, and at night it is dark.

But Zirel had an attic which she called her boudoir, and where hung a mirror as blue as water on the point of freezing. The mirror had a crack in the middle, and it was set in a golden frame which was decorated with snakes, knobs, roses, and adders. In front of the mirror lay a bearskin and close beside it was a chair with armrests of ivory and a cushioned seat. What could be more pleasant than to sit naked in this chair, and rest one's feet on the bearskin, and contemplate oneself? Zirel had much to gaze at. Her skin was white as satin, her breasts as full as wineskins, her hair fell across her shoulders, and her legs were as slender as a hind's. She would sit for hours on end delighting in her beauty. The door fastened and bolted, she would imagine that it opened to admit either a prince or a hunter or a knight or a poet. For everything hidden must be revealed, each secret longs to be disclosed, each love yearns to be betrayed, everything sacred must be desecrated. Heaven and earth conspire that all good beginnings should come to a bad end.

Well, once I learned of the existence of this luscious little tidbit, I determined that she would be mine. All that was required was a little patience. One summer day, as she sat staring at the nipple on her left breast, she caught sight of me in the mirror—there I was, black as tar, long as a shovel, with donkey's ears, a ram's horns, a frog's mouth, and a goat's beard. My eyes were all pupil. She was so surprised that she forgot to be frightened. Instead of crying, "Hear, O Israel," she burst out laughing.

"My, how ugly you are," she said.

"My, how beautiful you are," I replied.

She was pleased with my compliment. "Who are you?" she asked.

"Fear not," I said. "I am an imp, not a demon. My fingers have no nails, my mouth has no teeth, my arms stretch like licorice, my horns are as pliable as wax. My power lies in my tongue; I am a fool by trade, and I have come to cheer you up because you are alone."

"Where were you before?"

"In the bedroom behind the stove where the cricket chirps and the mouse rustles, between a dried wreath and a faded willow branch."

"What did you do there?"

"I looked at you."

"Since when?"

"Since your wedding night."

"What did you eat?"

"The fragrance of your body, the glow of your hair, the light of your eyes, the sadness of your face."

"Oh, you flatterer!" she cried. "Who are you? What are you doing here? Where do you come from? What is your errand?"

I made up a story. My father, I said, was a goldsmith and my mother a succubus; they copulated on a bundle of rotting rope in a cellar and I was their bastard. For some time I lived in a settlement of devils on Mount Seir where I inhabited a mole's hole. But when it was learned that my father was human I was driven out. From then on I had been homeless. She-devils avoided me because I reminded them of the sons of Adam; the daughters of Eve saw in me Satan. Dogs barked at me, children wept when they saw me. Why were they afraid? I harmed no one. My only desire was to gaze at beautiful women—to gaze and converse with them.

"Why converse? The beautiful aren't always wise."

"In Paradise the wise are the footstools of the beautiful."

"My teacher taught me otherwise."

"What did your teacher know? The writers of books have the brains of a flea; they merely parrot each other. Ask me when you want to know something. Wisdom extends no further than the first heaven. From there on everything is lust. Don't you know that angels are headless? The Seraphim play in the sand like children; the Cherubim can't count; the Aralim chew their cud before the throne of Glory. God himself is jovial. He spends his time pulling Leviathan by the tail and being licked by the Wild Ox; or else he tickles the Shekhinah, causing her to lay myriads of eggs each day, and each egg is a star."

"Now I know you're making fun of me."

"If that's not the truth may a funny bone grow on my nose. It's a long time since I squandered my quota of lies. I have no alternative but to tell the truth."

"Can you beget children?"

"No, my dear. Like the mule I am the last of a line. But this does not blunt my desire. I lie only with married women, for good actions are my sins; my prayers are blasphemies; spite is my bread; arrogance, my wine; pride, the marrow of my bones. There is only one other thing I can do besides chatter."

This made her laugh. Then she said: "My mother didn't bring me up to be a devil's whore. Away with you, or I'll have you exorcised."

"Why bother," I said. "I'll go. I don't force myself on anyone. *Auf wiedersehen.*"

I faded away like mist.

II

For seven days Zirel absented herself from her boudoir. I dozed inside the mirror. The net had been spread; the victim was ready. I knew she was curious. Yawning, I considered my next step. Should I seduce a rabbi's daughter? deprive a bridegroom of his manhood? plug up the synagogue chimney? turn the Sabbath wine into vinegar? give an elflock to a virgin? enter a ram's horn on Rosh Hashana? make a cantor hoarse? An imp never lacks for things to do, particularly during the Days of Awe when even the fish in the water tremble. And then as I sat dreaming of moon juice and turkey seeds, she entered. She looked for me, but could not see me. She stood in front of the mirror but I didn't show myself.

"I must have been imagining," she murmured. "It must have been a daydream."

She took off her nightgown and stood there naked. I knew that her husband was in town and that he had been with her the night before although she had not gone to the ritual bath—but as the Talmud puts it, "a woman would rather have one measure of debauchery than ten of modesty." Zirel, daughter of Roize Glike, missed me, and her eyes were sad. She is mine, mine, I thought. The Angel of Death stood ready with his rod; a zealous little devil busied himself preparing the cauldron for her in hell; a sinner, promoted to stoker, collected the kindling wood. Everything was prepared—the snow drift and the live coals, the hook for her tongue and the pliers for her breasts, the mouse that would eat her liver and the worm that would gnaw her bladder. But my little charmer suspected nothing. She stroked her left breast, and then her right. She looked at her belly, examined her thighs, scrutinized her toes. Would she read her book? trim her nails? comb her hair? Her husband had brought her perfumes from Lenczyc, and she smelled of rosewater and carnations. He had presented her with a coral necklace which hung around her neck. But what is Eve without a serpent? And what is God without Lucifer? Zirel was full of desire. Like a harlot she summoned me with her eyes. With quivering lips she uttered a spell:

"Swift is the wind,
Deep the ditch,
Sleek black cat,
Come within reach.
Strong is the lion,
Dumb the fish,
Reach from the silence,
And take your dish."

As she uttered the last word, I appeared. Her face lit up.

"So you're here."

"I was away," I said, "but I have returned."

"Where have you been?"

"To never-never land. I was at Rahab the Harlot's palace in the garden of the golden birds near the castle of Asmodeus."

"As far as that?"

"If you don't believe me, my jewel, come with me. Sit on my back, and hold on to my horns, and I'll spread my wings, and we'll fly together beyond the mountain peaks."

"But I don't have a thing on."

"No one dresses there."

"My husband won't have any idea where I am."

"He'll learn soon enough."

"How long a trip is it?"

"It takes less than a second."

"When will I return?"

"Those who go there don't want to return."

"What will I do there?"

"You'll sit on Asmodeus' lap and plait tresses in his beard. You'll eat almonds and drink porter; evenings you'll dance for him. Bells will be attached to your ankles, and devils will whirl with you."

"And after that?"

"If my master is pleased with you, you will be his. If not, one of his minions will take care of you."

"And in the morning?"

"There are no mornings there."

"Will you stay with me?"

"Because of you I might be given a small bone to lick."

"Poor little devil, I feel sorry for you, but I can't go. I have a husband and a father. I have gold and silver and dresses and furs. My heels are the highest in Krashnik."

"Well, then, good-by."

"Don't hurry off like that. What do I have to do?"

"Now you are being reasonable. Make some dough with the whitest of flour. Add honey, menstrual blood, and an egg with a bloodspot, a measure of pork fat, a thimbleful of suet, a goblet of libatory wine. Light a fire on the Sabbath and bake the mixture on the coals. Now call your husband to your bed and make him eat the cake you have baked. Awaken him with lies and put him to sleep with profanity. Then when he begins to snore, cut off one half of his beard and one earlock, steal his gold, burn his promissory notes, and tear up the marriage contract. After that throw your jewels under the pig butcher's window—this will be my engagement gift. Before leaving your house, throw the prayer book into the rubbish and spit on the *mezuzah,* at the precise spot where the word *Shadai* is written. Then come straight to me. I'll bear you on my wings from Krashnik to the desert. We'll fly over fields filled with toadstools, over woods inhabited by werewolves, over the ruins of Sodom where serpents are scholars, hyenas are singers, crows are preachers, and thieves are entrusted with the money for charity. There ugliness is beauty, and crooked is straight; tortures are amusement, and mockery, the height of exaltation. But hurry, for our eternity is brief."

"I'm afraid, little devil, I'm afraid."

"Everyone who goes with us is."

She wished to ask questions, to catch me in contradictions, but I made off. She pressed her lips against the mirror and met the end of my tail.

III

Her father wept; her husband tore his hair; her servants searched for her in the woodshed and in the cellar; her mother-in-law poked with a shovel in the chimney; carters and butchers hunted for her in the woods. At night, torches were lit and the voices of the searchers echoed and re-echoed: "Zirel, where are you? Zirel! Zirel!" It was suspected that she had run off to a convent, but the priest swore on the crucifix that this was not so. A wonder worker was sent for, and then a sorceress, an old Gentile woman who made wax effigies, and finally a man who located the dead or missing by means of a black mirror; a farmer lent them his blood hounds. But when I get my prey, it is reprieved by no one. I spread my wings and we were off. Zirel spoke to me, but I did not answer. When we came to Sodom, I hovered a moment over Lot's wife. Three oxen were busy licking her nose. Lot lay in a cave with his daughters, drunk as always.

In the vale of shadow which is known as the world everything is subject to change. But for us time stands still! Adam remains naked, Eve lustful, still in the act of being seduced by the serpent. Cain kills Abel, the flea lies with the elephant, the flood falls from heaven, the Jews knead clay in Egypt, Job scratches at his sore-covered body. He will keep scratching until the end of time, but he will find no comfort.

She wished to speak to me, but with a flutter of wings I disappeared. I had done my errand. I lay like a bat blinking sightless eyes on a steep cliff. The earth was brown, the heavens yellow. Devils stood in a circle wiggling their tails. Two turtles were locked in an embrace, and a male stone mounted a female stone. Shabriri and Bariri appeared. Shabriri had assumed the shape of a squire. He wore a pointed cap, a curved sword; he had the legs of a goose and a goat's beard. On his snout were glasses, and he spoke in a German dialect. Bariri was ape, parrot, rat, bat, all at once. Shabriri bowed low and began to chant like a jester at a wedding:

> *"Argin, margin,*
> *Here's a bargain.*
> *A pretty squirrel,*
> *Name of Zirel.*
> *Open the door,*
> *To love impure."*

He was about to take her in his arms when Bariri screamed, "Don't let him touch you. He has scabs on his head, sores on his legs, and what a woman needs he doesn't have. He acts the great lover, but a capon is more amorous. His father was like that also, and so was his grandfather. Let me be your lover. I am the grandson of the Chief Liar. In addition I am a man of wealth and good family. My grandmother was lady-in-waiting to Machlath, daughter of Naama. My mother had the honor to wash Asmodeus' feet. My father, may he stay in hell forever, carried Satan's snuffbox."

Shabriri and Bariri had grasped Zirel by the hair, and each time they pulled they tore out a tuft. Now Zirel saw how things were and she cried out, "Pity, pity!"

"What's this we have here?" asked Ketev Mariri.

"A Krashnik coquette."

"Don't they have better than that?"

"No, it's the best they've got."

"Who dragged her in?"

"A little imp."

"Let's begin."

"Help, help," Zirel moaned.

"Hang her," Wrath, the Son of Anger, screamed. "It won't help to cry out here. Time and change have been left behind. Do what you are told; you're neither young nor old."

Zirel broke into lamentations. The sound roused Lilith from her sleep. She thrust aside Asmodeus' beard and put her head out of the cave, each of her hairs, a curling snake.

"What's wrong with the bitch?" she asked. "Why all the screaming?"

"They're working on her."

"Is that all? Add some salt."

"And skim the fat."

This fun has been going on for a thousand years, but the black gang does not weary of it. Each devil does his bit; each imp makes his pun. They pull and tear and bite and pinch. For all that, the masculine devils aren't so bad; it's the females who really enjoy themselves, commanding: Skim boiling broth with bare hands! Plait braids without using the fingers! Wash the laundry without water! Catch fish in hot sand! Stay at home and walk the streets! Take a bath without getting wet! Make butter from stones! Break the cask without spilling the wine! And all the while the virtuous women in Paradise gossip; and the pious men sit on golden chairs, stuffing themselves with the meat of Leviathan, as they boast of their good deeds.

Is there a God? Is He all merciful? Will Zirel ever find salvation? Or is creation a snake primeval crawling with evil? How can I tell? I'm still only a minor devil. Imps seldom get promoted. Meanwhile generations come and go, Zirel follows Zirel, in a myriad of reflections—a myriad of mirrors.

Translated by Norbert Guterman

The Little Shoemakers

1 : *The Shoemakers and Their Family Tree*

The family of the little shoemakers was famous not only in Frampol but in the outlying district—in Yonev, Kreshev, Bilgoray, and even in Zamoshoh. Abba Shuster, the founder of the line, appeared in Frampol some time after Chmielnitzki's progroms. He brought himself a plot of ground on the stubby hill behind the butcher stalls, and there he built a house that remained standing until just the other day. Not that it was in such fine condition—the stone foundation settled, the small windows warped, and the shingled roof turned a moldy green and was hung with swallows' nests. The door, moreover, sank into the ground; the banisters became bowlegged; and instead of stepping up onto the threshold, one was obliged to step down. All the same, it did survive the innumerable fires that devastated Frampol in the early days. But the rafters were so rotten that mushrooms grew on them, and when wood dust was needed to staunch the blood of a circumcision, one had only to break off a piece of the outer wall and rub it between one's fingers. The roof, pitched so steeply that the chimneysweep was unable to climb onto it to look after the chimney, was always catching fire from the sparks. It was only by the grace of God that the house was not overtaken by disaster.

The name of Abba Shuster is recorded, on parchment, in the annals of the Frampol Jewish community. It was his custom to make six pairs of shoes every year for distribution among widows and orphans; in recognition of his philanthropy the synagogue called him to the reading of the Torah under the honorific title, *Murenu,* meaning "our teacher."

His stone in the old cemetery had vanished, but the shoemakers knew a sign for the grave—nearby grew a hazelnut tree. According to the old wives, the tree sprang from Reb Abba's beard.

Reb Abba had five sons; they settled, all but one, in the neighboring towns; only Getzel remained in Frampol. He continued his father's charitable practice of making shoes for the poor, and he too was active in the gravediggers' brotherhood.

The annals go on to say that Getzel had a son, Godel, and that to Godel was born Treitel, and to Treitel, Gimpel. The shoemaker's art was handed down from one generation to the next. A principle was fast established in the family, requiring the eldest son to remain at home and succeed his father at the workbench.

The shoemakers resembled one another. They were all short, sandy-haired, and sound, honest workmen. The people of Frampol believed that Reb Abba, the head of the line, had learned shoemaking from a master of the craft in Brod, who divulged to him the secret of strengthening leather and making it durable. In the cellar of their house the little shoemakers kept a vat for soaking hides. God knows what strange chemicals they added to the tanning fluid. They did not disclose the formula to outsiders, and it was handed on from father to son.

As it is not our business to deal with all the generations of the little shoemakers, we will confine ourselves to the last three. Reb Lippe remained without heir till his old age, and it was taken for a certainty that the line would end with him. But when he was in his late sixties his wife died and he married an overripe virgin, a milkmaid, who bore him six children. The eldest son, Feivel, was quite well to do. He was prominent in community affairs, attended all the important meetings, and for years served as sexton of the tailors' synagogue. It was the custom in this synagogue to select a new sexton every Simchath Torah. The man so selected was honored by having a pumpkin placed on his head; the pumpkin was set with lighted candles, and the lucky fellow was led about from house to house and refreshed at each stop with wine and strudel or honey-cakes. However, Reb Feivel happened to die on Simchath Torah, the day of rejoicing over the Law, while dutifully making these rounds; he fell flat in the market place, and there was no reviving him. Because Feivel had been a notable philanthropist, the rabbi who conducted his services declared that the candles he had borne on his head would light his way to Paradise. The will found in his strongbox requested that when he was carried to the cemetery, a hammer, an awl, and a last should be laid on the black cloth over his coffin, in sign of the fact that he was a man of peaceful industry who never cheated his customers. His will was done.

Feivel's eldest son was called Abba, after the founder. Like the rest of his stock, he was short and thickset, with a broad yellow beard, and a high forehead lined with wrinkles, such as only rabbis and shoemakers have. His eyes were also yellow, and the over-all impression he created was that of a sulky hen. Nevertheless he was a clever workman, charitable like his forbears, and unequaled in

Frampol as a man of his word. He would never make a promise unless he was sure he could fulfill it; when he was not sure he said: who knows, God willing, or maybe. Furthermore he was a man of some learning. Every day he read a chapter of the Torah in Yiddish translation and occupied his free time with chap-books. Abba never missed a single sermon of the traveling preachers who came to town, and he was especially fond of the Biblical passages which were read in the synagogue during the winter months. When his wife, Pesha, read to him, of a Sabbath, from the Yiddish translation of the stories in the Book of Genesis, he would imagine that he was Noah, and that his sons were Shem, Ham, and Japheth. Or else he would see himself in the image of Abraham, Isaac, or Jacob. He often thought that if the Almighty were to call on him to sacrifice his eldest son, Gimpel, he would rise early in the morning and carry out his commands without delay. Certainly he would have left Poland and the house of his birth and gone wandering over the earth where God sent him. He knew the story of Joseph and his brothers by heart, but he never tired of reading it over again. He envied the ancients because the King of the Universe revealed Himself to them and performed miracles for their sake, but consoled himself by thinking that from him, Abba, to the Patriarchs, there stretched an unbroken chain of generations—as if he too were part of the Bible. He sprang from Jacob's loins; he and his sons were of the seed whose number had become like the sand and the stars. He was living in exile because the Jews of the Holy Land had sinned, but he awaited the Redemption, and he would be ready when the time came.

Abba was by far the best shoemaker in Frampol. His boots were always a perfect fit, never too tight or too roomy. People who suffered from chilblains, corns, or varicose veins were especially pleased with his work, claiming that his shoes relieved them. He despised the new styles, the gimcrack boots and slippers with fancy heels and poorly stitched soles that fell apart with the first rain. His customers were respectable burghers of Frampol or peasants from the surrounding villages, and they deserved the best. He took their measurements with a knotted string, as in the old days. Most of the Frampol women wore wigs, but his wife, Pesha, covered her head with a bonnet as well. She bore him seven sons, and he named them after his forefathers—Gimpel, Getzel, Treitel, Godel, Feivel, Lippe, and Chananiah. They were all short and sandy-haired like their father. Abba predicted that he would turn them into shoemakers, and as a man of his word he let them look on at the workbench while they were still quite young, and at times taught them the old maxim—good work is never wasted.

He spent sixteen hours a day at the bench, a sack spread on his knees, gouging holes with the awl, sewing with a wire needle, tinting and polishing the leather or scraping it with a piece of glass; and while he worked he hummed snatches from the canticles of the Days of Awe. Usually the cat huddled nearby and watched the proceedings as though she were looking after him. Her mother and grandmother had caught mice, in their time, for the little shoemakers. Abba could look down the hill through the window and see the whole town and a considerable distance beyond, as far as the road to Bilgoray and the pine woods. He observed the groups of matrons who gathered every morning at the butcher stalls and the young men and idlers who went in and out of the courtyard of the synagogue; the girls going to the pump to draw water for tea, and the women hurrying at dusk to the ritual bath.

Evenings, when the sun was setting, the house would be pervaded by a dusky glow. Rays of light danced in the corners, flicked across the ceiling, and set Abba's beard gleaming with the color of spun gold. Pesha, Abba's wife, would be cooking *kasha* and soup in the kitchen, the children would be playing, neighboring women and girls would go in and out of the house. Abba would rise from his work, wash his hands, put on his long coat, and go off to the tailors' synagogue for evening prayers. He knew that the wide world was full of strange cities and distant lands, that Frampol was actually no bigger than a dot in a small prayer book; but it seemed to him that his little town was the navel of the universe and that his own house stood at the very center. He often thought that when the Messiah came to lead the Jews to the Land of Israel, he, Abba, would stay behind in Frampol, in his own house, on his own hill. Only on the Sabbath and on Holy Days would he step into a cloud and let himself be flown to Jerusalem.

II : *Abba and His Seven Sons*

Since Gimpel was the eldest, and therefore destined to succeed his father, he came foremost in Abba's concern. He sent him to the best Hebrew teachers and even hired a tutor who taught him the elements of Yiddish, Polish, Russian, and arithmetic. Abba himself led the boy down into the cellar and showed him the formula for adding chemicals and various kinds of bark to the tanning fluid. He revealed to him that in most cases the right foot is larger than the left, and that the source of all trouble in the fitting of shoes is usually to be found in the big toes. Then he taught Gimpel the principles for cutting soles and inner soles, snub-toed and pointed shoes, high heels and low; and for fitting customers with flat feet, bunions, hammer toes, and calluses.

On Fridays, when there was always a rush of work to get out, the older boys would leave *cheder* at ten in the morning and help their father in the shop. Pesha baked *chalah* and prepared their lunch. She would grasp the first loaf and carry it, hot from the oven, blowing on it all the while and tossing it from hand to hand, to show it to Abba, holding it up, front and back, till he nodded approval. Then she would return with a ladle and let him sample the fish soup, or ask him to taste a crumb of freshly baked cake. Pesha valued his judgment. When she went to buy cloth for herself or the children she brought home swatches for him to choose. Even before going to the butcher she asked his opinion—what should she get, breast or roast, flank or ribs? She consulted him not out of fear or because she had no mind of her own, but simply because she had learned that he always knew what he was talking about. Even when she was sure he was wrong, he would turn out to be right, after all. He never browbeat her, but merely cast a glance to let her know when she was being a fool. This was also the way he handled the children. A strap hung on the wall, but he seldom made use of it; he had his way by kindness. Even strangers respected him. The merchants sold him hides at a fair price and presented no objections when he asked for credit. His own customers trusted him and paid his prices without a murmur. He was always called sixth to the reading of the Torah in the tailors' synagogue—a considerable honor—and when he pledged or was assessed for money, it was never necessary to remind him. He paid up, without fail, right after the Sabbath. The town soon learned of his virtues, and though he was nothing but a plain shoemaker, and, if the truth be told, something of an ignoramus, they treated him as they would a distinguished man.

When Gimpel turned thirteen, Abba girded the boy's loins in sackcloth and put him to work at the bench. After Gimpel, Getzel, Treitel, Godel, and Feivel became apprentices. Though they were his own sons and he supported them out of his earnings, he nevertheless paid them a wage. The two youngest boys, Lippe and Chananiah, were still attending the elementary *cheder,* but they too lent a hand at hammering pegs. Abba and Pesha were proud of them. In the morning the six workers trooped into the kitchen for breakfast, washed their six pairs of hands with the appropriate benediction, and their six mouths chewed the roasted groats and corn bread.

Abba loved to place his two youngest boys one on each knee, and sing an old Frampol song to them:

"A mother had
Ten little boys,
Oh, Lord, ten little boys!

The first one was Avremele,
The second one was Berele,
The third one was called Gimpele,
The fourth one was called Dovid'l
The fifth one was called Hershele. . . ."

And all the boys came in on the chorus:

"Oh, Lord, Hershele!"

Now that he had apprentices, Abba turned out more work, and his income grew. Living was cheap in Frampol, and since the peasants often made him a present of a measure of corn or a roll of butter, a sack of potatoes or a pot of honey, a hen or a goose, he was able to save some money on food. As their prosperity increased, Pesha began to talk of rebuilding the house. The rooms were too narrow, the ceiling was too low. The floor shook underfoot. Plaster was peeling off the walls, and all sorts of maggots and worms crawled through the woodwork. They lived in constant fear that the ceiling would fall on their heads. Even though they kept a cat, the place was infested with mice. Pesha insisted that they tear down this ruin and build a larger house.

Abba did not immediately say no. He told his wife he would think it over. But after doing so, he expressed the opinion that he would rather keep things as they were. First of all, he was afraid to tear down the house, because this might bring bad luck. Second, he feared the evil eye —people were grudging and envious enough. Third, he found it hard to part with the home in which his parents and grandparents, and the whole family, stretching back for generations, had lived and died. He knew every corner of the house, each crack and wrinkle. When one layer of paint peeled off the wall, another, of a different color, was exposed; and behind this layer, still another. The walls were like an album in which the fortunes of the family had been recorded. The attic was stuffed with heirlooms—tables and chairs, cobbler's benches and lasts, whetstones and knives, old clothes, pots, pans, bedding, salting boards, cradles. Sacks full of torn prayer books lay spilled on the floor.

Abba loved to climb up to the attic on a hot summer's day. Spiders spun great webs, and the sunlight, filtering in through cracks, fell upon the threads in rainbows. Everything lay under a thick coat of dust. When he listened attentively he would hear a whispering, a murmuring and soft scratching, as of some unseen creature engaged in endless activity, conversing in an unearthly tongue. He was sure that the souls of his forefathers kept watch over the house. In much the same way he loved the ground on which it stood. The weeds were as high as a man's head. There was a dense growth of hairy and brambly vegetation all about the place—the very leaves and twigs would catch hold of one's clothing as though with teeth and claws. Flies and midges swarmed in the air and the ground crawled with worms and snakes of all descriptions. Ants had raised their hills in this thicket; field mice had dug their holes. A pear tree grew in the midst of this wilderness; every year, at the time of the Feast of the Tabernacle, it yielded small fruit with the taste and hardness of wood. Birds and bees flew over this jungle, great big golden-bellied flies. Toadstools sprang up after each rain. The ground was unkept, but an unseen hand guarded its fertility.

When Abba stood here looking up at the summer sky, losing himself in contemplation of the clouds, shaped like sailboats, flocks of sheep, brooms, and elephant herds, he felt the presence of God, His providence and His mercy. He could virtually see the Almighty seated on His throne of glory, the earth serving Him as a footstool. Satan was vanquished; the angels sang hymns. The Book of Memory in which were recorded all the deeds of men lay open. From time to time, at sunset, it even seemed to Abba that he saw the river of fire in the nether world. Flames leaped up from the burning coals; a wave of fire rose, flooding the shores. When he listened closely he was sure he heard the muffled cries of sinners and the derisive laughter of the evil host.

No, this was good enough for Abba Shuster. There was nothing to change. Let everything stand as it had stood for ages, until he lived out his allotted time and was buried in the cemetery among his ancestors, who had shod the sacred community and whose good name was preserved not only in Frampol but in the surrounding district.

III : *Gimpel Emigrates to America*

Therefore the proverb says: Man proposes, God disposes.

One day while Abba was working on a boot, his eldest son, Gimpel, came into the shop. His freckled face was heated, his sandy hair disheveled under the skullcap. Instead of taking his place at the bench, he stopped at his father's side, regarded him hesitantly, and at last said, "Father, I must tell you something."

"Well, I'm not stopping you," replied Abba.

"Father," he cried, "I'm going to America."

Abba dropped his work. This was the last thing he expected to hear, and up went his eyebrows.

"What happened? Did you rob someone? Did you get into a fight?"

"No, Father."

"Then why are you running away?"

"There's no future for me in Frampol."

"Why not? You know a trade. God willing, you'll marry some day. You have everything to look forward to."

"I'm sick of small towns; I'm sick of the people. This is nothing but a stinking swamp."

"When they get around to draining it," said Abba, "there won't be any more swamp."

"No, Father, that's not what I mean."

"Then what do you mean?" cried Abba angrily. "Speak up!"

The boy spoke up, but Abba couldn't understand a word of it. He laid into synagogue and state with such venom, Abba could only imagine that the poor soul was possessed: the Hebrew teachers beat the children; the women empty their slop pails right outside the door; the shopkeepers loiter in the streets; there are no toilets anywhere, and the public relieves itself as it pleases, behind the bathhouse or out in the open, encouraging epidemics and plagues. He made fun of Ezreal the Healer and of Mecheles the Marriage Broker, nor did he spare the rabbinical court and the bath attendant, the washerwoman and the overseer of the poorhouse, the professions and the benevolent societies.

At first Abba was afraid that the boy had lost his mind, but the longer he continued his harangue, the clearer it became that he had strayed from the path of righteousness. Jacob Reifman, the atheist, used to hold forth in Shebreshin, not far from Frampol. A pupil of his, a detractor of Israel, was in the habit of visiting an aunt in Frampol and had gathered quite a following among the good-for-nothings. It had never occurred to Abba that his Gimpel might fall in with this gang.

"What do you say, Father?" asked Gimpel.

Abba thought it over. He knew that there was no use arguing with Gimpel, and he remembered the proverb: A rotten apple spoils the barrel. "Well," he replied, "what can I do? If you want to go, go. I won't stop you."

And he resumed his work.

But Pesha did not give in so easily. She begged Gimpel not to go so far away; she wept and implored him not to bring shame on the family. She even ran to the cemetery, to the graves of her forefathers, to seek the intercession of the dead. But she was finally convinced that Abba was right: it was no use arguing. Gimpel's face had turned hard as leather, and a mean light showed in his yellow eyes. He had become a stranger in his own home. He spent that night out with friends, and returned in the morning to pack his prayer shawl and phylacteries, a few shirts, a blanket, and some hard-boiled eggs—and he was all set to go. He had saved enough money for passage. When his mother saw that it was settled, she urged him to take at least a jar of preserves, a bottle of cherry juice, bedding, pillows. But Gimpel refused. He was going to steal over the border into Germany, and he stood a better chance if he traveled light. In short, he kissed his mother, said good-by to his brothers and friends, and off he went. Abba, not wanting to part with his son in anger, took him in the wagon to the station at Reivetz. The train arrived in the middle of the night with a hissing and whistling, a racket and din. Abba took the headlights of the locomotive for the eyes of a hideous devil, and shied away from the funnels with their columns of sparks and smoke and their clouds of steam. The blinding lights only intensified the darkness. Gimpel ran around with his baggage like a madman, and his father ran after him. At the last moment the boy kissed his father's hand, and Abba called after him, into the darkness, "Good luck! Don't forsake your religion!"

The train pulled out, leaving a smell of smoke in

Abba's nostrils and a ringing in his ears. The earth trembled under his feet. As though the boy had been dragged off by demons! When he returned home and Pesha fell on him, weeping, he said to her, "The Lord gave and the Lord has taken away. . . ."

Months passed without word from Gimpel. Abba knew that this was the way with young men when they leave home—they forget their dearest ones. As the proverb says: Out of sight, out of mind. He doubted that he would ever hear from him, but one day a letter came from America. Abba recognized his son's handwriting. Gimpel wrote that he crossed the border safely, that he saw many strange cities and spent four weeks on board ship, living on potatoes and herring because he did not want to touch improper food. The ocean was very deep and the waves as high as the sky. He saw flying fish but no mermaids or mermen, and he did not hear them singing. New York is a big city, the houses reach into the clouds. The trains go over the roofs. The gentiles speak English. No one walks with his eyes on the ground, everybody holds his head high. He met a lot of his countrymen in New York; they all wear short coats. He too. The trade he learned at home has come in very handy. He is *all right;* he is earning a living. He will write again, a long letter. He kisses his father and mother and his brothers, and sends regards to his friends.

A friendly letter after all.

In his second letter Gimpel announced that he had fallen in love with a girl and bought her a diamond ring. Her name is Bessie; she comes from Rumania; and she works *at dresses.* Abba put on his spectacles with the brass frames and spent a long time puzzling this out. Where did the boy learn so many English words? The third letter stated that he was married and that *a reverend* had performed the service. He enclosed a snapshot of himself and wife.

Abba could not believe it. His son was wearing a gentleman's coat and a high hat. The bride was dressed like a countess in a white dress, with train and veil; she held a bouquet of flowers in her hand. Pesha took one look at the snapshot and began to cry. Gimpel's brothers gaped. Neighbors came running, and friends from all over town: they could have sworn that Gimpel had been spirited away by magic to a land of gold, where he had taken a princess to wife—just as in the storybooks the pack merchants brought to town.

To make a long story short, Gimpel induced Getzel to come to America, and Getzel brought over Treitel; Godel followed Treitel, and Feivel, Godel; and then all five brothers brought the young Lippe and Chananiah across. Pesha lived only for the mail. She fastened a charity box to the doorpost, and whenever a letter came she dropped a coin through the slot. Abba worked all alone. He no longer needed apprentices because he now had few expenses and could afford to earn less; in fact, he could have given up work altogether, as his sons sent him money from abroad. Nevertheless he rose at his usual early hour and remained at the bench until late in the evening. His hammer sounded away, joined by the cricket on the hearth, the mouse in its hole, the shingles crackling on the roof. But his mind reeled. For generations the little shoemakers had lived in Frampol. Suddenly the birds had flown the coop. Was this a punishment, a judgment, on him? Did it make sense?

Abba bored a hole, stuck in a peg, and murmured, "So—you, Abba, know what you're doing and God does not? Shame on you, fool! His will be done. Amen!"

IV : *The Sack of Frampol*

Almost forty years went by. Pesha had long since died of cholera, during the Austrian occupation. And Abba's sons had grown rich in America. They wrote every week, begging him to come and join them, but he remained in Frampol, in the same old house on the stubby hill. His own grave lay ready, next to Pesha's, among the little shoemakers; the stone had already been raised; only the date was missing. Abba put up a bench by the side of her grave, and on the eve of Rosh Hashonoh or during fasts, he went there to pray and read Lamentations. He loved it in the cemetery. The sky was so much clearer and loftier than in town, and a great, meaningful silence rose from the consecrated ground and the old gravestone overgrown with moss. He loved to sit and look at the tall white birches, which trembled even when no breeze blew, and at the crows balancing in the branches, like black fruit. Before she died Pesha made him promise that he would not remarry and that he would come regularly to her grave with news of the children. He kept his promise. He would stretch out alongside the mound and whisper into her ear, as if she were still alive, "Gimpel has another grandchild. Getzel's youngest daughter is engaged, thank God. . . ."

The house on the hill was nearly in ruins. The beams had rotted away, and the roof had to be supported by stone posts. Two of the three windows were boarded over because it was no longer possible to fit glass to the frames. The floor was all but gone, and the bare ground lay exposed to the feet. The pear tree in the garden had withered; the trunk and branches were covered with scales. The garden itself was now overgrown with poisonous berries and grapes, and there was a profusion of the burrs that children throw about on Tishe b'Av. People swore they saw strange fires burning there at night, and claimed that the attic was full of bats which fly into girls' hair. Be that as it may, an owl certainly did hoot somewhere near the house. The neighbors repeatedly warned Abba to move out of this ruin before it was too late—the least wind might knock it over. They pleaded with him to give up working—his sons were showering him with money. But Abba stubbornly rose at dawn and continued at the shoemaker's bench. Although yellow hair does not readily change color, Abba's beard had turned completely white, and the white, staining, had turned yellow again. His brows had sprouted like brushes and hid his eyes, and his high forehead was like a piece of yellow parchment. But he had not lost his touch. He could still turn out a stout shoe with a broad heel, even if it did take a little longer. He bored holes with awl, stitched with the needle, hammered his pegs, and in a hoarse voice sang the old shoemaker's song:

> "*A mother bought a billy goat,*
> *The* shochet *killed the billy goat,*
> *Oh, Lord, the billy goat!*
> *Avremele took its ears,*
> *Berele took its lung,*
> *Gimpele took the gullet,*
> *And Dovid'l took the tongue,*
> *Hershele took the neck. . . .*"

As there was no one to join him, he now sang the chorus alone:

> "*Oh, Lord, the billy goat!*"

His friends urged him to hire a servant, but he would not take a strange woman into the house. Occasionally one of the neighbor women came in to sweep and dust, but even this was too much for him. He got used to being alone. He learned to cook for himself and would prepare soup on the tripod, and on Fridays even put up the pudding for the Sabbath. Best of all, he liked to sit alone at the bench and follow the course of his thoughts, which had become more and more tangled with the years. Day and night he carried on conversations with himself. One voice asked questions, the other answered. Clever words came to his mind, sharp, timely expressions full of the wisdom of age, as though his grandfathers had come to life again and were conducting their endless disputations inside his head on matters pertaining to this world and the next. All his thoughts ran on one theme: What is life and what is death, what is time that goes on without stopping, and how far away is America? His eyes would close; the hammer would fall out of his hand; but he would still hear the cobbler's characteristic rapping—a soft tap, a louder one, and a third, louder still—as if a ghost sat at his side, mending unseen shoes. When one of the neighbors asked him why he did not go to join his sons, he would point to the heap on the bench and say, "*Nu,* and the shoes? Who will mend them?"

Years passed, and he had no idea how or where they vanished. Traveling preachers passed through Frampol with disturbing news of the outside world. In the tailors' synagogue, which Abba still attended, the young men spoke of war and anti-Semitic decrees, of Jews flocking to Palestine. Peasants who had been Abba's customers for years suddenly deserted him and took their trade to Polish shoemakers. And one day the old man heard that a new world war was imminent. Hitler—may his name vanish!—had raised his legions of barbarians and was threatening to grab up Poland. This scourge of Israel had expelled the Jews from Germany, as in the days of Spain. The old man thought of the Messiah and became terribly excited. Who knows? Perhaps this was the battle of Gog and Magog? Maybe the Messiah really was coming and the dead would rise again! He saw the graves opening and the little shoemakers stepping forth—Abba, Getzel, Treitel, Gimpel, his grandfather, his own father. He called them all into his house and set out brandy and cakes. His wife, Pesha, was ashamed to find the house in such condition, but "Never mind," he assured her, "we'll get someone to sweep up. As long as we're all together!" Suddenly a cloud appears, envelops the town of Frampol

—synagogue, House of Study, ritual bath, all the Jewish homes, his own among them—and carries the whole settlement off to the Holy Land. Imagine his amazement when he encounters his sons from America. They fall at his feet, crying, "Forgive us, Father!"

When Abba pictured this event his hammer quickened in tempo. He saw the little shoemakers dress for the Sabbath in silks and satins, in flowing robes with broad sashes, and go forth rejoicing in Jerusalem. They pray in the Temple of Solomon, drink the wine of Paradise, and eat of the mighty steer and Leviathan. The ancient Jochanan the Shoemaker, renowned for his piety and wisdom, greets the family and engages them in a discussion of Torah and shoemaking. Sabbath over, the whole clan returns to Frampol, which has become part of the Land of Israel, and re-enters the old home. Even though the house is as small as ever, it has miraculously grown roomy enough, like the hide of a deer, as it is written in the Book. They all work at one bench, Abbas, Gimpels, Getzels, Godels, the Treitels and the Lippes, sewing golden sandals for the daughters of Zion and lordly boots for the sons. The Messiah himself calls on the little shoemakers and has them take his measure for a pair of silken slippers.

One morning, while Abba was wandering among his thoughts, he heard a tremendous crash. The old man shook in his bones: the blast of the Messiah's trumpet! He dropped the boot he had been working on and ran out in ecstasy. But it was not Elijah the Prophet proclaiming the Messiah. Nazi planes were bombing Frampol. Panic spread through the town. A bomb fell near the synagogue, so loud that Abba felt his brain shudder in his skull. Hell opened before him. There was a blaze of lightning, followed by a blast that illuminated all of Frampol. A black cloud rose over the courtyard of the synagogue. Flocks of birds flapped about in the sky. The forest was burning. Looking down from his hill, Abba saw the orchards under great columns of smoke. The apple trees were blossoming and burning. Several men who stood near him threw themselves down on the ground and shouted to him to do the same. He did not hear them; they were moving their lips in dumbshow. Shaking with fright, his knees knocking together, he re-entered the house and packed a sack with his prayer shawl and phylacteries, a shirt, his shoemaker's tools, and the paper money he had put away in the straw mattress. Then he took up a stick, kissed the *mezzuzah,* and walked out the door. It was a miracle that he was not killed; the house caught fire the moment he left. The roof swung out like a lid, uncovering the attic with its treasures. The walls collapsed. Abba turned about and saw the shelf of sacred books go up in flames. The blackened pages turned in the air, glowing with fiery letters like the Torah given to the Jews on Mount Sinai.

V : *Across the Ocean*

From that day on, Abba's life was transformed beyond recognition—it was like a story he had read in the Bible, a fantastic tale heard from the lips of a visiting preacher. He had abandoned the house of his forefathers and the place of his birth and, staff in hand, gone wandering into the world like the Patriarch Abraham. The havoc in Frampol and the surrounding villages brought Sodom and Gomorrah to mind, burning like a fiery furnace. He spent his nights in the cemetery together with the other Jews, lying with his head on a gravestone—he too, as Jacob did at Beth-El, on the way from Beer Sheba to Haran.

On Rosh Hashonoh the Frampol Jews held services in the forest, with Abba leading the most solemn prayer of the Eighteen Benedictions because he was the only one with a prayer shawl. He stood under a pine tree, which served as an altar, and in a hoarse voice intoned the litany of the Days of Awe. A cuckoo and a woodpecker accompanied him, and all the birds roundabout twittered, whistled, and screeched. Late summer gossamers wafted through the air and trailed onto Abba's beard. From time to time a lowing sounded through the forest, like a blast on the ram's horn. As the Day of Atonement drew near, the Jews of Frampol rose at midnight to say the prayer for forgiveness, reciting it in fragments, whatever they could remember. The horses in the surrounding pastures whinnied and neighed, frogs croaked in the cool night. Distant gunfire sounded intermittently; the clouds shone red. Meteors fell; flashes of lightning played across the sky. Half-starved little children, exhausted from crying, took sick and died in their mothers' arms. There were many burials in the open fields. A woman gave birth.

Abba felt he had become his own great-great-grandfather, who had fled Chmielnitzki's pogroms, and whose name is recorded in the annals of Frampol. He was ready to offer himself in Sanctification of the Name. He dreamed of priests and Inquisitions, and when the wind blew among the branches he heard martyred Jews crying out, "Hear, O Israel, the Lord our God, the Lord is One!"

Fortunately Abba was able to help a good many Jews with his money and shoemaker's tools. With the money they hired wagons and fled south, toward Rumania; but often they had to walk long distances, and their shoes gave out. Abba would stop under a tree and take up his tools. With God's help, they surmounted danger and crossed the Rumanian frontier at night. The next morning, the day before Yom Kippur, an old widow took Abba into her house. A telegram was sent to Abba's sons in America, informing them that their father was safe.

You may be sure that Abba's sons moved heaven and earth to rescue the old man. When they learned of his whereabouts they ran to Washington and with great difficulty obtained a visa for him; then they wired a sum of money to the consul in Bucharest, begging him to help their father. The consul sent a courier to Abba, and he was put on the train to Bucharest. There he was held a week, then transferred to an Italian seaport, where he was shorn and deloused and had his clothes steamed. He was put on board the last ship for the United States.

It was a long and severe journey. The train from Rumania to Italy dragged on, uphill and down, for thirty-six hours. He was given food, but for fear of touching anything ritually unclean he ate nothing at all. His phylacteries and prayer shawl got lost, and with them he lost all track of time and could no longer distinguish between Sabbath and weekdays. Apparently he was the only Jewish passenger on board. There was a man on the ship who spoke German, but Abba could not understand him.

It was a stormy crossing. Abba spent almost the whole time lying down, and frequently vomited gall, though he took nothing but dry crusts and water. He would doze off and wake to the sound of the engines throbbing day and night, to the long, threatening signal blasts, which reeked of fire and brimstone. The door of his cabin was constantly slamming to and fro, as though an imp were swinging on it. The glassware in the cupboard trembled and danced; the walls shook; the deck rocked like a cradle.

During the day Abba kept watch at the porthole over his bunk. The ship would leap up as if mounting the sky, and the torn sky would fall as though the world were returning to original chaos. Then the ship would plunge back into the ocean, and once again the firmament would be divided from the waters, as in the Book of Genesis. The waves were a sulphurous yellow and black. Now they would saw-tooth out to the horizon like a mountain range, reminding Abba of the Psalmist's words: "The mountains skipped like rams, the little hills like lambs."

Then they would come heaving back, as in the miraculous Parting of the Waters. Abba had little learning, but Biblical references ran through his mind, and he saw himself as the prophet Jonah, who fled before God. He too lay in the belly of a whale and, like Jonah, prayed to God for deliverance. Then it would seem to him that this was not ocean but limitless desert, crawling with serpents, monsters, and dragons, as it is written in Deuteronomy. He hardly slept a wink at night. When he got up to relieve himself, he would feel faint and lose his balance. With great difficulty he would regain his feet and, his knees buckling under, go wandering, lost, down the narrow, winding corridor, groaning and calling for help until a sailor led him back to the cabin. Whenever this happened he was sure that he was dying. He would not even receive decent Jewish burial, but be dumped in the ocean. And he made his confession, beating his knotty fist on his chest and exclaiming, "Forgive me, Father!"

Just as he was unable to remember when he began his voyage, so he was unaware when it came to an end. The ship had already been made fast to the dock in New York harbor, but Abba hadn't the vaguest notion of this. He saw huge buildings and towers, but mistook them for the pyramids of Egypt. A tall man in a white hat came into the cabin and shouted something at him, but he remained motionless. At last they helped him dress and led him out on deck, where his sons and daughters-in-law and grandchildren were waiting. Abba was bewildered; a crowd of Polish landowners, counts and countesses, gentile boys and girls, leaped at him, hugged him, and kissed him, crying out in a strange language, which was both Yiddish and not Yiddish. They half led, half carried him away, and placed him in a car. Other cars arrived, packed with Abba's kinfolk, and they set out, speeding like shot arrows over bridges, rivers, and roofs. Buildings rose up and receded, as if by magic, some of the buildings touching the sky. Whole cities lay spread out before him; Abba thought of Pithom and Rameses. The car sped so fast, it seemed to him the people in the streets were moving backward. The air was full of thunder and lightning; a banging and trumpeting, it was a wedding and a conflagration at once. The nations had gone wild, a heathen festival . . .

His sons were crowding around him. He saw them as in a fog and did not know them. Short men with white hair. They shouted, as if he were deaf.

"I'm Gimpel!"

"Getzel!"

"Feivel!"

The old man closed his eyes and made no answer. Their voices ran together; everything was turning pell-mell, topsy-turvy. Suddenly he thought of Jacob arriving in Egypt, where he was met by Pharaoh's chariots. He felt, he had lived through the same experience in a previous incarnation. His beard began to tremble; a hoarse sob rose from his chest. A forgotten passage from the Bible stuck in his gullet.

Blindly he embraced one of his sons and sobbed out, "Is this you? Alive?"

He had meant to say: "Now let me die, since I have seen thy face, because thou art yet alive."

VI : *The American Heritage*

Abba's sons lived on the outskirts of a town in New Jersey. Their seven homes, surrounded by gardens, stood on the shore of a lake. Every day they drove to the shoe factory, owned by Gimpel, but on the day of Abba's arrival they took a holiday and prepared a feast in his honor. It was to be held in Gimpel's house, in full compliance with the dietary laws. Gimpel's wife, Bessie, whose father had been a Hebrew teacher in the old country, remembered all the rituals and observed them carefully, going so far as to cover her head with a kerchief. Her sisters-in-law did the same, and Abba's sons put on the skullcaps they had once worn during Holy Days. The grandchildren and great-grandchildren, who did not know a word of Yiddish, actually learned a few phrases. They had heard the legends of Frampol and the little shoemakers and the first Abba of the family line. Even the gentiles in the neighborhood were fairly well acquainted with this history. In the ads Gimpel published in the papers, he had proudly disclosed that his family belonged to the shoemaking aristocracy:

> Our experience dates back three hundred years to the Polish city of Brod, where our ancestor, Abba, learned the craft from a local master. The community of Frampol, in which our family worked at its trade for fifteen generations, bestowed on him the title of Master in recognition of his charitable services. This sense of public responsibility has always gone hand in hand with our devotion to the highest principles of the craft and our strict policy of honest dealing with our customers.

The day Abba arrived, the papers in Elizabeth carried a notice to the effect that the seven brothers of the famous shoe company were welcoming their father from Poland. Gimpel received a mass of congratulatory telegrams from rival manufacturers, relatives, and friends.

It was an extraordinary feast. Three tables were spread in Gimpel's dining-room; one for the old man, his sons, and daughters-in-law, another for the grandchildren, and the third for the great-grandchildren. Although it was broad daylight, the tables were set with candles—red, blue, yellow, green—and their flames were reflected from the dishes and silverware, the crystal glasses and the wine cups, the decanters reminiscent of the Passover Seder. There was an abundance of flowers in every available corner. To be sure, the daughters-in-law would have preferred to see Abba properly dressed for the occasion, but Gimpel put his foot down, and Abba was allowed to spend his first day in the familiar long coat, Frampol style. Even so, Gimpel hired a photographer to take pictures of the banquet—for publication in the newspapers—and invited a rabbi and a cantor to the feast to honor the old man with traditional song.

Abba sat in an armchair at the head of the table. Gimpel and Getzel brought in a bowl and poured water over his hands for the benediction before eating. The food was served on silver trays, carried by colored women. All sorts of fruit juices and salads were set before the old man, sweet brandies, cognac, caviar. But Pharaoh, Joseph, Potiphar's wife, the Land of Goshen, the chief baker, and the chief butler spun round and round in his head. His hands trembled so that he was unable to feed himself, and Gimpel had to help him. No matter how often his sons spoke to him, he still could not tell them apart. Whenever the phone rang he jumped—the Nazis were bombing Frampol. The entire house was whirling round and round like a carousel; the tables were standing on the ceiling and everyone sat upside down. His face was sickly pale in the light of the candles and the electric bulbs. He fell asleep soon after the soup course, while the chicken was being served. Quickly they led him to the bedroom, undressed him, and called a doctor.

He spent several weeks in bed, in and out of consciousness, fitfully dozing as in a fever. He even lacked the strength to say his prayers. There was a nurse at his bedside day and night. Eventually he recovered enough to take a few steps outdoors, in front of the house, but his senses remained disordered. He would walk into clothes closets, lock himself into the bathroom and forget how to come out; the doorbell and the radio frightened him; and he suffered constant anxiety because of the cars that raced past the house. One day Gimpel brought him to a synagogue ten miles away, but even here he was bewildered. The sexton was clean-shaven; the candelabra held electric lights; there was no courtyard, no faucet for washing one's hands, no stove to stand around. The cantor, instead of singing like a cantor should, babbled and croaked. The congregation wore tiny little prayer shawls, like scarves around their necks. Abba was sure he had been hauled into church to be converted. . . .

When spring came and he was no better, the daughters-in-law began to hint that it wouldn't be such a bad idea to put him in a home. But something unforeseen took place. One day, as he happened to open a closet, he noticed a sack lying on the floor which seemed somehow familiar. He looked again and recognized his shoemaker's equipment from Frampol: last, hammer and nails, his knife and pliers, the file and the awl, even a broken-down shoe. Abba felt a tremor of excitement; he could hardly believe his eyes. He sat down on a footstool and began to poke about with fingers grown clumsy and stale. When Bessie came in and found him playing with a dirty old shoe, she burst out laughing.

"What are you doing, Father? Be careful, you'll cut yourself, God forbid!"

That day Abba did not lie in bed dozing. He worked busily till evening and even ate his usual piece of chicken with greater appetite. He smiled at the grandchildren when they came in to see what he was doing. The next morning, when Gimpel told his brothers how their father had returned to his old habits, they laughed and thought nothing more of it—but the activity soon proved to be the old man's salvation. He kept at it day after day without tiring, hunting up old shoes in the clothes closets and begging his sons to supply him with leather and tools. When they gave in, he mended every last pair of shoes in the house—man, woman, and child's. After the Passover holidays the brothers got together and decided to build a little hut in the yard. They furnished it with a cobbler's bench, a stock of leather soles and hides, nails, dyes, brushes—everything even remotely useful in the craft.

Abba took on new life. His daughters-in-law cried, he

looked fifteen years younger. As in the Frampol days, he now rose at dawn, said his prayers, and got right to work. Once again he used a knotted string as a measuring tape. The first pair of shoes, which he made for Bessie, became the talk of the neighborhood. She had always complained of her feet, but this pair, she insisted, were the most comfortable shoes she had ever worn. The other girls soon followed her example and also had themselves fitted. Then came the grandchildren. Even some of the gentile neighbors came to Abba when they heard that in sheer joy of the work he was turning out custom-made shoes. He had to communicate with them, for the most part, in gestures, but they got along very well. As for the younger grandchildren and the great-grandchildren, they had long been in the habit of standing at the door to watch him work. Now he was earning money, and he plied them with candies and toys. He even whittled a stylus and began to instruct them in the elements of Hebrew and piety.

One Sunday, Gimpel came into the workshop and, no more than half in earnest, rolled up his sleeves and joined Abba at the bench. The other brothers were not to be outdone, and on the following Sunday eight work stools were set up in the hut. Abba's sons spread sackcloth aprons on their knees and went to work, cutting soles and shaping heels, boring holes and hammering pegs, as in the good old days. The women stood outside, laughing, but they took pride in their men, and the children were fascinated. The sun streamed in through the windows, and motes of dust danced in the light. In the high spring sky, lofting over the grass and the water, floated clouds in the form of brooms, sailboats, flocks of sheep, herds of elephants. Birds sang; flies buzzed; butterflies fluttered about.

Abba raised his dense eyebrows, and his sad eyes looked around at his heirs, the seven shoemakers: Gimpel, Getzel, Treitel, Godel, Feivel, Lippe, and Chananiah. Their hair was white, though yellow streaks remained. No, praise God, they had not become idolaters in Egypt. They had not forgotten their heritage, nor had they lost themselves among the unworthy. The old man rattled and bumbled deep in his chest, and suddenly began to sing in a stifled, hoarse voice:

> *"A mother had*
> *Ten little boys,*
> *Oh, Lord, ten little boys!*
>
> *The sixth one was called Velvele,*
> *The seventh one was Zeinvele,*
> *The eighth one was called Chenele,*
> *The ninth one was called Tevele,*
> *The tenth one was called Judele . . ."*

And Abba's sons came in on the chorus:

> *"Oh, Lord, Judele!"*

Translated by Isaac Rosenfeld

The Old Man

I

At the beginning of the great war, Chaim Sachar of Krochmalna Street in Warsaw was a rich man. Having put aside dowries of a thousand rubles each for his daughters, he was about to rent a new apartment, large enough to include a Torah-studying son-in-law. There would also have to be additional room for his ninety-year-old father, Reb Moshe Ber, a Turisk hassid, who had recently come to live with him in Warsaw.

But two years later, Chaim Sachar's apartment was almost empty. No one knew where his two sons, young giants, who had been sent to the front, had been buried. His wife and two daughters had died of typhus. He had accompanied their bodies to the cemetery, reciting the memorial prayer for the three of them, pre-empting the most desirable place at the prayer stand in the synagogue, and inviting the enmity of other mourners, who accused him of taking unfair advantage of his multiple bereavement.

After the German occupation of Warsaw, Chaim Sachar, a tall, broad man of sixty who traded in live geese, locked his store. He sold his furniture by the piece, in order to buy frozen potatoes and moldy dried peas, and prepared gritty blackish noodles for himself and his father, who had survived the grandchildren.

Although Chaim Sachar had not for many months been near a live fowl, his large caftan was still covered with goose down, his great broad-brimmed hat glistened with fat, and his heavy, snub-toed boots were stained with slaughterhouse blood. Two small eyes, starved and frightened, peered from beneath his dishevelled eyebrows; the red rims about his eyes were reminiscent of the time when he could wash down a dish of fried liver and hard-boiled eggs with a pint of vodka every morning after prayer. Now, all day long, he wandered through the market place, inhaling butchershop odors and those from restaurants, sniffing like a dog, and occasionally napping on porters' carts. With the refuse he had collected in a basket, he fed his kitchen stove at night; then, rolling the sleeves over his hairy arms, he would grate turnips on a grater. His father, meanwhile, sat warming himself at the open kitchen door, even though it was midsummer. An open Mishna treatise lay across his knees, and he complained constantly of hunger.

As though it were all his son's fault, the old man would mutter angrily, "I can't stand it much longer . . . this gnawing. . . ."

Without looking up from his book, a treatise on impurity, he would indicate the pit of his stomach and resume his mumbling in which the word "impure" recurred like a refrain. Although his eyes were a murky blue, like the eyes of a blind man, he needed no glasses, still retained some of his teeth, yellow and crooked as rusty nails, and awoke each day on the side on which he had fallen asleep. He was disturbed only by his rupture, which nevertheless, did not keep him from plodding through the streets of Warsaw with the help of his pointed stick, his "horse," as he called it. At every synagogue he would tell stories about wars, about evil spirits, and of the old days of cheap and abundant living when people dried sheepskins in cellars and drank spirits directly from the barrel through a straw. In return, Reb Moshe Ber was treated to raw carrots, slices of radish, and turnips. Finishing them in no time, he would then, with a trembling hand, pluck each crumb from his thinning beard—still not white—and speak of Hungary, where more than seventy years before, he had lived in his father-in-law's house. "Right after prayer, we were served a large decanter of wine and a side of veal. And with the soup there were hard-boiled eggs and crunchy noodles."

Hollow-cheeked men in rags, with ropes about their loins, stood about him, bent forward, mouths watering, digesting each of his words, the whites of their eyes greedily showing, as if the old man actually sat there eating. Young yeshiva students, faces emaciated from fasts, eyes shifty and restless as those of madmen, nervously twisted their long earlocks around their fingers, grimacing, as though to suppress stomach-aches, repeating ecstatically, "That was the time. A man had his share of heaven and earth. But now we have nothing."

For many months Reb Moshe Ber shuffled about searching for a bit of food; then, one night in late summer, on returning home, he found Chaim Sachar, his first-born, lying in bed, sick, barefoot, and without his caftan. Chaim Sachar's face was as red as though he had been to a steam bath, and his beard was crumpled in a knot. A neighbor woman came in, touched his forehead, and chanted, "Woe is me, it's that sickness. He must go to the hospital."

Next morning the black ambulance reappeared in the courtyard. Chaim Sachar was taken to the hospital; his apartment was sprayed with carbolic acid; and his father was led to the disinfection center, where they gave him a long white robe and shoes with wooden soles. The guards, who knew him well, gave him double portions of bread under the table and treated him to cigarettes. The Sukkoth holiday had passed by the time the old man, his shaven chin concealed beneath a kerchief, was allowed to leave the disinfection center. His son had died long before, and Reb Moshe Ber said the memorial prayer, *kaddish,* for him. Now alone in the apartment, he had to feed his stove with paper and wood shavings from garbage cans. In the ashes he baked rotten potatoes, which he carried in his scarf, and in an iron pot, he brewed chicory. He kept house, made his own candles by kneading bits of wax and suet around wicks, laundered his shirt beneath the kitchen faucet, and hung it to dry on a piece of string. He set the mousetraps each night and drowned the mice each morning. When he went out he never forgot to fasten the heavy padlock on the door. No one had to pay rent in Warsaw at that time. Moreover, he wore his son's boots and trousers. His old acquaintances in the Houses of Study, envied him. "He lives like a king!" they said, "He has inherited his son's fortune!"

The winter was difficult. There was no coal, and since several tiles were missing from the stove, the apartment was filled with thick black smoke each time the old man made a fire. A crust of blue ice and snow covered the window panes by November, making the rooms constantly dark or dusky. Overnight, the water on his night table froze in the pot. No matter how many clothes he piled over him in bed, he never felt warm; his feet remained stiff, and as soon as he began to doze, the entire pile of clothes would fall off, and he would have to climb out naked to make his bed once more. There was no kerosene; even matches were at a premium. Although he recited chapter upon chapter of the Psalms, he could not fall asleep. The wind, freely roaming about the rooms, banged the doors; even the mice left. When he hung up his shirt to dry, it would grow brittle and break, like glass. He stopped washing himself; his face became coal black. All day long he would sit in the House of Study, near the red-hot iron stove. On the shelves, the old books lay like piles of rags; tramps stood around the tin-topped tables, nondescript fellows with long matted hair and rags over their swollen feet—men who, having lost all they had in the war, were half-naked or covered only with torn clothes, bags slung over their shoulders. All day long, while orphans recited *kaddish,* women stood in throngs around the Holy Ark, loudly praying for the sick, and filling his ears with their moans and lamentations. The room, dim and stuffy, smelled like a mortuary chamber from the numerous anniversary candles that were burning. Every time Reb Moshe Ber, his head hanging down, fell asleep, he would burn himself on the stove. He had to be escorted home at night, for his shoes were hobnailed, and he was afraid he might slip on the ice. The other tenants in his house had given him up for dead. "Poor thing—he's gone to pieces."

One December day, Reb Moshe Ber actually did slip, receiving a hard blow on his right arm. The young man escorting him, hoisted Reb Moshe Ber on his back, and carried him home. Placing the old man on his bed without undressing him, the young man ran away as though he had committed a burglary. For two days the old man groaned, called for help, wept, but no one appeared. Several times each day he said his Confession of Sins, praying for death to come quickly, pounding his chest with his left hand. It was quiet outside in the daytime, as though everyone had died; a hazy green twilight came through the windows. At night he heard scratching noises as though a cat were trying to climb the walls; a hollow roar seemed to come repeatedly from underground. In the darkness the old man fancied that his bed stood in the middle of the room and all the windows were open. After sunset on the second day he thought he saw the door open suddenly, admitting a horse with a black sheet on its back. It had a head as long as a donkey's and innumerable eyes. The old man knew at once that this was the Angel of Death. Terrified, he fell from his bed, making such a racket that two neighbors heard it. There was a commotion in the courtyard; a crowd gathered, and an ambulance was summoned. When he came to his senses, Reb Moshe Ber found himself in a dark box, bandaged and covered up. He was sure this was his hearse, and it worried him that he had no heirs to say *kaddish,* and that therefore the peace of his grave would be disturbed. Suddenly he recalled the verses he would have to say to Duma, the Prosecuting Angel, and his bruised, swollen face twisted into a corpselike smile:

> *"What man is he that liveth and shall not see death?*
> *Shall he deliver his soul from the grave?"*

II

After Passover, Reb Moshe Ber was discharged from the hospital. Completely recovered, he once more had a great appetite but nothing to eat. All his possessions had been stolen; in the apartment only the peeling walls remained. He remembered Jozefow, a little village near the border of Galicia, where for fifty years he had lived and enjoyed great authority in the Turisk hassidic circle, because he had personally known the old rabbi. He inquired about the possibilities of getting there, but those he questioned merely shrugged their shoulders, and each said something different. Some assured him Jozefow had been burned to the ground, wiped out. A wandering beggar, on the other hand, who had visited the region, said that Jozefow was more prosperous than ever, that its inhabitants ate the Sabbath white bread even on week days. But Jozefow was on the Austrian side of the border, and whenever Reb Moshe Ber broached the subject of his trip, men smiled mockingly in their beards and waved their hands. "Don't be foolish, Reb Moshe Ber. Even a young man couldn't do it."

But Reb Moshe Ber was hungry. All the turnips, carrots, and watery soups he had eaten in public kitchens had left him with a hollow sensation in his abdomen. All night he would dream of Jozefow knishes stuffed with ground meat and onions, of tasty concoctions of tripe and calf's feet, chicken fat and lean beef. The moment he closed his eyes he would find himself at some wedding or circumcision feast. Large brown rolls were piled up on the long table, and Turisk hassidim in silken caftans with high velvet hats over their skull caps, danced, glasses of brandy in their hands, singing:

> *"What's a poor man*
> *Cooking for his dinner?*
> *Borscht and potatoes!*
> *Borscht and potatoes!*
> *Faster, faster, hop-hop-hop!"*

He was the chief organizer of all those parties; he quarreled with the caterers, scolded the musicians, supervised every detail, and having no time to eat anything, had to postpone it all for later. His mouth watering, he awoke each morning, bitter that not even in his dream had he tasted those wonderful dishes. His heart pounded; his body was covered with a cold perspiration. The light outside seemed brighter every day, and in the morning, rectangular patterns of sunlight would waver on the peeling wall, swirling, as though they mirrored the rushing waves of a river close by. Around the bare hook for a chandelier on the crumbling ceiling, flies hummed. The cool golden glow of dawn illumined the window panes, and the distorted image of a bird in flight was always reflected in them. Beggars and cripples sang their songs in the courtyard below, playing their fiddles and blowing little brass trumpets. In his shirt, Reb Moshe Ber would crawl down from the one remaining bed, to warm his feet and stomach and to gaze at the barefoot girls in short petticoats who were beating red comforters. In all directions feathers flew, like white blossoms, and there were familiar scents of rotton straw and tar. The old man, straightening his crooked fingers, pricking up his long hairy ears as though to hear distant noises, thought for the thousandth time that if he didn't get out of here this very summer, he never would.

"God will help me," he would tell himself. "If he wills it, I'll be eating in a holiday arbor at Jozefow."

He wasted a lot of time at first by listening to people who told him to get a passport and apply for a visa. After being photographed, he was given a yellow card, and then he had to stand with hordes of others for weeks outside the Austrian consulate on a crooked little street somewhere near the Vistula. They were constantly being cursed in German and punched with the butts of guns by bearded, pipe-smoking soldiers. Women with infants in their arms wept and fainted. It was rumored that visas were granted only to prostitutes and to men who paid in gold. Reb Moshe Ber, going there every day at sunrise, sat on the ground and nodded over his Beni Issachar treatise, nourishing himself with grated turnips and moldy red radishes. But since the crowd continued to increase, he decided one day to give it all up. Selling his cotton-padded caftan to a peddler, he bought a loaf of bread, and a bag in which he placed his prayer shawl and phylacteries, as well as a few books for good luck; and planning to cross the border illegally, he set out on foot.

It took him five weeks to get to Ivangorod. During the day, while it was warm, he walked barefoot across the fields, his boots slung over his shoulders, peasant fashion. He fed on unripened grain and slept in barns. German military police often stopped him, scrutinized his Russian passport for a long time, searched him to see that he was not carrying contraband, and then let him go. At various times, as he walked, his intestines popped out of place; he lay on the ground and pushed them back with his hands. In a village near Ivangorod he found a group of Turisk hassidim, most of them young. When they heard where he was going and that he intended to enter Galicia, they gaped at him, blinking, then, after whispering among themselves, they warned him, "You're taking a chance in times like these. They'll send you to the gallows on the slightest pretext."

Afraid to converse with him, lest the authorities grow suspicious, they gave him a few marks and got rid of him. A few days later, in that village, people spoke in hushed voices of an old Jew who had been arrested somewhere on the road and shot by a firing squad. But not only was Reb Moshe alive by then; he was already on the Austrian side of the border. For a few marks, a peasant had taken him across, hidden in a cart under a load of straw. The old man started immediately for Rajowiec. He fell ill with dysentery there and lay in the poorhouse for several days. Everyone thought he was dying, but he recovered gradually.

Now there was no shortage of food. Housewives treated Reb Moshe Ber to brown buckwheat with milk, and on Saturdays he even ate cold calf's foot jelly and drank a glass of brandy. The moment his strength returned, he was off again. The roads were familiar here. In this region, the peasants still wore the white linen coats and quadrangular caps with tassels that they had worn fifty years ago; they had beards and spoke Ukrainian. In Zamosc the old man was arrested and thrown into jail with two young peasants. The police confiscated his bag. He refused gentile food and accepted only bread and water. Every other day he was summoned by the commandant who, as though Reb Moshe Ber were deaf, screamed directly into his ear in a throaty language. Comprehending nothing, Reb Moshe Ber simply nodded his head and tried to throw himself at the commandant's feet. This went on until after Rosh Hashonah; only then did the Zamosc Jews learn that an old man from abroad was being held in jail. The rabbi and the head of the community obtained his release by paying the commandant a ransom.

Reb Moshe Ber was invited to stay in Zamosc until after Yom Kippur, but he would not consider it. He spent the night there, took some bread, and set out on foot for Bilgorai at daybreak. Trudging across harvested fields, digging turnips for food, he refreshed himself in the thick pinewoods with whitish berries, large, sour and watery, which grow in damp places and are called Valakhi in the local dialect. A cart gave him a lift for a mile or so. A few miles from Bilgorai, he was thrown to the ground by some shepherds who pulled off his boots and ran away with them.

Reb Moshe Ber continued barefoot, and for this reason did not reach Bilgorai until late at night. A few tramps, spending the night in the House of Study, refused to let him in, and he had to sit on the steps, his weary head on his knees. The autumnal night was clear and cold; against the dark yellow, dull glow of the starry sky, a flock of goats, silently absorbed, peeled bark from the wood that had been piled in the synagogue courtyard for winter. As though complaining of an unforgettable sorrow, an owl lamented in a womanish voice, falling silent and then beginning again, over and over. People with wooden lanterns in their hands came at daybreak to say the *Selichoth* prayers. Bringing the old man inside, they placed him near the stove and covered him with discarded prayer shawls from the chest. Later in the morning they brought him a heavy pair of hobnailed, coarse-leathered military boots. The boots pinched the old man's feet badly, but Reb Moshe Ber was determined to observe the Yom Kippur fast at Jozefow, and Yom Kippur was only one day off.

He left early. There were no more than about four

miles to travel, but he wanted to arrive at dawn, in time for the *Selichoth* prayers. The moment he had left town, however, his stiff boots began to cause him such pain, that he couldn't take a step. He had to pull them off and go barefoot. Then there was a downpour with thunder and lightning. He sank knee deep in puddles, kept stumbling, and became smeared with clay and mud. His feet swelled and bled. He spent the night on a haystack under the open sky, and it was so cold that he couldn't sleep. In the neighboring villages, dogs kept barking, and the rain went on forever. Reb Moshe Ber was sure his end had come. He prayed God to spare him until the *Nilah* prayer, so that he might reach heaven purified of all sin. Later, when on the eastern horizon, the edges of clouds began to glow, while the fog grew milky white, Reb Moshe Ber was infused with new strength and once again set off for Jozefow.

He reached the Turisk circle at the very moment when the hassidim had assembled in the customary way, to take brandy and cake. A few recognized the new arrival at once, and there was great rejoicing for he had long been thought dead. They brought him hot tea. He said his prayers quickly, ate a slice of white bread with honey, gefilte fish made of fresh carp, and kreplach, and took a few glasses of brandy. Then he was led to the steam bath. Two respectable citizens accompanied him to the seventh shelf and personally whipped him with two bundles of new twigs, while the old man wept for joy.

Several times during Yom Kippur, he was at the point of fainting, but he observed the fast until it ended. Next morning the Turisk hassidim gave him new clothes and told him to study the Torah. All of them had plenty of money, since they traded with Bosnian and Hungarian soldiers, and sent flour to what had been Galicia in exchange for smuggled tobacco. It was no hardship for them to support Reb Moshe Ber. The Turisk hassidim knew who he was—a hassid who had sat at the table of no less a man than Reb Motele of Chernobel! He had actually been a guest at the famous wonder-rabbi's home!

A few weeks later, the Turisk hassidim, timber merchants, just to shame their sworn enemies, the Sandzer hassidim, collected wood and built a house for Reb Moshe Ber and married him to a spinster, a deaf and dumb village girl of about forty.

Exactly nine months later she gave birth to a son—now he had someone to say *kaddish* for him. As though it were a wedding, musicians played at the circumcision ceremony. Well-to-do housewives baked cakes and looked after the mother. The place where the banquet was held, the assembly room of the Turisk circle, smelled of cinnamon, saffron, and the women's best Sabbath dresses. Reb Moshe Ber wore a new satin caftan and a high velvet hat. He danced on the table, and for the first time, mentioned his age:

"And Abraham was a hundred years old," he recited, "when his son Isaac was born unto him. And Sarah said: God hath made me laugh so that all who hear will laugh with me."

He named the boy Isaac.

Translated by Norbert Guterman
and Elaine Gottlieb

The Unseen

1 : *Nathan and Temerl*

They say that I, the evil spirit, after descending to earth in order to induce people to sin, will then ascend to heaven to accuse them. As a matter of fact, I am also the one to give the sinner the first push, but I do this so cleverly that the sin appears to be an act of virtue; thus, other infidels, unable to learn from the example, continue to sink into the abyss.

But let me tell you a story. There once lived a man in the town of Frampol who was known for his wealth and lavish ways. Named Nathan Jozefover, for he was born in Little Jozefov, he had married a Frampol girl and settled there. Reb Nathan, at the time of this story, was sixty, perhaps a bit more. Short and broad-boned, he had, like most rich people, a large paunch. Cheeks red as wine showed between the clumps of short black beard. Over small twinkling eyes his eyebrows were thick and shaggy. All his life, he had eaten, drunk, and made merry. For breakfast, his wife served him cold chicken and raisin bread, which, like a great landowner, he washed down with a glass of mead. He had a preference for dainties such as roast squab, necks stuffed with chopped milt, pancakes with liver, egg noodles with broth, etc. The townspeople whispered that his wife, Roise Temerl, prepared a noodle-pudding for him every day, and if he so desired made a Sabbath dinner in the middle of the week. Actually, she too liked to indulge.

Having plenty of money and no children, husband and wife apparently believed that good cheer was in order. Both of them, therefore, became fat and lazy. After their lunch, they would close the bedroom shutters and snore in their featherbeds as though it were midnight. During the winter nights, long as Jewish exile, they would get out of bed to treat themselves to gizzard, chicken livers, and jam, washed down with beet soup or apple juice. Then, back to their canopied beds they went to resume their dreams of the next day's porridge.

Reb Nathan gave little time to his grain business, which ran itself. A large granary with two oaken doors stood behind the house he had inherited from his father-in-law. In the yard there were also a number of barns, sheds, and other buildings. Many of the old peasants in the surrounding villages would sell their grain and flax to Nathan alone, for, even though others might offer them more, they trusted Nathan's honesty. He never sent anyone away empty-handed, and sometimes even advanced money for the following year's crop. The simple peasants, in gratitude, brought him wood from the forest, while their wives picked mushrooms and berries for him. An elderly servant, widowed in her youth, looked after the house and even assisted in the business. For the entire week, with the exception of market day, Nathan did not have to lift a finger.

He enjoyed wearing fine clothes and telling yarns. In the summer, he would nap on a bed among the trees of his orchard, or read either the Bible in Yiddish, or simply a story book. He liked, on the Sabbath, to listen to the preaching of a *magid,* and occasionally to invite a poor man to his house. He had many amusements: for example, he loved to have his wife, Roise Temerl, tickle his feet, and she did this whenever he wished. It was rumored that he and his wife would bathe together in his own bathhouse, which stood in his yard. In a silk dressing gown embroidered with flowers and leaves, and wearing pompommed slippers, he would step out on his porch in the afternoon, smoking a pipe with an amber bowl. Those who passed by greeted him, and he responded in a friendly fashion. Sometimes he would stop a passing girl, ask her this and that, and then send her off with a joke. After the reading of the *Perek* on Saturday, he would sit with the women on the bench, eating nuts or pumpkin seeds, listening to gossip, and telling of his own encounters with landowners, priests, and rabbis. He had traveled widely in his youth, visiting Cracow, Brody, and Danzig.

Roise Temerl was almost the image of her husband. As the saying goes: when a husband and wife sleep on one pillow finally they have the same head. Small and plump, she had cheeks still full and red despite her age, and a tiny talkative mouth. The smattering of Hebrew, with which she just found her way through the prayer books, gave her the right to a leading role in the women's section of the Prayer House. She often led a bride to the synagogue, was sponsor at a circumcision, and occasionally collected money for a poor girl's trousseau. Although a wealthy woman, she could apply cups to the sick, and would adroitly cut out the pip of a chicken. Her skills included embroidery and knitting. She possessed numerous jewels, dresses, coats, and furs, all of which she kept in oaken chests as protection against moths and thieves.

Because of her gracious manner, she was welcomed at the butcher's, at the ritual bath, and wherever else she went. Her only regret was that she had no children. To make up for this, she gave charitable contributions and engaged a pious scholar to pray in her memory after her death. She took pleasure in a nest-egg she had managed to save over the years, kept it hidden somewhere in a bag, and now and then enjoyed counting the gold pieces. However, since Nathan gave her everything she needed, she had no idea of how to spend the money. Although he knew of her hoard, he pretended ignorance, realizing that "stolen water is sweet to drink," and did not begrudge her this harmless diversion.

II : *Shifra Zirel the Servant*

One day their old servant became ill and soon died. Nathan and his wife were deeply grieved, not only because they had grown so accustomed to her that she was almost a blood relative, but she had also been honest, industrious, and loyal, and it would not be easy to replace her. Nathan and Roise Temerl wept over her grave, and Nathan said the first *kaddish*. He promised that after the thirty day mourning period, he would drive to Janow to order the tombstone she deserved. Nathan, actually did not come out a loser through her death. Having rarely spent any of her earnings, and being without a family, she had left everything to her employers.

Immediately after the funeral, Roise Temerl began to look for a new servant, but could not find any that compared to the first. The Frampol girls were not only lazy, but they could not bake and fry to Roise Temerl's satisfaction. Various widows, divorced women, and deserted wives were offered her, but none had the qualifications that Roise Temerl desired. Of every candidate presented at her house, she would make inquiries on how to prepare fish, marinate borscht, bake pastry, strudel, egg cookies, etc.; what to do when milk and borscht sour, when a chicken is too tough, a broth too fat, a Sabbath pudding overdone, a porridge too thick or too thin, and other tricky questions. The bewildered girl would lose her tongue and leave in embarrassment. Several weeks went by like this, and the pampered Roise Temerl, who had to do all the chores, could clearly see that it was easier to eat a meal than prepare one.

Well, I, the Seducer, could not stand by and watch Nathan and his wife starve; I sent them a servant, a wonder of wonders.

A native of Zamosc, she had even worked for wealthy families in Lublin. Although at first she had refused—even if she were paid her weight in gold—to go to an insignificant spot like Frampol, various people had intervened, Roise Temerl had agreed to pay a few gulden more than she had paid previously, and the girl, Shifra Zirel, decided to take the job.

In the carriage that had to be sent to Zamosc for her and her extensive luggage, she arrived with suitcases, baskets, and knapsacks, like a rich bride. Well along in her twenties, she seemed no more than eighteen or nineteen. Her hair was plaited in two braids coiled at the sides of her head; she wore a checkered shawl with tassels, a cretonne dress, and narrow heeled shoes. Her chin had a wolf-like sharpness, her lips were thin, her eyes shrewd and impudent. She wore rings in her ears and around her throat a coral necklace. Immediately, she found fault with the Frampol mud, the clay taste of the well water, and the lumpy home-made bread. Served over-cooked soup by Roise Temerl on the first day, she took a drop of it with her spoon, made a face, and complained, "It's sour and rancid!"

She demanded a Jewish or Gentile girl as an assistant, and Roise Temerl, after a strenuous search, found a Gentile one, the sturdy daughter of the bath attendant. Shifra Zirel began to give orders. She told the girl to scrub the floors, clean the stove, sweep the cobwebs in corners, and advised Roise Temerl to get rid of the superfluous pieces of furniture, various rickety chairs, stools, tables, and chests. The windows were cleaned, the dusty curtains removed, and the rooms became lighter and more spacious. Roise Temerl and Nathan were amazed by her first meal. Even the emperor could ask for no better cook. An appetizer of calves' liver and lungs, partly fried and partly boiled, was served before the broth, and its aroma titillated their nostrils. The soup was seasoned with herbs unobtainable at Frampol, such as paprika and capers, which the new servant had apparently brought from Zamosc. Dessert was a mixture of applesauce, raisins, and apricots, flavored with cinnamon, saffron, and cloves, whose fragrance filled the house. Then, as in the wealthy homes of Lublin, she served black coffee with chicory. After lunch, Nathan and his wife wanted to nap as usual, but Shifra Zirel warned them that it was unhealthful to sleep immediately after eating, because the vapors mount from the stomach to the brain. She advised her employers to walk back and forth in the garden a few times. Nathan was brimful of good food, and the coffee had gone to his head. He reeled and kept repeating. "Well, my dear wife, isn't she a treasure of a servant?"

"I hope no one will take her away," Roise Temerl said. Knowing how envious people were, she feared the Evil Eye, or those who might offer the girl better terms.

There is no sense going into detail about the excellent dishes Shifra Zirel prepared, the babkas and macaroons she baked, the appetizers she introduced. The neighbors found Nathan's rooms and his yard unrecognizable. Shifra Zirel had whitewashed the walls, cleaned the sheds and closets, and hired a laborer to weed the garden and repair the fence and railing of the porch. Like the mistress of the house rather than its servant, she supervised everything. When Shifra Zirel, in a woolen dress and pointed shoes, went for a stroll on Saturdays, after the pre-cooked *cholent* dinner, she was stared at not only by common laborers and poor girls, but by young men and women of good families as well. Daintily holding up her skirt, she walked, her head high. Her assistant, the bath-house attendant's daughter, followed, carrying a bag of fruit and cookies, for Jews could not carry parcels on the Sabbath. From the benches in front of their houses women observed her and shook their heads. "She's as proud as a landowner's wife!" they would comment, predicting that her stay in Frampol would be brief.

III : *Temptation*

One Tuesday, when Roise Temerl was in Janow visiting her sister, who was ill, Nathan ordered the Gentile girl to prepare a steam bath for him. His limbs and bones had been aching since morning, and he knew that the only remedy for this was to perspire abundantly. After putting a great deal of wood in the stove around the bricks, the girl lighted the fire, filled the vat with water, and returned to the kitchen.

When the fire had burnt itself out, Nathan undressed and then poured a bucket of water on the red hot bricks. The bathhouse filled with steam. Nathan, climbing the stairs to the high shelf where the steam was hot and dense, whipped himself with a twig broom that he had prepared previously. Usually Roise Temerl helped him with this. When he perspired she poured the buckets of water, and when she perspired he poured. After they had flogged each other with twig brooms, Roise Temerl would bathe him in a wooden tub and comb him. But this time Roise Temerl had had to go to Janow to her sick sister, and Nathan did not think it wise to wait for her return, since his sister-in-law was very old and might die and then Roise Temerl would have to stay there seven days. Never before had he taken his bath alone. The steam, as usual, soon settled. Nathan wanted to go down and pour more water on the bricks, but his legs felt heavy and he was lazy. With his belly protruding upward, he lay on his back, flogging himself with the broom, rubbing his knees and ankles, and staring at the bent beam on the smoke-blackened ceiling. Through the crack, a patch of clear sky stared in. This was the month of Elul, and Nathan was assailed by melancholy. He remembered his sister-in-law as a young woman full of life, and now she was on her deathbed. He too would not eat marchpanes nor sleep on eider down forever, it occurred to him, for some day he would be placed in a dark grave, his eyes covered with shards, and worms would consume the body that Roise Temerl had pampered for the nearly fifty years that she had been his wife.

Probing his soul, Nathan lay there, belly upward, when he suddenly heard the chain clank, the door creak. Looking about, he saw to his amazement, that Shifra Zirel had entered. Barefoot, with a white kerchief around her head, she was dressed only in a slip. In a choking voice, he cried out, "No!" and hastened to cover himself. Upset, and shaking his head, he beckoned her to leave, but Shifra Zirel said, "Don't be afraid, master, I won't bite you."

She poured a bucket of water over the hot bricks. A hissing noise filled the room, and white clouds of steam quickly rose, scalding Nathan's limbs. Then Shifra Zirel climbed the steps to Nathan, grabbed the twig broom, and began to flog him. He was so stunned, he became speechless. Choking, he almost rolled off the slippery shelf. Shifra Zirel, meanwhile, continued diligently to whip him and to rub him with a cake of soap she had brought. Finally, having regained his composure, he said, hoarsely, "What's the matter with you? Shame on you!"

"What's there to be ashamed about?" the servant asked airily, "I won't harm the master . . ."

For a long time she occupied herself combing and massaging him, rubbing him with soap, and drenching him with water, and Nathan was compelled to acknowledge that this devilish woman was more accomplished than Roise Temerl. Her hands, too, were smoother; they tickled his body and aroused his desire. He soon forgot that this was the month of Elul, before the Days of Awe, and told the servant to lock the wooden latch of the door. Then, in a waving voice, he made a proposition.

"Never, uncle!" she said resolutely, pouring a bucket of water on him.

"Why not?" he asked, his neck, belly, head, all his limbs dripping.

"Because I belong to my husband."

"What husband?"

"The one I'll have some day, God willing."

"Come on, Shifra Zirel," he said, "I'll give you something—a coral necklace, or a brooch."

"You're wasting your breath," she said.

"A kiss at least!" he begged.

"A kiss will cost twenty-five coins," Shifra Zirel said.

"Groszy or threepence pieces?" Nathan asked, efficiently, and Shifra Zirel answered, "Gulden."

Nathan reflected. Twenty-five gulden was no trifle. But I, the Old Nick, reminded him that one does not live forever, and that there was no harm in leaving a few gulden less behind. Therefore, he agreed.

Bending over him, placing her arms about his neck, Shifra Zirel kissed him on the mouth. Half kiss and half bite, it cut his breath. Lust arose in him. He could not climb down, for his arms and legs were trembling, and Shifra Zirel had to help him down and even put on his dressing gown. "So that's the kind you are . . ." he murmured.

"Don't insult me, Reb Nathan," she admonished, "I'm pure."

"Pure as a pig's knuckle," Nathan thought. He opened the door for her. After a moment, glancing anxiously about to make sure he was not seen, he left also. "Imagine such a thing happening!" he murmured. "What impudence! A real whore!" He resolved never again to have anything to do with her.

IV : *Troubled Nights*

Nathan lay at night on his eiderdown mattress, wrapped in a silken blanket, his head propped up by three pillows, but he was robbed of sleep by my wife Lilith and her companions. He had drowsed off, but was awake; he began to dream something, but the vision frightened him, and he rose with a start. Someone invisible whispered something into his ear. He fancied, for a moment, that he was thirsty. Then his head felt feverish. Leaving his bed, he slipped into his slippers and dressing gown, and went to the kitchen to scoop up a mug of water. Leaning over the barrel, he slipped and almost fell in. Suddenly he realized that he craved Shifra Zirel with the craving of a young man. "What's the matter with me?" he murmured, "This can only be a trick of the devil." He started to walk to his own room, but found himself going to the little room where the servant slept. Halting at the doorway, he listened. A rustling came from behind the stove, and in the dry wood something creaked. The pale glow of a lantern flashed outside; there was a sigh. Nathan recalled that this was Elul, that God-fearing Jews rise at dawn for the *Selichot* prayers. Just as he was about to turn back, the servant opened the door and asked in an alert tone, "Who's there?"

"I am," Nathan whispered.

"What does the master wish?"

"Don't you know?"

She groaned and was silent, as though wondering what to do. Then she said, "Go back to bed, master. It's no use talking."

"But I can't sleep," Nathan complained in a tone he sometimes used with Roise Temerl, "Don't send me away!"

"Leave, master," Shifra Zirel said in an angry voice, "or I'll scream!"

"Hush. I won't force you, God forbid. I'm fond of you. I love you."

"If the master loves me then let him marry me."

"How can I? I have a wife!" Nathan said, surprised.

"Well, what of it? What do you think divorce is for?" she said and sat up.

"She's not a woman," Nathan thought, "but a demon." Frightened by her and her talk he remained in the doorway, heavy, bewildered, leaning against the jamb. The Good Spirit, who is at the height of his power during the month of Elul, reminded him of *The Measure of Righteousness*—which he had read in Yiddish—stories of pious men, tempted by landowners' wives, she-demons, whores, but who had refused to succumb to the temptation. "I'll send her away at once, tomorrow, even if I must pay her wages for a year," Nathan decided. But he said, "What's wrong with you? I've lived with my wife for almost fifty years! Why should I divorce her now?"

"Fifty years is sufficient," the brazen servant answered.

Her insolence, rather than repelling him, attracted him the more. Walking to her bed, he sat on the edge. A vile warmth arose from her. Seized by a powerful desire, he said, "How can I divorce her? She won't consent."

"You can get one without her consent," said the servant, apparently well-informed.

Blandishments and promises would not change her mind. To all Nathan's arguments, she turned a deaf ear. Day was already breaking when he returned to his bed. His bedroom walls were gray as canvas. Like a coal glowing on a heap of ashes, the sun arose in the east, casting a light, scarlet as the fire of hell. A crow, alighting on the windowsill, began to caw with its curved black beak, as though trying to announce a piece of bad news. A shudder went through Nathan's bones. He felt that he was his own master no longer, that the Evil Spirit, having seized the reins, drove him along an iniquitous path, perilous and full of obstacles.

From then on Nathan did not have a moment's respite.

While his wife, Roise Temerl, observed the mourning period for her sister in Janow, he was roused each night, and driven to Shifra Zirel, who, each time, rejected him.

Begging and imploring, he promised valuable gifts, offered a rich dowry and inclusion in his will, but nothing availed him. He vowed not to return to her, but his vow was broken each time. He spoke foolishly, in a manner unbecoming to a respectable man, and disgraced himself. When he woke her, she not only chased him away, but scolded him. In passing from his room to hers in the darkness, he would stumble against doors, cupboards, stoves, and he was covered with bruises. He ran into a slop basin and spilled it. He shattered glassware. He tried to recite a chapter of the Psalms that he knew by heart and implored God to rescue him from the net I had spread, but the holy words were distorted on his lips and his mind was confused with impure thoughts. In his bedroom there was a constant buzz and hum from the glowworms, flies, moths, and mosquitoes with which I, the Evil One, had filled it. With eyes open and ears intent, Nathan lay wide awake, listening to each rustle. Roosters crowed, frogs croaked in the swamps, crickets chirped, flashes of lightning glowed strangely. A little imp kept reminding him: Don't be a fool, Reb Nathan, she's waiting for you; she wants to see if you're a man or a mouse. And the imp hummed: Elul or no Elul, a woman's a woman, and if you don't enjoy her in this world it's too late in the next. Nathan would call Shifra Zirel and wait for her to answer. It seemed to him that he heard the patter of bare feet, that he saw the whiteness of her body or of her slip in the darkness. Finally, trembling, afire, he would rise from his bed to go to her room. But she remained stubborn. "Either I or the mistress," she would declare. "Go, master!"

And grabbing a broom from the pile of refuse, she would smack him across the back. Then Reb Nathan Jozefover, the richest man in Frampol, respected by young and old, would return defeated and whipped to his canopied bed, to toss feverishly until sunrise.

V : *Forest Road*

Roise Temerl, when she returned from Janow and saw her husband, was badly frightened. His face was ashen; there were bags under his eyes; his beard, which until recently had been black, was now threaded with white; his stomach had become loose, and hung like a sack. Like one dangerously ill, he could barely drag his feet along. "Woe is me, even finer things than this are put in the grave!" she exclaimed. She began to question him, but since he could not tell her the truth, he said he was suffering from headaches, heartburn, stitches, and smiliar ailments. Roise Temerl, though she had looked forward to seeing her husband and had hoped to enjoy herself with him, ordered a carriage and horses and told him to see a doctor in Lublin. Filling a suitcase with cookies, jams, juices, and various other refreshments, she urged him not to spare money, but to find the best of doctors and to take all the medication he prescribed. Shifra Zirel too, saw her master depart, escorting the carriage on foot as far as the bridge, and wishing him a speedy recovery.

Late at night, by the light of the full moon, while the carriage drove along a forest road and shadows ran ahead, I, the Evil Spirit, came to Reb Nathan and asked, "Where are you going?"

"Can't you see? To a doctor."

"Your ailment can't be cured by a doctor," I said.

"What shall I do then? Divorce my old wife?"

"Why not?" I said to him, "Did not Abraham drive his bondwoman, Hagar, into the wilderness, with nothing but a bottle of water, because he preferred Sarah? And later, did he not take Keturah and have six sons with her? Did not Moses, the teacher of all Jews, take, in addition to Zipporah, another wife from the land of Kush; and when Miriam, his sister, spoke against him, did she not become leprous? Know ye, Nathan, you are fated to have sons and daughters, and according to the law, you should have divorced Roise Temerl ten years after marrying her? Well, you may not leave the world without begetting children, and Heaven, therefore, has sent you Shifra Zirel to lie in your lap and become pregnant and bear healthy children, who after your death will say *kaddish* for you and will inherit your possessions. Therefore do not try to resist, Nathan, for such is the decree of Heaven, and if you do not execute it, you will be punished, you will die soon, and Roise Temerl will be a widow anyway and you will inherit hell."

Hearing these words, Nathan became frightened. Shuddering from head to foot, he said, "If so, why do I go to Lublin? I should, rather, order the driver to return to Frampol."

And I replied, "No, Nathan. Why tell your wife what you're about to do? When she learns you plan to divorce her and take the servant in her place, she will be greatly grieved, and may revenge herself on you or the servant. Rather follow the advice Shifra Zirel gave you. Get divorce papers in Lublin and place them secretly in your wife's dresses; this will make the divorce valid. Then tell her that doctors had advised you to go to Vienna for an operation since you have an internal growth. And before leaving, collect all the money and take it along with you, leaving your wife only the house and the furniture and her personal belongings. Only when you are far from home, and Shifra Zirel with you, you may inform Roise Temerl that she is a divorcee. In this way you will avoid scandal. But do not delay, Nathan, for Shifra Zirel won't tarry, and if she leaves you, you might be punished and perish and lose this world as well as the next."

I made more speeches, pious and impious, and at daybreak, when he fell asleep, I brought him Shifra Zirel, naked, and showed him the images of the children she would bear, male and female, with side whiskers and curls, and I made him eat imaginary dishes she had prepared for him: they tasted of Paradise. He awoke from these visions, famished, and consumed with desire. Approaching the city, the carriage stopped at an inn, where Nathan was served breakfast and a soft bed prepared for him. But on his palate there remained the savor of the pancake he had tasted in his dream. And on his lips he could almost feel Shifra Zirel's kisses. Overcome with longing, he put on his coat again, and told his hosts he must hurry to meet merchants.

In a back alley where I led him, he discovered a miserly scribe, who for five gulden, wrote the divorce papers and had them signed by witnesses, as required by law. Then Nathan, after purchasing numerous bottles and pills from an apothecary, returned to Frampol. He told his wife he had been examined by three doctors, that they had all found he had a tumor in his stomach, and that he must go at once to Vienna to be treated by great specialists or he would not last the year. Shaken by the story, Roise Temerl said, "What's money? Your health means far more to me." She wanted to accompany him, but Nathan reasoned with her and argued, "The trip will cost double; moreover, our business here must be looked after. No, stay here, and God willing, if everything goes well, I'll be back, we'll be happy together." To make a long story short, Roise Temerl agreed with him and stayed.

The same night, after Rosie Temerl had fallen asleep, Nathan rose from bed and quietly placed the divorce papers in her trunk. He also visited Shifra Zirel in her room to inform her of what he had done. Kissing and embracing him, she promised to be a good wife and faithful mother to his children. But in her heart, jeering, she thought: You old fool, you'll pay dearly for falling in love with a whore.

And now starts the story of how I and my companions forced the old sinner, Nathan Jozefover, to become a man who sees without being seen, so that his bones would never be properly buried, which is the penalty for lechery.

VI : *Nathan Returns*

A year passed, Roise Temerl now had a second husband, having married a Frampol grain dealer, Moshe Mecheles, who had lost his wife at the same time as she had been divorced. Moshe Mecheles was a small red-bearded man, with heavy red eyebrows and piercing yellow eyes. He often disputed with the Frampol rabbi, put on two pairs of phylacteries while praying, and owned a water mill. He was always covered with white flour dust. He had been rich before, and after his marriage to Roise Temerl, he took over her granaries and customers and became a magnate.

Why had Roise Temerl married him? For one thing, other people intervened. Secondly, she was lonely, and thought that another husband might at least partially replace Nathan. Third, I, the Seducer, had my own reasons for wanting her married. Well, after marrying, she realized she had made a mistake. Moshe Mecheles had odd ways. He was thin, and she tried to fatten him, but he would not touch her dumplings, pancakes, and chickens. He preferred bread with garlic, potatoes in their skins, onions and radishes, and once a day, a piece of lean boiled beef. His stained caftan was never buttoned; he wore a string to hold up his trousers, refused to go to the bath Roise Temerl would heat for him, and had to be forced to change a shirt or a pair of underpants. Moreover he was rarely at home; he either traveled for business or attended community meetings. He went to sleep late, and groaned and snored in his bed. When the sun rose, so did Moshe Mecheles, humming like a bee. Although close to sixty, Roise Temerl still did not disdain what others like, but Moshe Mecheles came to her rarely, and then it was only a question of duty. The woman finally conceded that she had blundered, but what could be done? She swallowed her pride and suffered silently.

One afternoon around Elul time, when Roise Temerl went to the yard to pour out the slops, she saw a strange figure. She cried out; the basin fell from her hands, the slops spilled at her feet. Ten paces away stood Nathan, her former husband. He was dressed like a beggar, his caftan torn, a piece of rope around his loins, his shoes in shreds, and on his head only the lining of a cap. His once pink face was now yellow, and the clumps of his beard were gray; pouches hung from his eyes. From his disheveled eyebrows he stared at Roise Temerl. For a moment it occurred to her that he must have died, and this was his ghost before her. She almost called out: Pure Soul, return to your place of rest! But since this was happening in broad daylight, she soon recovered from her shock and asked in trembling voice:

"Do my eyes deceive me?"

"No," said Nathan, "It is I."

For a long time husband and wife stood silently gazing at each other. Roise Temerl was so stunned that she could not speak. Her legs began to shake, and she had to hold on to a tree to keep from falling.

"Woe is me, what has become of you?" she cried.

"Is your husband at home?" Nathan asked.

"My husband?" she was bewildered, "No . . ."

About to ask him in, Roise Temerl remembered that according to law, she was not permitted to stay under the same roof with him. Also, she feared that the servant might recognize him. Bending, she picked up the slop basin.

"What happened?" she asked.

Haltingly, Nathan told her how he had met Shifra Zirel in Lublin, married her, and been persuaded by her to go to her relatives in Hungary. At an inn near the border, she deserted him, stealing everything, even his clothes. Since then, he had wandered all over the country, slept in poorhouses, and like a beggar, made the rounds of private homes. At first he had thought he would obtain a writ signed by one hundred rabbis, enabling him to remarry, and he had set out for Frampol. Then he had learned that Roise Temerl had married again, and he had come to beg her forgiveness.

Unable to believe her eyes, Roise Temerl kept staring at him. Leaning on his crooked stick, as a beggar might, he never lifted his eyes. From his ears and nostrils, thatches of hair protruded. Through his torn coat, she saw the sackcloth, and through a slit in it, his flesh. He seemed to have grown smaller.

"Have any of the townspeople seen you?" she asked.

"No. I came through the fields."

"Woe is me. What can I do with you now?" she exclaimed, "I am married."

"I don't want anything from you," Nathan said, "Farewell."

"Don't go!" Roise Temerl said, "Oh, how unlucky I am!"

Covering her face with her hands, she began to sob. Nathan moved aside.

"Don't mourn for me," he said, "I haven't died yet."

"I wish you had," she replied, "I'd be happier."

Well, I, the Destroyer, had not yet tried all my insidious tricks. The scale of sins and punishment was not yet balanced. Therefore, in a vigorous move, I spoke to the woman in the language of compassion, for it is known that compassion, like any other sentiment, can serve evil as well as good purposes. Roise Temerl, I said, he is your husband; you lived with him for fifty years, and you cannot repudiate him, now that he has fallen. And when she asked, "What shall I do? After all, I cannot stand here and expose myself to derision," I made a suggestion. She trembled, raised her eyes, and beckoned Nathan to follow her. Submissively, he walked behind her, like any poor visitor who does everything that the lady of the house tells him to do.

VII : *The Secret of the Ruin*

In the yard, behind the granary, near the bathhouse, stood a ruin in which many years before, Roise Temerl's parents had lived. Unoccupied now, its ground floor windows were boarded, but on the second floor there were still a few well preserved rooms. Pigeons perched on the roof, and swallows had nested under the gutter. A worn broom had been stuck in the chimney. Nathan had often said the building should be razed, but Roise Temerl had insisted that while she was alive her parents' home would not be demolished. The attic was littered with old rubbish and rags. Schoolboys said that a light emanated from the ruin at midnight, and that demons lived in the cellar. Roise Temerl led Nathan there now. It was not easy to enter the ruin. Weeds that pricked and burned obstructed the path. Roise Temerl's skirt caught on thorns sharp as nails. Little mole-hills were everywhere. A heavy curtain of cobwebs barred the open doorway. Roise Temerl swept them away with a rotten branch. The stairs were rickety. Her legs were heavy and she had to lean on Nathan's arm. A thick cloud of dust arose, and Nathan began to sneeze and cough.

"Where are you taking me?" he asked, bewildered.

"Don't be afraid," Roise Temerl said, "It's all right."

Leaving him in the ruin, she returned to the house. She told the servant to take the rest of the day off, and the servant did not have to be told twice. When she had gone, Roise Temerl opened the cabinets that were still filled with Nathan's clothes, took his linen from the chest, and brought everything to the ruin. Once more she left, and when she returned it was with a basket containing a meal of rice and pot roast, tripe with calves' feet, white bread, and stewed prunes. After he had gobbled his supper and licked off the prune plate, Roise Temerl drew a bucket of water from the well and told him to go to another room to wash. Night was falling, but the twilight lingered a long time. Nathan did as Roise Temerl instructed, and she could hear him splash and sigh in the next room. Then he changed his clothes. When Roise Temerl saw him, tears streamed from her eyes. The full moon that shone through the window made the room bright as daylight, and Nathan, in a clean shirt, his dressing gown embroidered with leaves and flowers, in his silken cap and velvet slippers, once again seemed his former self.

Moshe Mecheles happened to be out of town, and Roise Temerl was in no hurry. She went again to the house and returned with bedding. The bed only needed to be fitted with boards. Not wanting to light a candle, lest someone notice the glow, Roise Temerl went about in the dark, climbed to the attic with Nathan, and groped until she found some old slats for the bed. Then she placed a mattress, sheets, and pillow on it. She had even remembered to bring some jam and a box of cookies so that Nathan could refresh himself before going to sleep. Only then did she sit down on the unsteady stool to rest. Nathan sat on the edge of the bed.

After a long silence, he said, "What's the use? Tomorrow I must leave."

"Why tomorrow?" said Rosie Temerl," Rest up. There's always time to rot in the poorhouse."

Late into the night they sat, talking, murmuring. Roise Temerl cried and stopped crying, began again and was calm again. She insisted that Nathan confess everything to her, without omitting details, and he told her again how he had met Shifra Zirel, how they had married, how she had persuaded him to go with her to Pressburg, and how she had spent the night full of sweet talk and love play with him at an inn. And at daybreak, when he fell asleep, she had arisen and untied the bag from his neck. He also told Roise Temerl how he had been forced to discard all shame, to sleep in beggars' dormitories, and eat at strangers' tables. Although his story angered her, and she called him blockhead, stupid fool, ass, idiot, her heart almost dissolved with pity.

"What is there to do now?" she kept murmuring to herself, over and over again. And I, the Evil Spirit, answered: Don't let him go. The beggar's life is not for him. He might die of grief or shame. And when Roise Temerl argued that because she was a married woman she had no right to stay with him, I said: Can the twelve lines of a bill of divorcement separate two souls who have been fused by fifty years of common life? Can a brother and sister be transformed by law into strangers? Hasn't Nathan become part of you? Don't you see him every night in your dreams? Isn't all your fortune the result of his industry and effort? And what is Moshe Mecheles? A stranger, a lout. Wouldn't it be better to fry with Nathan in hell, rather than serve as Moshe Mecheles' footstool in Heaven? I also recalled to her an incident in a story book, where a landowner, whose wife had eloped with a bear tamer, later forgave her and took her back to his manor.

When the clock in the Frampol church chimed eleven, Roise Temerl returned home. In her luxurious, canopied bed, she tossed, like one in a fever. For a long time, Nathan stood beside his window, looking out. The Elul sky was full of stars. The owl on the roof of the synagogue screeched with a human voice. The caterwauling of cats reminded him of women in labor. Crickets chirped, and unseen saws seemed to be buzzing through tree trunks. The neighing of horses that had grazed all night came through the fields with the calls of shepherds. Nathan, because he stood on an upper floor, could see the whole little town at a glance, the synagogue, the church, the slaughterhouse, the public bathhouse, the market, and the side streets where Gentiles lived. He recognized each shed, shack, and board in his own yard. A goat stripped some bark from a tree. A field mouse left the granary to return to its nest. Nathan watched for a long time. Everything about him was familiar and yet strange, real and ghostly, as though he were no longer among the living—only his spirit floated there. He recalled that there was a Hebrew phrase which applied to him, but he could not remember it exactly. Finally, after trying for a long time, he remembered: *one who sees without being seen.*

VIII : *One Who Sees Without Being Seen*

In Frampol the rumor spread the Roise Temerl, having quarreled with her maid, had dismissed her in the middle of her term. This surprised the housewives, because the girl was reputedly industrious and honest. Actually, Roise Temerl had dismissed the girl to keep her from discovering that Nathan lived in the ruin. As always, when I seduce sinners, I persuaded the couple that all this was provisional, that Nathan would stay only until he had recovered from his wandering. But I made certain that Roise Temerl welcomed the presence of her hidden guest and that Nathan enjoyed being where he was. Even though they discussed their future separation each time they were together, Roise Temerl gave Nathan's quarters an air of permanency. She resumed her cooking and frying for him, and once more brought him her tasty dishes. After a few days, Nathan's appearance changed remarkably. From pastries and puddings, his face became pink again, and once more, like that of a man of wealth, his paunch protruded. Once more he wore embroidered shirts, velvet slippers, silken dressing gowns, and carried batiste handkerchiefs. To keep him from being bored by his idleness, Roise Temerl brought him a Bible in Yiddish, a copy of the *Inheritance of the Deer,* and numerous story books. She even managed to procure some tobacco for his pipe, for he enjoyed smoking one, and she brought from the cellar bottles of wine and mead that Nathan had stored for years. The divorced couple had banquets in the ruin.

I made certain that Moshe Mecheles was seldom at home; I sent him to all kinds of fairs, and even recommended him as arbiter in disputes. It did not take long for the ruin behind the granary to become Roise Temerl's only comfort. Just as a miser's thoughts constantly dwell on the treasure he has buried far from sight, so Roise Temerl thought only of the ruin and the secret in her heart. Sometimes she thought that Nathan had died and she had magically resurrected him for a while; at other times, she imagined the whole thing a dream. Whenever she looked out of her window at the moss-covered roof of the ruin, she thought: No! It's inconceivable for Nathan to be there; I must be deluded. And immediately, she had to fly there, up the rickety stairs, to be met half-way by Nathan in person, with his familiar smile and his pleasant odor. "Nathan, you're here?" she would ask, and he would respond, "Yes, Roise Temerl, I'm here and waiting for you."

"Have you missed me?" she would ask, and he would answer:

"Of course. When I hear your step, it's a holiday for me."

"Nathan, Nathan," she would continue, "Would you have believed a year ago that it would end like this?"

And he would murmur, "No, Roise Temerl, it is like a bad dream."

"Oh Nathan, we have already lost this world, and I'm afraid we'll lose the other also," Roise Temerl said.

And he replied, "Well, that's too bad, but hell too is for people, not for dogs."

Since Moshe Mecheles belonged to the Hassidim, I,

Old Rebel, sent him to spend the Days of Awe with his rabbi. Alone, Roise Temerl bought Nathan a prayer shawl, a white robe, a prayer book, and prepared a holiday meal for him. Since on Rosh Hashonah, there is no moon, he ate the evening meal in darkness, blindly dunked a slice of bread in honey, and tasted an apple, a carrot, the head of a carp, and offered a blessing for the first fruit, over a pomegranate. He stood praying during the day in his robe and prayer shawl. The sound of the ram's horn came faintly to his ears from the synagogue. At the intermission between the prayers, Roise Temerl visited him in her golden dress, her white, satin-lined coat, and the shawl embroidered with silver threads, to wish him a happy new year. The golden chain he had given her for their betrothal hung around her neck. A brooch he had brought to her from Danzig, quivered on her breast, and from her wrist dangled a bracelet he had bought her at Brody. She exuded an aroma of honey cake and the women's section of the synagogue. On the evening before the Day of Atonement, Roise Temerl brought him a white rooster as a sacrificial victim and prepared for him the meal to be eaten before commencing the fast. Also, she gave the synagogue a wax candle for his soul. Before leaving for the *Minchah* prayer at the synagogue, she came to bid him good-by, and she began to lament so loudly that Nathan feared she would be heard. Falling into his arms, she clung to him and would not be torn away. She drenched his face with tears and howled as though possessed. "Nathan, Nathan," she wailed, "may we have no more unhappiness," and other things that are said when a member of a family dies, repeating them many times. Fearing she might faint and fall, Nathan had to escort her downstairs. Then, standing at the window, he watched the people of Frampol on their way to the synagogue. The women walked quickly and vigorously, as though hurrying to pray for someone on his deathbed; they held up their skirts, and when two of them met, they fell into each other's arms and swayed back and forth as if in some mysterious struggle. Wives of prominent citizens knocked at doors of poor people and begged to be forgiven. Mothers, whose children were ill, ran with arms outstretched, as though chasing someone, crying like madwomen. Elderly men, before leaving home, removed their shoes, put on white robes, prayer shawls, and white skull caps. In the synagogue yard, the poor sat with alms boxes on benches. A reddish glow spread over the roofs, reflecting in the window panes, and illuminating pale faces. In the west, the sun grew enormous; clouds around it caught fire, until half the sky was suffused with flames. Nathan recalled the River of Fire, in which all souls must cleanse themselves. The sun sank soon below the horizon. Girls, dressed in white, came outside and carefully closed shutters. Little flames played on the high windows of the synagogue, and inside, the entire building seemed to be one great flicker. A muted hum arose from it, and bursts of sobbing. Removing his shoes, Nathan wrapped himself in his shawl and robe. Half reading and half remembering, he chanted the words of Kol Nidre, the song that is recited not only by the living but by the dead in their graves. What was he, Nathan Jozefover, but a dead man, who instead of resting in his grave, wandered about in a world that did not exist?

IX : *Footprints in the Snow*

The High Holidays were over. Winter had come. But Nathan was still in the ruin. It could not be heated, not only because the stove had been dismantled, but because smoke, coming from the chimney, would make people suspicious. To keep Nathan from freezing, Roise Temerl provided him with warm clothes and a coal pot. At night he covered himself with two feather quilts. During the day he wore his fox fur and had felt boots on his feet. Roise Temerl also brought him a little barrel of spirits with a straw in it, which he sipped each time he felt cold, while eating a piece of dried mutton. From the rich food with which Roise Temerl plied him, he grew fat and heavy. In the evenings he stood at the window watching with curiosity the women who went to the ritual bath. On market days he never left the window. Carts drove into the yard and peasants unloaded sacks of grain. Moshe Mecheles, in a cotton padded jacket, ran back and forth, crying out hoarsely. Although it pained Nathan to think that this ridiculous fellow disposed of his possessions and lay with his wife, Moshe Mecheles' appearance made him laugh, as though the whole thing were a kind of prank that he, Nathan, had played on his competitor. Sometimes he felt like calling to him: Hey, there, Moshe Mecheles! while throwing him a bit of plaster or a bone.

As long as there was no snow, Nathan had everything he needed. Roise Temerl visited him often. At night Nathan would go out for a walk on a path that led to the river. But one night a great deal of snow fell, and the next day Roise Temerl did not visit him, for she was afraid someone might notice her tracks in the snow. Nor could Nathan go out to satisfy his natural needs. For two days he had nothing warm to eat, and the water in the pail turned to ice. On the third day Roise Temerl hired a peasant to clear the snow between the house and the granary and she also told him to clear the snow between the granary and the ruin. Moshe Mecheles, when he came home was surprised and asked, "Why?", but she changed the subject, and since he suspected nothing, he soon forgot about it.

Nathan's life, from then on, became increasingly difficult. After each new snowfall, Roise Temerl cleared the path with a shovel. To keep her neighbors from seeing what went on in the yard, she had the fence repaired. And as a pretext for going to the ruin, she had a ditch for refuse dug close to it. Whenever she saw Nathan, he said it was time for him to take his bundle and leave, but

Roise Temerl prevailed on him to wait. "Where will you go?" she asked. "You might, God forbid, drop from exhaustion." According to the almanac, she argued, the winter would be a mild one, and summer would begin early, weeks before Purim, and he only had to get through half the month of Kislev, besides Teveth and Shevat. She told him other things. At times, they did not even speak, but sat silently, holding hands and weeping. Both of them were actually losing strength each day. Nathan grew fatter, more blown up; his belly was full of wind; his legs seemed leaden; and his sight was dimming. He could no longer read his story books. Roise Temerl grew thin, like a consumptive, lost her appetite, and could not sleep. Some nights she lay awake, sobbing. And when Moshe Mecheles asked her why, she said it was because she had no children to pray for her after she was gone.

One day a downpour washed away the snow. Since Roise Temerl had not visited the ruin for two days, Nathan expected her to arrive at any moment. He had no food left; only a bit of brandy remained at the bottom of the barrel. For hours on end he stood waiting for her at the window, which was misted over with frost, but she did not come. The night was pitch black and icy. Dogs barked, a wind blew. The walls of the ruin shook; a whistling sound ran through the chimney, and the eaves rattled on the roof. In Nathan's house, now the house of Moshe Mecheles, several lamps seemed to have been lighted; it seemed extraordinarily bright, and the light made the surrounding darkness thicker. Nathan thought he heard the rolling of wheels, as though a carriage had driven to the house. In the darkness, someone drew water from the well, and someone poured out the slops. The night wore on, but despite the late hour, the shutters remained open. Seeing shadows run back and forth, Nathan thought important visitors might have come and were being treated to a banquet. He remained staring into the night until his knees grew weak, and with his last bit of strength, he dragged himself to his bed and fell into a deep sleep.

The cold awoke him early next morning. With stiff limbs he arose and barely propelled himself to the window. More snow had fallen during the night, and a heavy frost had set in. To his amazement, Nathan saw a group of men and women standing around his house. He wondered, anxiously, what was going on. But he did not have to wonder long, for suddenly the door swung open, and four men carried out a coffin hearse covered with a black cloth. "Moshe Mecheles is dead!" Nathan thought. But then he saw Moshe Mecheles following the coffin. It was not he, but Roise Temerl who had died.

Nathan could not weep. It was as though the cold had frozen his tears. Trembling and shaking, he watched the men carrying the coffin, watched the beadle rattling his alms box and the mourners wading through deep snowdrifts. The sky, pale as linen, hung low, meeting the blanketed earth. As though drifting on a flood, the trees in the fields seemed to be afloat in whiteness. From his window, Nathan could see all the way to the cemetery. The coffin moved up and down; the crowd, following it, thinned out and at times vanished entirely, seemed to sink into the ground and then emerge again. Nathan fancied for a moment that the cortege had stopped and no longer advanced, and then, that the people, as well as the corpse, were moving backward. The cortege grew gradually smaller, until it became a black dot. Because the dot ceased to move, Nathan realized that the pall bearers had reached the cemetery, and that he was watching his faithful wife being buried. With the remaining brandy, he washed his hands, for the water in his pail had turned to ice, and he began to murmur the prayer for the dead.

x : *Two Faces*

Nathan had intended to pack his things and leave during the night, but I, the Chief of the devils, prevented him from carrying out his plan. Before sunrise he was seized with powerful stomach cramps; his head grew hot and his knees so weak that he could not walk. His shoes had grown brittle; he could not put them on; and his legs had become fat. The Good Spirit counseled him to call for help, to shout until people heard and came to rescue him, because no man may cause his own death, but I said to him: Do you remember the words of King David: "Let me rather fall into God's hands, than into the hands of people?" You don't want Moshe Mecheles and his henchmen to have the satisfaction of revenging themselves on you and jeering. Rather die like a dog. In short, he listened to me, first, because he was proud, and second, because he was not fated to be buried according to law.

Gathering together his last remnants of strength, he pushed his bed to the window, to lie there and watch. He fell asleep early and awoke. There was day, and then night. Sometimes he heard cries in the yard. At other times he thought someone called him by name. His head, he fancied, had grown monstrously large and burdensome, like a millstone carried on his neck. His fingers were wooden, his tongue hard; it seemed bigger than the space it occupied. My helpers, goblins, appeared to him in dreams. They screamed, whistled, kindled fires, walked on stilts, and carried on like Purim players. He dreamed of floods, then of fires, imagined the world had been destroyed, and then that he hovered in the void with bats' wings. In his dreams he also saw pancakes, dumplings, broad noodles with cheese, and when he awoke his stomach was as full as though he had actually eaten; he belched and sighed, and touched his belly that was empty and aching all over.

Once, sitting up, he looked out of the window, and saw

to his surprise that people were walking backward, and marveled at this. Soon he saw other extraordinary things. Among those who passed, he recognized men who had long been dead. "Do my eyes deceive me?" he wondered, "Or has Messiah come, and has he resurrected the dead?" The more he looked the more astonished he became. Entire generations passed through the town, men and women with packs on their shoulders and staffs in their hands. He recognized, among them, his father and grandfather, his grandmothers and great-aunts. He watched workers build the Frampol synagogue. They carried bricks, sawed wood, mixed plaster, nailed on eaves. Schoolboys stood about, staring upward and calling a strange word he could not understand, like something in a foreign tongue. As in a dance around the Torah, two storks circled the building. Then the building and builders vanished, and he saw a group of people, barefooted, bearded, wild-eyed, with crosses in their hands, lead a Jew to the gallows. Though the black-bearded young man cried heart-rendingly, they dragged him on, tied in ropes. Bells were ringing; the people in the streets ran away and hid. It was midday, but it grew dark as the day of an eclipse of the sun. Finally, the young man cried out: "Shema Yisroel, the Lord our God, the Lord is One," and was left hanging, his tongue lolling out. His legs swayed for a long time, and hosts of crows flew overhead, cawing hoarsely.

On his last night, Nathan dreamed that Roise Temerl and Shifra Zirel were one woman with two faces. He was overjoyed at her apperance. "Why have I not noticed this before?" he wondered. "Why did I have to go through this trouble and anxiety?" He kissed the two-faced female, and she returned his kisses with her doubled lips, pressing against him her two pairs of breasts. He spoke words of love to her, and she responded in two voices. In her four arms and two bosoms, all his questions were answered. There was no longer life and death, here nor there, beginning nor end. "The truth is twofold." Nathan exclaimed, "This is the mystery of all mysteries!"

Without a last confession of his sins, Nathan died that night. I at once transported his soul to the nether abyss. He still wanders to this day in desolate spaces, and has not yet been granted admittance to hell. Moshe Mecheles married again, a young woman this time. She made him pay dearly, soon inherited his fortune, and squandered it. Shifra Zirel became a harlot in Pressburg and died in the poorhouse. The ruin still stands as before, and Nathan's bones still lie there. And, who can tell, perhaps another man, who sees without being seen, is hiding in it.

Translated by Norbert Guterman and Elaine Gottlieb

The Spinoza of Market Street

I

Dr. Nahum Fischelson paced back and forth in his garret room in Market Street, Warsaw. Dr. Fischelson was a short, hunched man with a grayish beard, and was quite bald except for a few wisps of hair remaining at the nape of the neck. His nose was as crooked as a beak and his eyes were large, dark, and fluttering like those of some huge bird. It was a hot summer evening, but Dr. Fischelson wore a black coat which reached to his knees, and he had on a stiff collar and a bow tie. From the door he paced slowly to the dormer window set high in the slanting room and back again. One had to mount several steps to look out. A candle in a brass holder was burning on the table and a variety of insects buzzed around the flame. Now and again one of the creatures would fly too close to the fire and sear its wings, or one would ignite and glow on the wick for an instant. At such moments Dr. Fischelson grimaced. His wrinkled face would twitch and beneath his disheveled moustache he would bite his lips. Finally he took a handkerchief from his pocket and waved it at the insects.

"Away from there, fools and imbeciles," he scolded. "You won't get warm here; you'll only burn yourself."

The insects scattered but a second later returned and once more circled the trembling flame. Dr. Fischelson wiped the sweat from his wrinkled forehead and sighed, "Like men they desire nothing but the pleasure of the moment." On the table lay an open book written in Latin, and on its broad-margined pages were notes and comments printed in small letters by Dr. Fischelson. The book was Spinoza's *Ethics* and Dr. Fischelson had been studying it for the last thirty years. He knew every proposition, every proof, every corollary, every note by heart. When he wanted to find a particular passage, he generally opened to the place immediately without having to search for it. But, nevertheless, he continued to study the *Ethics* for hours every day with a magnifying glass in his bony hand, murmuring and nodding his head in agreement. The truth was that the more Dr. Fischelson studied, the more puzzling sentences, unclear passages, and cryptic remarks he found. Each sentence contained hints unfathomed by any of the students of Spinoza. Actually the philosopher had anticipated all of the criticisms of pure reason made by Kant and his followers. Dr. Fischelson was writing a commentary on the *Ethics.* He had drawers full of notes and drafts, but it didn't seem that he would ever be able to complete his work. The stomach ailment which had plagued him for years was growing worse from day to day. Now he would get pains in his stomach after only a few mouthfuls of oatmeal. "God in Heaven, it's difficult, very difficult," he would say to himself using the same intonation as had his father, the late Rabbi of Tishevitz. "It's very, very hard."

Dr. Fischelson was not afraid of dying. To begin with, he was no longer a young man. Secondly, it is stated in the fourth part of the *Ethics* that "a free man thinks of nothing less than of death and his wisdom is a meditation not of death, but of life." Thirdly, it is also said that "the human mind cannot be absolutely destroyed with the human body but there is some part of it that remains eternal." And yet Dr. Fischelson's ulcer (or perhaps it was a cancer) continued to bother him. His tongue was always coated. He belched frequently and emitted a different foul-smelling gas each time. He suffered from heartburn and cramps. At times he felt like vomiting and at other times he was hungry for garlic, onions, and fried foods. He had long ago discarded the medicines prescribed for him by the doctors and had sought his own remedies. He found it beneficial to take grated radish after meals and lie on his bed, belly down, with his head hanging over the side. But these home remedies offered only temporary relief. Some of the doctors he consulted insisted there was nothing the matter with him. "It's just nerves," they told him. "You could live to be a hundred."

But on this particular hot summer night, Dr. Fischelson felt his strength ebbing. His knees were shaky, his pulse weak. He sat down to read and his vision blurred. The letters on the page turned from green to gold. The lines became waved and jumped over each other, leaving white gaps as if the text had disappeared in some mysterious way. The heat was unbearable, flowing down directly from the tin roof; Dr. Fischelson felt he was inside of an oven. Several times he climbed the four steps to the window and thrust his head out into the cool of the evening breeze. He would remain in that position for so long his knees would become wobbly. "Oh it's a fine breeze," he would murmur, "really delightful," and he would recall that according to Spinoza, morality and happiness were identical, and that the most moral deed a man could perform was to indulge in some pleasure which was not contrary to reason.

II

Dr. Fischelson, standing on the top step at the window and looking out, could see into two worlds. Above him were the heavens, thickly strewn with stars. Dr. Fischelson had never seriously studied astronomy but he could differentiate between the planets, those bodies which like the earth, revolve around the sun, and the fixed stars, themselves distant suns, whose light reaches us a hundred or even a thousand years later. He recognized the constellations which mark the path of the earth in space and that nebulous sash, the Milky Way. Dr. Fischelson owned a small telescope he had bought in Switzerland where he had studied and he particularly enjoyed looking at the moon through it. He could clearly make out on the moon's surface the volcanoes bathed in sunlight and the dark, shadowy craters. He never wearied of gazing at these cracks and crevasses. To him they seemed both near and distant, both substantial and insubstantial. Now and then he would see a shooting star trace a wide arc across the sky and disappear, leaving a fiery trail behind it. Dr. Fischelson would know then that a meteorite had reached our atmosphere, and perhaps some unburned fragment of it had fallen into the ocean or had landed in the desert or perhaps even in some inhabited region. Slowly the stars which had appeared from behind Dr. Fischelson's roof rose until they were shining above the house across the street. Yes, when Dr. Fischelson looked up into the heavens, he became aware of that infinite extension which is, according to Spinoza, one of God's attributes. It comforted Dr. Fischelson to think that although he was only a weak, puny man, a changing mode of the absolutely infinite Substance, he was nevertheless a part of the cosmos, made of the same matter as the celestial bodies; to the extent that he was a part of the Godhead, he knew he could not be destroyed. In such moments, Dr. Fischelson experienced the *Amor Dei Intellectualis* which is, according to the philosopher of Amsterdam, the highest perfection of the mind. Dr. Fischelson breathed deeply, lifted his head as high as his stiff collar permitted and actually felt he was whirling in company with the earth, the sun, the stars of the Milky Way, and the infinite host of galaxies known only to infinite thought. His legs became light and weightless and he grasped the window frame with both hands as if afraid he would lose his footing and fly out into eternity.

When Dr. Fischelson tired of observing the sky, his glance dropped to Market Street below. He could see a long strip extending from Yanash's market to Iron Street with the gas lamps lining it merged into a string of fiery dots. Smoke was issuing from the chimneys on the black, tin roofs; the bakers were heating their ovens, and here and there sparks mingled with the black smoke. The street never looked so noisy and crowded as on a summer evening. Thieves, prostitutes, gamblers, and fences loafed in the square which looked from above like a pretzel covered with poppy seeds. The young men laughed coarsely and the girls shrieked. A peddler with a keg of lemonade on his back pierced the general din with his intermittent cries. A watermelon vendor shouted in a savage voice, and the long knife which he used for cutting the fruit dripped with the blood-like juice. Now and again the street became even more agitated. Fire engines, their heavy wheels clanging, sped by; they were drawn by sturdy black horses which had to be tightly curbed to prevent them from running wild. Next came an ambulance, its siren screaming. Then some thugs had a fight among themselves and the police had to be called. A passer-by was robbed and ran about shouting for help. Some wagons loaded with firewood sought to get through into the courtyards where the bakeries were located but the horses could not lift the wheels over the steep curbs and the drivers berated the animals and lashed them with their whips. Sparks rose from the clanging hoofs. It was now long after seven, which was the prescribed closing time for stores, but actually business had only begun. Customers were led in stealthily through back doors. The Russian policemen on the street, having been paid off, noticed nothing of this. Merchants continued to hawk their wares, each seeking to outshout the others.

"Gold, gold, gold," a woman who dealt in rotten oranges shrieked.

"Sugar, sugar, sugar," croaked a dealer of overripe plums.

"Heads, heads, heads," a boy who sold fishheads roared.

Through the window of a *Chassidic* study house across the way, Dr. Fischelson could see boys with long sidelocks swaying over holy volumes, grimacing and studying aloud in sing-song voices. Butchers, porters, and fruit dealers were drinking beer in the tavern below. Vapor drifted from the tavern's open door like steam from a bathhouse, and there was the sound of loud music. Outside of the tavern, streetwalkers snatched at drunken soldiers and at workers on their way home from the factories. Some of the men carried bundles of wood on their shoulders, reminding Dr. Fischelson of the wicked who are condemned to kindle their own fires in Hell. Husky record players poured out their raspings through open windows. The liturgy of the high holidays alternated with vulgar vaudeville songs.

Dr. Fischelson peered into the half-lit bedlam and cocked his ears. He knew that the behavior of this rabble was the very antithesis of reason. These people were immersed in the vainest of passions, were drunk with emotions, and, according to Spinoza, emotion was never good. Instead of the pleasure they ran after, all they succeeded in obtaining was disease and prison, shame and the suffering that resulted from ignorance. Even the cats which loitered on the roofs here seemed more savage and passionate than those in other parts of the town. They caterwauled with the voices of women in labor, and like demons scampered up walls and leaped onto eaves and balconies. One of the toms paused at Dr. Fischelson's window and let out a howl which made Dr. Fischelson shudder. The doctor stepped from the window and, picking up a broom, brandished it in front of the black beast's glowing, green eyes. "Scat, begone, you ignorant savage!"—and he rapped the broom handle against the roof until the tom ran off.

III

When Dr. Fischelson had returned to Warsaw from Zurich where he had studied philosophy, a great future had been predicted for him. His friends had known that he was writing an important book on Spinoza. A Jewish Polish journal had invited him to be a contributor; he had been a frequent guest at several wealthy households and he had been made head librarian at the Warsaw synagogue. Although even then he had been considered an old bachelor, the matchmakers had proposed several rich girls for him. But Dr. Fischelson had not taken advantage of these opportunities. He had wanted to be as independent as Spinoza himself. And he had been. But because of his heretical ideas he had come into conflict with the rabbi and had had to resign his post as librarian. For years after that, he had supported himself by giving private lessons in Hebrew and German. Then, when he had become sick, the Berlin Jewish community had voted him a subsidy of five hundred marks a year. This had been made possible through the intervention of the famous Dr. Hildesheimer with whom he corresponded about philosophy. In order to get by on so small a pension, Dr. Fischelson had moved into the attic room and had begun cooking his own meals on a kerosene stove. He had a cupboard which had many drawers, and each drawer was labelled with the food it contained—buckwheat, rice, barley, onions, carrots, potatoes, mushrooms. Once a week Dr. Fischelson put on his widebrimmed black hat, took a basket in one hand and Spinoza's *Ethics* in the other, and went off to the market for his provisions. While he was waiting to be served, he would open the *Ethics*. The merchants knew him and would motion him to their stalls.

"A fine piece of cheese, Doctor—just melts in your mouth."

"Fresh mushrooms, Doctor, straight from the woods."

"Make way for the Doctor, ladies," the butcher would shout. "Please don't block the entrance."

During the early years of his sickness, Dr. Fischelson had still gone in the evening to a café which was frequented by Hebrew teachers and other intellectuals. It had been his habit to sit there and play chess while drinking a half a glass of black coffee. Sometimes he would stop at the bookstores on Holy Cross Street where all sorts of old books and magazines could be purchased cheap. On one occasion a former pupil of his had arranged to meet him at a restaurant one evening. When Dr. Fischelson arrived, he had been surprised to find a group of friends and admirers who forced him to sit at the head of the table while they made speeches about him. But these were things that had happened long ago. Now people were no longer interested in him. He had isolated himself completely and had become a forgotten man. The events of 1905 when the boys of Market Street had begun to organize strikes, throw bombs at police stations, and shoot strike breakers so that the stores were closed even on weekdays had greatly increased his isolation. He began to despise everything associated with the modern Jew—Zionism, socialism, anarchism. The young men in question seemed to him nothing but an ignorant rabble intent on destroying society, society without which no reasonable existence was possible. He still read a Hebrew magazine occasionally, but he felt contempt for modern Hebrew which had no roots in the Bible or the Mishnah. The spelling of Polish words had changed also.

Dr. Fischelson concluded that even the so-called spiritual men had abandoned reason and were doing their utmost to pander to the mob. Now and again he still visited a library and browsed through some of the modern histories of philosophy, but he found that the professors did not understand Spinoza, quoted him incorrectly, attributed their own muddled ideas to the philosopher. Although Dr. Fischelson was well aware that anger was an emotion unworthy of those who walk the path of reason, he would become furious, and would quickly close the book and push it from him. "Idiots," he would mutter, "asses, upstarts." And he would vow never again to look at modern philosophy.

IV

Every three months a special mailman who only delivered money orders brought Dr. Fischelson eighty rubles. He expected his quarterly allotment at the beginning of July but as day after day passed and the tall man with the blond moustache and the shiny buttons did not appear, the Doctor grew anxious. He had scarcely a groshen left. Who knows—possibly the Berlin Community had rescinded his subsidy; perhaps Dr. Hildesheimer had died, God forbid; the post office might have made a mistake. Every event has its cause, Dr. Fischelson knew. All was determined, all necessary, and a man of reason had no right to worry. Nevertheless, worry invaded his brain, and buzzed about like the flies. If the worst came to the worst, it occurred to him, he could commit suicide, but then he remembered that Spinoza did not approve of suicide and compared those who took their own lives to the insane.

One day when Dr. Fischelson went out to a store to purchase a composition book, he heard people talking about war. In Serbia somewhere, an Austrian Prince had been shot and the Austrians had delivered an ultimatum to the Serbs. The owner of the store, a young man with a yellow beard and shifty yellow eyes, announced, "We are about to have a small war," and he advised Dr. Fischelson to store up food because in the near future there was likely to be a shortage.

Everything happened so quickly. Dr. Fischelson had not even decided whether it was worthwhile to spend four groshen on a newspaper, and already posters had been hung up announcing mobilization. Men were to be seen walking on the street with round, metal tags on their lapels, a sign that they were being drafted. They were followed by their crying wives. One Monday when Dr. Fischelson descended to the street to buy some food with his last kopecks, he found the stores closed. The owners and their wives stood outside and explained that merchandise was unobtainable. But certain special customers were pulled to one side and let in through the back doors. On the street all was confusion. Policemen with swords unsheathed could be seen riding on horseback. A large crowd had gathered around the tavern where, at the command of the Tsar, the tavern's stock of whiskey was being poured into the gutter.

Dr. Fischelson went to his old café. Perhaps he would find some acquaintances there who would advise him. But he did not come across a single person he knew. He decided, then, to visit the rabbi of the synagogue where he had once been librarian, but the sexton with the six-sided skull cap informed him that the rabbi and his family had gone off to the spas. Dr. Fischelson had other old friends in town but he found no one at home. His feet ached from so much walking; black and green spots appeared before his eyes and he felt faint. He stopped and waited for the giddiness to pass. The passers-by jostled him. A dark-eyed high school girl tried to give him a coin. Although the war had just started, soldiers eight abreast were marching in full battle dress—the men were covered with dust and were sunburnt. Canteens were strapped to their sides and they wore rows of bullets across their chests. The bayonets on their rifles gleamed with a cold, green light. They sang with mournful voices. Along with the men came cannons, each pulled by eight horses; their blind muzzles breathed gloomy terror. Dr. Fischelson felt nauseous. His stomach ached; his intestines seemed about to turn themselves inside out. Cold sweat appeared on his face.

"I'm dying," he thought. "This is the end." Nevertheless, he did manage to drag himself home where he lay down on the iron cot and remained, panting and gasping. He must have dozed off because he imagined that he was in his home town, Tishevitz. He had a sore throat and his mother was busy wrapping a stocking stuffed with hot salt around his neck. He could hear talk going on in the house; something about a candle and about how a frog had bitten him. He wanted to go out into the street but they wouldn't let him because a Catholic procession was passing by. Men in long robes, holding double edged axes in their hands, were intoning in Latin as they sprinkled holy water. Crosses gleamed; sacred pictures waved in the air. There was an odor of incense and corpses. Suddenly the sky turned a burning red and the whole world started to burn. Bells were ringing; people rushed madly about. Flocks of birds flew overhead, screeching. Dr. Fischelson awoke with a start. His body was covered with sweat and his throat was now actually sore. He tried to meditate about his extraordinary dream, to find its rational connection with what was happening to him and to comprehend it *sub specie eternitatis,* but none of it made sense. "Alas, the brain is a receptacle for nonsense," Dr. Fischelson thought. "This earth belongs to the mad."

And he once more closed his eyes; once more he dozed; once more he dreamed.

V

The eternal laws, apparently, had not yet ordained Dr. Fischelson's end.

There was a door to the left of Dr. Fischelson's attic room which opened off a dark corridor, cluttered with boxes and baskets, in which the odor of fried onions and laundry soap was always present. Behind this door lived a spinster whom the neighbors called Black Dobbe. Dobbe was tall and lean, and as black as a baker's shovel. She had a broken nose and there was a mustache on her upper lip. She spoke with the hoarse voice of a man and she wore men's shoes. For years Black Dobbe had sold breads, rolls, and bagels which she had bought from the baker at the gate of the house. But one day she and the baker had quarreled and she had moved her business to the market place and now she dealt in what were called "wrinklers" which was a synonym for cracked eggs. Black Dobbe had no luck with men. Twice she had been engaged to baker's apprentices but in both instances they had returned the engagement contract to her. Some time afterwards she had received an engagement contract from an old man, a glazier who claimed that he was divorced, but it had later come to light that he still had a wife. Black Dobbe had a cousin in America, a shoemaker, and repeatedly she boasted that this cousin was sending her passage, but she remained in Warsaw. She was constantly being teased by the women who would say, "There's no hope for you, Dobbe. You're fated to die an old maid." Dobbe always answered, "I don't intend to be a slave for any man. Let them all rot."

That afternoon Dobbe received a letter from America. Generally she would go to Leizer the Tailor and have him read it to her. However, that day Leizer was out and so Dobbe thought of Dr. Fischelson whom the other tenants considered a convert since he never went to prayer. She knocked on the door of the doctor's room but there was no answer. "The heretic is probably out," Dobbe thought but, nevertheless she knocked once more, and this time the door moved slightly. She pushed her way in and stood there frightened. Dr. Fischelson lay fully clothed on his bed; his face was as yellow as wax; his Adam's apple stuck out prominently; his beard pointed upward. Dobbe screamed; she was certain that he was dead, but—no—his body moved. Dobbe picked up a glass which stood on the table, ran into the corridor, filled the glass with water from the faucet, hurried back, and threw the water into the face of the unconscious man. Dr. Fischelson shook his head and opened his eyes.

"What's wrong with you?" Dobbe asked. "Are you sick?"

"Thank you very much. No."

"Have you a family? I'll call them."

"No family," Dr. Fischelson said.

Dobbe wanted to fetch the barber from across the street but Dr. Fischelson signified that he didn't wish the barber's assistance. Since Dobbe was not going to the market that day, no "wrinklers" being available, she decided to do a good deed. She assisted the sick man to get off the bed and smoothed down the blanket. Then she undressed Dr. Fischelson and prepared some soup for him on the kerosene stove. The sun never entered Dobbe's room, but here squares of sunlight shimmered on the faded walls. The floor was painted red. Over the bed hung a picture of a man who was wearing a broad frill around his neck and had long hair. "Such an old fellow and yet he keeps his place so nice and clean," Dobbe thought approvingly. Dr. Fischelson asked for the *Ethics,* and she gave it to him disapprovingly. She was certain it was a gentile prayer book. Then she began bustling about, brought in a pail of water, swept the floor. Dr. Fischelson ate; after he had finished, he was much stronger and Dobbe asked him to to read her the letter.

He read it slowly, the paper trembling in his hands. It

came from New York, from Dobbe's cousin. Once more he wrote that he was about to send her a "really important letter" and a ticket to America. By now, Dobbe knew the story by heart and she helped the old man decipher her cousin's scrawl. "He's lying," Dobbe said. "He forgot about me a long time ago." In the evening, Dobbe came again. A candle in a brass holder was burning on the chair next to the bed. Reddish shadows trembled on the walls and ceiling. Dr. Fischelson sat propped up in bed, reading a book. The candle threw a golden light on his forehead which seemed as if cleft in two. A bird had flown in through the window and was perched on the table. For a moment Dobbe was frightened. This man made her think of witches, of black mirrors and corpses wandering around at night and terrifying women. Nevertheless, she took a few steps toward him and inquired, "How are you? Any better?"

"A little, thank you."

"Are you really a convert?" she asked although she wasn't quite sure what the word meant.

"Me, a convert? No, I'm a Jew like any other Jew," Dr. Fischelson answered.

The doctor's assurances made Dobbe feel more at home. She found the bottle of kerosene and lit the stove, and after that she fetched a glass of milk from her room and began cooking kasha. Dr. Fischelson continued to study the *Ethics,* but that evening he could make no sense of the theorems and proofs with their many references to axioms and definitions and other theorems. With trembling hand he raised the book to his eyes and read, "The idea of each modification of the human body does not involve adequate knowledge of the human body itself. . . . The idea of the idea of each modification of the human mind does not involve adequate knowledge of the human mind."

VI

Dr. Fischelson was certain he would die any day now. He made out his will, leaving all of his books and manuscripts to the synagogue library. His clothing and furniture would go to Dobbe since she had taken care of him. But death did not come. Rather his health improved. Dobbe returned to her business in the market, but she visited the old man several times a day, prepared soup for him, left him a glass of tea, and told him news of the war. The Germans had occupied Kalish, Bendin, and Cestechow, and they were marching on Warsaw. People said that on a quiet morning one could hear the rumblings of the cannon. Dobbe reported that the casualties were heavy. "They're falling like flies," she said. "What a terrible misfortune for the women."

She couldn't explain why, but the old man's attic room attracted her. She liked to remove the gold-rimmed books from the bookcase, dust them, and then air them on the window sill. She would climb the few steps to the window and look out through the telescope. She also enjoyed talking to Dr. Fischelson. He told her about Switzerland where he had studied, of the great cities he had passed through, of the high mountains that were covered with snow even in the summer. His father had been a rabbi, he said, and before he, Dr. Fischelson, had become a student, he had attended a yeshiva. She asked him how many languages he knew and it turned out that he could speak and write Hebrew, Russian, German, and French, in addition to Yiddish. He also knew Latin. Dobbe was astonished that such an educated man should live in an attic room on Market Street. But what amazed her most of all was that although he had the title "Doctor," he couldn't write prescriptions. "Why don't you become a real doctor?" she would ask him. "I am a doctor," he would answer. "I'm just not a physician." "What kind of a doctor?" "A doctor of philosophy." Although she had no idea of what this meant, she felt it must be very important. "Oh my blessed mother," she would say, "where did you get such a brain?"

Then one evening after Dobbe had given him his crackers and his glass of tea with milk, he began questioning her about where she came from, who her parents were, and why she had not married. Dobbe was surprised. No one had ever asked her such questions. She told him her story in a quiet voice and stayed until eleven o'clock. Her father had been a porter at the kosher butcher shops. Her mother had plucked chickens in the slaughterhouse. The family had lived in a celler at No. 19 Market Street. When she had been ten, she had become a maid. The man she had worked for had been a fence who bought stolen goods from thieves on the square. Dobbe had had a brother who had gone into the Russian army and had never returned. Her sister had married a coachman in Praga and had died in childbirth. Dobbe told of the battles between the underworld and the revolutionaries in 1905, of blind Itche and his gang and how they collected protection money from the stores, of the thugs who attacked young boys and girls out on Saturday afternoon strolls if they were not paid money for security. She also spoke of the pimps who drove about in carriages and abducted women to be sold in Buenos Aires. Dobbe swore that some men had even sought to inveigle her into a brothel, but that she had run away. She complained of a thousand evils done to her. She had been robbed; her boy friend had been stolen; a competitor had once poured a pint of kerosene into her basket of bagels; her own cousin, the shoemaker, had cheated her out of a hundred rubles before he had left for America. Dr. Fischelson listened to her attentively. He asked her questions, shook his head, and grunted.

"Well, do you believe in God?" he finally asked her.

"I don't know," she answered. "Do you?"

"Yes, I believe."

"Then why don't you go to synagogue?" she asked.

"God is everywhere," he replied. "In the synagogue. In the marketplace. In this very room. We ourselves are parts of God."

"Don't say such things," Dobbe said. "You frighten me."

She left the room and Dr. Fischelson was certain she had gone to bed. But he wondered why she had not said "good night." "I probably drove her away with my philosophy," he thought. The very next moment he heard her footsteps. She came in carrying a pile of clothing like a peddler.

"I wanted to show you these," she said. "They're my trousseau." And she began to spread out, on the chair, dresses—woolen, silk, velvet. Taking each dress up in turn, she held it to her body. She gave him an account of every item in her trousseau—underwear, shoes, stockings.

"I'm not wasteful," she said. "I'm a saver. I have enough money to go to America."

Then she was silent and her face turned brick-red. She looked at Dr. Fischelson out of the corner of her eyes, timidly, inquisitively. Dr. Fischelson's body suddenly began to shake as if he had the chills. He said, "Very nice, beautiful things." His brow furrowed and he pulled at his beard with two fingers. A sad smile appeared on his toothless mouth and his large fluttering eyes, gazing into the distance through the attic window, also smiled sadly.

VII

The day that Black Dobbe came to the rabbi's chambers and announced that she was to marry Dr. Fischelson, the rabbi's wife thought she had gone mad. But the news had already reached Leizer the Tailor, and had spread to the bakery, as well as to other shops. There were those who thought that the "old maid" was very lucky; the doctor, they said, had a vast hoard of money. But there were others who took the view that he was a run-down degenerate who would give her syphilis. Although Dr. Fischelson had insisted that the wedding be a small, quiet one, a host of guests assembled in the rabbi's rooms. The baker's apprentices who generally went about barefoot, and in their underwear, with paper bags on the tops of their heads, now put on light-colored suits, straw hats, yellow shoes, gaudy ties, and they brought with them huge cakes and pans filled with cookies. They had even managed to find a bottle of vodka although liquor was forbidden in wartime. When the bride and groom entered the rabbi's chamber, a murmur arose from the crowd. The women could not believe their eyes. The woman that they saw was not the one they had known. Dobbe wore a wide-brimmed hat which was amply adorned with cherries, grapes, and plumes, and the dress that she had on was of white silk and was equipped with a train; on her feet were high-heeled shoes, gold in color, and from her thin neck hung a string of imitation pearls. Nor was this all: her fingers sparkled with rings and glittering stones. Her face was veiled. She looked almost like one of those rich brides who were married in the Vienna Hall. The bakers' apprentices whistled mockingly. As for Dr. Fischelson, he was wearing his black coat and broad-toed shoes. He was scarcely able to walk; he was leaning on Dobbe. When he saw the crowd from the doorway, he became frightened and began to retreat, but Dobbe's former employer approached him saying, "Come in, come in, bridegroom. Don't be bashful. We are all brethren now."

The ceremony proceeded according to the law. The rabbi, in a worn satin gabardine, wrote the marriage contract and then had the bride and groom touch his handkerchief as a token of agreement; the rabbi wiped the point of the pen on his skullcap. Several porters who had been called from the street to make up the quorum supported the canopy. Dr. Fischelson put on a white robe as a reminder of the day of his death and Dobbe walked around him seven times as custom required. The light from the braided candles flickered on the walls. The shadows wavered. Having poured wine into a goblet, the rabbi chanted the benedictions in a sad melody. Dobbe uttered only a single cry. As for the other women, they took out their lace handkerchiefs and stood with them in their hands, grimacing. When the baker's boys began to whisper wisecracks to each other, the rabbi put a finger to his lips and murmured, "*Eh nu oh,*" as a sign that talking was forbidden. The moment came to slip the wedding ring on the bride's finger, but the bridegroom's hand started to tremble and he had trouble locating Dobbe's index finger. The next thing, according to custom, was the smashing of the glass, but though Dr. Fischelson kicked the goblet several times, it remained unbroken. The girls lowered their heads, pinched each other gleefully, and giggled. Finally one of the apprentices struck the goblet with his heel and it shattered. Even the rabbi could not restrain a smile. After the ceremony the guests drank vodka and ate cookies. Dobbe's former employer came up to Dr. Fischelson and said, "*Mazel tov,* bridegroom. Your luck should be as good as your wife." "Thank you, thank you," Dr. Fischelson murmured, "but I don't look forward to any luck." He was anxious to return as quickly as possibly to his attic room. He felt a pressure in his stomach and his chest ached. His face had become greenish. Dobbe had suddenly become angry. She pulled back her veil and called out to the crowd, "What are you laughing at? This isn't a show." And without picking up the cushion-cover in which the gifts were wrapped, she returned with her husband to their rooms on the fifth floor.

Dr. Fischelson lay down on the freshly made bed in his room and began reading the *Ethics.* Dobbe had gone back to her own room. The doctor had explained to her that he was an old man, that he was sick and without strength. He had promised her nothing. Nevertheless she returned wearing a silk nightgown, slippers with pompoms, and with her hair hanging down over her shoulders. There was a smile on her face, and she was bashful and hesitant. Dr. Fischelson trembled and the *Ethics* dropped from his hands. The candle went out. Dobbe groped for Dr. Fischelson in the dark and kissed his mouth. "My dear husband," she whispered to him, "*Mazel tov.*"

What happened that night could be called a miracle. If Dr. Fischelson hadn't been convinced that every occurrence is in accordance with the laws of nature, he would have thought that Black Dobbe had bewitched him. Powers long dormant awakened in him. Although he had had only a sip of the benediction wine, he was as if intoxicated. He kissed Dobbe and spoke to her of love. Long forgotten quotations from Klopfstock, Lessing, Goethe, rose to his lips. The pressures and aches stopped. He embraced Dobbe, pressed her to himself, was again a man as in his youth. Dobbe was faint with delight; crying, she murmured things to him in a Warsaw slang which he did not understand. Later, Dr. Fischelson slipped off into the deep sleep young men know. He dreamed that he was in Switzerland and that he was climbing mountains—running, falling, flying. At dawn he opened his eyes; it seemed to him that someone had blown into his ears. Dobbe was snoring. Dr. Fischelson quietly got out of bed. In his long nightshirt he approached the window, walked up the steps and looked out in wonder. Market Street was asleep, breathing with a deep stillness. The gas lamps were flickering. The black shutters on the stores were fastened with iron bars. A cool breeze was blowing. Dr. Fischelson looked up at the sky. The black arch was thickly sown with stars—there were green, red, yellow, blue stars; there were large ones and small ones, winking and steady ones. There were those that were clustered in dense groups and those that were alone. In the higher sphere, apparently, little notice was taken of the fact that a certain Dr. Fischelson had in his declining days married someone called Black Dobbe. Seen from above even the Great War was nothing but a temporary play of the modes. The myriads of fixed stars continued to travel their destined courses in unbounded space. The comets, planets, satellites, asteroids kept circling these shining centers. Worlds were born and died in cosmic upheavals. In the chaos of nebulae, primeval matter was being formed. Now and again a star tore loose, and swept across the sky, leaving behind it a fiery streak. It was the month of August when there are showers of meteors. Yes, the divine substance was extended and had neither beginning nor end; it was absolute, indivisible, eternal, without duration, infinite in its attributes. Its waves and bubbles danced in the universal cauldron, seething with change, following the unbroken chain of causes and effects, and he, Dr. Fischelson, with his unavoidable fate, was part of this. The doctor closed his eyelids and allowed the breeze to cool the sweat on his forehead and stir the hair of his beard. He breathed deeply of the midnight air, supported his shaky hands on the window sill and murmured, "Divine Spinoza, forgive me. I have become a fool."

Translated by Martha Glicklich
and Cecil Hemley

The Black Wedding

I

Aaron Naphtali, Rabbi of Tzivkev, had lost three-fourths of his followers. There was talk in the rabbinical courts that Rabbi Aaron Naphtali alone had been responsible for driving away his Chassidim. A rabbinical court must be vigilant, more adherents must be acquired. One has to find devices so that the following will not diminish. But Rabbi Aaron Naphtali was apathetic. The study house was old and toadstools grew unmolested on the walls. The ritual bath fell to ruin. The beadles were tottering old men, deaf and half-blind. The rabbi passed his time practicing miracle-working cabala. It was said that Rabbi Aaron Naphtali wanted to imitate the feats of the ancient ones, to tap wine from the wall and create pigeons through combinations of holy names. It was even said that he molded a golem secretly in his attic. Moreover, Rabbi Naphtali had no son to succeed him, only one daughter named Hindele. Who would be eager to follow a rabbi under these circumstances? His enemies contended that

Rabbi Aaron Naphtali was sunk in melancholy, as were his wife and Hindele. The latter, at fifteen, was already reading esoteric books and periodically went into seclusion like the holy men. It was rumored that Hindele wore a fringed garment underneath her dress like that worn by her saintly grandmother after whom she had been named.

Rabbi Aaron Naphtali had strange habits. He shut himself in his chamber for days and would not come out to welcome visitors. When he prayed, he put on two pairs of phylacteries at once. On Friday afternoons, he read the prescribed section of the Pentateuch—not from a book but from the parchment scroll itself. The rabbi had learned to form letters with the penmanship of the ancient scribes, and he used this script for writing amulets. A little bag containing one of these amulets hung from the neck of each of his followers. It was known that the rabbi warred constantly with the evil ones. His grandfather, the old Rabbi of Tzivkev, had exorcised a dybbuk from a young girl and the evil spirits had revenged themselves upon the grandson. They had not been able to bring harm to the old man because he had been blessed by the Saint of Kozhenitz. His son, Rabbi Hirsch, Rabbi Aaron Naphtali's father, died young. The grandson, Rabbi Aaron Naphtali, had to contend with the vengeful devils all his life. He lit a candle, they extinguished it. He placed a volume on the bookshelf, they knocked it off. When he undressed in the ritual bath, they hid his silk coat and his fringed garment. Often, sounds of laughter and wailing seemed to come from the rabbi's chimney. There was a rustling behind the stove. Steps were heard on the roof. Doors opened by themselves. The stairs would screech although nobody had stepped on them. Once the rabbi laid his pen on the table and it sailed out through the open window as if carried by an unseen hand. The rabbi's hair turned white at forty. His back was bent, his hands and feet trembled like those of an ancient man. Hindele often suffered attacks of yawning;

red flushes spread over her face, her throat ached, there was a buzzing in her ears. At such times incantations had to be made to drive away the evil eye.

The rabbi used to say, "They will not leave me in peace, not even for a moment." And he stamped his foot and asked the beadle to give him his grandfather's cane. He rapped it against each corner of the room and cried out, "You will not work your evil tricks on me!"

But the black hosts gained ascendancy just the same. One autumn day the rabbi became ill with erysipelas and it was soon apparent that he would not recover from his sickness. A doctor was sent for from a nearby town, but on the way the axle of his coach broke and he could not complete the journey. A second physician was called for, but a wheel of his carriage came loose and rolled into a ditch, and the horse sprained his leg. The rabbi's wife went to the memorial chapel of her husband's deceased grandfather to pray, but the vindictive demons tore her bonnet from her head. The rabbi lay in bed with a swollen face and a shrunken beard, and for two days he did not speak a word. Quite suddenly he opened an eye and cried out, "They have won!"

Hindele, who would not leave her father's bed, wrung her hands and began to wail in despair, "Father, what's to become of me?"

The rabbi's beard trembled. "You must keep silent if you are to be spared."

There was a great funeral. Rabbis had come from half of Poland. The women predicted that the rabbi's widow would not last much longer. She was white as a corpse. She hadn't enough strength in her feet to follow the hearse and two women had to support her. At the burial she tried to throw herself into the grave and they could barely restrain her. All through the Seven Days of Mourning, she ate nothing. They tried to force a spoon of chicken broth into her mouth, but she was unable to swallow it. When the Thirty Days of Mourning had passed, the rabbi's wife still had not left her bed. Physicians were brought to her but to no avail. She herself foresaw the day of her death and she foretold it to the minute. After her funeral, the rabbi's disciples began to look around for a young man for Hindele. They had tried to find a match for her even before her father's death, but her father had been difficult to please. The son-in-law would eventually have to take the rabbi's place and who was worthy to sit in the Tzivkev rabbinical chair? Whenever the rabbi finally gave his approval, his wife found fault with the young man. Besides, Hindele was known to be sick, to keep too many fast days and to fall into a swoon when things did not go her way. Nor was she attractive. She was short, frail, had a large head, a skinny neck, and flat breasts. Her hair was bushy. There was an insane look in her black eyes. However, since Hindele's dowry was a following of thousands of Chassidim, a candidate was found, Reb Simon, son of the Yampol Rabbi. His older brother having died, Reb Simon would become Rabbi of Yampol after his father's death. Yampol and Tzivkev had much in common. If they were to unite, the glory of former times would return. True, Reb Simon was a divorced man with five children. But as Hindele was an orphan, who would protest? The Tzivkev Chassidim had one stipulation—that after his father's death, Reb Simon should reside in Tzivkev.

Both Tzivkev and Yampol were anxious to bring the union about. Immediately after the marriage contract was written, wedding preparations were begun, because the Tzivkev rabbinical chair had to be filled. Hindele had not yet seen her husband-to-be. She was told that he was a widower, and nothing was said about the five children. The wedding was a noisy one. Chassidim came from all parts of Poland. The followers of the Yampol court and those of the Tzivkev court began to address one another by the familiar "thou." The inns were full. The innkeeper brought straw mattresses down from the attic and put them out in corridors, granaries, and tool sheds, to accommodate the large crowd. Those who opposed the match foretold that Yampol would engulf Tzivkev. The Chassidim of Yampol were known for their crudeness. When they played, they became boisterous. They drank long draughts of brandy from tin mugs and became drunk. When they danced, the floors heaved under them. When an adversary of Yampol spoke harshly of their rabbi, he was beaten. There was a custom in Yampol that when the wife of a young man gave birth to a girl, the father was placed on a table and lashed thirty-nine times with a strap.

Old women came to Hindele to warn her that it would not be easy to be a daughter-in-law in the Yampol court. Her future mother-in-law, an old woman, was known for her wickedness. Reb Simon and his younger brothers had wild ways. The mother had chosen large women for her sons and the frail Hindele would not please her. Reb Simon's mother had consented to the match only because of Yampol's ambitions regarding Tzivkev.

From the time that the marriage negotiations started until the wedding, Hindele did not stop crying. She cried at the celebration of the writing of the marriage contract, she cried when the tailors fitted her trousseau, she cried when she was led to the ritual bath. There she was ashamed to undress for the immersion before the attendants and the other women, and they had to tear off her stays and her underpants. She would not let them remove from her neck the little bag which contained an amber charm and the tooth of a wolf. She was afraid to immerse herself in the water. The two attendants who led her into the bath, held her tightly by her wrists and she trembled like the sacrificial chicken the day before Yom Kippur. When Reb Simon lifted the veil from Hindele's face after the wedding, she saw him for the first time. He was a tall man with a broad fur hat, a pitch-black disheveled beard, wild eyes, a broad nose, thick lips, and a long moustache. He gazed at her like an animal. He breathed noisily and smelled of perspiration. Clusters of hair grew out of his nostrils and ears. His hands, too, had a growth of hair as thick as fur. The moment Hindele saw him she knew what she had suspected long before—that her bridegroom was a demon and that the wedding was nothing but black magic, a satanic hoax. She wanted to call out "Hear, O Israel" but she remembered her father's deathbed admonition to keep silent. How strange that the moment Hindele understood that her husband was an evil spirit, she could immediately discern what was true and what was false. Although she saw herself sitting in her mother's living room, she knew she was really in a forest. It appeared to be light, but she knew it was dark. She was surrounded by Chassidim with fur hats and satin gabardines, as well as by women who wore silk bonnets and velvet capes, but she knew it was all imaginary and that the fancy garments hid heads grown with elflocks, goose-feet, unhuman navels, long snouts. The sashes of the young men were snakes in reality, their sable hats were actually hedgehogs, their beards clusters of worms. The men spoke Yiddish and sang familiar songs, but the noise they made was really the bellowing of oxen, the hissing of vipers, the howling of wolves. The musicians had tails, and horns grew from their heads. The maids who attended Hindele had canine paws, hoofs of calves, snouts of pigs. The wedding jester was all beard and tongue. The so-called relatives on the groom's side were lions, bears, boars. It was raining in the forest and the wind was blowing. It thundered and flashed lightning. Alas, this was not a human wedding, but a Black Wedding. Hindele knew, from reading the holy books, that demons sometimes married human virgins whom they later carried away behind the black mountains to cohabit with them and sire their children. There was only one thing to do in such a case—not to comply with them, never willingly submit to them, to let them get everything by force as one kind word spoken to Satan is equivalent to sacrificing to the idols. Hindele remembered the story of Joseph De La Rinah and the misfortune that befell him when he felt sorry for the evil one and gave him a pinch of tobacco.

II

Hindele did not want to march to the wedding canopy, and she planted her feet subbornly on the floor, but the bridesmaids dragged her. They half-pulled her, half-carried her. Imps in the images of girls held the candles and formed an aisle for her. The canopy was a braid of reptiles. The rabbi who performed the ceremony was under contract to Samael. Hindele submitted to nothing. She refused to hold out her finger for the ring and had to be forced to do so. She would not drink from the goblet and they poured some wine into her mouth. Hobgoblins performed all the wedding rites. The evil spirit who appeared in the likeness of Reb Simon was wearing a white robe. He stepped on the bride's foot with his hoof so that he might rule over her. Then he smashed the wine glass. After the ceremony, a witch danced toward the bride carrying a braided bread. Presently the bride and groom were served the so-called soup, but Hindele spat everything into her handkerchief. The musicians played a Kossack, an Angry Dance; a Scissors Dance and a Water Dance. But their webbed roosters' feet peeped out from under their robes. The wedding hall was nothing but a forest swamp, full of frogs, mooncalves, monsters, each with his ticks and grimaces. The Chassidim presented the couple with assorted gifts, but these were devices to ensnare Hindele in the net of evil. The wedding jester recited sad poems and funny poems, but his voice was that of a parrot.

They called Hindele to dance the Good-Luck dance, but she did not want to get up, knowing it was actually a

Bad-Luck dance. They urged her, pushed her, pinched her. Little imps stuck pins into her thighs. In the middle of the dance, two she-demons grabbed her by the arms and carried her away into a bedroom which was actually a dark cave full of thistles, scavengers, and rubbish. While these females whispered to her the duties of a bride, they spat in her ear. Then she was thrown upon a heap of mud which was supposed to be linen. For a long while, Hindele lay in that cave, surrounded by darkness, poison weeds and lice. So great was her anxiety that she couldn't even pray. Then the devil to whom she was espoused entered. He assailed her with cruelty, tore off her clothes, martyred her, abused her, shamed her. She wanted to scream for help but she restrained herself knowing that if she uttered a sound she would be lost forever.

All night long Hindele felt herself lying in blood and pus. The one who had raped her snored, coughed, hissed like an adder. Before dawn a group of hags ran into the room, pulled the sheet from under her, inspected it, sniffed it, began to dance. That night never ended. True, the sun rose. It was not really the sun, though, but a bloody sphere which somebody hung in the sky. Women came to coax the bride with smooth talk and cunning but Hindele did not pay any attention to their babble. They spat at her, flattered her, said incantations, but she did not answer them. Later a doctor was brought to her, but Hindele saw that he was a horned buck. No, the black powers could not rule her, and Hindele kept on spiting them. Whatever they bade her do, she did the opposite. She threw the soup and marchpane into the slop can. She dumped the chickens and squab which they baked for her into the outhouse. She found a page of a psalter in the mossy forest and she recited psalms furtively. She also remembered a few passages of the Torah and of the prophets. She acquired more and more courage to pray to God-Almighty to save her. She mentioned the names of holy angels as well those of her illustrious ancestors like the Baal Shem, Rabbi Leib Sarah's, Rabbi Pinchos Korzer and the like.

Strange, that although she was only one and the others were multitudes, they could not overcome her. The one who was disguised as her husband tried to bribe her with sweet-talk and gifts, but she did not satisfy him. He came to her but she turned away from him. He kissed her with his wet lips and petted her with clammy fingers, but she did not let him have her. He forced himself on her, but she tore at his beard, pulled at his sidelocks, scratched his forehead. He ran away from her bloody. It became clear to Hindele that her power was not of this world. Her father was interceding for her. He came to her in his shroud and comforted her. Her mother revealed herself to her and gave her advice. True, the earth was full of evil spirits, but up above angels were hovering. Sometimes, Hindele heard the angel Gabriel fighting and fencing with Satan. Bevies of black dogs and crows came to help him, but the saints drove them away with their palm leaves and hosannahs. The barking and the crowing were drowned out by the song which Hindele's grandfather used to sing Saturday evenings and which was called "The Sons of the Mansion."

But horror of horrors, Hindele became pregnant. A devil grew inside her. She could see him through her own belly as through a cobweb: half-frog, half-ape, with eyes of a calf and scales of a fish. He ate her flesh, sucked her blood, scratched her with his claws, bit her with his pointed teeth. He was already chattering, calling her mother, cursing with vile language. She had to get rid of him, stop his gnawing at her liver. Nor was she able to bear his blasphemy and mockery. Besides, he urinated in her and defiled her with his excrement. Miscarriage was the only way out, but how bring it on? Hindele struck her stomach with her fist. She jumped, threw herself down, crawled, all to get rid of that devil's bastard, but to no avail. He grew quickly and showed inhuman strength, pushed and tore at her insides. His skull was of copper, his mouth of iron. He had capricious urges. He told her to eat lime from the wall, the shell of an egg, all kinds of garbage. And if she refused, he squeezed her gall bladder. He stank like a skunk and Hindele fainted from the stench. In her swoon, a giant appeared to her with one eye in his forehead. He talked to her from a hollowed tree saying, "Give yourself up, Hindele, you are one of us."

"No, never."

"We will take revenge."

He flogged her with a fiery rod and yelled abuses. Her head became as heavy as a millstone from fear. The fingers of her hands became big and hard like rolling pins. Her mouth puckered as from eating unripe fruit. Her ears felt as if they were full of water. Hindele was not free any more. The hosts rolled her in muck, mire, slime. They immersed her in baths of pitch. They flayed her skin. They pulled the nipples of her breasts with pliers. They tortured her ceaselessly but she remained mute. Since the males could not persuade her, the female devils attacked her. They laughed with abandon, they braided their hair around her, choked her, tickled her, and pinched her. One giggled, another cried, another wiggled like a whore. Hindele's belly was big and hard as a drum and Belial sat in her womb. He pushed with elbows and pressed with his skull. Hindele lay in labor. One she-devil was a mid-wife and the other an aide. They had hung all kinds of charms over her canopied bed and they put a knife and a Book of Creation under her pillow, the way the evil ones imitate the humans in all manners. Hindele was in her birth throes, but she remembered that she was not allowed to groan. One sigh and she would be lost. She must restrain herself in the name of her holy forbears.

Suddenly the black one inside her pushed with all his might. A piercing scream tore itself from Hindele's throat and she was swallowed in darkness. Bells were ringing as on a gentile holiday. A hellish fire flared up. It was as red as blood, as scarlet as leprosy. The earth opened like in the time of Korah, and Hindele's canopied bed began to sink into the abyss. Hindele had lost everything, this world and the world to come. In the distance she heard the crying of women, the clapping of hands, blessings and good wishes, while she flew straight into the castle of Asmodeus where Lilith, Namah, Machlath, Hurmizah rule.

In Tzivkev and in the neighborhood the tidings spread that Hindele had given birth to a male child by Reb Simon of Yampol. The mother had died in childbirth.

Translated by Martha Glicklich

A Tale of Two Liars

I

A lie can only thrive on truth; lies, heaped one upon another, lack substance. Let me tell you how I manipulated two liars by pulling the strings, making them dance to my tune.

The woman of the pair, Glicka Genendel, arrived in Janov several weeks before Passover, claiming to be the widow of the Zosmir rabbi; she was childless, she said, and anxious to remarry. She was not required to participate first in the levirate marriage ceremony, she explained, since her husband had been an only son. She was settling in Janov because a soothsayer had prophesied that she would meet a mate in this town. She boasted that her late husband had studied the Talmud with her, and, to prove it, she sprinkled her conversation with quotations. She was a source of constant wonder to the townspeople. True, she was no beauty. Her nose sloped like a ram's horn, but she did have a pleasantly pale complexion, and large, dark eyes; in addition, her chin was pointed and her tongue glib. There was a bounce to her walk, and she scattered witticisms wherever she went.

No matter what occurred, she could remember a similar experience; for every sorrow, she offered comfort, for every illness, a remedy. She was dazzling in her high-buttoned shoes, woolen dress, fringed silk shawl, and head-band festooned with precious gems. There was slush on the ground, and so she skipped nimbly from stone to stone and plank to plank, holding her skirt daintily in one hand, and her satchel in the other. She brought joy wherever she went, although she did solicit donations, but the donations were not for herself, God forbid. What she got, she turned over to poor brides and indigent mothers-to-be. Because she was such a doer of good deeds, she boarded at the inn free of charge. The guests enjoyed her quips and yarns, and, you may be sure, the innkeeper lost nothing by the arrangement.

She was immediately showered with proposals, and she accepted them all. In almost no time, the town's widowers and divorcees were at each other's throats, each determined to have this remarkable "catch" for himself. Meanwhile, she ran up bills for dresses and underclothing, and dined well on roast squab and egg-noodles. She was also active in community affairs, helping in the preparation of the mill for Passover, examining the sheaves of Pashcal wheat, assisting in the baking of the matzoths, joking with the bakers as they kneaded, rolled, perforated, poured, and cut. She even went to the rabbi so that the ceremony of selling the leavened bread which she had left behind in Zosmir could be performed. The rabbi's wife invited Glicka Genendel to the Seder. She came adorned in a white satin gown and heavy with jewelry, and chanted the Haggadah as fluently as any man. Her coquetry made the rabbi's daughters and daughters-in-law jealous. The widows and divorcees of Janov were simply consumed with rage. It seemed as if this crafty woman would snare for herself the wealthiest widower in town, and, without as much as a by-your-leave, become the richest matron in Janov. But it was I, the Arch-Devil, who saw to it that she was supplied with a mate.

He showed up in Janov during Passover, arriving in an ornate *britska* which had been hired for the occasion. His story was that he had come from Palestine to solicit charity, and he, like Glicka, had also recently lost his spouse. His trunk was banded with brass; he smoked a hookah, and the bag in which he carried his prayer shawl was made of leather. He put on two sets of phylacteries when he prayed, and his conversation was sprinkled with Aramaic. His name was Reb Yomtov, he said. He was a tall, thin man, with a pointed beard, and though he dressed like any other townsman in caftan, fur cap, breeches, and high hose, his swarthy face and burning eyes brought to mind a Sephardic Jew from Yemen or Persia. He insisted that he had seen with his own eyes Noah's Ark on Mount Ararat, and that the splinters he sold at six farthings a piece had been carved from one of its planks. He also had in his possession coins over which Yehudah the Chassid had cast a spell, along with a sack of chalky earth from Rachel's grave. This sack, apparently, had no bottom as it never grew empty.

He too put up at the inn, and soon he and Glicka Genendel were friends, to their mutual delight. When they traced back their ancestry, they discovered that they were distant relatives, both descended from some saint or other. They would chat with each other and plot deep into the night. Glicka Genendel hinted that she found Reb Yomtov attractive. She didn't have to spell it out for him—they understood each other.

Those two were in a hurry. That is—I, Sammael, spurred them on. So the Articles of Engagement were drawn up, and after the prospective bride had signed, her husband-to-be gave as his gifts an engagement ring and a necklace of pearls. He had received them, he said, from his first wife who had been an heiress in Baghdad. In return, Glicka Genendel presented to her betrothed a sapphire-studded cover for the Sabbath loaf which she had inherited from her late father, the famous philanthropist.

Then, just at the end of Passover, there was a great to-do in town. One of the very substantial citizens, a Reb Kathriel Abba, complained to the rabbi that Glicka Genendel was engaged to him and that he had given her thirty gulden for a trousseau.

The widow was enraged at these allegations.

"It's just spite," she said, "because I wouldn't sin with him."

She demanded that her slanderer pay her thirty gulden as restitution. But Reb Kathriel Abba stood by the truth of his accusation, and offered to take an oath before the Holy Scroll. Glicka Genendel was just as determined to defend her statement in front of the Black Candles. However an epidemic was raging in the town at the time and the women were fearful that all this oath-taking would end up costing them the lives of their children, and so the rabbi finally ruled that Glicka was obviously a good woman and he commanded that Reb Kathriel Abba apologize and pay the settlement.

Immediately after that, a beggar arrived from Zosmir and surprised everyone by explaining that the late rabbi's wife could not be visiting in Janov, since she was in Zosmir, God be praised, with her husband who was not the least bit dead. There was great excitement and the townspeople rushed to the inn to punish the fraudulent widow for her infamous lie. She was not at all upset and merely explained that she had said "Kosmir," not "Zosmir." Once more all was well, and the preparations for the wedding continued. The wedding had been set for the thirty-third day of the Feast of Omer.

But there was one additional incident before the wedding. For one reason or another, Glicka Genendel thought it wise to consult a goldsmith about the pearls which Reb Yomtov had given her. The jeweler weighed and examined the pearls and declared them to be paste. The wedding was off, Glicka Genendel announced, and informed the bridegroom to that effect. He speedily rose to his own defense; in the first place, the jeweler was incompetent; there couldn't be any doubt of that since he, Reb Yomtov, had personally paid ninety-five drachmas for the pearls in Stamboul; in the second place, immediately after the ceremony, God willing, he would replace the counterfeits with the genuine article, and finally he wanted to point out, just in passing, that the cover Glicka Genendel had given him was not embroidered with sapphires, but with beads, and beads, mind you, that sold for three groshen a dozen in the market. Therefore the two liars were quits, and with their differences patched up, stood under the marriage canopy together.

However, later that night, the delegate from the Holy Land discovered that he had not married a spring chicken. She took off her wig, releasing a mass of gray hair. A hag stood before him, and he ransacked his brain to find a solution. But since he was a professional he didn't show his irritation. Nevertheless, Glicka Genendel was taking no chances; to make sure of her husband's love, she fashioned a love charm. She plucked hair from a private place and wove it around a button of her dear one's dressing gown; in addition, she washed her breasts in water which she then poured into a potion for him to drink. As she went about performing this significant business, she sang:

"As a tree has its shadow,
Let me have my love.
As wax melts in a fire,
Let him burn to my touch.
Now and forever,

In me be his trust,
Trapped in desire
Until all turn to dust.
Amen. Selah."

II

"Is there any reason why we should stay in Janov?" Reb Yomtov asked when the seven days of nuptial benediction were over. "I would prefer to return to Jerusalem. After all we have a fine house waiting for us near the Wailing Wall. But first I must visit a few towns in Poland to make collections. There are my yeshiva students to think of and then also funds are required to erect a prayer house on the grave of Reb Simon Bar Johai. The last is a very expensive project and will require a good deal of money."

"What towns will you visit? And how long will you be away?" Glicka Genendel asked.

"I intend to stop off at Lemberg, Brod, and some of the other towns in their immediate vicinity. I should be back by midsummer, God willing. We should be in Jerusalem in time to celebrate the High Holy days."

"That's fine," she said. "I'll use the time to visit the graves of my dear ones and to say goodbye to my relatives in Kalish. God speed, and don't forget the way home."

They embraced warmly, and she presented him with some preserves and cookies, and a jar of chicken fat. She also gave him an amulet to protect him from highwaymen, and he set off on his journey.

When he arrived at the River San he halted, turned his carriage around, and drove off on the Lublin road. His destination was Piask, a small town on the outskirts of Lublin. The inhabitants of Piask had a fine reputation. It was said that you did not put on a prayer shawl there, if you didn't want your phylacteries stolen; the point being that in Piask you dared not cover your eyes even that long. Well, it was in that splendid place that the legate sought out the assistant rabbi and had the scribe write out a Bill of Divorcement for Glicka Genendel. He then sent the papers by messenger to Janov. The whole thing cost Reb Yomtov five gulden, but he considered it money well spent.

This done, Reb Yomtov rode into Lublin and preached at the famous Marshall Synagogue. He had a tongue of silver, and chose a Lithuanian accent for his sermon. Beyond the Cossack Steppes and the land of the Tartars, he explained, dwelt the last of the Chazars. This ancient people were cave-dwellers, fought with bow and arrow, sacrificed in the Biblical manner, and spoke Hebrew. He had in his possession a letter from their chieftain, Yedidi Ben Achitov, a grandson of the Chazar king, and he exhibited a parchment scroll which bore the name of many witnesses. These distant Jews who were waging such a stubborn war against the enemies of Israel and who were the only ones who knew the secret road to the river Sambation, were in dire need of funds, he pointed out, and he went through the crowd collecting money for them.

As he circulated among the people, he was approached by a blond-haired young man who asked him his name.

"Solomon Simeon," Reb Yomtov replied, merely lying out of habit.

The young man wished to know where he was staying, and when he heard that it was at the inn, he shook his head.

"Such a needless expense," he said. "And why associate with riff-raff? I have a large house, God be praised. In it there is a guest room and holy books to spare. I am at business all day, and I have no children (may you be spared my fate), so you won't be disturbed. My wife would be honored to have a scholar in the house, and my mother-in-law, who is visiting us, is a learned woman, and a matchmaker in the bargain. Should you need a wife, she will find you one, and a real catch, I can assure you."

"Alas, I am a widower," the spurious Reb Solomon Simeon said, putting on a glum expression, "but I cannot think of marriage at this time. My dear wife was a true grandchild of Rabbi Sabbatai Kohen, and though she is gone three years now, I cannot forget her." And Reb Yomtov continued to sigh mournfully.

"Who are we to question the wisdom of the Almighty?" the young man asked. "It is written in the Talmud that one must not grieve too long."

On their way to the young man's house, the two carried on a lively discussion concerning the Torah, with occasional digressions to more worldly matters. The young man was amazed at his guest's knowledge and intellect.

As he mounted the steps of the young man's house, Reb Yomtov was almost overcome by the odors he smelled. His mouth watered. Fowl was being roasted, cabbage boiled. "Praised be His name," he thought to himself, "Lublin looks like it will be very satisfactory. If his wife wants a learned man, she will certainly have one. And who can tell, I may be strong enough to produce a miracle, and they may yet have a son and heir. Nor if a rich bride becomes available, will I turn her down either."

The doors swung open, admitting Reb Yomtov to a kitchen whose walls were covered with copper pans. An oil lamp hung from the ceiling. In the room were two women, the lady of the house and a servant girl; they stood at the stove in which a goose was being roasted. The young man introduced his guest (it was obvious that he was proud to have brought home such a man) and his wife smiled warmly at Reb Yomtov.

"My husband does not praise everyone so highly," she said. "You must be a very unusual man. It is good to have you here. My mother is in the dining room, and will make you welcome. Should you want anything, don't hesitate to let her know."

Reb Yomtov thanked his hostess, and walked in the direction she had indicated, but his host lingered for a moment in the kitchen, no doubt anxious to amplify further on what a distinguished visitor they were entertaining.

Piously Reb Yomtov kissed the *mezuzah,* and opened the door to the adjoining room. What lay beyond was even better than what had gone before. The room which he was entering was most elegantly furnished. But then he stopped. What was this he saw? His heart dropped, and words failed him. No, it couldn't be; he was dreaming. He was seeing a mirage. No, it was witchcraft. For there stood his former bride, his Janov sweetheart. There could be no doubt about it. This was Glicka Genendel.

"Yes, it is me," she said, and once more he heard that familiar shrewish voice.

"What are you doing here?" he asked. "You said you were going to Kalish."

"I have come to visit my daughter."

"Your daughter? You told me you had no children."

"I thought you were on your way to Lemberg," she said.

"Didn't you get the divorce papers?"

"What divorce papers?"

"Those I sent by messenger."

"I tell you I've received nothing. May all my bad dreams be visited on your head."

Reb Yomtov saw how things were: he had fallen into a trap; there was no means of escape. His host would enter at any moment, and he would be exposed.

"I have been guilty of a great foolishness," he said, summoning up all of his courage. "These people are under the impression that I am a traveler just returned from the land of the Chazars. It's to your interest to protect me. You don't want to have me driven out of town and remain a deserted wife forever. Don't say anything, and I swear by my beard and earlocks that I'll make it worthwhile for you."

Glicka Genendel had a good many abusive things that she was longing to say, but just then her son-in-law entered. He was beaming.

"We have a most distinguished guest in the house," he said. "This is Reb Solomon Simeon of Lithuania. He has just returned from a visit to the Chazars, who, as you know, live very close to the Lost Ten Tribes." And to Reb Yomtov he explained, "My mother-in-law is to depart shortly for the Holy Land. She is married to a Reb Yomtov, a delegate from Jerusalem and a descendant of the house of David. Possibly you've heard of him?"

"I most certainly have," Reb Yomtov said.

By this time, Glicka Genendel had recovered her composure sufficiently to say, "Do be seated, Reb Solomon Simeon, and tell us all about the Lost Ten Tribes. Did you actually see the River Sambation hurling stones? Were you able to cross over safely and meet the king?"

But the moment her son-in-law left the room, she was on her feet hissing, "Well, what about it, Reb Solomon Simeon? Where is my payment?"

Before he had a chance to say anything, she grabbed him by his lapels and thrust her hand into the inside pocket of his coat. There she found a pouch of ducats, and it took only a very few seconds for her to transfer them to her stocking. For good measure, she pulled a handful of hair from his beard.

"I'm going to teach you a lesson," she said. "Don't think that you're going to get away from here in one piece. Your descendants to the tenth generation will beware of being such an outrageous liar." And she spat in his face. He took out his handkerchief and wiped himself off. Then the lady of the house and the servant girl came in and set the table for supper. In honor of the visitor, the host descended to the wine cellar to fetch a bottle of dry wine.

III

After supper, Glicka Genendel made up a bed for the guest.

"Now get in there," she said, "and I don't want you to do so much as stir a whisker. After the others are asleep, I'll be back for a little chat."

And to prevent him from escaping she inpounded his overcoat, cap, and shoes. Reb Yomtov said his prayers and went to bed. He lay there trying to think of some way out of his predicament; and it was at this point that I, the Evil One, materialized.

"Why hang around here like a trussed calf awaiting the slaughterer?" I said. "Open the window and run."

"Just how am I to manage that," he asked, "with no clothes or shoes?"

"It's warm enough outside," I told him. "You're not going to get sick. Just find your way to Piask, and once there, you'll make out all right. Anything is better than remaining with this termagant."

As usual he heeded my counsel. He rose from the bed, threw open the window, and began the descent. I saw to it, however, that there was an obstacle in his path, and he lost his footing and fell, spraining his ankle. For a moment he lay on the ground unconscious. But I revived him.

He forced himself to his feet. It was a very dark night. Barefoot, half-naked, limping, he started off down the Piask road.

While this was going on, Glicka Genendel was occupied otherwise. She could hear the snores of her daughter and son-in-law coming from their bedroom, and so she got up, put on her wrapper, and tiptoed to the chamber of her best beloved. To her astonishment she saw that the bed was unoccupied and the window open. Before she could scream, however, I appeared to her.

"Now what's the sense of that?" I asked her. "It's not a crime for a man to get out of bed, is it? He hasn't stolen anything. The fact is it's you who've done the stealing, and if he's caught, he'll tell about the money you took from him. You're the one who'll suffer."

"Well, what shall I do?" she asked me.

"Don't you see? Steal your daughter's jewel box; then begin to yell. If he's apprehended he'll be the one who's thrown in jail. That way your revenge is certain."

The idea appealed to her and she took my advice. A few shrieks and she had awakened the household. Right away it was discovered that the jewelry was missing, and the ensuing din brought in the neighbors. A posse of men, equipped with lanterns and cudgels, took off after the thief.

I saw that the noble young altruist was quite shaken by what his guest had done, and so I took the opportunity to taunt him.

"You see what happens when you bring a guest home," I pointed out.

"So long as I live there'll be no more poor strangers in this house," he promised.

By this time the posse was busy searching the streets for the fugitive. They were joined by the night watch and the magistrate's constables. It wasn't very difficult to hunt down Reb Yomtov, lame and half-clothed as he was. They found him seated under a balcony, futilely attempting to set his dislocated ankle. Immediately they began to beat him with their clubs despite his protestations of innocence.

"Of course," they laughed, "innocent men always leave a house by the window in the middle of the night."

His hostess followed, screaming invectives at every step. "Thief! Murderer! Criminal! My jewels! My jewels!"

He kept repeating that he knew nothing about the

robbery, but to no avail. The guards threw him into a cell and wrote down the names of the witnesses.

Glicka Genendel returned to bed. It was sweet to lie under the warm comforter while one's enemy rotted in jail. She thanked God for the favor he had bestowed upon her, and promised to donate eighteen groshen to charity. All the running about had exhausted her, and she longed for sleep, but I came to her and would not permit her to rest.

"Why such great elation?" I inquired. "Yes, he's in jail all right, but now you won't get a divorce from him. He'll tell everyone whose husband he is, and you and your whole family will be disgraced."

"What should I do?" she asked.

"He sent you a divorce by a messenger to Janov. Go to Janov and get the papers. First of all, you'll be rid of him. Secondly, if you're not here, you can't be called as a witness. And if you're not at the trial, who will believe his story? When the excitement is over, you can return."

My argument convinced her, and the very next morning she arose at sunrise, and explained to her daughter that she was off to Warsaw to meet her husband, Reb Yomtov. Her daughter was still in a state of shock and so did not put up much resistance. Actually Glicka Genendel wanted to put back the jewelry she had stolen from her daughter, but I talked her out of it.

"What's the rush?" I asked. "If the jewels are found, they'll let the liar out, and who's that going to harm, but you? Let him stay behind bars. He'll learn that one doesn't trifle with such a fine, upstanding woman as you."

So to make a long story short, Glicka Genendel set out for Janov, with the intention of either meeting the messenger there in person, or at least getting some clue as to his whereabouts. When she walked into the market place, everyone stared at her. They all knew about the messenger and the divorce papers. She sought out the rabbi and the rabbi's wife snubbed her; his daughter, who was the one who let her in, did not bid her welcome, nor ask her to sit down. But, at any rate, the rabbi gave her the facts: a messenger had come to Janov to present her with divorce papers, but not being able to locate her in town, had left. He remembered that the messenger was named Leib and that he came from Piask. Leib, he recalled, had yellow hair and a red beard. When Glicka Genendel heard this, she immediately engaged a carriage to take her to Piask. There was no point in staying in Janov any longer as the townspeople avoided her.

Reb Yomtov was still in jail. He sat surrounded by thieves and murderers. Vermin-infested rags were his only clothing. Twice daily he fed on bread and water.

And then, at length, the day of his trial rolled round, and he stood before the judge, who turned out to be an irascible man who was hard of hearing.

"Well, what about the jewels?" the judge growled. "Did you steal them?"

Reb Yomtov pleaded not guilty. He was no thief.

"All right, you're no thief. But why did you run out of the house in the middle of the night?"

"I was running away from my wife," Reb Yomtov explained.

"What wife?" the judge asked angrily.

Patiently Reb Yomtov began his elucidation: The mother-in-law of the man at whose house he had been staying was none other than his, Reb Yomtov's wife, but the judge did not allow him to proceed further.

"That's a fine story," he shouted. "You certainly are a brazen-faced liar."

Nevertheless, he did send for Glicka Genendel. Since she had already left town, her daughter came in her place, and testified that it was quite true that her mother was married, but that it was to a highly respectable man from Jerusalem, the famous scholar Reb Yomtov. As a matter of fact, she was even then on her way to meet him.

The prisoner lowered his eyes and cried out, "I am Reb Yomtov."

"You Reb Yomtov," the woman shouted. "Everyone knows you are Reb Solomon Simeon." And she began to curse him with the choicest oaths at her command.

"The farce is over," the judge said sternly. "We have enough scoundrels here already. We don't need any foreign importations." And he decreed that the prisoner be given twenty-five lashes, and then hanged.

It did not take long for the Jews of Lublin to hear of the decree; one of their own, and a scholar at that, was to be hanged, and immediately they sent a delegation to intercede with the governor in the prisoner's behalf. But this time they could accomplish nothing.

"Why are you Jews always so anxious to buy back your criminals?" the governor asked. "We know how to deal with ours, but you let yours off scot free. No wonder there are so many crooks among you." And he had the delegation chased off by dogs, and Reb Yomtov remained in jail.

He lay in his cell, chained hand and foot, awaiting execution. As he tossed about on his bundle of straw, mice darted out from chinks in the wall, and gnawed at his limbs. He cursed them and sent them scurrying back to cover. Outside the sun shone, but in his dungeon all was black as night. His situation, he saw, was comparable to that of the Prophet Jonah when he had been deep inside the stomach of the whale. He opened his lips to pray, but I, Satan the Destroyer, came to him and said, "Are you stupid enough to still believe in the power of prayer? Remember how the Jews prayed during the Black Plague, and, nevertheless, how they perished like flies? And what about the thousands the Cossacks butchered? There was enough prayer, wasn't there, when Chmielnicki came? How were those prayers answered? Children were buried alive, chaste wives raped—and later their bellies ripped open and cats sewed inside. Why should God bother with your prayers? He neither hears nor sees. There is no judge. There is no judgment."

This is the way I spoke to him, after the fashion of the philosophers, and shortly his lips had lost their inclination to pray.

"How can I save myself?" he asked. "What is your advice?"

"Become a convert," I told him. "Let the priests sprinkle a little holy water over you. That way you can stay alive and have revenge in the bargain. You do want to revenge yourself, don't you, on your enemies? And who are your enemies but the Jews, the Jews who are quite willing to see you hang because of the lies that a Jewess has invented to destroy you?"

He listened carefully to these words of wisdom and when the turnkey brought him his food, told him that he had a desire to be converted. This news was brought to the priests, and a monk was dispatched to interview the prisoner.

"What is your motive in wanting to become a Christian?" the monk inquired. "Is it merely to save your skin? Or has Jesus Christ entered your heart?"

It had happened while he was asleep, Reb Yomtov explained. His grandfather had come to him in a vision. Jesus, the saintly man had told him, was among the most exalted in Heaven, and sat with the Patriarchs in Paradise. No sooner did Reb Yomtov's words reach the bishop, than the prisoner was taken out of his cell, and washed and combed. Dressed in clean raiment, he was put in the company of a friar who instructed him in the catechism; and while he learned of the significance of the host and the cross, he dined on delicious food. What is more, the best families in the neighborhood came to visit him. Then, at last, he was led at the head of a procession to the monastery and converted to Christianity. Now he was certain that his troubles were over, and that he would shortly be a free man, but instead he was led back to his cell.

"When one is sentenced to death," the priest told him, "there's no way out. But don't be sorrowful; you will go with a clean soul into the next world."

Now Reb Yomtov realized that he had cut himself off from all of his worlds. His sorrow was so extreme that he lost his power of speech and spoke not one word as the hangman tightened the noose around his neck.

IV

On her way from Janov to Piask, Glicka Genendel stopped to visit a relative. She spent the Sabbath and Pentecost in the small village in which this relative lived. As she helped her hostess decorate the windows for the holiday, she munched on butter-cookies. And then the day after Pentecost she resumed her journey to Piask.

Of course, it never entered her mind that she was already a widow. Nor did it occur to her, you may be sure, that she was walking into a trap, a trap that I had baited. She traveled leisurely, stopping at all the inns on the way, stuffing herself with egg-cookies and brandy. She did not forget the coachman, but bought him egg-cookies and brandy as well, and to show his gratitude, he arranged a comfortable seat for her in the wagon, and helped her to mount and alight. He looked her over lecherously, but she couldn't bring herself to lie with so low a fellow.

The weather was mild. The fields were green with wheat. Storks circled overhead; frogs croaked, crickets chirped; butterflies were everywhere. At night as the wagon rolled through the deep forest, Glicka Genendel stretched herself out on the matting like a queen, and loosened her blouse, and permitted the soft breezes to cool her skin. She was well along in years, but her body had resisted old age, and passion still burnt in her as brightly as ever. Already she was making plans to get a new husband.

Then early one morning she arrived in Piask, just as the merchants were opening their shops. The grass was still wet with dew. Troops of barefoot girls, carrying ropes and baskets, were on their way into the forest to gather firewood and mushrooms. Glicka Genendel sought out the assistant rabbi and asked him what he knew of her divorce. He received her cordially, explaining that the Bill of Divorcement had been drawn up by him personally and signed in his presence. The papers were now in the hands of Leib the Coachman. When Glicka Genendel suggested that the beadle be sent to fetch the man, the assistant rabbi made a counter proposal.

"Why don't you go to his house yourself?" he said. "Then you can settle the whole thing with him personally."

So Glicka Genendel went to Leib's house which was a hut that squatted on a hilltop behind the slaughterhouses. The roof of the building was made of rotting straw, and the windows were covered with cow-bladders instead of glass. Although it was summer, the earth around the house was wet and slimy, but this did not bother the ragged, half-naked children who were entertaining themselves there with worn-out brooms and poultry feathers. Scrawny goats, as grimy as pigs, scurried about this way and that.

Leib the Coachman had neither wife nor children. He was a short, broad-shouldered man, with large hands and feet; there was a growth on his forehead and his beard was a fiery red. He was dressed in a short jacket and straw shoes; on his head he wore the lining of a cap which could not quite conceal his bristling tufts of yellow hair.

The sight of him repelled Glicka Genendel, but, nevertheless, she said, "Are you Leib?"

"Well, we can be sure of one thing, you're not Leib," he answered insolently.

"Do you have the divorce papers?"

"What business is that of yours?" he wanted to know.

"I am Glicka Genendel. The divorce was drawn up for me."

"That's your story," he said. "How do I know you're telling me the truth? I don't see your name written on your forehead."

Glicka Genendel realized that this was going to be a difficult man to deal with, and she asked, "What's the matter? Are you after money?— Don't worry I'll give you a handsome tip."

"Come back tonight," he said.

And when she inquired why that was necessary, he told her that one of his horses was dying, and he couldn't bear any further conversation. He conducted her into an alleyway. There lay an emaciated nag with a mangy skin, foam frothing from its mouth, its stomach rising and falling like a bellows. Droves of flies buzzed around the dying creature, and overhead were circling crows, cawing as they waited.

"Very well, I'll come back this evening," Glicka Genendel said, now thoroughly disgusted. And her high buttoned shoes moved as fast as she could make them go, taking her away from the ruin and poverty.

It just happened that the night before the Piask thieves had been out on business; they had invaded Lenchic with carts and covered wagons, and had emptied the stores. It had been the evening before market day and so there had been more than enough goods to take. But this rich haul had not been sufficient to satisfy the raiders; they had also broken into the church and had divested it of its gold chains, crowns, plates, and jewels. The holy statues had been left naked. Then they had beaten a hasty retreat homewards, and, as a matter of fact, the horse that Glicka Genendel had seen expiring had been a casualty of the expedition; it had been whipped so mercilessly during the withdrawal that it had collapsed as soon as the robbers had reached home.

Of course, Glicka Genendel knew nothing of this. She went to an inn and ordered a roast chicken. To get the sight of the dying horse out of her mind, she drank a pint of mead. Inevitably, she made friends with all the male guests, inquiring of each his name, home town, and business in this vicinity. Inevitably also, she spoke of her background: her noble descent, her knowledge of Hebrew, her wealth, her jewels, her skill at cooking, sewing, and crocheting. Then when dinner was finished she went to her room and took a nap.

She awoke to find that the sun was setting and that the cows were being driven home from pasture. From the chimneys of the village smoke was issuing as the housewives prepared the evening meal.

Once more Glicka Genendel took the path that led to Leib's. When she entered the house she left behind the purple dusk, and found herself in a night that was almost as black as the inside of a chimney. There was only one small candle burning—inside of a shard. She could just make out Leib who sat astride an inverted bucket. He was mending a saddle. Leib was not a thief himself; he just drove for the thieves.

Glicka Genendel began to talk business immediately, and he took up his old complaint. "How do I know that it's your divorce?"

"Here take these two gulden and stop this nonsense," she said.

"It's not a question of money," he grumbled.

"What's eating you, anyway?" she wanted to know.

He hesitated for a moment.

"I am a man too," he said, "not a dog. I like the same things everyone else does." And he winked lecherously and pointed toward a bench-bed heaped with straw. Glicka Genendel was almost overcome with disgust, but

I, the Prince of Darkness, hastened to whisper in her ear, "It doesn't pay to haggle with such an ignoramus."

She begged him to give her the divorce papers first. It was merely a question of lessening the sin. Didn't he see that it would be better for all concerned if he went to bed with a divorcee rather than a married woman? But he was too shrewd for that.

"Oh, no," he said, "as soon as I serve you with the papers, you'll change your mind."

He bolted the door and put out the candle. She wanted to scream but I muffled her voice. Oddly enough she was only half afraid; the other half of her was alive with lust. Leib pulled her down onto the straw; he stank of leather and horses. She lay there in silence and astonishment.

That such a thing should happen to me! she marveled to herself.

She did not know that it was I, the Arch-Fiend, who stoked her blood and muddled her reason. Outside destruction already lay in wait for her.

Suddenly there was the sound of horsemen. The door was splintered open as if by a hurricane, and dragoons and guardsmen, carrying torches, burst into the room. All this happened so quickly that the adulterers did not even get a chance to stop what they were doing. Glicka Genendel screamed and fainted.

This foray had been led by the Lenchic squire himself who came with his troops to punish the thieves. His men broke into the homes of all known criminals. An informer accompanied the platoon. Leib wilted at the first blow and confessed that he was a driver for the gang. Two soldiers hustled him out, but before they left one of them asked Glicka Genendel, "Well, whore, who are you?"

And he ordered that she be searched.

Of course, she protested that she knew nothing of the sacking of Lenchic, but the informer said, "Don't listen to that tart!" He thrust his hand inside her bosom and drew out a treasure trove: her daughter's jewelry and Reb Yomtov's pouch of gold. Under the glow of the torches, the ducats, diamonds, sapphires, and rubies gleamed wickedly. Now Glicka Genendel could not doubt that misfortune had overtaken her, and she threw herself at the squire's feet, begging for mercy. But despite her entreaties she was clapped into irons and taken along with the other thieves to Lenchic.

At her trial, she swore that the jewels were her own. But the rings did not fit her fingers, nor the bracelets her wrists. She was asked how much money was in the pouch, but she did not know because Reb Yomtov had coins from Turkey in his hoard. When the prosecutor wanted to know where she had obtained the ducats, she replied, "From my husband."

"And where is your husband?"

"In Lublin," she blurted out in her confusion, "in prison."

"The husband is a jailbird," the prosecutor said. "And she is a whore. The jewelry is obviously not hers, and she doesn't even know how much money is in her possession. Is there any doubt about the conclusion?"

Everyone agreed that there was not.

Now Glicka Genendel saw that her chances were indeed slim, and it occurred to her that her only hope was to announce that she had a daughter and son-in-law in Lublin, and that the jewelry belonged to her daughter. But I said to her, "First of all, no one's going to believe you. And suppose they do, look what happens. They fetch your daughter here and she finds out that not only have you stolen her jewelry, but also that you've fornicated with that scab-head like a common harlot. The disgrace will kill her, and so you'll have your punishment anyway. Incidentally, Reb Yomtov will be released, and believe me, he'll find your situation amusing. No, better keep quiet. Rather perish than yield to your enemies."

And although my advice led to the abyss, she did not object, for it is well known that my people are vain and will lay down their lives for their vanity. For what is the pursuit of pleasure but pride and delusion?

So Glicka Genendel was sentenced to the gallows.

The night before the execution I came to her and urged her to become a convert, just as I had in the case of the late, unlamented Reb Yomtov, but she said, "Is it any greater honor to have a convert for a mother than a prostitute? No, I'll go to my death a good Jewess."

Don't think I didn't do my best! I pleaded with her over and over again, but, as it is written: A female has nine measures of stubbornness.

The following day, a gallows was erected in Lenchic. When the town's Jews learend that a daughter of Israel was to be hanged, they became frantic and petitioned the Squire. But a church had been pillaged, and he would not grant mercy. And so from the surrounding areas the peasants and gentry drove in, coverging on the place of execution in coaches and wagons. Hog-butchers hawked salamis. Beer and whiskey were guzzled.

A darkness fell upon the Jews, and they closed their shutters at mid-day. Just before the execution, there was a near-riot among the peasants as to who would stand closest to the gallows in order to get a piece of the rope for a good luck charm.

First they hanged the thieves, Leib the Coachman among them. Then Glicka Genendel was led up the steps. Before the hood was placed over her head, they asked her if she had a final request, and she begged that the rabbi be summoned to hear her confession. He came, and she told him the true story. It was probably the first time in her life she had ever told the truth. The rabbi recited the Confession for her and promised her Paradise.

It seems, however, that the Lenchic rabbi had little influence in Heaven because before Glicka Genendel and

Reb Yomtov were admitted to Paradise, they had to atone for every last sin. No allowances are made up there for anything.

When I told this story to Lilith, she found it very amusing and decided to see these two sinners in Gehenna. I flew with her to purgatory and showed her how they hung suspended by their tongues, which is the prescribed punishment for liars.

Under their feet were braziers of burning hot coals. Devils flogged their bodies with fiery rods. I called out to the sinners, "Now, tell me whom did you fool with those lies? Well, you have only yourselves to thank. Your lips spun the thread, and your mouths wove the net. But be of good cheer. Your stay in Gehenna lasts only for twelve months, including Sabbaths and holidays."

Translated by Cecil Hemley
and June Ruth Flaum

The Beggar Said So

I

One hot summer day a big wagon, drawn by one horse, lumbered into the market place of Yanov. It was piled high with motley rags and bedding, laden with cans and buckets, and from the axle between the rear wheels a lantern hung. On top of everything a flower pot and a cage with a little yellow bird swayed precariously. The driver of the wagon was dark, with a pitch-black beard. He wore a cap with a leather visor and a coat not cut in the usual style. At first glance one could have taken him for an ordinary Russian. But the woman with him wore on her head the familiar Jewish coif. Jews, then, after all. Instantly, from all the little shops round about, the Jews of the town rushed out to meet the new arrivals. The stranger stood there in the market place with his whip in his hand.

"Wher-r-re's your magistr-r-rate?" he demanded. He pronounced his "r's" in the dialect of Great Poland, hard and sharp.

"And what would you need the magistrate for?"

"I want to be a chimney sweep," said the newcomer.

"And why should a Jew want to be a chimney sweep?"

"I served in the Army for twenty-five years. I have my working papers."

"There's a chimney sweep in town already."

"But the beggar said there wasn't," the newcomer insisted.

"What beggar?"

"Why, the one that came to our town."

It seemed that the man—his name was Moshe—had been a chimney sweep in some small town on the other side of the river Vistula, not far from the Prussian border. One day a beggar who traveled from place to place had come to that town and had said something about a chimney sweep being needed in Yanov. Moshe and his wife had lost no time; they had loaded all their worldly goods onto a wagon and set out for Yanov.

The young men watching them smiled, nudged each other and exchanged meaningful glances. The older householders shrugged their shoulders.

"Why didn't you write a letter first?" they asked Moshe.

"I can't w-r-rite," was the answer.

"So you can get someone else to write for you. Beggars have made up stories before."

"But the beggar said. . . ."

All talk and counter-arguments proved vain. To every question the man had only one answer: "The beggar said so." One might have thought his wife would have had more sense, but she, too, had the same stock rejoinder: "The beggar said so." The crowd of townspeople grew swiftly and the strange tale passed from mouth to mouth. The onlookers began to whisper to each other about it; they shook their heads and made crude puns. One of the men, a flour dealer, called out:

"Just think, believing a poor tramp like that!"

"Maybe the beggar was the Prophet Elijah in disguise," jeered another.

The school children came out from the *Cheder* and mimicked the new arrivals. "The beggar said so," they hooted after them. The young girls giggled while the older women wrung their hands and lamented the lot of these poor fools from Great Poland. In the meantime Moshe the chimney sweep filled one of his cans with water at the town pump and gave his horse a drink. Then he proceeded to fasten a bag of oats around the animal's jaws. From the horse's collar which was studded with bits of brass two pine branches protruded stiffly. The shaft was painted blue. Everyone soon saw that the two travelers had with them, besides the horse and the bird, an odd assortment of geese, ducks, chickens, and one black rooster with a red comb—all in one big cage.

In Yanov at the time there were no vacant dwellings; temporarily, therefore, the two strangers were put up at the poorhouse. A coachman took their horse into his own stable, and someone else bought the fowl. Moshe's spouse, Mindel, immediately joined the other *shnorrers'* wives in the kitchen of the poorhouse where she cooked some porridge. Moshe, himself, went off to the study house to recite a few chapters from the Book of Psalms. And a new byword became fashionable in Yanov: "But the beggar said so." The schoolboys never tired of questioning Moshe and of laughing up their sleeves.

"Tell us," they would query, "just what did he look like, that beggar?"

"Like all other beggars," Moshe would reply.

"What kind of a beard did he have?"

"Yellow."

"Don't you know that men who grow yellow hair are cheaters?"

"How should I know?" Moshe would report. "I'm a

simple man. The beggar said so, and I believed him."

"If he had told you that the rabbi's wife lays eggs, would you have believed that too?"

Moshe did not answer. He was a man well into his fifties, though still without one grey hair. His face was tanned like that of a gypsy. His back was straight; his shoulders and chest, broad. He produced for the school teacher's inspection two medals which he had gotten in the Tsar's service for proficiency in riding and marksmanship, and he told of his experiences as a soldier. He had been one of the young boys inducted by force. His father had been a blacksmith. He, Moshe, had still been a student at the *Cheder* when a child-snatcher from the Tsar's army had taken him away. But he, Moshe, had refused to eat forbidden foods and had fasted until he was faint with hunger. The village priest had tried to convert him, but he had a *mezuzah* which his mother had given him as well as the fringed ritual garment worn next to the body to remind him of his God at all times. Yes, they had whipped him, flogged him too with wet switches, but he had not given in. He had remained a Jew. When they tortured him, he had cried out, "Hear, O Israel, the Lord our God is One."

Moshe also told about the time, years later, when he had fallen asleep while on sentry duty and his gun had slipped from his hand. If he had been caught napping, he would have been sent to Siberia. But lo, his dead grandfather had appeared to him in a dream and awakened him. He had had another close call: while crossing a frozen river, he had been stranded on an ice floe. Once too he had been attacked by a wild ox. But he had managed to grab the beast by its horns—he still bore the scar on his wrist. The Tsar's veterans had a reputation for telling tall tales, but everyone believed Moshe; it was clear from the way he told his stories that he had not made them up.

Not long after the arrival of Moshe and his wife, a

room was found for them to live in and a stable for the horse. Just at that time one of the Yanov water carriers died; Moshe procured a wooden yoke and became a water carrier. His wife, Mindel, went every Thursday to knead dough in the baking troughs and, besides that job, she stripped feathers for the bedding of new brides. Gradually the two newcomers grew accustomed to Yanov. Yet one question still burrowed deep in the heart of Moshe. Why should the beggar have deceived him so? Had not he, Moshe, given his guest, the beggar, his own bed while he himself tossed about on the ground all night? Not to brag about it, but on that Sunday morning, hadn't he given his guest a loaf of bread and a slab of cheese to take on the way? Why, then, should the beggar have wanted to make a fool of him? Moshe often discussed the riddle with his wife. But she did not know the answer either, and each time he broached the subject, she would say:

"Moshe, take my advice and stop thinking about it."

"But . . . why should the beggar have said so if it wasn't true?" he would persist.

Moshe knew that wandering beggars can turn up anywhere. Every Sabbath he looked over the transients gathered at the synagogue entrance to see if this one beggar was among them. But the years passed and the beggar never came. Was the man afraid that Moshe might take revenge? Or, perhaps, Moshe thought, God had punished him and he had died on the road. In time, the odd thing was that Moshe was not even angry any longer. He had made up his mind that he would not even give the beggar a beating if he were to meet him again. He would simply take him by the neck and say:

"Why did you make a fool of me, contemptible creature?"

Several coachmen tried to persuade Moshe to sell his horse. The wells from which water was drawn for the town of Yanov were nearby so that a water carrier had no need of a horse. And why, they argued, should he have to feed an animal for nothing? But Moshe refused to part with his old mare. He and his wife were fond of animals. God had not granted them any children, but a variety of living things—stray dogs, cats, birds that could no longer fly—had joined their household. The wife would buy a live carp for the Sabbath, but instead of cleaning it and chopping it up she would let it swim about in a washtub for weeks until it finally died of natural causes. Even though one beggar had misused their kindness, these two did not take out their chagrin on other little people. Moshe's wife carried groats to the poorhouse, and every Friday night Moshe would take a wayfarer home as his guest for the Sabbath. To every one of them he would tell the story of what had happened to him and at the end he would ask, "Now why should the beggar have said so?"

II

Late one winter night, Moshe was sitting in his chair soaking his feet in a tub of water. His wife had opened the door of a little cage and a tiny yellow bird was flying about the room. They had taught it a number of tricks. For instance, Moshe would place some millet seeds between his fingers and the bird would take them. Or else he would put one single grain on his lips and the bird would snatch it with its beak, exchanging a kiss with the master.

The oven was warm and the door locked tightly against the cold outside. The woman sat in a corner darning socks. Suddenly, Moshe's head sank down on his chest; he fell asleep and at once began to dream. He dreamed that the soot in the chimney of the poorhouse had caught fire. A bright flame shot out from the chimney and was melting all the snow on the shingle roof. Moshe awoke with a start.

"Mindel," he called to his wife. "There's a fire at the poorhouse."

"How do you know?"

"I saw it in a dream."

"A dream can fool."

"No, it's true," said Moshe.

In vain did his wife argue that it was bitter outside and that he might catch cold—Heaven forbid—if he went out so soon after soaking his feet. Hurrying, Moshe put on his boots, his fur coat and his sheepskin cap. In his closet he still had his chimney sweep's broom, with the rope and iron plummet. He took them with him now as he left the house. He walked through Lublin Street and the Street of the Synagogue and then arrived at the poorhouse. There he saw everything exactly as it had been in his dream. The chimney spouted fiery sparks. The snow near it had melted. Moshe began to shout as hard as he could but the people in the poorhouse did not hear him. Indeed, even if they had waked immediately, they would hardly have been able to save themselves for all of them were old, sick and lame. There was no ladder. Moshe attempted to scale the wall. He caught hold of a giant icicle but that broke off. Then he clung to a shingle but it, too, fell from the eaves before he could climb up. Already, a part of the roof was on fire. In desperation, Moshe grabbed his broom with the iron plummet and with a forceful heave aimed it at the chimney. Amazingly, at the first try it landed in the chimney. The rope hung out; Moshe grasped it and, like an acrobat, he swung himself onto the roof. There was no water; quickly he scooped up snow and patting it into balls threw them into the chimney, all the while bellowing at the top of his voice. But no one heard him. The poorhouse was some distance away from the town; besides, the wind was howling. And the people of Yanov were sound sleepers.

When Moshe failed to return home, his wife put on her

boots and padded jacket and went to the poorhouse to see what was keeping him. The dream was true: there he was, standing on the roof. The fire was out but the chimney was still smoking. Pale moonlight shone on the eery scene. By now some of the old people inside had waked and come out, carrying a scoop and shovel. They crowded around. All declared that had it not been for Moshe, the building would have burned to cinders and they would all have perished inside. What with the wind blowing in the direction of the town, the fire could have spread to the synagogue, the bathhouse, the study house and, yes, even to the houses in the market place. And then not only would the houses have been burned-out shells, but there would have been more deaths from cold and exposure.

By the next day the report of the feat of Moshe the water carrier had spread through the town. The mayor appointed a commission to inspect all the chimneys, and the investigation revealed that the town chimney sweep had not done his job in months. They found him in his room, dead drunk, with a straw in his mouth, still sipping vodka from a cask. He was sent packing and, in his place, Moshe became the official chimney sweep of the town of Yanov.

And now a marvelous thing came to pass.

A few days later, when Moshe went to the poorhouse and the inmates crowded round him to thank him and to shower him with blessings, he noticed someone whose features seemed familiar. The man's beard was a mixture of yellow and gray. He was lying on a straw sack covered with rags. The face from which the eyes bulged out was yellow with jaundice. Moshe stopped short and thought in wonder: Where have I met him before? I could swear that I know this man. And then he clasped his hands together in amazement. Why, this was none other than the beggar, the very same one who, years ago, had told him that they needed a chimney sweep in Yanov. A stream of tears gushed forth from Moshe's eyes.

Yes, it was the beggar. He had long forgotten his words but he did recall that in that year and at that time he had spent the Sabbath in that village in Great Poland. He even recalled that he had stayed with some chimney sweep there.

And what was the fruit of all this questioning, of this investigation? Why, it had become quite clear to Moshe that the whole chain of events had been directed from On High. Years ago, this one beggar had been ordained to find a man who would one day save him and all the other people of Yanov from death. It was plain, then, that this beggar had been an instrument of God. Besides, his words had come true after all. Not at the time he said them, to be sure, but much later, for now Moshe had indeed become the official chimney sweep of Yanov. The longer Moshe thought about it, the more clearly did he see the hand of Divine Providence in it all. It was beyond his grasp. Imagine! Holy angels in Heaven thinking of Moshe the Chimney Sweep and sending him messengers with prophecies, just as in the story of Father Abraham!

Moshe was overcome by awe and humility. Had the poorhouse floor not been so dirty he would have fallen upon his face right there and prostrated himself and given thanks to the Almighty. A sob came from his throat and his beard grew sodden with his tears. After he had recovered his composure, he lifted the beggar's frail body in his arms and bore him home upon his shoulders. He washed him, bathed him, dressed him in a clean shirt and laid him on his bed. Mindel immediately went to the stove and made some soup. And the people of the town who for so many years had poked fun at Moshe and had dubbed him "But-The-Beggar-Said-So" took the events to heart and told their children to stop using that name.

III

For over three months the beggar lay in Moshe's bed while Moshe slept on the floor. Gradually the poor man regained some of his strength and wanted to go on the road again, but Moshe and his wife would not hear of it. The beggar had neither wife nor child and he was much too old and weak to wander about. He remained with the pair. Regularly he went to the study house to pray and recite psalms. His eyes failed and he grew almost blind. Other wayfarers told story after story of noblemen, merchants and rabbis, but this beggar was silent. When he finished his reading of the Book of Psalms, he would immediately start all over again. He had also memorized whole passages from the Mishnah. When the Talmud students came to him to inquire why, so many years ago, he had told Moshe that there was no chimney sweep in Yanov, he would raise his eyebrows, shrug his shoulders and answer:

"I really don't know."

"And where do you come from?" they would ask him.

He would give some sort of reply, but his words did not come out clearly. The people thought he was deaf. And yet he had no trouble at all hearing the Reader's prayers from his remote corner of the study house. Mindel catered to him, pampering him with chicken and oatmeal, but he ate less and less as time went by. He would absently raise a spoonful of soup to his lips and then forget to put it in his mouth. The little bird which Moshe had brought with him to Yanov had long since died, but his wife had bought another bird from the gypsies. The cage was never closed, and the bird would fly out and perch on the beggar's shoulder for hours on end.

After some time had passed, the beggar was taken ill again. Moshe and his wife sent for a doctor who spared neither time nor remedies, but apparently the man had no more years left. He died during the Passover month and was buried on a Friday. The burial society set aside a plot for him among the graves of residents of long standing. Half of Yanov followed the funeral procession. When Moshe and Mindel returned home from the cemetery they found that their bird had gone. It never came back. And in Yanov the word went around that the old beggar who had died had been a *Lamed-Vavnik,* one of the Thirty-Six Righteous Men who, living out their days in obscurity, were keeping the world from destruction by the strength of their virtues.

One night, not long after the beggar's death, Moshe and his wife could not sleep. They began to speak of all sorts of things, talking on till sunrise. That morning Moshe announced in the study house that he and his wife wanted to have a new Scroll of the Law made for the community.

The scribe of Yanov labored over the Scroll for three years, and during all that time Moshe and Mindel talked of their Scroll as if it had been their only daughter. Mindel skimped and saved on household expenses, but for the Scroll she bought remnants of silk and velvet, golden thread, and she hired poor maidens to fashion these into embroidered mantelets. Moshe went all the way to Lublin to order the rollers, a crown with bells, a breastplate and a silver pointer, all to adorn the Scroll. Both the mantelets and the rollers bore the beggar's name—Abraham, the son of Chaim.

On the day the Scroll was dedicated, Moshe gave a festive meal for all the poor of Yanov. Just before dusk the guests assembled in the courtyard of the synagogue. The final sheet of the Scroll had been left incomplete, and after evening services the respected citizens of the community each bought the privilege of having one letter on the last sheet inscribed in their behalf. When all the ink had dried on the parchment and the sheet had been sewn into place, the festive procession began. A wedding canopy was spread out on its poles, and held aloft by four of the most distinguished members of the congregation. Beneath the canopy marched the rabbi, carrying the new Scroll in his arms. The little bells on the shining crown tinkled softly. The men and boys sang; the maidens held up braided candles. Waxen tapers had been lit. Moshe and his wife shone in their holiday best. Simple man that he was, Moshe had pinned his two Russian medals to his lapel. Some of the more learned congregants took this amiss and wanted to tell him in no uncertain terms to take them off, but the rabbi would not allow them to humiliate Moshe in public.

Not even the very old in the congregation could recall ever having witnessed a dedication feast like this one. Two bands played without pause. The night was mild and the moon shone brightly. The sky looked like a star-studded curtain for a Heavenly Ark. The girls and the women danced together, apart from the men. One young man strode about merrily on stilts, and a jester serenaded the host and hostess—Moshe and his wife. There was plenty of wine and ginger cake, supplied by Moshe and Mindel. The band played a real wedding march, a Shear Dance, an Angry Dance, and a Good Morning Dance; it was all just like a regular wedding feast. And then Moshe hitched up his coattails and Mindel her skirts and they danced a *Kasatzke* together, bumping fronts and backsides as they pranced about.

Moshe called out:

"The Beggar-r-r's right next to God!"

And Mindel sang out in reply:

"We are not worthy even of the dust of his feet."

Moshe and Mindel still lived on for quite a few years after this celebration. Before he died, Moshe reserved a burial place for himself next to the grave of the beggar, and he asked to have the broom, the rope and the plummet, with which he had saved the old people at the poorhouse, placed in his coffin.

And as for Mindel—each day she went to the study

house and drew aside the velvet curtain of the Ark to bestow a reverent kiss upon her own beloved Scroll. Early every morning without fail, until the last day of her life, she performed this ritual. And in her last will and testament she stipulated that she be buried next to her husband and the beggar who had, after all, spoken the truth.

Translated by Gertrude Hirschler

The Man Who Came Back

You may not believe it but there are people in the world who were called back. I myself knew such a one, in our town of Turbin, a rich man. He was taken with a mortal illness, the doctors said a lump of fat had formed under his heart, God forbid it should happen to any of us. He made a journey to the hot springs, to draw off the fat, but it didn't help. His name was Alter, and his wife's name was Shifra Leah; I can see them both, as if they were standing right before my eyes.

She was lean as a stick, all skin and bones, and black as a spade; he was short and fair, with a round paunch and a small round beard. A rich man's wife, but she wore a pair of broken-down clodhoppers and a shawl thrown over her head, and was forever looking out for bargains. When she heard of a village where one could pick up cheap a measure of corn or a pot of buckwheat, she would go all the way on foot and haggle there with the peasant until he let her have it for next to nothing. I beg her pardon—but the family she came from was scum. He was a lumber merchant, a partner in the sawmill; half the town bought their lumber from him. Unlike his wife, he was fond of good living, dressing like a count, always in a shortcoat and fine leather boots. You could count each hair in his beard, it was so carefully combed and brushed.

He liked a good meal too. His old woman stinted on everything for herself—but for him no delicacy was too dear. Because he favored rich broths, with circlets of fat floating on top, she bullied the butcher, demanding fat meat, with a marrow bone thrown in, for her husband's broth with the gold coins in it, as she explained. In my time, when people got married they loved each other; who ever thought of divorce? But this Shifra Leah was so wrapped up in her Alter that people laughed in their fists. My husband this, and my husband that; heaven and earth and Alter. They had no children, and it's well known that when a woman is childless she turns all her love on her husband. The doctor said he was to blame, but who can be sure about such things?

Well, to make the story short. The man took sick and it looked bad. The biggest doctors came to see him—it didn't help; he lay in bed and sank from day to day. He still ate well, she feeding him roast pigeons and marzipans and all sorts of other delicacies, but his strength was ebbing away. One day I came to bring him a prayer book that my father—rest in peace—had sent over to him. There he lay on the sofa in a green dressing gown and white socks, a handsome figure. He looked healthy, except that his paunch was blown up like a drum, and when he spoke he puffed and he panted. He took the prayer book from me, and gave me a cookie together with a pinch on the cheek.

A day or two later the news was that Alter was dying. The menfolk gathered; the burial society waited at the door. Well, listen to what happened. When she saw that

Alter was at his final gasp, Shifra Leah ran for the doctor. But by the time she got back with the doctor in tow, there was Leizer Godl, the elder of the burial society, holding a feather to her Alter's nostrils. It was all over, they were ready to lift him off the bed, as the custom is. The instant Shifra Leah took it in, she flew into a frenzy; God help us, her screaming and wailing could be heard at the edge of town. "Beasts, murderers, thugs! Out of my house! He'll live! He'll live!' She seized a broom and began to lay about her—everybody thought she had gone out of her mind. She knelt by the corpse: "Don't leave me! Take me with you!" and ranting and raving, she shook and jostled him with lamentations louder than those you'd hear on Yom Kippur.

You know you are not allowed to shake a corpse, and they tried to restrain her, but she threw herself prone on the dead man and screeched into his ear: "Alter, wake up! Alter! Alter!" A living man couldn't have stood it—his eardrums would have burst. They were just making a move to pull her away when suddenly the corpse stirred and let out a deep sigh. She had called him back. You should know that when a person dies his soul does not go up to heaven at once. It flutters at the nostrils and longs to enter the body again, it's so used to being there. If someone screams and carries on, it may take fright and fly back in, but it seldom remains long, because it cannot stay inside a body ruined by disease. But once in a great while it does, and when that happens, you have a person who was called back.

Oh, it's forbidden. When the time comes for a man to die, he should die. Besides, one who has been called back is not like other men. He wanders about, as the saying goes, between worlds; he is here, and yet he isn't here; he would be better off in the grave. Still, the man breathes and eats. He can even live with his wife. Only one thing, he casts no shadow. They say there was a man once in Lublin who had been called back. He sat all day in the prayer house and never said a word for twelve years; he did not even recite the Psalms. When he died at last, all that was left of him was a sack of bones. He had been rotting all those years and his flesh had turned to dust. Not much was left to bury.

Alter's case was different. He immediately began to recover, talking and wisecracking as if nothing had happened. His belly shrank, and the doctor said that the fat was gone from his heart. All Turbin was agog, people even coming from other towns to get a look at him. There was muttering that the burial society put living men into the ground; for if it was possible to call Alter back, then why not others? Perhaps others were also merely cataleptic?

Shifra Leah soon drove everyone away, she allowed no one to enter her house, not even the doctor. She kept the door locked and the curtains drawn, while she tended and watched over her Alter. A neighbor reported he was already sitting up, taking food and drink, and even looking into his account books.

Well, my dear people, it wasn't a month before he showed up at the market place, with his cane and his pampered beard and his shiny boots. Folks greeted him, gathering round and wishing him health, and he answered, "So you thought you were rid of me, eh? Not so soon! Plenty of water will yet run under the bridge before I go." People asked, "What happened after you stopped breathing?" And he said: "I ate of the Leviathan and dipped it in mustard." He was always ready with the usual wisecrack. It was said that the Rabbi summoned him and they were locked up together in the judgment chamber. But no one ever knew what talk passed between them.

Anyhow, it was Alter, only now he had a nickname: the One Who Was Called Back. He was soon back at his trading in boards and logs. The gravediggers' brethren went about with long faces; they had hoped to pick up a juicy bone at the funeral. At first people were a bit afraid of him. But what was there to be afraid of? He was the same merchant. His illness had cost quite a sum, but he had enough left over. On Saturdays he came to prayer, he was called to the reading, offered thanksgiving. He was also expected to contribute to the poorhouse and to give a feast for the townsfolk, but Alter played dumb. As for his wife, Shifra Leah, she strutted like a peacock, looking down her nose at everyone. A small matter?—she had brought a dead man back to life! Ours was quite a big town. Other men fell ill and other wives tried to call them back, but no one had a mouth like hers. If everybody could be recalled, the Angel of Death would have to put aside his sword.

Well, things took a turn. Alter had a partner in his mill, Falik Weingarten; in those days people were not called by their family names, but Falik was a real aristocrat. One day Falik came to the rabbi with a queer story: Alter, his partner, had become a swindler. He stole money from the partnership, he pulled all sorts of tricks and was trying to push him, Falik, out of the business. The rabbi couldn't believe it: when a man had gone through such an ordeal, would he suddenly become a crook? It didn't stand to reason. But Falik was not one to make up tales, and they sent for Alter. He went into a song and dance—black was white, and white was black. He dug up ancient bills and accounts all the way back from King Sobieski's time. He showed bundles of claims. To hear him tell it, his partner still owed *him* a small fortune, and what's more, he threatened to start court action.

The townspeople tried arguing with Alter: "You've done business together for so many years, what's gone wrong all of a sudden?" But Alter was a changed man—he seemed to be looking for quarrels. He started litigation, and the case dragged on and cost a fortune. Falik took it so to heart that he died. Who won, I don't remember, I only remember that the sawmill went over to creditors, and Falik's widow was left penniless. The rabbi rebuked Alter: "Is this how you thank the Lord for putting you back on your feet and raising you from the dead?" Alter's answer was no better than the barking of a dog: "It was not God who did it. It was Shifra Leah." And he said further: "There is no other world. I was good and dead, and I can tell you there is nothing—no hell and no paradise." The rabbi decided he had lost his mind—perhaps so. But wait, hear the rest.

His wife, Shifra Leah, was the worst kind of draggletail—people said that a pile of dirt sprang up wherever she stood. Suddenly Alter began to demand that she should dress up, deck herself out. "A wife's place," he said, "is not only under the quilt. I want you to go promenading with me on Lublin Street." The whole town buzzed. Shifra Leah ordered a new cotton dress made, and on Sabbath afternoon, after the *cholent* meal, there were Alter and his wife Shifra Leah on the promenade, along with the tailors' helpers and shoemakers' apprentices. It was a sight—whoever had the use of his limbs ran out to look.

Alter even trimmed his beard. He became—what's it called? an atheist. Nowadays, they're all over the place; every fool puts on a short jacket and shaves his chin. But in my time we had only one atheist—the apothecary. People began to say that when Shifra Leah called Alter back with her screams, the soul of a stranger had entered his body. Souls come flying when someone dies, souls of kinsfolk and others, and, who knows, evil souls too, ready to take possession. Reb Arieh Vishnitzer, a pupil of the old rabbi, declared that Alter was no longer Alter. True, it was not the same Alter. He talked differently, he laughed differently, he looked at you differently. His eyes were like a hawk's, and when he stared at a woman, it was enough to make a shudder pass through you. He hung out with the musicians and all sorts of riffraff. At first his wife said amen to everything, whatever Alter said or did was all right with her. I beg her pardon, but she was a cow. But then a certain female arrived in our town, from Warsaw. She came to visit her sister, who wasn't much to boast of and whose husband was a barber; on market days he shaved the peasants, and he also bled them. You can expect anything from such people: he had a cage full of birds, twittering all day long, and he also had a dog. His own wife had never shaved off her hair, and the sister from Warsaw was a divorcee—no one knew who her husband was. She came among us bedecked and bejeweled, but who ever looked at her twice? A broomstick can be dressed up too. She showed the women the long stockings she was wearing, hooked, if you'll pardon the word, to her drawers. It was not hard to guess that she had come to trap some man. And who do you think fell into her clutches? Alter. When the townsfolk heard that Alter was running around with the barber's sister-in-law, they couldn't believe it; even coopers and skinners, in those days, had some regard for decency. But Alter was a changed man. God forbid, he had lost all shame. He strolled with the divorcee in the market place, and people looked from all the windows, shaking their heads and spitting in disgust. He went with her to the tavern, for all the world like a peasant with his woman. There they sat, in the middle of the week, guzzling wine.

When Shifra Leah heard it, she knew she was in trouble. She came running to the tavern, but her husband turned on her with the vilest abuse. The newcomer, the slut, also jeered at her and taunted her. Shifra Leah tried to appeal to him: "Have you no shame before the world?" "The world can kiss what we sit on," says he. Shifra Leah cried to the other one: "He is my husband!" "Mine, also," answers she. The tavern keeper tried to put a word in, but Alter and the slut belabored him too; a woman depraved is worse than the worst man. She opened such a mouth that she shocked even the tavern keeper. People said she grabbed a pitcher and threw it at him. Turbin is not Warsaw. The town was in an uproar. The rabbi sent the sexton to summon Alter to him, but Alter refused to come. Then the community threatened him with the three letters of excommunication. It didn't help, he had connections with the authorities and defied one and all.

After a couple of weeks, the divorced slut left town, and people thought things would quiet down. Before the week was out, the man who was called back from the dead came to his wife with a tale. He had an opportunity, he said, to buy a wood in Wolhynia, an unusual bargain, and he must leave at once. He collected all his money, and told Shifra Leah that he had to pawn her jewelry too. He bought a barouche and two horses. People suspected he was up to something crooked and warned his wife, but the faith she had in him, he could have been a wonder rabbi. She packed his suits and underwear; roasted chickens and prepared jams for him for the journey. Just before he set off he handed her a small box: "In here," he said, "are three promissory notes. On Thursday, eight days from today, take the notes to the rabbi. The money was left with him." He spun her a story, and she swallowed it. Then he was off.

Thursday, eight days later, she opened the box and discovered a writ of divorce. She let out a scream and fell into a faint. When she came to, she ran to the Rabbi, but he took one look at the paper and said: "There is nothing to be done. A writ of divorce can be hung on your doorknob, or it can be slipped under your door." You can imagine what went on in Turbin that day. Shifra Leah pulled at her cheeks, screaming: "Why didn't I let him croak? May he drop dead wherever he is!" He had cleaned her out—even her holiday kerchief was gone. The house was there still, but it was mortgaged to the barber. In olden times, runners would have been sent after such a shameless betrayer. The Jews once had power and authority, and there was a pillory in the synagogue court, to which a wretch would have been bound. But among our Gentile officials a Jew was of small consequence—they couldn't care less. Besides, Alter had taken care to bribe his way.

Well, Shifra Leah took sick, climbed into her bed and refused to get up. She would take nothing to eat, and kept cursing him with the deadliest curses. Then suddenly she started beating her breast and lamenting: "It's all my fault. I did not do enough to please him." She wept and she laughed—she was like one possessed by an evil spirit. The barber, who claimed now to be the legal owner of the house, wanted to throw her out of her home, but the community wouldn't let him, and she remained, in a room in the attic.

In time, after a few weeks, she recovered, and she went out with a peddler's pack, like a man, to trade among the peasants. She turned out to be a good hand at buying and selling; soon the matchmakers were approaching her with proposals of marriage. She wouldn't hear of it; all she talked about, she bent your ear if you would listen, was her Alter. "You wait," she said, "he'll come back to me. The other one didn't want him, she was after his money. She'll clean him out and leave him flat." "And you'd take such riffraff back again?" folks asked her, to which she answered: "Only let him come. I'll wash his feet and drink the water." She still had a trunk left and she collected linens and woolens, like a bride. "This will be my dowry for when he returns," she boasted. "I'll marry him again." Nowadays you call it infatuation; we called it plumb crazy.

Whenever people came from the big cities, she ran to them: "Have you run into my Alter?" But no one had seen him: it was rumored that he had become an apostate. Some said he had married a she-demon. Such things happen. The years went by, and people began to think that Alter would never be heard of again.

One Sabbath afternoon, when Shifra Leah was dozing on her bench-bed (she had never learned to read the Holy Book, as the women do), the door opened and in stepped a soldier. He took out a sheet of paper. "Are you Shifra Leah, the wife of the scoundrel Alter?" She turned white as chalk; she could not understand Russian, and an interpreter was brought in. Well, Alter was in prison, a serious crime, because he was sentenced to life. He was being kept in the Lublin jail, and he had managed to bribe the soldier, who was going home on leave, to bring a letter to Shifra Leah. Who knows where Alter got the money to bribe in prison? He must have hidden it somewhere in his cot when he was first brought in. Those who read the letter said that it would have melted a stone; he wrote to his former wife: "Shifra Leah, I have sinned against you. Save me! Save me! I am going under. Death is better than such a life." The other one, the slut, the barber's sister-in-law, had stripped him of everything and left him only his shirt. She probably informed on him too.

The town buzzed with excitement. But what could anyone do to help him?—you may be sure he was not put away for reading the Holy Book. But Shifra Leah ran to all the important people in town. "It is not his fault," she cried, "it comes from his sickness." She was not yet sobered up, the old cow. People asked her: "What do you need that lecher for?" She would not allow a speck to fall on his name. She sold everything, even her Passover dishes; she borrowed money, she got what she could from high and low. Then she took herself off to Lublin, and there she must have turned heaven and earth, for she finally got him freed from jail.

Back she came to Turbin with him, and young and old ran out to meet them. When he stepped out from the covered wagon, you couldn't reocgnize him: without a beard, only a thick mustache, and he had on a short caftan and high boots. It was a *goy,* not Alter. On looking closer, you saw that it was Alter after all: the same walk, the same swagger. He called each man by his name and asked about all kinds of detail. He wisecracked and said things to make the women blush. They asked him: "Where's your beard?" He answers: "I pawned it with a moneylender." They asked him: "How does a Jew take up such ways?" He replies: "Are you any better? Everybody is a thief." On the spot he gave a recital of everybody's secret sins. It was plain to see that he was in the hands of the Evil One.

Shifra Leah tried to make excuses for him and to restrain him; she fluttered over him like a mother hen. She forgot that they were divorced and wanted to take him home, but the rabbi sent word that they must not live under the same roof; it was even wrong for her, he said, to have traveled with him in the same wagon. Alter might scoff at Jewishness, but the law still remained. The women took a hand. The pair were separated for twelve days, while she took the prescribed ablutions, and then they were led under the wedding canopy. A bride must go to the ritual bath even if she is taking back her own husband.

Well, a week after the wedding he started thieving. On market days he was among the carts, picking pockets. He went off to the villages to steal horses. He was no longer plump, but lean as a hound. He clambered over roofs, forced locks, broke open stable doors. He was strong as iron and nimble as a devil. The peasants got together and posted a watch with dogs and lanterns. Shifra Leah was ashamed to show her face and kept her window shuttered; you can imagine what must have gone on between man and wife. Soon Alter became the leader of a band of roughnecks. He guzzled at the tavern with them, and they sang a Polish song in his honor; I remember the words to this day: "Our Alter is a decent sort, he hands out beer by the quart."

There is a saying: a thief will end up on the gallows.

One day, as Alter was drinking with his toughs, a squadron of Cossacks came riding up to the tavern with drawn swords. Orders had come from the governor to throw him into irons and bring him to the jail. Alter saw at once that this was the end, and he grabbed a knife; his drinking pals ran off—they left him to fight it out alone. The tavern keeper said afterwards that he fought with the strength of a demon, chopping away at the Cossacks as though they were a field of cabbages. He turned over tables and threw barrels at them; he was no longer a young man, but for a while it almost looked as though he might get the better of them all. Still, as the saying goes, one is none. The Cossacks slashed and hacked at him till there was no more blood left in his veins. Someone brought the bad news to Shifra Leah, and she came running like crazy to his side. There he lay, and she wanted to call him back again, but he said one word to her: "Enough!" Shifra Leah fell silent. The Jews ransomed his body from the officials.

I didn't see him dead. But those who did swore that he looked like an old corpse that had been dug up from the grave. Pieces were dropping from his body. The face could not be recognized, it was a shapeless pulp. It was said that when he was being cleansed for burial, an arm came off, and then a foot; I wasn't there, but why should people lie? Men who are called back rot while they are alive. He was buried in a sack outside the graveyard fence, at midnight. After his death, an epidemic struck our town, and many innocent children died. Shifra Leah, that deluded woman, put up a stone for him and went to visit his grave. What I mean to say is—it is not proper to recall the dying. If she had let him go at his appointed hour, he would have left behind a good name. And who knows how many men who were called back are out in the world today? All our misfortunes come from them.

Translated by Mirra Ginsburg

In the Poorhouse

I

There was a warm, homelike feeling about the poorhouse today. The rich man of the town, Reb Leizer Lemkes, married off his youngest daughter, Altele. And he gave a feast for the poor. In addition to gorging themselves on carp, *kreplach* with soup, *chalah,* beef and carrot stew, and washing it all down with wine, each of the paupers was given something to take home: a slice of honey cake, a chicken drumstick, an apple, a piece of pastry. Everyone had eaten his fill. Most of them had overeaten. The poorhouse overseer had also had his share and did not stint today: he piled the stove full of firewood. Such heat came from its iron door that Hodele the beggar asked someone to open the chimney, she was in such a sweat.

After the feast everybody fell asleep. Night descended quickly. None of the men had prayed that evening. But after some hours of sleep, the little family began to wake. First to open his eyes was Leibush Scratch. He had hidden a roast chicken in the straw. And he began to put it away now, for fear that someone might steal it during the long night, or else the mice might get at it.

The second to wake up was Jonah the Thief. He had slipped under his pillow a head of a carp wrapped in cabbage leaves—a present from Serele the servant girl. Bashe the Whore, who had hidden three macaroons in her stocking, could not sleep either. The sounds of munching, chewing, gnawing mingled with the snuffling and snoring of the sleepers. Outside, fresh snow had fallen, and the moon was bright. After a while, Leibush Scratch asked:

"Jonah, my friend, are you eating or sleeping on it?"

"Chewing is no sin," Jonah the Thief retorted smartly.

"Leave him alone, Reb Leibush," put in Bashe the Whore, "or he may swallow a bone."

"What are you crunching there?" asked Leibush. "Last Passover's matzos?"

"A bit of a macaroon."

"I thought you had something. Who gave it to you, eh?"

"The little Tsipele."

"Give me a piece. . . ."

Bashe did not answer.

Jonah the Thief laughed: "Her kind doesn't give anything for nothing."

"I can give her my bellyache."

"If you have an ache, you can keep it to yourself," replied Bashe.

"I have plenty to spare for you too."

"Don't curse, Reb Leibush, I am cursed enough," said Bashe. At any other time she would not trouble to talk to Leibush, but the food and the wine and the glowing stove softened all hearts. People forgot their quarrels for a while. Besides, the night was long, and they could not go back to sleep.

For a while it was quiet again. Leibush could be heard

cracking the chicken bones and sucking the marrow. Then he asked:

"I wonder how late it is?"

"I sent my watch for repair," joked Jonah the Thief.

"Once upon a time I had no need of watches. In the daytime I could tell the hour by the sun. At night I looked at the stars, or sniffed the wind. But you can't tell anything in this stench. Why are no roosters crowing?"

"All the roosters were slaughtered for the wedding," said Bashe.

"Tell us a story, Reb Leibush," asked Jonah the Thief.

"What story? I've told you everything. Old Getsl makes up his stories, but I don't like to make them up. What's the good of that? I can tell you that I was Count Pototsky once upon a time, or that Radziwill used to heat the bath house for me. What will come of that? Did I ever tell you about the mannikin?"

"In the glass of whiskey? With the magician?"

"Yes."

"You told us that one."

"And about the hail?"

"The hail too."

"And the ox?"

"The way the ox attacked you on the way to night prayers?"

"Yes."

"You did, you told us that one too."

"Well, what can I tell you, then? You are a thief, you have many stories to tell. I spent my life over the grindstone."

"Hey, you, Bashe, why don't you ever tell us anything?" asked Jonah.

Bashe was silent. They no longer expected her to answer. Suddenly her voice was heard:

"What can I tell you?"

"Tell us how you became a whore, and all the rest of it."

"The moment I open my mouth, the women begin to curse."

"The women are asleep."

"They'll wake soon enough. They don't let me live. God has forgiven long ago, but they won't forgive. What harm have I done them? I am not from these parts. I have never sinned with their husbands. I lie here and never hurt a fly, but they eat me up alive with their eyes. They spit into my face. Whenever anyone brings a plate of soup or a bowl of *kashe,* they begin to hiss like snakes: 'Not for her! Not for her!' If it were up to them, I would have died of hunger long ago. But kind people have pity. If I had my legs, I'd not be lying here. I'd run from here to where black pepper grows."

"But you have none."

"And that's my bitter misfortune. I long for death, but it doesn't come. Healthy people go, but I lie here and rot alive. It's lucky they put me here. The women used to pinch me, they used to tear out lumps of my flesh. They threw garbage at me. They spilled their night slops over me. . . ."

"We know, we know it all."

"You don't know one thousandth of it. When a man hits someone, everybody sees it and there's a hullaballoo. But women can dig your heart out on the sly. Now they cannot reach me with their hands, so they stick needles into me with their eyes. They can't forgive me that I lie here among the men. When I lie dead, with my feet toward the door and a straw under my head, they will still envy me."

"I thought you were going to tell us a story."

"What have I to tell? I've had troubles from my childhood on. My mother, may she intercede for me, had three daughters before me. My father wanted a boy. He made a journey to a rabbi, and the rabbi promised him a boy. When the midwife told him it was a girl, he would not believe her. He demanded to be shown. . . . My father was a Hasid, and it was a custom in the study house that a man whose wife gave birth to one daughter after another was given a whipping. The Hasidim stretched my father out on the table, and whipped him with their sashes. He never wanted to look at me. He would not even call me by my name. He never hit me either. Just as if I were a step-child. When I called him 'father,' he pretended he did not hear me. Was it my fault? My mother used to say: 'You were born in a black hour.' When I was nine, I left home."

"Why did you leave home?"

"Because I slaughtered three ducks."

"What? You slaughtered ducks?"

"Yes, I was growing up a wild thing. Whatever I saw, I imitated. One day my mother sent me to the *shochet,* to have him slaughter a hen. I saw him standing there with the knife slaughtering the fowl, and I liked it. We had three ducks locked in the pantry. I took a pocket knife, spit on a stone, sharpened it, and cut the throats of the three ducks. Suddenly the door opened, and my father came in. He turned white as chalk. He ran to my mother, screaming: 'Either she goes, or I do . . .' On the following day they packed a few things into a bundle and sent me into service in Lublin."

"But how did you become a whore?"

"How did you become a horse thief? Little by little. A young fellow promises to lead you under the bridal canopy. Then he tells you to go and whistle."

"Who was the first one?"

"A teacher's helper."

"A teacher's helper, eh? And then?"

"He went away, and that was the last of him. Try and find a teacher's helper in God's world. After him came a tailor's assistant, and after the tailor, a hat-maker. When a girl loses her virtue, she is anybody's game. Whoever wants to, has the use of her. A bridal canopy is only a few lengths of velvet and four posts. But without it, a girl is less than the dirt under your nail."

"We know that. When did you enter a brothel?"

"When I got a belly full."

"And what happened there?"

"What could happen there? Nothing."

"And the child, what became of it?"

"It was left on the church steps."

"One child?"

"Three."

"And then what?"

"Nothing."

"This is no story."

"The story comes later."

"What happened?"

"I'm ashamed to tell it before Reb Leibush."

"What? But he's sleeping."

"He fell asleep?"

"Don't you hear him snoring?"

"Yes. But he was talking just now!"

"At his age you can talk one minute, doze off the next, and a minute later you make bye-bye, and it's all over. And with me you don't have to feel ashamed."

"No."

"Let's hear it, then."

"I'm afraid the women are listening."

"They're sleeping like the dead. Talk quietly. I am not deaf."

"There are times when you want to talk. I was already in Warsaw at that time. I was with a madam. She had three of us, and I was the prettiest. Don't look at me today. I am a broken vessel. I have no legs, my hair is gone, my teeth are gone. I am an old scarecrow. But in my young days I was a beauty. The queen! That's what they called me. People could not look into my face—it dazzled like the sun. Whenever a guest had me, he never wanted anyone else. The other two stood at the gate all night, but I sat on my bed and they came to me as if I were a doctor. The madam had a tongue like a whip, but when she spoke to me, it was as through a silken cloth. I had a fiancé—that's what we called them—Yankel, and he was crazy about me. He bought me whatever I wanted. If the madam said an unkind word to me, right away he'd pull the knife out of his boot. He was a wild one, too. A guest is a guest, after all. But suddenly he'd get jealous. He'd grab the man by the collar and throw him down the whole flight of stairs, if he just dared to kiss me. The madam would yell murder, but he'd yell back: 'Shut up, or I'll knock out all your teeth.' He wanted to marry me, too, but his years were short. He caught the smallpox and was covered with blisters all over. They took him in an ambulance to the hospital, and there they poisoned everybody."

"Poisoned? Why?"

"Just so."

"And then what?"

"He died and was buried. After that my luck changed. I was taken over by another fellow, but that one had only money on his mind. Sender was his name, Sender the Bum. He did not care for me, and I did not care for him. When the madam saw that things were going badly with me, she began to lord it over me. I could not run away because I had a yellow passport. And where can our kind escape? Only to the grave. The madam began to abuse me, and the other two sluts made my life miserable. A woman must have someone to protect her, or else she's nine feet deep in trouble.

"Once in two weeks we had our day off. When Yankel was alive, he used to take me everywhere. We even drove out in a *droshky*. He bought me chocolates, marmalade, halvah and licorice from a Turk—whatever my heart desired. There was a carousel in Voiny Place, and we used to go round and round in it. But when Yankel was gone,

I was all alone. The madam lived on Nizka Street, and I went out walking along the Dzhika. Were you ever in Warsaw? I had nothing to do. So I leaned on a lamp-post, cracking sunflower seeds. I was not out to catch anyone. I put on a cotton dress and a shawl over my shoulders, like an honest girl.

"I stand there, and think about my life. Suddenly a tall young man comes over to me, in a wide-brimmed hat, with a shock of long hair and a cape down to the sidewalk. I was so startled, I cried out. He looked strange, pale and disheveled like a free-thinker. In those years workers were organizing unions and throwing bombs at the Tsar. I thought he was one of that company. I wanted to get away, but he put out a long hand and grabbed me. 'Fraulein,' says he, 'do not run away. I do not eat people.' 'What does the gentleman want?' I ask. And he says: 'Do you want to earn some money?' 'Who doesn't want money?' I say, 'But I have no time. I must be back at the old woman's in an hour.' 'It won't take an hour,' says he. He starts talking so fast that I cannot understand anything at first. He is in love, he tells me, with a girl, and she is making him sweat. So he wants me to come with him and he'll introduce me as his fiancée. 'What will come of it?' I ask, '—besides, I must get back very soon.' And he says: 'I want to test her.' 'How do you know who I am?' I ask. So he tells me he lives across the street and he sees me at the gate. It seems he followed me.

"I was afraid because I could not stay out long, and Sender was free with his fists. Anything not to his liking, and he could beat you to death. But before I could say a word, I was sitting in a *droshky*. 'Take off your shawl,' says he. On Nalewki Street there was a miliner. He tells the *droshky* to wait and picks out a hat for me, with a wide brim, for three roubles. I put it on, and I don't know my own face in the mirror. He takes my shawl and hides it under his cloak. We drive out on Mead Street, and there he buys me a handbag. All the customers haggle. They bargain the shopkeeper down to half the asking price. But he doesn't bargain, he pays whatever they ask. The salesgirls laugh at him and pinch one another. My mother used to say: 'Send a fool to market, and the shopkeepers rejoice.' To make it short and sweet, I was now a lady from Marshalkovski Street.

"From Mead Street we drove back to Franciscan Boulevard. The driver was already beginning to grumble that it was more than a single fare zone. So the man takes a half a rouble from his pocket and hands it to him. He is throwing money around like a lord.

"Then we come to a leather goods store, and there's a girl inside. There are no customers. He lets me walk ahead and then follows me in. Respect for the ladies, we called it in Warsaw. She was an ordinary girl. I could not tell what he saw in her. Her eyes were black and sharp. You could tell she was a shrew. She took one look at him and turned white as chalk. He takes me under the arm and leads me to the counter. 'Leah, my dear,' he says, 'this is my fiancée.' I thought the jade would catch apoplexy on the spot. If she could, she would have swallowed me up alive. 'Why did you bring your fiancée here?' she asked, 'Do you want me to congratulate her?' 'No,' he answers, 'this wasn't the reason. I want a pair of shoes made for her, and I know your father sells the best leather. Give her first-class goods. The price is no object.' If the girl did not catch a stroke, she was stronger than iron. 'You cannot buy leather without a shoemaker,' she says. 'You have to know the size and the trimmings.' 'You can take her size,' says he, and tells me to sit down on the stool. He lefts up my dress, tears off a strip of paper and measures my foot. And he says: 'Leah my dear, did you ever see such a foot? It's the smallest foot in Warsaw.' I really had small feet. He tickles me with his long fingers, and I can hardly keep a straight face. The girl says: 'Don't think you are fooling me. You could have gotten your leather somewhere else. You came here to tease me.

So I can tell you: whoever begrudges you, let him have nothing himself. And she isn't your fiancée either. You picked someone up in the street. I know your tricks. I don't need your trade. Get out of here and don't come back. If you show up again, alone or with her, I'll call the policeman!' My gentleman turns white and says nothing. He drops my foot, and I sit there with one shoe and one stocking. And then he cries out: 'Yes, you are right. She is a girl from the street, but I swear to God I'll marry her this very day! Tonight she'll be my wife, and I'll forget all about you. I'll tear you from my heart. I'll love her with my whole soul. Even if she is an unfortunate one, she has more decency than you. . . .' Those were his words. He started abusing her in the vilest language. He caught me by the hand and screamed:

"'Come to the rabbi, my bride! Tonight we shall be man and wife.'

"I was so mixed up that I left one shoe in the store."

II

Leibush Scratch woke up.

"You're talking? Talk. What happened after that?"

"Have you heard it, then?" Jonah the Thief asked. "But you were sleeping!"

"I dozed off, but I heard. At my age sleep isn't what it used to be. I dream I am at a fair, and I know I am lying here at the poorhouse. I am here, and I am there. I am Leibush, and I am the rabbi. Why did you leave your shoe, eh?"

"I was afraid a crowd would gather."

"How could you walk around in one shoe?"

"Just as I stood there, the shoe flew after me from the store. I ran to catch it, and a cart almost knocked me over. My fine gentleman dropped down on his knees in the middle of the gutter and put the shoe on my foot. Just like a play in the theatre. The whole street laughed. The *droshky* was gone, and he pulled me and yelled: 'Where do you find a rabbi around here?' People pointed out a house across the street. And then, my friends, I saw that I had no luck. We were already in front of the steps, when I was suddenly afraid. I said to him: 'You love the other girl, not me.' 'I'll love you, I'll love you,' he answers. 'I am a trained pharmacist. I can live in Petersburg, in Moscow, anywhere in Russia. We'll leave this city, and I'll pluck her out of my heart. I'll love and cherish you, and you will be the mother of my children.' I remember every word as if it happened yesterday. I did not know what a pharmacist was. Later someone explained to me it meant a druggist. An educated man. But I say: 'Do you know what I do?' 'I know,' he cries, 'but I don't want to know. I'll forgive you everything . . .' 'But you don't even know me,' I say, but he screams: 'I do not need to know you. You are more pure than she is . . .' I look at him: he is foaming at the mouth. His eyes are like a madman's. I suddenly felt sick. I broke away and began to run. I ran out of the gates, and heard him running after me and calling: 'Where are you running? Where are you running? Come back! . . .' I ran as if he were a murderer. I came to the butcher stalls in the market, and there I got away from him. The place was so crowded that you could not drop a needle. It was only after I cooled off that I realized that I was done for. Where was I running, woe is me? Back to the mire.

"When I came home and they saw me with the stylish hat and handbag, there was an uproar. The old woman asks: 'Where is the shawl?' And I don't have the shawl. He hid it under his cape. Well, there was no end of talk and laughter. They wouldn't believe me, either. When Sender came and they told him everything, he took away the hat and the handbag. He gave me a punch too, into the bargain. He had a fiancée somewhere, and he took everything to her. And, my dear people, I'll tell you something else: the old woman deducted from my wages for the shawl, or may I never have a holy burial."

For a long while everyone was silent. Then Leibush Scratch asked:

"You are sorry now, eh?"

"Why not? I wouldn't be rotting here today."

"If he lived across the street, why didn't you seek him out?" asked Jonah the Thief.

"They would not give me any days off after that. I thought he would come, but he never did."

"Perhaps he made up with the girl from the leather store?"

"Perhaps."

"There is a saying: forge the iron while it's hot," Leibush Scratch said reflectively.

"That's true."

"And yet, if it is not written for you, it isn't. Was it you, then, who was running? Your feet carried you. Or take me. Did I have to end up lying here on a bundle of straw? Not more than you have to dance on the roof. I was not rich, but I was a man of some property. I owned a house, a small mill. I had a wife . . . But if they want it up in heaven that a man should fall, they find a way. First my wife sickened and died. Then the house went up in smoke. Nobody knew how it started. A few splinters were smoldering under the tripod. Then suddenly there was a burst of fire as though hell itself had opened. There wasn't even any wind. My house stood right next to Chaim the Cooper's, but never a spark touched his place, while I was ruined. Can anyone understand that?"

"No."

"Someone saw a little flame sit on the bed. It rolled over and made somersaults. It was all from the evil ones."

"What did the evil ones have against you?"

"I was destined to take up a beggar's sack. . . ."

Jonah the Thief began to crack his knuckles, first one hand, then the other.

"Isn't it the truth, though? That night when I went to the village of Bysht I knew well enough that I should not go. The peasants had heard of me. I was warned that they were sleeping in the stables. Wojciech the village elder had posted a watch with a rattle. I needed the whole business like a hole in the head. Just a few days before that I pulled in a big haul. Zeldele, may she rest in peace, begged me: 'Jonah, don't try to grab the whole world. I'd rather eat dry bread than see you making this kind of a living.' And what did we need? There were only the two of us. Zelig the horse merchant wanted to hire me as a driver. I could have become a horse dealer myself. Sometimes you earn more, sometimes less, but it's honest money. I was already going to bed that night. I closed the shutters and pulled off my boots. Suddenly I put them on again and started out for Bysht. I walked with a heavy heart. I kept stopping and wanting to turn back. But I never walked back—they brought me home in a wheelbarrow."

"What did they do it with? Sticks?" asked Leibush.

"Whatever they could lay their hands on. A whole village against one man. . . ."

"I'll tell you the truth—it's a wonder you came out alive. This was before your day. There was a certain Itchele Nonie—that's what they called him because he had a long nose—and he went to Boyares to steal a horse. The peasants ambushed him and burned him alive. All that was left of him was a heap of ashes. The gravediggers' brotherhood had nothing to bury . . ."

"I know. I've heard of it. He had better luck than I."

"When did your wife die? I don't remember any more."

"Six months later."

"From all that trouble, eh?"

"No, from pleasure."

"Well, everything is destined. Everything is written for us above, to the last breath. As my grandmother used to say: Nobody is mightier than the Almighty."

"Who writes it all? God?"

"Not you."

"Where does he get so much paper?"

"Don't let your brains dry up in worrying about that."

"Man has his share of responsibility too."

"No, he hasn't. . . ."

It became quiet at the poorhouse. Hodele the beggar moaned in her sleep, muttered unintelligible words. A cricket chirped once. Leibush Scratch resumed his snoring, whistling through his nose. Jonah the Thief asked:

"Do you still have a piece of macaroon? I have a bitter taste in my mouth. . . ."

Bashe did not answer.

Translated by Mirra Ginsburg

Taibele and Her Demon

I

In the town of Lashnik, not far from Lublin, there lived a man and his wife. His name was Chaim Nossen, hers Taibele. They had no children. Not that the marriage was barren; Taibele had borne her husband a son and two daughters, but all three had died in infancy—one of whooping cough, one of scarlet fever, and one of diphtheria. After that Taibele's womb closed up, and nothing availed: neither prayers, nor spells, nor potions. Grief drove Chaim Nossen to withdraw from the world. He kept apart from his wife, stopped eating meat, and no longer slept at home, but on a bench in the prayer house. Taibele owned a dry-goods store, inherited from her parents, and she sat there all day, with a yardstick on her right, a pair of shears on her left, and the Women's Prayer Book in Yiddish in front of her. Chaim Nossen, tall, lean, with black eyes and a wedge of a beard, had always been a morose, silent man even at the best of times. Taibele was small and fair, with blue eyes and a round face. Although punished by the Almighty, she still smiled easily, the dimples playing on her cheeks. She had no one else to cook for now, but she lit the stove or the tripod every day and cooked some porridge or soup for herself. She also went on with her knitting—now a pair of stockings, now a vest; or else she would embroider something on canvas. It wasn't in her nature to rail at fate or cling to sorrow.

One day Chaim Nossen put his prayer shawl and phylacteries, a change of underwear, and a loaf of bread into a sack and left the house. Neighbors asked where he was going; he answered: "Wherever my eyes lead me."

When people told Taibele that her husband had left her, it was too late to catch up with him. He was already across the river. It was discovered that he had hired a cart to take him to Lublin. Taibele sent a messenger to seek him out, but neither her husband nor the messenger was ever seen again. At thirty-three, Taibele found herself a deserted wife.

After a period of searching, she realized that she had nothing more to hope for. God had taken both her children and her husband. She would never be able to marry again; from now on she would have to live alone. All she had left was her house, her store, and her belongings. The townspeople pitied her, for she was a quiet woman, kindhearted and honest in her business dealings. Everyone asked: how did she deserve such misfortunes? But God's ways are hidden from man.

Taibele had several friends among the town matrons whom she had known since childhood. In the daytime housewives are busy with their pots and pans, but in the evening Taibele's friends often dropped in for a chat. In the summer, they would sit on a bench outside the house, gossiping and telling each other stories.

One moonless summer evening when the town was as dark as Egypt, Taibele sat with her friends on the bench, telling them a tale she had read in a book bought from a peddler. It was about a young Jewish woman, and a demon who had ravished her and lived with her as man and wife. Taibele recounted the story in all its details. The women huddled closer together, joined hands, spat to ward off evil, and laughed the kind of laughter that comes from fear. One of them asked:

"Why didn't she exorcise him with an amulet?"

"Not every demon is frightened of amulets," answered Taibele.

"Why didn't she make a journey to a holy rabbi?"

"The demon warned her that he would choke her if she revealed the secret."

"Woe is me, may the Lord protect us, may no one know of such things!" a woman cried out.

"I'll be afraid to go home now," said another.

"I'll walk with you," a third one promised.

While they were talking, Alchonon, the teacher's helper who hoped one day to become a wedding jester, happened to be passing by. Alchonon, five years a widower, had the reputation of being a wag and a prankster, a man with a screw loose. His steps were silent because the soles of his shoes were worn through and he walked on his bare feet. When he heard Taibele telling the story, he halted to listen. The darkness was so thick, and the women so engrossed in the weird tale, that they did not see him. This Alchonon was a dissipated fellow, full of cunning goatish tricks. On the instant, he formed a mischievous plan.

After the women had gone, Alchonon stole into Taibele's yard. He hid behind a tree and watched through the window. When he saw Taibele go to bed and put out the candle, he slipped into the house. Taibele had not bolted the door; thieves were unheard of in that town. In the hallway, he took off his shabby caftan, his fringed garment, his trousers, and stood as naked as his mother bore him. Then he tiptoed to Taibele's bed. She was almost asleep, when suddenly she saw a figure looming in the dark. She was too terrified to utter a sound.

"Who is it?" she whispered, trembling.

Alchonon replied in a hollow voice: "Don't scream, Taibele. If you cry out, I will destroy you. I am the demon Hurmizah, ruler over darkness, rain, hail, thunder, and wild beasts. I am the evil spirit who espoused the young woman you spoke about tonight. And because you told the story with such relish, I heard your words from the abyss and was filled with lust for your body. Do not try to resist, for I drag away those who refuse to do my will beyond the Mountains of Darkness—to Mount Sair, into a wilderness where man's foot is unknown, where no beast dares to tread, where the earth is of iron and the sky of copper. And I roll them in thorns and in fire, among adders and scorpions, until every bone of their body is ground to dust, and they are lost for eternity in the nether depths. But if you comply with my wish, not a hair of your head will be harmed, and I will send you success in every undertaking. . . ."

Hearing these words, Taibele lay motionless as in a swoon. Her heart fluttered and seemed to stop. She thought her end had come. After a while, she gathered courage and murmured:

"What do you want of me? I am a married woman!"

"Your husband is dead. I followed in his funeral procession myself." The voice of the teacher's helper boomed out. "It is true that I cannot go to the rabbi to testify and free you to remarry, for the rabbis don't believe our kind. Besides, I don't dare step across the threshold of the rabbi's chamber—I fear the Holy Scrolls. But I am not lying. Your husband died in an epidemic, and the worms have already gnawed away his nose. And even were he alive, you would not be forbidden to lie with me, for the laws of the *Shulchan Aruch* do not apply to us."

Hurmizah the teacher's helper went on with his persuasions, some sweet, some threatening. He invoked the names of angels and devils, of demonic beasts and of vampires. He swore that Asmodeus, King of the Demons, was his step-uncle. He said that Lilith, Queen of the Evil Spirits, danced for him on one foot and did every manner of thing to please him. Shibtah, the she-devil who stole babies from women in childbed, baked poppyseed cakes for him in Hell's ovens and leavened them with the fat of wizards and black dogs. He argued so long, adducing such witty parables and proverbs, that Taibele was finally obliged to smile, in her extremity. Hurmizah vowed that he had loved Taibele for a long time. He described to her the dresses and shawls she had worn that year and the year before; he told her the secret thoughts that came to her as she kneaded dough, prepared her Sabbath meal, washed herself in the bath, and saw to her needs at the outhouse. He also reminded her of the morning when she had wakened with a black and blue mark on her breast. She had thought it was the pinch of a ghoul. But it was really the mark left by a kiss of Hurmizah's lips, he said.

After a while, the demon got into Taibele's bed and had his will of her. He told her that from then on he would visit her twice a week, on Wednesdays and on Sabbath evenings, for those were the nights when the unholy ones were abroad in the world. He warned her, though, not to divulge to anyone what had befallen her, or even hint at it, on pain of dire punishment: he would pluck out the hair from her skull, pierce her eyes, and bite out her navel. He would cast her into a desolate wilderness where bread was dung and water was blood, and where the wailing of Zalmaveth was heard all day and all night. He commanded Taibele to swear by the bones of her mother that she would keep the secret to her last day. Taibele saw that there was no escape for her. She put her hand on his thigh and swore an oath, and did all that the monster bade her.

Before Hurmizah left, he kissed her long and lustfully,

and since he was a demon and not a man, Taibele returned his kisses and moistened his beard with her tears. Evil spirit though he was, he had treated her kindly. . . .

When Hurmizah was gone, Taibele sobbed into her pillow until sunrise.

Hurmizah came every Wednesday night and every Sabbath night. Taibele was afraid that she might find herself with child and give birth to some monster with tail and horns—an imp or a mooncalf. But Hurmizah promised to protect her against shame. Taibele asked whether she need go to the ritual bath to cleanse herself after her impure days, but Hurmizah said that the laws concerning menstruation did not extend to those who consorted with the unclean host.

As the saying goes, may God preserve us from all that we can get accustomed to. And so it was with Taibele. In the beginning she had feared that her nocturnal visitant might do her harm, give her boils or elflocks, make her bark like a dog or drink urine, and bring disgrace upon her. But Hurmizah did not whip her or pinch her or spit on her. On the contrary, he caressed her, whispered endearments, made puns and rhymes for her. Sometimes he pulled such pranks and babbled such devil's nonsense, that she was forced to laugh. He tugged at the lobe of her ear and gave her love-bites on the shoulder, and in the morning she found the marks of his teeth on her skin. He persuaded her to let her hair grow under her cap and he wove it into braids. He taught her charms and spells, told her about his night-brethren, the demons with whom he flew over ruins and fields of toadstools, over the salt marshes of Sodom, and the frozen wastes of the Sea of Ice. He did not deny that he had other wives, but they were all she-devils; Taibele was the only human wife he possessed. When Taibele asked him the names of his wives, he enumerated them: Namah, Machlath, Aff, Chuldah, Zluchah, Nafkah, and Cheimah. Seven altogether.

He told her that Namah was black as pitch and full of rage. When she quarreled with him, she spat venom and blew fire and smoke through her nostrils.

Machlath had the face of a leech, and those whom she touched with her tongue were forever branded.

Aff loved to adorn herself with silver, emeralds, and diamonds. Her braids were of spun gold. On her ankles she wore bells and bracelets; when she danced, all the deserts rang out with their chiming.

Chuldah had the shape of a cat. She meowed instead of speaking. Her eyes were green as gooseberries. When she copulated, she always chewed bear's liver.

Zluchah was the enemy of brides. She robbed bridegrooms of potency. If a bride stepped outside alone at night during the Seven Nuptial Benedictions, Zluchah danced up to her and the bride lost the power of speech or was taken by a seizure.

Nafkah was lecherous, always betraying him with other demons. She retained his affections only by her vile and insolent talk, which delighted his heart.

Cheimah should have, according to her name, been as vicious as Namah should have been mild, but the reverse was true: Cheimah was a she-devil without gall. She was forever doing charitable deeds, kneading dough for housewives when they were ill, or bringing bread to the homes of the poor.

Thus Hurmizah described his wives, and told Taibele how he disported himself with them, playing tag over roofs and engaging in all sorts of pranks. Ordinarily, a woman is jealous when a man consorts with other women, but how can a human be jealous of a female devil? Quite the contrary. Hurmizah's tales amused Taibele, and she was always plying him with questions. Sometimes he revealed to her mysteries no mortal may know—about God, his angels and seraphs, his heavenly mansions, and the seven heavens. He also told her how sinners, male and female, were tortured in barrels of pitch and cauldrons of fiery coals, on beds studded with nails and in pits of snow, and how the Black Angels beat the bodies of the sinners with rods of fire.

The greatest punishment in hell was tickling, Hurmizah said: There was a certain imp in hell by the name of Lekish. When Lekish tickled an adulteress on her soles or under the arms, her tormented laughter echoed all the way to the island of Madagascar.

In this way, Hurmizah entertained Taibele all through the night, and soon it came about that she began to miss him when he was away. The summer nights seemed too short, for Hurmizah would leave soon after cockcrow. Even winter nights were not long enough. The truth was that she now loved Hurmizah, and though she knew a woman must not lust after a demon, she longed for him day and night.

II

Although Alchonon had been a widower for many years, matchmakers still tried to marry him off. The girls they proposed were from mean homes, widows and divorcees, for a teacher's helper was a poor provider, and Alchonon had besides the reputation of being a shiftless ne'er-do-well. Alchonon dismissed the offers on various pretexts: one woman was too ugly, the other had a foul tongue, the third was a slattern. The matchmakers wondered: how could a teacher's helper who earned nine groschen a week presume to be such a picker and chooser? And how long could a man live alone? But no one can be dragged by force to the wedding canopy.

Alchonon knocked around town—long, lean, tattered, with a red disheveled beard, in a crumpled shirt, with his pointed Adam's apple jumping up and down. He waited for the wedding jester Reb Zekele to die, so that he could take over his job. But Reb Zekele was in no hurry to die;

he still enlivened weddings with an inexhaustible flow of quips and rhymes, as in his younger days. Alchonon tried to set up on his own as a teacher for beginners, but no householder would entrust his child to him. Mornings and evenings, he took the boys to and from the *cheder*. During the day he sat in Reb Itchele the Teacher's courtyard, idly whittling wooden pointers, or cutting out paper decorations which were used only once a year, at Pentecost, or modeling figurines from clay. Not far from Taibele's store there was a well, and Alchonon came there many times a day, to draw a pail of water or to take a drink, spilling the water over his red beard. At these times, he would throw a quick glance at Taibele. Taibele pitied him: why was the man knocking about all by himself? And Alchonon would say to himself each time: "Woe, Taibele, if you knew the truth! . . ."

Alchonon lived in a garret, in the house of an old widow who was deaf and half-blind. The crone often chided him for not going to the synagogue to pray like other Jews. For as soon as Alchonon had taken the children home, he said a hasty evening prayer and went to bed. Sometimes the old woman thought she heard the teacher's helper get up in the middle of the night and go off somewhere. She asked him where he wandered at night, but Alchonon told her that she had been dreaming. The women who sat on benches in the evenings, knitting socks and gossiping, spread the rumor that after midnight Alchonon turned into a werewolf. Some women said he was consorting with a succubus. Otherwise, why should a man remain so many years without a wife? The rich men would not trust their children to him any longer. He now escorted only the children of the poor, and seldom ate a spoonful of hot food, but had to content himself with dry crusts.

Alchonon became thinner and thinner, but his feet remained as nimble as ever. With his lanky legs, he seemed to stride down the street as though on stilts. He must have suffered constant thirst, for he was always coming down to the well. Sometimes he would merely help a dealer or peasant to water his horse. One day, when Taibele noticed from the distance how his caftan was torn and ragged, she called him into her shop. He threw a frightened glance and turned white.

"I see your caftan is torn," said Taibele. "If you wish, I will advance you a few yards of cloth. You can pay it off later, five pennies a week."

"No."

"Why not?" Taibele asked in astonishment. "I won't haul you before the Rabbi if you fall behind. You'll pay when you can."

"No."

And he quickly walked out of the store, fearing she might recognize his voice.

In summertime it was easy to visit Taibele in the middle of the night. Alchonon made his way through back lanes, clutching his caftan around his naked body. In winter, the dressing and undressing in Taibele's cold hallway became increasingly painful. But worst of all were the nights after a fresh snowfall. Alchonon was worried that Taibele or one of the neighbors might notice his tracks. He caught cold and began to cough. One night he got into Taibele's bed with his teeth chattering; he could not warm up for a long time. Afraid that she might discover his hoax, he invented explanations and excuses. But Taibele neither probed nor wished to probe too closely. She had long discovered that a devil had all the habits and frailties of a man. Hurmizah perspired, sneezed, hiccuped, yawned. Sometimes his breath smelled of onion, sometimes of garlic. His body felt like the body of her husband, bony and hairy, with an Adam's apple and a navel. At times, Hurmizah was in a jocular mood, at other times a sigh broke from him. His feet were not goose feet, but human, with nails and frost-blisters. Once Taibele asked him the meaning of these things, and Hurmizah explained:

"When one of us consorts with a human female, he assumes the shape of a man. Otherwise, she would die of fright."

Yes, Taibele got used to him and loved him. She was no longer terrified of him or his impish antics. His tales were inexhaustible, but Taibele often found contradictions in them. Like all liars, he had a short memory. He had told her at first that devils were immortal. But one night he asked:

"What will you do if I die?"

"But devils don't die!"

"They are taken to the lowest abyss. . . ."

That winter there was an epidemic in town. Foul winds came from the river, the woods, and the swamps. Not only children, but adults as well were brought down with the ague. It rained and it hailed. Floods broke the dam on the river. The storms blew off an arm of the windmill. On Wednesday night, when Hurmizah came into Taibele's bed, she noticed that his body was burning hot, but his feet were icy. He shivered and moaned. He tried to entertain her with talk of she-devils, of how they seduced young men, how they cavorted with other devils, splashed about in the ritual bath, tied elflocks in old men's beards, but he was weak and unable to possess her. She had never seen him in such a wretched state. Her heart misgave her. She asked:

"Shall I get you some raspberries with milk?"

Hurmizah replied: "Such remedies are not for our kind."

"What do you do when you get sick?"

"We itch and we scratch. . . ."

He spoke little after that. When he kissed Taibele, his breath was sour. He always remained with her until cockcrow, but this time he left early. Taibele lay silent, listening to his movements in the hallway. He had sworn to her that he flew out of the window even when it was closed and sealed, but she heard the door creak. Taibele knew that it was sinful to pray for devils, that one must curse them and blot them from memory; yet she prayed to God for Hurmizah.

She cried out in anguish: "There are so many devils, let there be one more. . . ."

On the following Sabbath Taibele waited in vain for Hurmizah until dawn; he never came. She called him inwardly and muttered the spells he had taught her, but the hallway was silent. Taibele lay benumbed. Hurmizah had once boasted that he had danced for Tubal-cain and Enoch, that he had sat on the roof of Noah's Ark, licked the salt from the nose of Lot's wife, and plucked Ahasuerus by the beard. He had prophesied that she would be reincarnated after a hundred years as a princess, and that he, Hurmizah, would capture her, with the help of his slaves Chittim and Tachtim, and carry her off to the palace of Bashemath, the wife of Esau. But now he was probably lying somewhere ill, a helpless demon, a lonely orphan—without father or mother, without a faithful wife to care for him. Taibele recalled how his breath came rasping like a saw when he had been with her last; when he blew his nose, there was a whistling in his ear. From Sunday to Wednesday Taibele went about as one in a dream. On Wednesday she could hardly wait until the clock struck midnight, but the night went, and Hurmizah did not appear. Taibele turned her face to the wall.

The day began, dark as evening. Fine snow dust was falling from the murky sky. The smoke could not rise from the chimneys; it spread over the roofs like ragged sheets. The rooks cawed harshly. Dogs barked. After the miserable night, Taibele had no strength to go to her store. Nevertheless, she dressed and went outside. She saw four pallbearers carrying a stretcher. From under the snowswept coverlet protruded the blue feet of a corpse. Only the sexton followed the dead man. Taibele asked who it was, and the sexton answered:

"Alchonon, the teacher's helper."

A strange idea came to Taibele—to escort Alchonon, the feckless man who had lived alone and died alone, on his last journey. Who would come to the store today? And what did she care for business? Taibele had lost everything. At least, she would be doing a good deed. She followed the dead on the long road to the cemetery. There she waited while the gravedigger swept away the snow and dug a grave in the frozen earth. They wrapped Alchonon the teacher's helper in a prayer shawl and a cowl, placed shards on his eyes, and stuck between his fingers a myrtle twig that he would use to dig his way to the Holy Land when the Messiah came. Then the grave was closed and the gravedigger recited the Kaddish. A cry broke from Taibele. This Alchonon had lived a lonely life, just as she did. Like her, he left no heir. Yes, Alchonon the teacher's helper had danced his last dance. From Hurmizah's tales, Taibele knew that the deceased did not go straight to heaven. Every sin creates a devil, and these devils are a man's children after his death. They come to demand their share. They call the dead man Father and roll him through forest and wilderness until the measure of his punishment is filled and he is ready for purification in hell. . . .

From then on Taibele remained alone, doubly deserted—by an ascetic and by a devil. She aged quickly. Nothing was left to her of the past except a secret that could never be told and would be believed by no one. There are secrets that the heart cannot reveal to the lips. They are carried to the grave. The willows murmur of them, the rooks caw about them, the gravestones converse about them silently, in the language of stone. The dead will awaken one day, but their secrets will abide with the Almighty and His Judgment until the end of all generations.

Translated by Mirra Ginsburg

Blood

I

The cabalists know that the passion for blood and the passion for flesh have the same origin, and this is the reason "Thou shalt not kill" is followed by "Thou shalt not commit adultery."

Reb Falik Ehrlichman was the owner of a large estate not far from the town of Laskev. He was born Reb Falik but because of his honesty in business his neighbors had called him *ehrlichman* for so long that it had become a part of his name. By his first wife Reb Falik had had two children, a son and a daughter, who had both died young and without issue. His wife had died too. In later years he had married again, according to the Book of Ecclesiastes: "In the morning sow thy seed, and in the evening withhold not thy hand." Reb Falik's second wife was thirty years younger than he and his friends had tried to dissuade him from the match. For one thing Risha had been widowed twice and was considered a man-killer. For another, she came of a coarse family and had a bad name.

It was said of her that she had beaten her first husband with a stick, and that during the two years her second husband had lain paralyzed she had never called in a doctor. There was other gossip as well. But Reb Falik was not frightened by warnings or whisperings. His first wife, peace be with her, had been ill for a long time before she died of consumption. Risha, corpulent and strong as a man, was a good housekeeper and knew how to manage a farm. Under her kerchief she had a full head of red hair and eyes as green as gooseberries. Her bosom was high and she had the broad hips of a childbearer. Though she had not had children by either of her first two husbands, she contended it was their fault. She had a loud voice and when she laughed one could hear her from far off. Soon after marrying Reb Falik, she began to take charge: she sent away the old bailiff who drank and hired in his place a young and diligent one; she supervised the sowing, the reaping, the cattle breeding; she kept an eye on the peasants to make sure they did not steal eggs, chickens, honey from the hives. Reb Falik hoped Risha would bear him a son to recite Kaddish after his death, but the years passed without her becoming pregnant. She said he was too old. One day she took him with her to Laskev to the notary public where he signed all his property over to her.

Reb Falik gradually ceased to attend to the affairs of the estate at all. He was a man of moderate height with a snowy white beard and rosy cheeks flushed with that half-faded redness of winter apples characteristic of affluent and meek old men. He was friendly to rich and poor alike and never shouted at his servants or peasants. Every spring before Passover he sent a load of wheat to Laskev for the poor, and in the fall after the Feast of Tabernacles he supplied the poorhouse with firewood for the winter as well as sacks of potatoes, cabbages, and beets. On the estate was a small study house which Reb Falik had built and furnished with a bookcase and Holy Scroll. When there were ten Jews on the estate to provide a quorum, they could pray there. After he had signed over all his possessions to Risha, Reb Falik sat almost all day long in this study house, reciting psalms, or sometimes dozing on the sofa in a side room. His strength began to leave him; his hands trembled; and when he spoke his head shook sidewise. Nearly seventy, completely dependent on Risha, he was, so to speak, already eating the bread of mercy. Formerly, the peasants could come to him for relief when one of their cows or horses wandered into his fields and the bailiff demanded payment for damages. But now that Risha had the upper hand, the peasant had to pay to the last penny.

On the estate there lived for many years a ritual slaughterer named Reb Dan, an old man who acted as beadle in the study house, and who, together with Reb Falik, studied a chapter of the Mishnah every morning. When Reb Dan died, Risha began to look about for a new slaughterer. Reb Falik ate a piece of chicken every evening for supper; Risha herself liked meat. Laskev was too far to visit every time she wanted an animal killed. Moreover, in both fall and spring, the Laskev road was flooded. Asking around, Risha heard that among the Jews in the nearby village of Krowica there was a ritual slaughterer named Reuben whose wife had died giving birth to their first child and who, in addition to being a butcher, owned a small tavern where the peasants drank in the evenings.

One morning Risha ordered one of the peasants to harness the britska in order to take her to Krowica to talk to Reuben. She wanted him to come to the estate from time to time to do their slaughtering. She took along several chickens and a gander in a sack so tight it was a wonder the fowl did not choke.

When she reached the village, they pointed out Reuben's hut near the smithy. The britska stopped and Risha, followed by the driver carrying the bag of poultry, opened the front door and went in. Reuben was not there but looking out a window into the courtyard behind she saw him standing by a flat ditch. A barefooted woman handed him a chicken which he slaughtered. Unaware he was being watched from his own house, Reuben was being playful with the woman. Jokingly, he swung the slaughtered chicken as if about to toss it into her face. When she handed him the penny fee, he clasped her wrist and held it. Meanwhile the chicken, its throat slit, fell to the ground where it fluttered about, flapping its wings in its attempt to fly and spattering Reuben's boots with blood. Finally the little rooster gave a last start and then lay still, one glassy eye and its slit neck facing up to God's heaven. The creature seemed to say: "See, Father in Heaven, what they have done to me. And still they make merry."

II

Reuben, like most butchers, was fat with a big stomach and a red neck. His throat was short and fleshy. On his cheeks grew bunches of pitchblack hair. His dark eyes held the cold look of those born under the sign of Mars. When he caught sight of Risha, mistress of the large neighboring estate, he became confused and his face turned even redder than it was. Hurriedly, the woman with him picked up the slaughtered bird and scurried away. Risha went into the courtyard, directing the peasant to set the sack with the fowl near Reuben's feet. She could see that he did not stand on his dignity, and she spoke to him lightly, half-jokingly, and he answered her in kind. When she asked if he would slaughter the birds in the sack for her, he answered: "What else should I do? Revive dead ones?" And when she remarked how important it was to her husband that his food be strictly kosher, he said: "Tell him he shouldn't worry. My knife is as smooth as a fiddle!"—and to show her he drew the bluish edge of the blade across the nail of his index finger. The peasant untied the sack and handed Reuben a yellow chicken. He promptly turned back its head, pulled a tuft of down from the center of its throat and slit it. Soon he was ready for the white gander.

"He's a tough one," said Risha. "All the geese were afraid of him."

"He won't be tough much longer," Reuben answered.

"Don't you have any pity?" Risha teased. She had never seen a slaughterer who was so deft. His hands were thick with short fingers matted with dense black hair.

"With pity, one doesn't become a slaughterer," answered Reuben. A moment later, he added, "When you scale a fish on the Sabbath, do you think the fish enjoys it?"

Holding the fowl, Reuben looked at Risha intently, his gaze traveling up and down her and finally coming to rest on her bosom. Still staring at her, he slaughtered the gander. Its white feathers grew red with blood. It shook its neck menacingly and suddenly went up in the air and flew a few yards. Risha bit her lip.

"They say slaughterers are destined to be born murderers but become slaughterers instead," Risha said.

"If you're so soft-hearted, why did you bring me the birds?" Reuben asked.

"Why? One has to eat meat."

"If someone has to eat meat, someone has to do the slaughtering."

Risha told the peasant to take away the fowl. When she paid Reuben, he took her hand and held it for a moment in his. His hand was warm and her body shivered pleasurably. When she asked him if he would be willing to come to the estate to slaughter, he said yes if in addition to paying him she would send a cart for him.

"I won't have any herd of cattle for you," Risha joked.

"Why not?" Reuben countered. "I have slaughtered cattle before. In Lublin I slaughtered more in one day than I do here in a month," he boasted.

Since Risha did not seem to be in any hurry, Reuben asked her to sit down on a box and he himself sat on a log. He told her of his studies in Lublin and explained how he had happened to come to this God-forsaken village where his wife, peace be with her, had died in childbirth due to the lack of an experienced midwife.

"Why haven't you remarried?" Risha questioned. "There's no shortage of women—widows, divorcees, or young girls."

Reuben told her the matchmakers were trying to find him a wife but the destined one had not yet appeared.

"How will you know the one who is destined for you?" Risha asked.

"My stomach will know. She will grab me right here" —and Reuben snapped his fingers and pointed at his navel. Risha would have stayed longer, except that a girl came in with a duck. Reuben arose. Risha returned to the britska.

On the way back Risha thought about the slaughterer Reuben, his levity and his jocular talk. Though she came to the conlusion that he was thick-skinned and his future wife would not lick honey all her life, still she could not get him out of her mind. That night, retiring to her canopied bed across the room from her husband's, she tossed and turned sleeplessly. When she finally dozed off, her dreams both frightened and excited her. She got up in the morning full of desire, wanting to see Reuben as quickly as possible, wondering how she might arrange it, and worried that he might find some woman and leave the village.

Three days later Risha went to Krowica again even though the larder was still full. This time she caught the birds herself, bound their legs, and shoved them into the sack. On the estate was a black rooster with a voice clear as a bell, a bird famous for its size, its red comb, and its crowing. There was also a hen that laid an egg every day and always at the same spot. Risha now caught both of these creatures, murmuring, "Come, children, you will soon taste Reuben's knife," and as she said these words a tremor ran down her spine. She did not order a peasant to drive the britska but, harnessing the horse herself, went off alone. She found Reuben standing at the threshold of his house as if he were waiting impatiently for her, as in fact he was. When a male and a female lust after each other, their thoughts meet and each can foresee what the other will do.

Reuben ushered Risha in with all the formality due a guest. He brought her a pitcher of water, offered her liqueur and a slice of honey cake. He did not go into the courtyard but untrussed the fowl indoors. When he took out the black rooster, he exclaimed, "What a fine cavalier!"

"Don't worry. You will soon take care of him," said Risha.

"No one can escape my knife," Reuben assured her. He slaughtered the rooster on the spot. The bird did not exhale its spirit immediately but finally, like an eagle caught by a bullet, it slumped to the floor. Then Reuben set the knife down on the whetstone, turned, and came over to Risha. His face was pale with passion and the fire in his dark eyes frightened her. She felt as if he were about to slaughter her. He put his arms around her without a word and pressed her against his body.

"What are you doing? Have you lost your mind?" she asked.

"I like you," Reuben said hoarsely.

"Let me go. Somebody might come in," she warned.

"Nobody will come," Reuben assured her. He put up the chain on the door and pulled Risha into a windowless alcove.

Risha wrangled, pretending to defend herself, and exclaimed, "Woe is me. I'm a married woman. And you—a pious man, a scholar. We'll roast in Gehenna for this . . ." But Reuben paid no attention. He forced Risha down on his bench-bed and she, thrice married, had never before felt desire as great as on that day. Though she called him murderer, robber, highwayman, and reproached him for bringing shame to an honest woman, yet at the same time she kissed him, fondled him, and responded to his masculine whims. In their amorous play, she asked him to slaughter her. Taking her head, he bent it back and fiddled with his finger across her throat. When Risha finally arose, she said to Reuben: "You certainly murdered me that time."

"And you, me," he answered.

III

Because Risha wanted Reuben all to herself and was afraid he might leave Krowica or marry some younger woman, she determined to find a way to have him live on the estate. She could not simply hire him to replace Reb Dan, for Reb Dan had been a relative whom Reb Falik would have had to provide for in any case. To keep a man just to slaughter a few chickens every week did not make sense and to propose it would arouse her husband's suspicions. After puzzling for a while, Risha found a solution.

She began to complain to her husband about how little profit the crops were bringing; how meagre the harvests were; if things went on this way, in a few years they would be ruined. Reb Falik tried to comfort his wife saying that God had not forsaken him hitherto and that one must have faith, to which Risha retorted that faith could not be eaten. She proposed that they stock the pastures with cattle and open a butcher shop in Laskev—that way there would be a double profit both from the dairy and from the meat sold at retail. Reb Falik opposed the plan as impractical and beneath his dignity. He argued that the butchers in Laskev would raise a commotion and that the community would never agree to him, Reb Falik, becoming a butcher. But Risha insisted. She went to Laskev, called a meeting of the community elders, and told them that she intended to open a butcher shop. Her meat would be sold at two cents a pound less than the meat in the other shops. The town was in an uproar. The rabbi warned her he would prohibit the meat from the estate. The butchers threatened to stab anyone who interfered with their livelihood. But Risha was not daunted. In the first place she had influence with the government, for the *starosta* of the neighborhood had received many fine gifts from her, often visited her estate and went hunting in her wood. Moreover, she soon found allies among the Laskev poor who could not afford to buy much meat at the usual high prices. Many took her side, coachmen, shoemakers, tailors, furriers, potters, and they announced that if the butchers did her any violence, they would retaliate by burning the butcher shops. Risha invited a mob of them to the estate, gave them bottles of homemade beer from her brewery, and got them to promise her their support. Soon afterwards she rented a store in Laskev and employed Wolf Bonder, a fearless man known as a horse-thief and brawler. Every other day, Wolf Bonder drove to the estate with his horse and buggy to cart meat to the city. Risha hired Reuben to do the slaughtering.

For many months the new business lost money, the rabbi having proscribed Risha's meat. Reb Falik was ashamed to look the townspeople in the face, but Risha had the means and strength to wait for victory. Since her meat was cheap, the number of her customers increased steadily, and soon because of competition several butchers were forced to close their shops and of the two Laskev slaughterers, one lost his job. Risha was cursed by many.

The new business provided the cover Risha needed to conceal the sins she was committing on Reb Falik's estate. From the beginning it was her custom to be present when Reuben slaughtered. Often she helped him bind an ox or a cow. And her thirst to watch the cutting of throats and the shedding of blood soon became so mixed with carnal desire that she hardly knew where one began and the other ended. As soon as the business became profitable, Risha built a slaughtering shed and gave Reuben an apartment in the main house. She bought him fine clothes and he ate his meals at Reb Falik's table. Reuben grew sleeker and fatter. During the day he seldom slaughtered but wandered about in a silken robe, soft slippers on his feet, skullcap on his head, watching the peasants working in the fields, the shepherds caring for the cattle. He enjoyed all the pleasures of the outdoors and, in the afternoons, often went swimming in the river. The aging Reb Falik retired early. Late in the evening Reuben, accompanied by Risha, went to the shed where she stood next to him as he slaughtered and while the animal was throwing itself about in the anguish of its death throes she would discuss with him their next act of lust. Sometimes she gave herself to him immediately after the slaughtering. By then all the peasants were in their huts asleep except for one old man, half deaf and nearly blind, who aided them at the shed. Sometimes Reuben lay with her on a pile of straw in the shed, sometimes on the grass just outside, and the thought of the dead and dying creatures near them whetted their enjoyment. Reb Falik disliked Reuben. The new business was repulsive to him but he seldom said a word in opposition. He accepted the annoyance with humility, thinking that he would soon be dead anyway and what was the point of starting a quarrel? Occasionally it occurred to him that his wife was overly familiar with Reuben, but he pushed the suspicion out of his mind since he was by nature honest and righteous, a man who gave everyone the benefit of the doubt.

One transgression begets another. One day Satan, the father of all lust and cunning, tempted Risha to take a hand in the slaughtering. Reuben was alarmed when she first suggested this. True, he was an adulterer, but nevertheless he was also a believer as many sinners are. He argued that for their sins they would be whipped, but why should they lead other people into iniquity, causing them to eat non-kosher carcasses? No, God forbid he and Risha should do anything like that. To become a slaughterer it was necessary to study the *Shulchan Aruch* and the Commentaries. A slaughterer was responsible for any blemish on the knife, no matter how small, and for any sin one of his customers incurred by eating impure meat. But Risha was adamant. What difference did it make? she asked. They would both toss on the bed of needles anyhow. If one committed sins, one should get as much enjoyment as possible out of them. Risha kept after Reuben constantly, alternating threats and bribes. She promised him new excitements, presents, money. She swore that if he would let her slaughter, immediately upon Reb Falik's death she would marry him and sign over all her property so that he could redeem some part of his iniquity through acts of charity. Finally Reuben gave in. Risha took such pleasure in killing that before long she was doing all the slaughtering herself, with Reuben acting merely as her assistant. She began to cheat, to sell tallow for kosher fat, and she stopped extracting the forbidden sinews in the thighs of the cows. She began a price war with the other Laskev butchers until those who remained became her hired employees. She got the contract to supply meat to the Polish army barracks, and since the officers took bribes, and the soldiers received only the worst meat, she earned vast sums. Risha became so rich that even she did not know how large her fortune was. Her malice grew. Once she slaughtered a horse and sold it as kosher beef. She killed some pigs too, scalding them in boiling water like the pork butchers. She managed never to be caught. She got so much satisfaction from deceiving the community that this soon became as powerful a passion with her as lechery and cruelty.

Like all those who devote themselves entirely to the pleasures of the flesh, Risha and Reuben grew prematurely old. Their bodies became so swollen they could barely meet. Their hearts floated in fat. Reuben took to drink. He lay all day long on his bed, and when he woke drank liquor from a carafe with a straw. Risha brought him refreshments and they passed their time in idle talk, chattering as do those who have sold their souls for the vanities of this world. They quarreled and kissed, teased and mocked, bemoaned the fact that time was passing and the grave coming nearer. Reb Falik was now sick most of the time but, though it often seemed his end was near, somehow his soul did not forsake his body. Risha toyed with ideas of death and even thought of poisoning Reb Falik. Another time, she said to Reuben: "Do you know, already I am satiated with life! If you want, slaughter me and marry a young woman."

After saying this, she transferred the straw from Reuben's lips to hers and sucked until the carafe was empty.

IV

There is a proverb: Heaven and earth have sworn together that no secret can remain undivulged. The sins of Reuben and Risha could not stay hidden forever. People began to murmur that the two lived too well together. They remarked how old and feeble Reb Falik had become, how much oftener he stayed in bed than on his feet, and they concluded that Reuben and Risha were having an affair. The butchers Risha had forced to close their businesses had been spreading all kinds of calumny about her ever since. Some of the more scholarly housewives found sinews in Risha's meat which, according to the Law, should have been removed. The Gentile butcher to whom Risha had been accustomed to sell the forbidden flanken complained that she had not sold him anything for months. With this evidence, the former butchers went in a body to the rabbi and community leaders and demanded an investigation of Risha's meat. But the council of elders was hesitant to start a quarrel with her. The rabbi quoted the Talmud to the effect that one who suspects the righteous deserves to be lashed, and added that, as long as there were no witnesses to any of Risha's transgressions, it was wrong to shame her, for the one who shames his fellow man loses his portion in the world to come.

The butcher, thus rebuffed by the rabbi, decided to hire a spy and they chose a tough youth named Jechiel. This young man, a ruffian, set out from Laskev one night after dark, stole into the estate, managing to avoid the fierce dogs Risha kept, and took up his position behind the slaughtering shed. Putting his eye to a large crack, he saw Reuben and Risha inside and watched with astonishment as the old servant led in the hobbled animals and Risha, using a rope, threw them one by one to the ground. When the old man left, Jechiel was amazed in the torchlight to see Risha catch up a long knife and begin to cut the throats of the cattle one after the other. The steaming blood gurgled and flowed. While the beasts were bleeding, Risha threw off all her clothes and stretched out naked on a pile of straw. Reuben came to her and they were so fat their bodies could barely join. They puffed and panted. Their wheezing mixed with the death-rattles of the animals made an unearthly noise; contorted shadows fell on the walls; the shed was saturated with the heat of blood. Jechiel was a hoodlum, but even he was terrified because only devils could behave like this. Afraid that fiends would seize him, he fled.

At dawn, Jechiel knocked on the rabbi's shutter. Stammering, he blurted out what he had witnessed. The rabbi roused the beadle and sent him with his wooden hammer to knock at the windows of the elders and summon them at once. At first no one believed Jechiel could be telling the truth. They suspected he had been hired by the butchers to bear false witness and they threatened him with beating and excommunication. Jechiel, to prove he was not lying, ran to the Ark of the Holy Scroll which stood in the Judgment Chamber, opened the door, and before those present could stop him swore by the Scroll that his words were true.

His story threw the town into a turmoil. Women ran out into the streets, striking their heads with their fists, crying and wailing. According to the evidence, the townspeople had been eating non-kosher meat for years. The wealthy housewives carried their pottery into the market place and broke it into shards. Some of the sick and several pregnant women fainted. Many of the pious tore their lapels, strewed their heads with ashes, and sat down to mourn. A crowd formed and ran to the butcher shops to punish the men who sold Risha's meat. Refusing to listen to what the butchers said in their own defense, they beat up several of them, threw whatever carcasses were on hand outdoors, and overturned the butcher blocks. Soon voices arose suggesting they go to Reb Falik's estate and the mob began to arm itself with bludgeons, rope, and knives. The rabbi, fearing bloodshed, came out into the street to stop them, warning that punishment must wait until the sin had been proved intentional and a verdict had been passed. But the mob wouldn't listen. The rabbi decided to go with them, hoping to calm them down on the way. The elders followed. Women trailed after them, pinching their cheeks and weeping as if at a funeral. Schoolboys dashed alongside.

Wolf Bonder, to whom Risha had given gifts and whom she had always paid well to cart the meat from the estate to Laskev, remained loyal to her. Seeing how ugly the temper of the crowd was becoming, he went to his stable, saddled a fast horse, and galloped out toward the estate to warn Risha. As it happened, Reuben and Risha had stayed overnight in the shed and were still there. Hearing hoofbeats, they got up and came out and watched with surprise as Wolf Bonder rode up. He explained what had happened and warned them of the mob on its way. He advised them to flee, unless they could prove their innocence; otherwise the angry men would surely tear them to pieces. He himself was afraid to stay any longer lest before he could get back the mob turn against him. Mounting his horse, he rode away at a gallop.

Reuben and Risha stood frozen with shock. Reuben's face turned a fiery red, then a deadly white. His hands trembled and he had to clutch at the door behind him to remain on his feet. Risha smiled anxiously and her face turned yellow as if she had jaundice, but it was Risha who moved first. Aprpoaching her lover, she stared into his eyes. "So, my love," she said, "the end of a thief is the gallows."

"Let's run away." Reuben was shaking so violently that he could hardly get the words out.

But Risha answered that it was not possible. The estate had only six horses and all of them had been taken early that morning by peasants going to the forest for wood. A yoke of oxen would move so slowly that the rabble could overtake them. Besides, she, Risha, had no intention of abandoning her property and wandering like a beggar. Reuben implored her to flee with him, since life is more precious than all possessions, but Risha remained stubborn. She would not go. Finally they went into the main house where Risha rolled some linen up into a bundle for Reuben, gave him a roast chicken, a loaf of bread, and a pouch with some money. Standing outdoors, she watched as he set out, swaying and wobbling across the wooden bridge that led into the pine woods. Once in the forest he would strike the path to the Lublin road. Several times Reuben turned about-face, muttered and waved his hand as if calling her, but Risha stood impassively. She had already learned he was a coward. He was only a hero against a weak chicken and a tethered ox.

V

As soon as Reuben was out of sight, Risha moved towards the fields to call in the peasants. She told them to pick up axes, scythes, shovels, explained to them that a mob was on its way from Laskev, and promised each man a gulden and a pitcher of beer if he would help defend her. Risha herself seized a long knife in one hand and brandished a meat cleaver in the other. Soon the noise of the crowd could be heard in the distance and before long the mob was visible. Surrounded by her peasant guard, Risha mounted a hill at the entrance to the estate. When those who were coming saw peasants with axes and scythes, they slowed down. A few even tried to retreat. Risha's fierce dogs ran among them snarling, barking, growling.

The rabbi, seeing that the situation could lead only to bloodshed, demanded of his flock that they return home, but the tougher of the men refused to obey him. Risha called out taunting them: "Come on, let's see what you can do! I'll cut your heads off with this knife—the same knife I used on the horses and pigs I made you eat." When a man shouted that no one in Laskev would buy her meat anymore and that she would be excommunicated, Risha shouted back: "I don't need your money. I don't need your God either. I'll convert. Immediately!" And she began to scream in Polish, calling the Jews cursed Christ-killers and crossing herself as if she were already a Gentile. Turning to one of the peasants beside her, she said: "What are you waiting for, Maciek? Run and summon the priest. I don't want to belong to this filthy sect anymore." The peasant went and the mob became silent. Everyone knew that converts soon became enemies of Israel and invented all kinds of accusations against their former brethren. They turned away and went home. The Jews were afraid to instigate the anger of the Christians.

Meanwhile Reb Falik sat in his study house and recited the Mishnah. Deaf and half-blind, he saw nothing and heard nothing. Suddenly Risha entered, knife in hand, screaming: "Go to your Jews. What do I need a synagogue here for?" When Reb Falik saw her with her head uncovered, a knife in her hand, her face contorted by abuse, he was seized by such anguish that he lost his tongue. In his prayer shawl and phylacteries, he rose to ask her what had happened, but his feet gave way and he collapsed to the floor dead. Risha ordered his body placed in an ox cart and she sent his corpse to the Jews in Laskev without even linen for a shroud. During the time the Laskev Burial Society cleansed and laid out Reb Falik's body, and while the burial was taking place and the rabbi speaking the eulogy, Risha prepared for her conversion. She sent men out to look for Reuben, for she wanted to persuade him to follow her example, but her lover had vanished.

Risha was now free to do as she pleased. After her conversion she reopened her shops and sold non-kosher meats to the Gentiles of Laskev and to the peasants who came in on market days. She no longer had to hide anything. She could slaughter openly and in whatever manner she pleased pigs, oxen, calves, sheep. She hired a Gentile slaughterer to replace Reuben and went hunting with him in the forest and shot deer, hares, rabbits. But she no longer took the same pleasure in torturing creatures; slaughtering no longer incited her lust; and she got little satisfaction from lying with the pig butcher. Fishing in the river, sometimes when a fish dangled on her hook or danced in her net, a moment of joy came to her heart imbedded in fat and she would mutter: "Well, fish, you are worse off than I am . . . !"

The truth was that she yearned for Reuben. She missed

their lascivious talk, his scholarship, his dread of reincarnation, his terror of Gehenna. Now that Reb Falik was in his grave, she had no one to betray, to pity, to mock. She had bought a pew in the Christian church immediately upon conversion and for some months went every Sunday to listen to the priest's sermon. Going and coming, she had her driver take her past the synagogue. Teasing the Jews gave her some satisfaction for a while, but soon this too palled.

With time Risha became so lazy that she no longer went to the slaughtering shed. She left everything in the hands of the pork butcher and did not even care that he was stealing from her. Immediately upon getting up in the morning, she poured herself a glass of liqueur and crept on her heavy feet from room to room talking to herself. She would stop at a mirror and mutter: "Woe, woe, Risha. What has happened to you? If your saintly mother should rise from her grave and see you—she would lie down again!" Some mornings she tried to improve her appearance but her clothes would not hang straight, her hair could not be untangled. Frequently she sang for hours in Yiddish and in Polish. Her voice was harsh and cracked and she invented the songs as she went along, repeating meaningless phrases, uttering sounds that resembled the cackling of fowls, the grunting of pigs, the death-rattles of oxen. Falling onto her bed she hiccuped, belched, laughed, cried. At night in her dreams, phantoms tormented her: bulls gored her with their horns; pigs shoved their snouts into her face and bit her; roosters cut her flesh to ribbons with their spurs. Reb Falik appeared dressed in his shroud, covered with wounds, waving a bunch of palm leaves, screaming: "I cannot rest in my grave. You have defiled my house."

Then Risha, or Maria Pawlowska as she was now called, would start up in bed, her limbs numb, her body covered with a cold sweat. Reb Falik's ghost would vanish but she could still hear the rustle of the palm leaves, the echo of his outcry. Simultaneously she would cross herself and repeat a Hebrew incantation learned in childhood from her mother. She would force her bare feet down to the floor and would begin to stumble through the dark from one room to another. She had thrown out all Reb Falik's books, had burned his Holy Scroll. The study house was now a shed for drying hides. But in the dining room there still remained the table on which Reb Falik had eaten his Sabbath meals, and from the ceiling hung the candelabra where his Sabbath candles had once burned. Sometimes Risha remembered her first two husbands whom she had tortured with her wrath, her greed, her curses and shrewish tongue. She was far from repenting, but something inside her was mourning and filling her with bitterness. Opening a window, she would look out into the midnight sky full of stars and cry out: "God, come and punish me! Come Satan! Come Asmodeus! Show your might. Carry me to the burning desert behind the dark mountains!"

VI

One winter Laskev was terrified by a carnivorous animal lurking about at night and attacking people. Some who had seen the creature said it was a bear, others a wolf, others a demon. One woman, going outdoors to urinate, had her neck bitten. A yeshiva boy was chased through the streets. An elderly night-watchman had his face clawed. The women and children of Laskev were afraid to leave their houses after nightfall. Everywhere shutters were bolted tight. Many strange things were recounted about the beast: someone had heard it rave with a human voice; another had seen it rise on its hind legs and run. It had overturned a barrel of cabbage in a courtyard, had opened chicken coops, thrown out the dough set to rise in the wooden trough in the bakery, and it had defiled the butcher blocks in the kosher shops with excrement.

One dark night the butchers of Laskev gathered with axes and knives determined either to kill or capture the monster. Splitting up into small groups they waited, their eyes growing accustomed to the darkness. In the middle of the night there was a scream and running toward it they caught sight of the animal making for the outskirts of town. A man shouted that he had been bitten in the shoulder. Frightened, some of the men dropped back, but others continued to give chase. One of the hunters saw it and threw his axe. Apparently the animal was hit, for with a ghastly scream it wobbled and fell. A horrible howling filled the air. Then the beast began to curse in Polish and Yiddish and to wail in a high-pitched voice like a woman in labor. Convinced that they had wounded a she-devil, the men ran home.

All that night the animal groaned and babbled. It even dragged itself to a house and knocked at the shutters. Then it became silent and the dogs began to bark. When day dawned, the bolder people came out of their houses. They discovered to their amazement that the animal was Risha. She lay dead dressed in a skunk fur coat wet with blood. One felt boot was missing. The hatchet had buried itself in her back. The dogs had already partaken of her entrails. Nearby was the knife she had used to stab one of her pursuers. It was now clear that Risha had become a werewolf. Since the Jews refused to bury her in their cemetery and the Christians were unwilling to give her a plot in theirs, she was taken to the hill on the estate where she had fought off the mob, and a ditch was dug for her there. Her wealth was confiscated by the city.

Some years later a wandering stranger lodged in the poorhouse of Laskev became sick. Before his death, he summoned the rabbi and the seven elders of the town and divulged to them that he was Reuben the slaughterer, with whom Risha had sinned. For years he had wandered from town to town, eating no meat, fasting Mondays and Thursdays, wearing a shirt of sack cloth, and repenting his abominations. He had come to Laskev to die because it was here his parents were buried. The rabbi recited the confession with him and Reuben revealed many details of the past which the townspeople had not known.

Risha's grave on the hill soon became covered with refuse. Yet long afterwards it remained customary for the Laskev schoolboys on the thirty-third day of Omer, when they went out carrying bows and arrows and a provision of hard-boiled eggs, to stop there. They danced on the hill and sang:

"Risha slaughtered
Black horses
Now she's fallen
To evil forces.

A pig for an ox
Sold Risha the witch
Now she's roasting
In sulphur and pitch."

Before the children left, they spat on the grave and recited:

"Thou shalt not suffer a witch to live
A witch to live thou shalt not suffer
Suffer a witch to live thou shalt not."

Translated by The Author and Elizabeth Pollet

Esther Kreindel the Second

I

A Talmud teacher named Meyer Zissl lived in the town of Bilgoray. He was a short, broad-shouldered man with a round face, black beard, red cheeks, cherry-black eyes, a mouth full of jutting teeth, and a furry head with hair that blanketed his neck. Meyer Zissl liked to eat well; he could drink down half a pint of brandy at one draught, and he liked to sing and dance at weddings until dawn. He had no patience for teaching, but still the wealthy sent him their sons as pupils.

When Meyer Zissl was thirty-six years old his wife died, leaving him with six children. Half a year later he married a widow, Reitze, from the village of Krashnik, a tall, lean, silent woman with a long nose and many freckles. This Reitze had been a milkmaid before marrying a rich man of seventy, Reb Tanchum Izhbitzer, by whom she had one daughter, Simmele. Before his death, Reb Tanchum had gone bankrupt leaving his widow with nothing but their one beloved child. Simmele knew how to write and she could read the Bible in Yiddish. Her father, returning from business trips, had always brought her gifts—a shawl, an apron, slippers, an embroidered handkerchief, and a new storybook. Simmele, bringing all her possessions, came to live with her mother and stepfather in Bilgoray.

Meyer Zissl's brood, four girls and two boys, were a greedy, ragged lot, fighters, gluttons, screamers, full of spiteful tricks, always ready to beg or steal. They immediately attacked Simmele, robbed her of all her treasures, and nicknamed her Miss Stuck-up. Simmele was delicate. She had a narrow waist, long legs, a thin face, white skin, black hair, gray eyes. She was afraid of the dogs in the courtyard, shrank at the way the family snatched food from each other's plates, and was ashamed to undress before her stepsisters. Before long she stopped talking to Meyer Zissl's children, nor did she make friends with any of the girls in the neighborhood. When she went into the street, the urchins threw stones after her and called her a fraidy-cat. Simmele stayed home, read books, and wept.

From childhood on Simmele had liked to listen to stories. Her mother had always been able to calm her so, and when Reb Tanchum was alive he had regularly put her to sleep with a fairytale. A ready subject for storytelling was Reb Zorach Lipover, a great friend of Reb Tanchum's who lived in Zamosc. Reb Zorach was known throughout half of Poland for his wealth. His wife, Esther Kreindel, also came from a rich home. Simmele loved to hear about this famous family, their wealth, and well-bred children.

One day Meyer Zissl came home for lunch with the news that Zorach Lipover's wife had died. Simmele opened her eyes wide. The name brought back memories of Krashnik, of her dead father, of the time when she had had her own room, a bed with two pillows, a silken coverlet in an embroidered linen case, a maid to serve refreshments. Now she sat here in an untidy room, wore a torn dress, ripped shoes; her hair had chicken feathers in it; she went unwashed; and she was surrounded by nasty brats who watched for every opportunity to do her mischief. Hearing of Esther Kreindel's death, Simmele covered her face with both hands and wept. The girl didn't know herself whether she was bemoaning Esther Kreindel's fate or her own, the fact that the pampered Esther Kreindel was now rotting in the grave or that her own, Simmele's, life had come to a dismal end.

II

When Simmele slept alone on her bench-bed, Meyer Zissl's children tormented her, so Reitze often took Simmele into her own bed to sleep. This was not a good arrangement because Meyer Zissl often wanted to come to his wife and then Simmele, though she understood well enough what the adults were up to, had to pretend to sleep through it all.

One night when Simmele was in bed with her mother, Meyer Zissl returned from a wedding drunk. He lifted the sleeping girl from his wife's side, only to discover that Reitze had left a heap of wet wash on the bench-bed. Because his desire was so strong, Meyer Zissl set his stepdaughter down on top of the oven among the rags. Simmele dozed off. Some time later she awoke to hear Meyer Zissl snoring. She pulled a flour sack over herself to keep warm. Then she heard a rustling sound as if somebody's fingers were scratching at a board. Lifting her head, she was astonished to see a bright spot of light on the wall nearest her. The shutters were closed; the fire in the oven was long since extinct; no lamp was lit. Where could it come from? As Simmele stared the brightness began to shake and tremble, the rings of light to coagulate. Simmele, bewildered, forgot to be afraid. A woman began to materialize, forehead first, then eyes, nose, chin, throat. The woman opened her mouth and began to speak, words that sounded as if they came from the Yiddish Bible.

"Simmele, my daughter," the voice said, "be it known to you that I am Esther Kreindel, the spouse of Reb Zorach Lipover. It is not usual for the dead to break their slumber, but because my husband longs for me endlessly day and night, I am unable to remain in peace. Though the thirty days of mourning have passed, he does not cease his lamentations and cannot put me out of his mind. If I could throw off death, I would gladly rise and return to him. But my body is buried under seven feet of ground, my eyes have already been consumed by the worms. Therefore, I, the spirit of Esther Kreindel, have been permitted to find myself another body. Because your father, Reb Tanchum, was like a brother to my Zorach, I have chosen you, Simmele. You are indeed no stranger to me but almost a relative. Simmele, I will enter your body soon, and you will become me. Have no fear, for nothing evil will befall you. In the morning rise, cover your head, and announce to your family and to the townspeople what has happened. The wicked will contradict you and accuse you, but I will protect you. Heed my words, Simmele, for you must do all that I bid you. Go to Zamosc to my sorrowing husband, and be a wife to him. Lie in his lap and serve him faithfully as I have done for forty years. Zorach may doubt at first that I have returned to him, but I will give you signs with which to convince him. You must not tarry because Zorach is consumed with longing and soon, God forbid, it may be too late. God willing, when the time comes for you to pass away, both you and I will be Zorach's footstools in Paradise. He will rest his right foot on me and his left on you; we will be like Rachel and Leah; my children will be yours. It will be as if they had issued from your womb . . ."

Esther Kreindel went on speaking, telling Simmele those intimacies only a wife can know. Not until the rooster in the coop crowed and the midnight moon was visible through the chinks of the shutters did she stop. Then Simmele felt something hard like a pea enter her nostrils and penetrate her skull. For a moment her head ached, but then the pain ceased and she felt her hands and feet stretching, her belly, her breasts ripening. Her mind was maturing too, her thoughts becoming those of a wife, a mother, a grandmother, who is used to commanding a large house with menservants, maids, cooks. It was all too wonderful. "I put myself into Thy hands," Simmele murmured. Soon she sank into sleep, and immediately Esther Kreindel reappeared in her dream and stayed with her until Simmele opened her eyes in the morning.

III

The delicate Simmele usually stayed in bed late but that morning she awoke with the rest of the family. Her stepbrothers and stepsisters, seeing her on top of the oven with a meal sack pulled over her, began to laugh, to spray water up at her, to tickle her bare feet with straws. Reitze drove them away. Simmele, sitting up, smiled benignly and recited, "I thank Thee." And though it is not the custom to set a pitcher of water near a girl's bed for morning ablutions, Simmele asked her mother for water and a basin. Reitze shrugged her shoulders. When Simmele was dressed, Reitze handed her a slice of bread and a cup of chicory, but Simmele said she wanted to pray first, and taking out her Saturday kerchief, she covered her head. Meyer Zissl watched the conduct of his stepdaughter with amazement. Simmele recited from the prayer book, bowed down, beat her breast, and after the words, "He makes peace on high," retreated three steps. Then, before eating, she washed her hands up to the wrists and recited the Benediction. The children flocked around, mimicking, mocking, but she only smiled in a motherly fashion and called out, "Please, children, let me say my prayers." She kissed the smallest girl on the head, pinched the youngest boy in the cheek, and made the older boy wipe his nose on her apron. Reitze gaped. Meyer Zissl scratched his head.

"What sort of stunts are these? I scarcely recognize the girl," said Meyer Zissl.

"She's matured overnight," said Reitze.

"She shakes like Yentl the Pious One," scoffed the oldest boy.

"Simmele, what's going on?" Reitze asked.

The girl didn't answer immediately, but went on chewing slowly the bread in her mouth. It was not like her to act with such quiet deliberation. When she had swallowed the last crumb, she said:

"I am no longer Simmele."

"Then who are you?" Meyer Zissl inquired.

"I am Esther Kreindel, the wife of Reb Zorach Lipover. Last night her soul entered me. Take me to Zamosc to my husband and children. My home is being neglected. Zorach needs me."

The older children burst out laughing; the younger gawked. Reitze turned white. Meyer Zissl clutched his beard, and said, "The girl is possessed by a dybbuk."

"No, not a dybbuk, but the sacred soul of Esther Kreindel has entered me. She could not remain in her grave because her husband, Zorach Lipover, is expiring of grief. His affairs are topsy-turvy. His fortune is disappearing. She has told me all her secrets. If you don't believe me, I will furnish proof." And Simmele began to repeat some of the things Esther Kreindel had confided to her while she was awake and while asleep. As Simmele's mother and Meyer Zissl listened, they became more and more amazed. Simmele's words, phrases, her whole style, were those of an experienced woman, of one who is accustomed to running a business and a large household. She referred to matters that it was impossible for one as young as Simmele to know. She described Esther Kreindel's final illness, told how the doctors had made her worse with their pills and salves, bleeding her by cupping and leeches.

The neighbors were soon aware that something strange was happening as people are wont in a town where they listen behind doors and peer through keyholes. The story spread and a crowd began to gather at Meyer Zissl's. When the rabbi heard what had happened, he sent a message ordering the girl to be brought to him. At the rabbi's the council of elders was assembled along with the most distinguished matrons of the community. After Simmele's arrival, the rabbi's wife chained the door and the interrogation began. It was necessary to find out if the girl was trying to deceive them, if she was possessed by a devil or by one of those insolent demons who try to outsmart the righteous and entrap them. After hours of interrogation, everyone was convinced that Simmele was telling the truth. They had all met Esther Kreindel and not only did Simmele talk like the dead woman but her gestures, her smile, the way she tossed her head and brushed her brow with her kerchief was exactly like the deceased. Her manner too was certainly that of someone who had always been accustomed to affluence. Moreover, if an evil spirit had possessed the girl, it would have become abusive whereas Simmele was respectful and answered all questions politely and judiciously. Soon, the men began tugging at their beards; the women wrung their hands, straightened their bonnets, and tightened their aprons. The members of the Burial Society, usually so tough and unemotional, wiped tears from their eyes. Even a blind man could see that Esther Kreindel's soul had returned.

While the interrogation was still in process, Zeinvel the coachman harnessed his horse and buggy and taking several witnesses with him set out for Zamosc to bring Reb Zorach Lipover the news. Reb Zorach wept when he was informed. He ordered the coachman to bring a four-horse carriage and he, a son and two daughters got in. The coachman did not spare the whip. The road was dry, the horses galloped, and by nightfall Zorach Lipover and his family had arrived in Bilgoray. Simmele was staying at the rabbi's and was being cared for by the rabbi's wife to escape the morbid and the curious. She sat in the kitchen knitting, something Reitze swore she had never known how to do before. Simmele had been reminiscing to those present of long forgotten events: dreadful winters three decades past, heat waves following the Feast of Tabernacles, snows in summer, winds that broke windmills, hails that shattered roofs, rainfalls of fish and toads. She had also chattered of roasting, baking; the illnesses women were susceptible to in pregnancy; she had discussed the rituals pertaining to cohabitation and the menstrual period. The women in the kitchen sat in stunned silence. To them it was like listening to a corpse speak. Suddenly there was the noise of wheels as Reb Zorach's carriage rolled into the courtyard. When Zorach entered, Simmele, having put down her knitting, rose and announced:

"Zorach, I have returned."

The women burst into a wail. Zorach just kept on staring. The questioning began again and continued until past midnight. Later there were many conflicting statements about what was said, and these disagreements led to protracted quarrels. But from the very beginning everyone admitted that the woman who received Zorach was no one but Esther Kreindel. Soon Zorach began to cry in a heartrending voice; Zorach's son called Simmele mother. The daughters did not give in so quickly but sought to prove that Simmele was a liar, anxious to assume their mother's prerogatives. Slowly they too realized that the matter was not that simple. First the younger became silent and then the older one bowed her head. Before daybreak both daughters had uttered the word they had been avoiding for hours: Mother!

IV

According to the law, Zorach Lipover could have married Simmele immediately, but Reb Zorach had a third daughter, Bina Hodel, who remained stubbornly unconvinced. She argued that Simmele could have learned all about Esther Kreindel from her own parents or from some maid Esther Kreindel had dismissed. Or Simmele might be a witch or could be in league with an imp.

Bina Hodel was not the only one who suspected Simmele. In Zamosc there were widows and divorcees who thought of Reb Zorach as a catch. None of these had any intention of letting Simmele grab Zorach without opposition, and they went around town saying that she was a sly fox, a scheming wanton, a pig trying to put its snout into someone else's garden. When the rabbi of Zamosc heard of Simmele's claim he ordered her to be brought before him for examination. Suddenly Zamosc found itself divided. The wealthy, the scholarly, and those with sharp tongues were dubious of Simmele's claims and wanted to examine her closely. Esther Kreindel's neighbors and friends also wanted to interrogate the girl.

When Reitze heard how things stood in Zamosc and how her daughter was likely to be treated, she protested that she did not want her child dragged around and made the talk of the town and that Simmele was not interested in Reb Zorach Lipover's fortune. But Meyer Zissl had different plans. He was tired of teaching, and he had long wanted to move to Zamosc, a larger and gayer city than Bilgoray, full of rich men, gay youths, handsome women, taverns and wine cellars. Meyer Zissl persuaded Reitze to let him take Simmele to Zamosc. He had already received a sum of money from Zorach Lipover.

In Zamosc a large crowd gathered outside the rabbi's house to watch Simmele arrive with Meyer Zissl. Meyer Zissl and those on his side saw to it that only the most influential citizens were admitted. Simmele was dressed in Reitze's holiday dress and had a silk kerchief on her head. In recent weeks, she had grown taller, plumper, and more mature. Attacked from all sides with questions, she answered with so much good taste and breeding that finally even those who had come to mock her became silent. Esther Kreindel herself could not have given better answers. At the beginning, she was asked much about the other world. Simmele told of her death agony, the cleansing of her body, her burial; she described how the Angel Dumah had approached the grave with his fiery rod and asked her her name; then how evil spirits and hobgoblins had tried to fasten themselves to her and how she had been saved by the Kaddish of her pious sons. Her good deeds and transgressions were weighed against each other on the scale at her trial in heaven. Satan had plotted against her, but holy angels defended her. She told of her encounter with her parents, her grandparents, her great grandparents and other souls who had long been residing in Paradise. But on her way to judgment she had been permitted to look at Gehenna through a window. When she spoke of the terrors of Gehenna, the torture beds, the piles of snow and beds of coals whereon the wicked were turned, the glowing hooks on which the spiteful were hung by their tongues or breasts, the whole assemblage sighed. Even the scornful and the impenitent trembled. Simmele identified by name many residents of Zamosc who were being punished, some by immersion in barrels of boiling pitch, other by being forced to gather wood for the pyres on which they were burned; still others were poisoned by snakes, or eaten by vipers and hedgehogs. A stranger would never have heard of most of these people, nor of their cimes.

Next Simmele described the diamond pillars of Paradise among which the just sit on golden chairs with crowns on their heads, feasting on Leviathan and the Wild Ox, drinking the wine which God keeps for his beloved ones while angels divulge to them the secrets of the

Torah. Simmele explained that the righteous don't use their wives as footstools; rather the holy women sit near their husbands, but on chairs whose gold heads are somewhat lower than those of the men. The women of Zamosc, gladdened by this news, began to cry and laugh. Reb Zorach Lipover covered his face with both hands and tears ran down his beard.

After the interrogation at the rabbi's house, Simmele was taken to Reb Zorach's where his children, relatives, and neighbors had gathered. There she was closely questioned again, this time about Esther Kreindel's friends, merchants, and servants. Simmele knew everything and remembered everybody. Reb Zorach's daughters pointed to drawers in the closets and sideboards and Simmele listed the linens and other objects contained within. She remarked of one embroidered table cloth that Zorach had bought it for her as a gift in Leipzig; of an incense box that he had purchased it at a fair in Prague. She spoke familiarly to all the aging women, Esther Kreindel's contemporaries. "Treina, do you still have heartburn after meals? . . . Riva Gutah, has the boil on your left breast healed?" And she joked good naturedly with Reb Zorach's daughters, remarking to one, "Do you still hate radishes?" and to another, "Do you remember the day I took you to Doctor Palecki and a pig frightened you?" She recalled the words the women of the Burial Society had spoken while cleansing her. When the questioning slackened, Simmele repeated that the yearning of her husband Zorach had not allowed her to rest in peace, and that the Lord of the living, taking pity on Zorach, had sent her back to him. She explained that when Zorach died she would die also for all of her years were used up, and she was living now only for his sake. No one took this prediction seriously, so young and healthy did she seem.

Zamosc had expected Simmele's interrogation to last many days but most of those who questioned her at the rabbi's and then later at Reb Zorach's were soon satisfied that she was truly the reincarnation of Esther Kreindel. Even the cat recognized her old mistress, meowing excitedly and running to rub its head against her ankles. By the end of the day, only a small group still held out. Esther Kreindel's friends covered Simmele with kisses; all Zorach's daughters except for Bina Hodel wept and embraced their mother; his sons did her honor. The grandchildren kissed her fingers. Everyone ignored the scoffers. Reb Zorach Lipover and Meyer Zissl set the marriage day.

The wedding was noisy. For though the soul was Esther Kreindel's, the body was that of a virgin.

V

Esther Kreindel had returned. But nevertheless it was hard for Zorach and the town to believe in the occurrence of such a miracle. When Esther Kreindel the second went to the market place, followed by her maid, girls peeped at her from the windows and those on the street stopped to stare. In the half-holidays of Passover and of the Feast of Tabernacles young people from all over traveled to Zamosc to see the woman who had returned from the grave. Crowds gathered in front of Reb Zorach's house and the door had to be chained to keep out the intruders. Zorach Lipover himself went around in a trance; his children, in the presence of their resurrected mother, blushed and stammered.

The town sceptics constantly reverted to the subject, referring to Zorach as an old goat; they asserted that he had arranged the miracle with Reitze, and speculated on how much he had paid—some said a thousand guldens—for her young daughter. One night two pranksters stealthily set a ladder against the wall of Zorach's house and peered through the shutter into his bedroom. In the tavern later they told how they had watched Esther Kreindel the second recite her prayers, bring a pitcher of water for the morning ablutions; how they had seen her herself remove Zorach's boots, tickle his soles, he lasciviously pulling at her earlobes. Even the Gentiles in their winehouse discussed the matter, several of them predicting that the court would enter the case and investigate the imposter, who was very likely a witch and in league with Lucifer.

For many months the new couple spent their nights talking. Zorach did not stop questioning Esther Kreindel about her departure from this world and what she had seen in the hereafter. He kept on looking for irrefutable proofs that she was what she claimed. He told her many times of the anguish he had endured while she lay sick and dying, and of the despair he felt while sitting *shiva* and during the thirty days of mourning. Esther Kreindel affirmed again and again that she had longed for him in her grave, that his agony had not let her rest, that she had gone as a supplicant before the Throne of Glory, while cherubim sang her praise and demons howled accusations. She kept on adding particulars about her encounters with dead relatives, their adventures in their graves, in Tophet, and later in the garden of Eden. When daybreak came, husband and wife were still talking.

On those nights that Esther Kreindel went to the ritual bath and Zorach came to her bed, he proclaimed that her body was more beautiful than it had been even in the first weeks of their first marriage. He said to her: "Perhaps I too will die and reappear as a young man." Esther Kreindel scolded him good-naturedly, assured him that she loved him more than she could possibly love any young fellow, and her only wish was to have him live to be a hundred and twenty.

Gradually everyone grew accustomed to the situation. Soon after the wedding Reitze and her stepchildren came to live in Zamosc in a house that Reb Zorach gave them. Reb Zorach took Meyer Zissl into his business, and put him in charge of loans to the local gentry. Meyer Zissl's boys who had so recently slapped, kicked, and spat on Simmele, now came to bid Esther Kreindel a good Sabbath and to be treated to almond bread and wine. The name Simmele was soon forgotten. Even Reitze no longer called her daughter Simmele. Esther Kreindel had been nearly sixty when she died; Simmele now treated Reitze like one of her daughters. It was strange to hear the younger woman calling Reitze child, giving her advice on baking, cooking, and bringing up children. The second Esther Kreindel like the first had a talent for business and her husband, Zorach, would make no decisions without consulting her.

In the community too the second Esther Kreindel assumed the position of the first. She was invited to accompany brides to the synagogue, to be the matron of honor at weddings, to hold the babies at circumcisions. And she conducted herself as if she had been accustomed to such honors for years. At first the younger women tried to make her their friend, but she treated them as if they belonged to another generation. At the wedding people had predicted that Esther Kreindel the second would soon conceive, but when several years passed and she did not, everyone began to remark that the returned Esther Kreindel was aging prematurely, her flesh shrinking, her skin drying up. Moreover she dressed like an old woman, wearing a cape with raised shoulders and a ribboned bonnet when she went out. She often wore tucked tops and pleated skirts with long trains. Every morning she entered the women's section of the synagogue carrying a gold-rimmed prayer book and a book of supplications. On the day before the new moon she fasted and attended the prayers to which only the old women went. During the months of Elul and Nissan when it is customary to visit the graves of relatives, the second Esther Kreindel visited the cemetery and prostrated herself on the grave of the first Esther Kreindel, weeping and begging forgiveness. It seemed then as if the corpse buried within had emerged to mourn and eulogize itself.

The years passed and Zorach grew older and weaker. Both his stomach and his feet pained him. Having stopped attending to his business, he sat all day long in an armchair, reading. Esther Kreindel brought him food and medicines. Sometimes she played "goat and wolf" or even cards with him; other times she read aloud to him. She took over the entire management of the business since his sons were lazy and incompetent. Every day she reported to him what had happened. Husband and wife talked of the old days as if they were really the same age. He reminded her of their early struggles, when the children were small. They recalled family worries and business complications with creditors, nobles, competitors. Esther Kreindel knew and remembered all the details. Often she reminded him of things he had forgotten. Other times they sat in silence for hours, Esther Kreindel knitting socks, Zorach Lipover watching her in amazement. The second Esther Kreindel had grown more and more like the first, had developed her high bosom, the wrinkles and folds in the face, the double chin, the bags under the eyes. Like the former Esther Kreindel, the present one wore her glasses on the point of her nose, scratched her ear with a knitting needle, refreshed herself with cherry wine and jam while muttering to herself or to the cat. Even her smell of fresh linen and lavender was that of the first Esther Kreindel. When she stopped going to the ritual bath everyone assumed she was undergoing her menopause. Even Reitze her mother could recognize nothing of the former Simmele.

Some of the first Esther Kreindel's contemporaries hinted that not only had their friend's soul returned from the grave but her body as well. The shoemaker insisted that the feet of the reincarnated woman were duplicates of the first. A wart had sprouted on the throat of the second in exactly the same spot where one had been on the throat of the first. There were those in Zamosc who said that if the grave of Esther Kreindel were opened, God forbid that anyone should commit such a sacrilege, the body exhumed would be not of Esther Kreindel but Simmele's.

Because a female cannot completely take over the place of a male, much of the responsibility for running Zorach Lipover's business passed to Meyer Zissl. The former Talmud teacher began to spend money lavishly. He got up late, drank wine from a silver goblet, sported a pipe with an amber bowl. Reb Zorach had always bowed and raised his hat to the squires but Meyer Zissl tried to be their equal. He dressed in a squire's costume with silver buttons, wore a sable hat with a feather, dined with the nobles, went hunting with them. When he was tipsy he threw coins to the peasants. His sons were sent to study in Italy, his daughters were married off to rich boys in Bohemia. After a while the Gentiles of Zamosc addressed him as Pan. Esther Kreindel reproached him, said it was not good for a Jew to indulge in worldly pleasures, that it made the Christians jealous, and that the money was being squandered, but Meyer Zissl paid no attention. There came a time when he ceased to go into Reitze's bedroom. Gossips spread the rumor that he had begun an affair with a Countess Zamoyska. There was a scandal over a woman of pleasure. Meyer Zissl and a noble fought a duel and the latter was wounded in the thigh. Meyer Zissl finally stopped coming to the synagogue except on the High Holidays.

Reb Zorach Lipover had become extremely feeble. His final illness was long and protracted. Esther Kreindel sat up with her husband for many nights, refusing to let others watch him. When he died, she fell on the corpse in her anguish and would not allow it to be laid out. The men of the Burial Society had to pull her away. Following the funeral, Esther Kreindel returned home surrounded by all of Zorach's sons and daughters who had come to sit the seven days of mourning with her. Because Zorach had been so old when he died, his children sat on small stools in their stocking feet and babbled of everyday matters. There were frequent references to his will: they all knew he had made one but what it contained they could not say. They assumed Zorach had left his widow a fortune and were already preparing to haggle with her. These men and women who had called the second Esther Kreindel mother for years now avoided looking her in the face. Esther Kreindel took her Bible and opened it to the Book of Job. Weeping, she read the words of Job and his companions. Bina Hodel, who hadn't cried once during her father's final illness, muttered loud enough to be heard: "God's thief."

Esther Kreindel closed the Bible and stood up. "Children, I want to take leave of you."

"Are you going somewhere?" Bina Hodel asked, lifting her brows.

"Tonight I will be with your father," Esther Kreindel replied.

"Tell us that next year," quipped Bina Hodel.

At supper that night Esther Kreindel hardly touched the food on her plate. Afterwards she stood at the east wall. She bowed, beat her breast and confessed her sins as if it were Yom Kippur. Reitze washed dishes in the kitchen. Meyer Zissl had gone to a ball. When Esther Kreindel was finished, she went to the bedroom and ordered the maid to make up the bed there. The maid demurred, muttering that the lady should sleep elsewhere. The master had died in that room. A wick was still burning in a shard, and the customary glass of water stood on the night table with the piece of linen inside prepared for the soul to cleanse itself. Who would spend the night in a room from which a corpse had so recently been taken out? But Esther Kreindel bade the girl do as she had been told.

Esther Kreindel undressed. The instant she stretched out on the bed her face began to change, and became yellow and sunken. The maid ran to summon the family. A doctor was sent for. Those who watched Esther Kreindel die testified later that she looked exactly like the first Esther Kreindel in her death throes. Her eyes remained open but opaque and unseeing. She was addressed but did not answer. A spoonful of chicken soup poured into her mouth dribbled out. All at once she heaved a sigh and the soul left the body. Bina Hodel threw herself down at the foot of the bed calling out, "My good mother. My sacred mother."

The funeral was a large one. Esther Kreindel the second was buried near Esther Kreindel the first. The most venerable woman of the town sewed her shroud. The rabbi delivered a eulogy. When the funeral was over, Meyer Zissl presented to the rabbi two wills. In one Zorach Lipover willed his wife three-quarters of his fortune; in the other Esther Kreindel left a third of her inheritance to charity and two-thirds to Reitze and her children. Meyer Zissl was the executor.

Not many months later Bina Hodel died and Meyer Zissl, without Esther Kreindel's stablizing influence, became reckless. He gave credit to insolvent merchants, accepted mortgages without evaluating the property, and continued to lose large sums of money. He was forever initiating law suits. More and more often he had to hide from his creditors and from the King's tax collectors. One day a group of squires accompanied by marshals, bailiffs, and soldiers came to Meyer Zissl's palace. The governor of Lublin had authorized a public auction of all his property. Meyer Zissl was arrested, shackled, and thrown into prison. Reitze tried to raise money from the community to get him released, but because he had ignored the Jews and Jewishness, the elders refused him assistance. The squires with whom he had drunk and caroused did not even bother to answer his letters of supplication. One morning nine months later when the jailer entered Meyer Zissl's cell with a loaf of bread and a bowl of hot water he found the prisoner hanging from the window grating. Meyer Zissl had torn his shirt into strips and braided it into a rope. The Jews took away the corpse and buried it behind the fence.

VI

Years later the people in Zamosc, in Bilgoray, in Krashnik, even in Lublin continued to discuss the case of the girl who went to sleep Simmele and woke up Esther Kreindel. Reitze had long since died in the poorhouse. Her children who lived in foreign lands had completely forsaken their faith. Of Zorach Lipover's great fortune nothing was left. But the controversy still went on. A wedding jester wrote a poem about Simmele. Seamstresses sang a ballad about her. On long winter nights girls and women, plucking feathers, chopping cabbage, knitting jackets, reviewed the facts. Even *cheder* boys told one another the story of how the soul of Esther Kreindel was reincarnated. Some contended that the whole thing had been mere fraud. What fools Reb Zorach Lipover and his family had been to let themselves be tricked by a girl. They claimed that the mastermind was Meyer Zissl. He had wanted to give up teaching and enjoy Zorach's wealth. One man concluded after much thought that Meyer Zissl had copulated with his stepdaughter and persuaded her to be a party in the plot. Another said Reitze had initiated the conspiracy and had primed her daughter for the part. In Zamosc there was a Dr. Ettinger who argued that miraculous though it was for a woman to rise from her grave and return to her husband, it was an even greater miracle for a fourteen-year-old girl to deceive the elders of Zamosc. After all Zamosc, unlike Chelm, was not a town of fools. In addition, how had it happened that Simmele had not become pregnant and had died the night after her husband's burial? No one can make a contract with the Angel of Death.

In any case, there is a birch tree growing from Zorach Lipover's grave. Birds nest in its branches. The leaves never stop trembling and their perpetual rustle rings like tiny bells. The tombstones of Esther Kreindel the first and Esther Kreindel the second lean against each other and have been made almost one by time. The world is full of puzzles. It is possible that not even Elijah will be able to answer all our questions when the Messiah comes. Even God in seventh Heaven may not have solved all the mysteries of His Creation. This may be the reason He conceals His face.

Translated by The Author
and Elizabeth Pollet

The Fast

I

Itche Nokhum was always a small eater, but after Roise Genendel had left him and his father, may he live long, had ordered him to send for a writ of divorce, Itche Nokhum had given himself over to fasting. It was easy to fast in the house of the Bekhever rebbe. The rebbetsin, his wife, was dead. Aunt Peshe, who kept house, never paid attention to whether one ate or didn't. The servant, Elke Dobe, often forgot to bring Itche Nokhum his meals. Under his window there was a pit where refuse was dumped. Itche Nokhum threw the food out the window. Dogs, cats and birds ate the scraps. It was only now, at the age of forty, that Itche Nokhum understood why the sages of old had fasted from Sabbath to Sabbath. An empty stomach, a pure bowel, is an exquisite pleasure. The body is light as though freed of gravity; the mind is clear. At first there is a slight gnawing at the stomach and the mouth waters, but after the first two days all hunger ceases. Itche Nokhum had long felt a repugnance to eating meat or anything that came from living creatures. Ever since he had seen Leizer the *shokhet* slaughter an ox at the slaughterhouse, meat made him nauseous. Even milk, drawn from udders, and eggs, laid by hens, were repellent. All of these had to do with blood, veins, gut. True, the Holy Books permitted the eating of meat, but only to saints, who have the power to deliver the sinful souls incarnated in kine and fowl. Itche Nokhum would have none of it.

Even bread, potatoes and greens were too much. It was enough to eat just to sustain life. And for that, a bite or two sufficed for several days. Anything more was self-indulgence. Why yield to gluttony? Since Roise Genendel, daughter of the Bialer rebbe, had left Itche Nokhum, he had discovered that a man can curb every desire. There is something in the heart that lusts, but one can thumb his nose at it. It wants to think carnal thoughts, but one compels it to pore over the Holy Book. It tempts one into longings and imaginings, but just to thwart it one recites the Psalms. In the morning it wants to sleep till nine, but one awakens it at daybreak. What this enemy within hates most of all is a cold ritual bath. But there is a little spot in the brain that has the final word, and when it commands the feet to go, they go, be the water cold as ice. In time, opposing this lusting creature becomes a habit. One bends it, gags it, or else one lets it babble on without answering—as it is written: "Answer not a fool according to his folly."

Itche Nokhum paced his room, back and forth—small, lean, with a wispy straw-colored beard, a face white as chalk, with a reddish, pointed nose and watery-blue eyes under shaggy yellow eyebrows. Over his forehead sat a crumpled skullcap with bits of straw and feathers clinging to it. Since Itche Nokhum had lost weight, everything hung loosely on his body: his trousers, held up by a sash, his gabardine, down to his ankles, his creased, unbuttoned shirt. Even his slippers and white socks were now too big. He did not walk, but shuffled. When the tempter became too strong, Itche Nokhum fooled him with a pinch of snuff or a pipe. Tobacco dulls the appetite. Itche

Nokhum grappled with the enemy without respite. One moment he was seized with lust for Roise Genendel, the next—with anger at his father, may he live long, for urging him to divorce her; now he wanted to sleep under a quilt, and now he was consumed with thirst for a cup of coffee. When he tired of pacing, he lay down on a bench, with his handkerchief under his head in place of a pillow. The boards pressed against his ribs, made it impossible to remain long in one position. If Itche Nokhum managed to doze off, he was immediately attacked by dreams—not one after another, as in the past, but in a swarm, like locusts, as though the visions and delusions had hovered over him, just waiting till he closed his eyes. Roise Genendel appeared to him, as naked as mother Eve, spoke perverse words, laughed shamelessly. Itche Nokhum ate pastries, marzipans, drank wine, swooped through the air like a bat. Musicians played, drums pounded. It was both Purim and Simkhas Torah. "How can this be?" Itche Nokhum wondered. "The Messiah must have come—Sabbati Zevi himself . . ."

He woke with a start, drenched with perspiration. For a while he still remembered all the apparitions, absurdities and delusions, but soon they vanished from his mind, leaving only the image of Roise Genendel. Her body dazzled. He heard the echo of her laughter. "I shouldn't have divorced her!" Itche Nokhum muttered to himself. "I should have left her and disappeared, so that she wouldn't know where my bones were resting. Too late now . . ." People were saying in Bekhev that she was about to become the daughter-in-law of a Galician, the wife of the Komarner rebbe. A Hassid who knew the Komarner rebbe said that he was tall up to the ceiling, black as a Gypsy and three times a widower . . .

Itche Nokhum caught himself in a sin. Why did he want to leave her a deserted wife? Out of revenge. He had mentally broken the Mosaic precept: Thou shalt not avenge nor bear any grudge. Itche Nokhum took *The*

Beginning of Wisdom from the bookshelf. What were the penances for vengefulness? He turned the yellowed pages, scanning them. There was a long list of sins, but revenge was not among them. Itche Nokhum grimaced. This was not the first time that he cursed Roise Genendel in his mind, wishing her ill. He had imagined her sick, dying, dead. He knew that he was consumed with rancor, hatred, evil thoughts. The stiff-necked body refused to yield. It was full of spite.

Itche Nokhum opened a drawer where he had put a handful of pebbles collected in the courtyard, some nettles he had gathered by the fence, and burrs, such as the urchins throw on Tishe b'Ov. Itche Nokhum latched the door, removed his slippers and put in the pebbles: let them cut his soles. He held the nettles against his arms and neck, and rubbed his chest with them. They stung, but not too badly. The blisters would come later. "And now I'll treat you to a cold immersion!" he said to himself. "Come along! . . ." He unlocked the door and started down the stairs. Itche Nokhum was no longer one man, but two. One meted out punishment, and the other resisted. One Itche Nokhum dragged the other to the ritual bath, and the other babbled obscenities, cursed, blasphemed. Itche Nokhum raised his hand and gave himself a slap on the face:

"Wanton!"

II

It was the fifth day of Itche Nokhum's fast. He had begun the fast on Sabbath evening, and now it was Thursday night. At first, Itche Nokhum had wanted to prove to himself that what the men of old could do, could also be done today. If Rabbi Zadock of Jerusalem had been able to nourish himself for forty years by sucking at a fig, he, Itche Nokhum, could surely abstain from glutting for a week. Secondly, the other one, the adversary, had become altogether too obstreperous. He sat in Itche Nokhum like a dybbuk, forever doing spite. One Itche Nokhum prayed, and the other grabbled rhymes like a clown. One applied the phylacteries, and the other belched, hiccuped, spat. One recited the Eighteen Benedictions, and the other conjured pictures of the Komarner disporting himself with Roise Genendel. Itche Nokhum no longer knew what he was doing. He repeated the same prayer three times. He was no longer in a wrestling bout, but in a fight for life or death. Itche Nokhum stopped sleeping. If a man cannot overcome the enemy by fasting, by lying on thorns, by cold immersions, then how is he to drive him out? By destroying himself? But that is forbidden! A man is expected to break the casket without spilling the wine. Yet how could this be done? Itche Nokhum lay on the bench in his trousers and socks, with a stone for a pillow, like the patriarch Jacob. His skin tingled, but he refused to scratch. Beads of sweat trickled down his neck, but he would not wipe it. The evil one thought of a different trick every minute. Itche Nokhum's hair pricked his skull. His ear buzzed as if a gnat had gotten into it. His nostrils itched to sneeze, his mouth tried to yawn. His knees ached. His belly swelled as though overstuffed with food. Itche Nokhum felt ants running up and down his back. He muttered in the dark "Go on, torment me, tear at my flesh! . . ."

For a while the other relented and Itche Nokhum dozed off. A huge frog opened its maw, ready to swallow him. The church bell rang out. Itche Nokhum started up, trembling. Was there a fire or some other disaster? He waited for the bell to ring again. But there was only a distant, hollow echo. Itche Nokhum felt a need to urinate. He stood by the pail, but nothing came. He washed his hands, preparing to say the prayer proper for the occasion, but the urge returned. He felt a burning and a throbbing. His entrails contracted with cramps. A bitterness flooded his mouth, as on the verge of vomiting.

"Shall I take a drink of water?" Itche Nokhum asked himself. He went to the stool, where a pitcher stood, half-filled with water for ritual hand-washing, and turned it over reluctantly. One of his socks became wet. "I'll not give in to him!" Itche Nokhum whispered. "Show a dog a finger and he'll snap up the whole hand . . ."

Itche Nokhum stretched out again on his bench, his limbs numb. The pains and aches, the gnawing hunger, the dryness of thirst had suddenly vanished. He was neither asleep nor awake. The brain was thinking, but Itche Nokhum did not know what it thought. The other, the spiteful one, was gone, and there was once again only one Itche Nokhum. He was no longer divided. "Am I dying?" he asked himself. All fear of death had disappeared. He was ready to go. When a funeral is held on Friday afternoon, he thought, the newly dead is spared interrogation and torture by the Black Angel. Itche Nokhum watched his strength ebbing away. His mind slipped over a stretch of time, leaving a blank. It was as if Purah, the Angel of Forgetfulness, had plucked out a piece of Itche Nokhum's memory. He marveled at it in the dark. The lapse may have lasted a minute, an hour, or a day and a night. Itche Nokhum had once read a story about a bewitched young man who bent over a barrel to dip some water, and when he straightened up it was seventy years later.

Suddenly Itche Nokhum was petrified. Something began to stir in the dark by the door—a coiling wisp of vapor, airy and misty. Itche Nokhum was so astonished that he forgot to be frightened. A figure loomed up, an apparition with head and shoulders, neck and hair—a woman. Her face seemed to glow with its own light. Itche Nokhum recognized her: Roise Genendel! The upper part of her body was now quite distinct; the face swayed as if trying to speak. The eyesockets grinned. Below, the phantasm trailed off in ragged wisps and shreds. Itche Nokhum heard his own voice:

"What do you want?"

He tried to rise, but his legs were numb and heavy. The specter flowed toward him, dragging its tail of slime like a chick prematurely breaking out of a shell. "The Primeval Substance!" something cried in Itche Nokhum. He recalled the Psalm: "Thine eyes did see my substance, yet being unperfect." He wanted to speak to the night-creature, but he was robbed of the power of speech. For a time he watched dumbly as she approached, half woman, half shapeless ooze, a monstrous fungus straining to break away from its root, a creature put together in haste. After a while she began to melt away. Pieces dropped from her. The face dissolved, the hair scattered, the nose stretched out and became a snout, as in the manikins that people put on window sills in winter to mock the frost. She spat out her tongue. Roise Genendel vanished, and the sun flashed in the east sharp as a knife. Bloody stains spattered the walls, the ceilings, the floor. The morning had slaughtered Roise Genendel and splashed her blood. A last bubble of life had burst, and everything returned to the void. Itche Nokhum sat up and rocked as men do over a corpse.

"Roise Genendel! . . . Woe is me! . . ."

III

They were blowing the ram's horn in Bekhev. Elul breezes blew in from the willows in the cemetery. Bright gossamer floated high in the air over the courtyard. Ripe fruit dropped from the trees in the rebbe's orchard. Desolation rustled in the prayer house. Sparrows skipped over the tables. The community goat wandered into the antechamber, leaned against the box with torn, discarded prayerbooks and tired to chew at the corner of a psalmbook. It was Thursday again, and Itche Nokhum had not tasted food since the Sabbath evening meal, but no one paid any attention. When a man fasts all year, he does not begin to eat in Elul, the month of repentance. Itche

Nokhum sat in his room, turning the pages of *The Covenant of Rest.* He mumbled for a while. Then he leaned his head on the back of the chair and dozed off.

Suddenly Itche Nokhum heard steps and loud voices. Someone was coming rapidly upstairs to him. The door was flung open and Itche Nokhum saw Roise Genendel and behind her, Yente, her maidservant. It was not the Roise Genendel who revealed herself to him in the nights and through whom he could see as through the weave of his sash, but Roise Genendel in the living flesh: tall, narrow, with a crooked nose, fiery black eyes, thick lips and a long neck. She was dressed in a black shawl, a silk cloak and high-heeled shoes. She was scolding her servant and made her a sign to follow her no further. Roise Genendel entered Itche Nokhum's room, leaving the door open—evidently in order not to remain alone with him. Yente remained standing half-way up the stairs. Itche Nokhum was astounded. "Have I already attained such power?" the thought flashed through his brain. For a long while she stood upon the threshold, holding up her skirt, appraising him with a sidelong stare, in which anger mingled with silent pity. Then she said:

"White as a corpse!"

"What do you want?" asked Itche Nokhum in a faint voice that he could scarcely hear himself.

"What are you doing? Fasting, eh?" Roise Genendel asked mockingly.

Itche Nokhum did not answer.

"Itche Nokhum, I must speak to you!"

Roise Genendel slammed the door to.

"What is it?"

"Itche Nokhum, leave me in peace!" Roise Genendel almost shouted. "We were divorced, we are strangers now, I want to marry, and you can also marry. Everything must have an end!"

"I don't know what you mean."

"You know, you know. You're sitting here and casting

spells. I was already on the eve of marriage, and I had to postpone it. Why don't you let me be? You'll drive me from this world. I'll throw myself into the well!"

Roise Genendel stamped her foot. She truculently placed her hand on the doorpost. A diamond ring flashed on her finger. She breathed both fear and strength. Itche Nokhum raised his eyebrows. His heart knocked once and seemed to stop.

"I swear, I don't know . . ."

"You wake me up! You scream into my ear! What do you want of me? It wasn't right between us. From the very first. Forgive me, but you're not a man. Why do you torment me, then? Will you tell me?"

"What am I doing?"

"You come to me, you pinch me, you flay me. I hear your steps. I don't eat and I don't sleep because of you. I am losing weight. People see you in our courtyard, they see you, I'm not mad! . . . Yente almost died of fright. I'll call her in, she will tell you herself. She was going, if you will pardon me, to the outhouse, and you floated toward her. She raised such screams that everybody in the yard came running . . . Just before sunrise you came and sat on my bed, and I could not move my feet. What are you, a devil?"

Itche Nokhum was silent.

"We've kept it secret," Roise Genendel went on. "But I can't suffer forever. I'll tell the whole world who you are and what you're doing. You will be excommunicated. I'm only sorry for your old father . . ."

Itche Nokhum wanted to answer, but he could not utter a single word. Everything in him shrank and dried up. He began to gasp and croak like a grandfather clock before striking. Something inside him leaped like a snake. Itche Nokhum was filled will a strange fluttering. An icy feather brushed down his spine. He shook his head from side to side, as if to say, "No."

"I've come to warn you! Swear that you will release me.

If not, I'll raise such a commotion that all Bekhev will come running. I'll put aside all shame. Come down to the prayer house and swear upon the Holy Scrolls. It's either my death or yours! . . ."

Itche Nokhum made another effort and began to mumble in a choked voice, as if he were being strangled.

"I swear to you, I am not to blame."

"Who is then? You're using Sacred Names. You've plunged yourself into the Cabala. You've lost this world—you'll lose the next one too. My father, may he live long, has sent me to you. He also has intercessors in heaven. You're dealing with the evil ones, woe is me. You'll be driven behind the Black Mountains! You'll be thrown into the Hollow of the Sling! Mooncalf! . . ."

"Roise Genendel!"

"Fiend! Satan! Asmodeus!"

Roise Genendel was suddenly stricken mute. She stared at Itche Nokhum with her enormous black eyes, recoiling from him. The room became so still that one could hear the buzzing of a single fly. Itche Nokhum strained to speak. His throat contracted as if he had swallowed something.

"Roise Genendel, I cannot . . . I cannot forget you!"

"Miserable leech! I'm in your power . . ."

Roise Genendel's mouth twisted. She covered her face with both hands and broke into a hoarse wail.

Translated by Mirra Ginsburg

The Last Demon

ꙮꙮꙮꙮꙮ

I

I, a demon, bear witness that there are no more demons left. Why demons, when man himself is a demon? Why persuade to evil someone who is already convinced? I am the last of the persuaders. I board in an attic in Tishevitz and draw my sustenance from a Yiddish storybook, a left-over from the days before the great catastrophe. The stories in the book are pablum and duck milk, but the Hebrew letters have a weight of their own. I don't have to tell you that I am a Jew. What else, a Gentile? I've heard that there are Gentile demons, but I don't know any, nor do I wish to know them. Jacob and Esau don't become in-laws.

I came here from Lublin. Tishevitz is a God-forsaken village; Adam didn't even stop to pee there. It's so small that a wagon goes through town and the horse is in the market place just as the rear wheels reach the toll gate. There is mud in Tishevitz from Succoth until Tishe b'Ov. The goats of the town don't need to lift their beards to chew at the thatched roofs of the cottages. Hens roost in the middle of the streets. Birds build nests in the women's bonnets. In the tailor's synagogue a billy goat is the tenth in the quorum.

Don't ask me how I managed to get to this smallest letter in the smallest of all prayer books. But when Asmodeus bids you go, you go. After Lublin the road is familiar as far as Zamosc. From there on you are on your own. I was told to look for an iron weathercock with a crow perched upon its comb on the roof of the study house. Once upon a time the cock turned in the wind, but for years now it hasn't moved, not even in thunder and lightning. In Tishevitz even iron weathercocks die.

I speak in the present tense as for me time stands still. I arrive. I look around. For the life of me I can't find a single one of our men. The cemetery is empty. There is no outhouse. I go to the ritual bathhouse, but I don't hear a sound. I sit down on the highest bench, look down on the stone on which the buckets of water are poured each Friday, and wonder. Why am I needed here? If a little demon is wanted, is it necessary to import one all the way from Lublin? Aren't there enough devils in Zamosc? Outside the sun is shining—it's close to the summer solstice—but inside the bathhouse it's gloomy and cold. Above me is a spider web, and within the web a spider wiggling its legs, seeming to spin but drawing no thread. There's no sign of a fly, not even the shell of a fly. "What does the creature eat?" I ask myself, "its own insides?" Suddenly I hear it chanting in a Talmudic singsong: "A lion isn't satisfied by a morsel and a ditch isn't filled up with dirt from its own walls."

I burst out laughing.

"Is that so? Why have you disguised youself as a spider?"

"I've already been a worm, a flea, a frog. I've been sitting here for two hundred years without a stitch of work to do. But you need a permit to leave."

"They don't sin here?"

"Petty men, petty sins. Today someone covets another man's broom; tomorrow he fasts and puts peas in his shoes. Ever since Abraham Zalman was under the illusion that he was Messiah, the son of Joseph, the blood of the people has congealed in their veins. If I were Satan, I wouldn't even send one of our first-graders here."

"How much does it cost him?"

"What's new in the world?" he asks me.

"It's not been so good for our crowd."

"What's happened? The Holy Spirit grows stronger?"

"Stronger? Only in Tishevitz is he powerful. No one's heard of him in the large cities. Even in Lublin he's out of style."

"Well, that should be fine."

"But it isn't," I say. " 'All Guilty is worse for us than All Innocent.' It has reached a point where people want to sin beyond their capacities. They martyr themselves for the most trivial of sins. If that's the way it is, what are we needed for? A short while ago I was flying over Levertov Street, and I saw a man dressed in a skunk's coat. He had a black beard and wavy sidelocks; an amber cigar holder was clamped between his lips. Across the street from him an official's wife was walking, so it occurs to me to say, 'That's quite a bargain, don't you think, Uncle?' All I expected from him was a thought. I had my handkerchief ready if he should spit on me. So what does the man do? 'Why waste your breath on me?' he calls out angrily. 'I'm willing. Start working on her.' "

"What sort of a misfortune is this?"

"Enlightenment! In the two hundred years you've been sitting on your tail here, Satan has cooked up a new dish of kasha. The Jews have now developed writers. Yiddish ones, Hebrew ones, and they have taken over our trade. We grow hoarse talking to every adolescent, but they print their *kitsch* by the thousands and distribute it to Jews everywhere. They know all our tricks—mockery, piety. They have a hundred reasons why a rat must be kosher. All that they want to do is to redeem the world. Why, if you could corrupt nothing, have you been left here for two hundred years? And if you could do nothing in two hundred years, what do they expect from me in two weeks?"

"You know the proverb, 'A guest for a while sees a mile.' "

"What's there to see?"

"A young rabbi has moved here from Modlv Bozyc. He's not yet thirty, but he's absolutely stuffed with knowledge, knows the thirty-six tractates of the Talmud by heart. He's the greatest Cabalist in Poland, fasts every Monday and Thursday, and bathes in the ritual bath when the water is ice cold. He won't permit any of us to talk to him. What's more he has a handsome wife, and that's bread in the basket. What do we have to tempt him with? You might as well try to break through an iron wall. If I were asked my opinion, I'd say that Tishevitz should be removed from our files. All I ask is that you get me out of here before I go mad."

"No, first I must have a talk with this rabbi. How do you think I should start?"

"You tell me. He'll start pouring salt on your tail before you open your mouth."

"I'm from Lublin. I'm not so easily frightened."

II

On the way to the rabbi, I ask the imp, "What have you tried so far?"

"What haven't I tried?" he sanswers.

"A woman?"

"Won't look at one."

"Heresy?"

"He knows all the answers."

"Money?"

"Doesn't know what a coin looks like."

"Reputation?"

"He runs from it."

"Doesn't he look backwards?"

"Doesn't even move his head."

"He's got to have some angle."

"Where's it hidden?"

The window of the rabbi's study is open, and in we fly. There's the usual paraphernalia around: an ark with the Holy Scroll, bookshelves, a mezuzah in a wooden case. The rabbi, a young man with a blond beard, blue eyes, yellow sidelocks, a high forehead, and a deep widow's peak sits on the rabbinical chair peering in the Gemara. He's fully equipped: *yarmulka,* sash, and fringed garment with each of the fringes braided eight times. I listen to his skull: pure throughts! He sways and chants in Hebrew, *"Rachel t'unah v'gazezah,"* and then translates, "a wooly sheep fleeced."

"In Hebrew Rachel is both a sheep and a girl's name," I say.

"So?"

"A sheep has wool and a girl has hair."

"Therefore?"

"If she's not androgynous, a girl has pubic hair."

"Stop babbling and let me study," the rabbi says in anger.

"Wait a second," I say, "Torah won't get cold. It's true that Jacob loved Rachel, but when he was given Leah instead, she wasn't poison. And when Rachel gave him Bilhah as a concubine, what did Leah do to spite her sister? She put Zilpah into his bed."

"That was before the giving of Torah."

"What about King David?"

"That happened before the excommunication by Rabbi Gershom."

"Before or after Rabbi Gershom, a male is a male."

"Rascal. *Shaddai kra Satan,*" the rabbi exclaims. Grabbing both of his sidelocks, he begins to tremble as if assaulted by a bad dream. "What nonsense am I thinking?" He takes his ear lobes and closes his ears. I keep on talking but he doesn't listen; he becomes absorbed in a difficult passage and there's no longer anyone to speak to. The little imp from Tishevitz says, "He's a hard one to hook, isn't he? Tomorrow he'll fast and roll in a bed of thistles. He'll give away his last penny to charity."

"Such a believer nowadays?"

"Strong as a rock."

"And his wife?"

"A sacrificial lamb."

"What of the children?"

"Still infants."

"Perhaps he has a mother-in-law?"

"She's already in the other world."

"Any quarrels?"

"Not even half an enemy."

"Where do you find such a jewel?"

"Once in a while something like that turns up among the Jews."

"This one I've got to get. This is my first job around here. I've been promised that if I succeed, I'll be transferred to Odessa."

"What's so good about that?"

"It's as near paradise as our kind gets. You can sleep twenty-four hours a day. The population sins and you don't lift a finger."

"So what do you do all day?"

"We play with our women."

"Here there's not a single one of your girls." The imp sighs. "There was one old bitch but she expired."

"So what's left?"

"What Onan did."

"That doesn't lead anywhere. Help me and I swear by

Asmodeus' beard that I'll get you out of here. We have an opening for a mixer of bitter herbs. You only work Passovers."

"I hope it works out, but don't count your chickens."

"We've taken care of tougher than he."

III

A week goes by and our business has not moved forward; I find myself in a dirty mood. A week in Tishevitz is equal to a year in Lublin. The Tishevitz imp is all right, but when you sit two hundred years in such a hole, you become a yokel. He cracks jokes that didn't amuse Enoch and convulses with laughter; he drops names from the Haggadah. Every one of his stories wears a long beard. I'd like to get the hell out of here, but it doesn't take a magician to return home with nothing. I have enemies among my colleagues and I must beware of intrigue. Perhaps I was sent here just to break my neck. When devils stop warring with people, they start tripping each other.

Experience has taught that of all the snares we use, there are three that work unfailingly—lust, pride, and avarice. No one can evade all three, not even Rabbi Tsots himself. Of the three, pride has the strongest meshes. According to the Talmud a scholar is permitted the eighth part of an eighth part of vanity. But a learned man generally exceeds his quota. When I see that the days are passing and that the rabbi of Tishevitz remains stubborn, I concentrate on vanity.

"Rabbi of Tishevitz," I say, "I wasn't born yesterday. I come from Lublin where the streets are paved with exegeses of the Talmud. We use manuscripts to heat our ovens. The floors of our attics sag under the weight of Cabala. But not even in Lublin have I met a man of your eminence. How does it happen," I ask, "that no one's heard of you? True saints should hide themselves, perhaps, but silence will not bring redemption. You should be the leader of this generation, and not merely the rabbi of this community, holy though it is. The time has come for you to reveal yourself. Heaven and earth are waiting for you. Messiah himself sits in the Bird Nest looking down in search of an unblemished saint like you. But what are you doing about it? You sit on your rabbinical chair laying down the law on which pots and which pans are kosher. Forgive me the comparison, but it is as if an elephant were put to work hauling a straw."

"Who are you and what do you want?" the rabbi asks in terror. "Why don't you let me study?"

"There is a time when the service of God requires the neglect of Torah," I scream. "Any student can study the Gemara."

"Who sent you here?"

"I was sent; I am here. Do you think they don't know about you up there? The higher-ups are annoyed with you. Broad shoulders must bear their share of the load. To put it in rhyme: the humble can stumble. Hearken to this: Abraham Zalman was Messiah, son of Joseph, and you are ordained to prepare the way for Messiah, son of David, but stop sleeping. Get ready for battle. The world sinks to the forty-ninth gate of uncleanliness, but you have broken through to the seventh firmament. Only one cry is heard in the mansions, the man from Tishevitz. The angel in charge of Edom has marshalled a clan of demons against you. Satan lies in wait also. Asmodeus is undermining you. Lilith and Namah hover at your bedside. You don't see them, but Shabriri and Briri are treading at your heels. If the Angels were not defending you, that unholy crowd would pound you to dust and ashes. But you do not stand alone, Rabbi of Tishevitz. Lord Sandalphon guards your every step. Metratron watches over you from his luminescent sphere. Everything hangs in the balance, man of Tishevitz; you can tip the scales."

"What should I do?"

"Mark well all that I tell you. Even if I command you to break the law, do as I bid."

"Who are you? What is your name?"

"Elijah the Tishbite. I have the ram's horn of the Messiah ready. Whether the redemption comes, or we wander in the darkness of Egypt another 2,689 years is up to you."

The rabbi of Tishevitz remains silent for a long time. His face becomes as white as the slips of paper on which he writes his commentaries.

"How do I know you're speaking the truth?" he asks in a trembling voice. "Forgive me, Holy Angel, but I require a sign."

"You are right. I will give you a sign."

And I raise such a wind in the rabbi's study that the slip of paper on which he is writing rises from the table and starts flying like a pigeon. The pages of the Gemara turn by themselves. The curtain of the Holy Scroll billows. The rabbi's *yarmulka* jumps from his head, soars to the ceiling, and drops back onto his skull.

"Is that how Nature behaves?" I ask.

"No."

"Do you believe me now?"

The rabbi of Tishevitz hesitates.

"What do you want me to do?"

"The leader of this generation must be famous."

"How do you become famous?"

"Go and travel in the world."

"What do I do in the world?"

"Preach and collect money."

"For what do I collect?"

"First of all collect. Later on I'll tell you what to do with the money."

"Who will contribute?"

"When I order, Jews give."

"How will I support myself?"

"A rabbinical emissary is entitled to a part of what he collects."

"And my family?"

"You will get enough for all."

"What am I supposed to do right now?"

"Shut the Gemara."

"Ah, but my soul yearns for Torah," the rabbi of Tishevitz groans. Nevertheless he lifts the cover of the book, ready to shut it. If he had done that, he would have been through. What did Joseph de la Rinah do? Just hand Samael a pinch of snuff. I am already laughing to myself, "Rabbi of Tishevitz, I have you all wrapped up." The little bathhouse imp, standing in a corner, cocks an ear and turns green with envy. True, I have promised to do him a favor, but the jealousy of our kind is stronger than anything. Suddenly the rabbi says, "Forgive me, my Lord, but I require another sign."

"What do you want me to do? Stop the sun?"

"Just show me your feet."

The moment the rabbi of Tishevitz speaks these words, I know everything is lost. We can disguise all the parts of our body but the feet. From the smallest imp right up to Ketev Meriri we all have the claws of geese. The little imp in the corner bursts out laughing. For the first time in a thousand years I, the master of speech, lose my tongue.

"I don't show my feet," I call out in rage.

"That means you're a devil. *Pik,* get out of here," the rabbi cries. He races to his bookcase, pulls out the *Book of Creation* and waves it menacingly over me. What devil can withstand the *Book of Creation?* I run from the rabbi's study with my spirit in pieces.

To make a long story short, I remain stuck in Tishevitz. No more Lublin, no more Odessa. In one second all my stratagems turn to ashes. An order comes from Asmodeus himself, "Stay in Tishevitz and fry. Don't go further than a man is allowed to walk on the Sabbath."

How long am I here? Eternity plus a Wednesday. I've seen it all, the destruction of Tishevitz, the destruction of Poland. There are no more Jews, no more demons. The women don't pour out water any longer on the night of the winter solstice. They don't avoid giving things in even numbers. They no longer knock at dawn at the antechamber of the synagogue. They don't warn us before emptying the slops. The rabbi was martyred on a Friday in the month of Nisan. The community was slaughtered, the holy books burned, the cemetery desecrated. The *Book of Creation* has been returned to the Creator. Gentiles wash themselves in the ritual bath. Abraham Zalman's chapel has been turned into a pig sty. There is no longer an Angel of Good nor an Angel of Evil. No more sins, no more temptations! The generation is already guilty seven times over, but Messiah does not come. To whom should he come? Messiah did not come for the Jews, so the Jews went to Messiah. There is no further need for demons. We have also been annihilated. I am the last, a refugee. I can go anywhere I please, but where should a demon like me go? To the murderers?

I found a Yiddish storybook between two broken barrels in the house which once belonged to Velvel the Barrelmaker. I sit there, the last of the demons. I eat dust. I sleep on a feather duster. I keep on reading gibberish. The style of the book is in our manner: Sabbath pudding cooked in pig's fat: blasphemy rolled in piety. The moral of the book is: neither judge, nor judgment. But nevertheless the letters are Jewish. The alphabet they could not squander. I suck on the letters and feed myself. I count the words, make rhymes, and tortuously interpret and reinterpret each dot.

Aleph, the abyss, what else waited?
Bet, the blow, long since fated.
Geemel, God, pretending he knew,
Dalet, death, its shadow grew.

Hey, the hangman, he stood prepared;
Wov, wisdom, ignorance bared.
Zayeen, the zodiac, signs distantly loomed;
Chet, the child, prenatally doomed.
Tet, the thinker, an imprisoned lord;
Jod, the judge, the verdict a fraud.

Yes, as long as a single volume remains, I have something to sustain me. As long as the moths have not destroyed the last page, there is something to play with. What will happen when the last letter is no more, I'd rather not bring to my lips.

When the last letter is gone,
The last of the demons is done.

Translated by Martha Glicklich
and Cecil Hemley

Alone

I

Many times in the past I have wished the impossible to happen—and then it happened. But though my wish came true, it was in such a topsy-turvy way that it appeared the Hidden Powers were trying to show me I didn't understand my own needs. That's what occurred that summer in Miami Beach. I had been living in a large hotel full of South American tourists who had come to Miami to cool off, as well as with people like myself who suffered from hay fever. I was fed up with the whole business—splashing about in the ocean with those noisy guests; hearing Spanish all day long; eating heavy meals twice each day. If I read a Yiddish newspaper or book, the others looked at me with astonishment. So it happened that taking a walk one day, I said out loud: "I wish I were alone in a hotel." An imp must have overheard me for immediately he began to set a trap.

When I came down to breakfast the next morning, I found the hotel lobby in confusion. Guests stood about in small groups, their voices louder than usual. Valises were piled all over. Bellboys were running about pushing carts loaded with clothing. I asked someone what was the matter. "Didn't you hear the announcement over the public address system? They've closed the hotel." "Why?" I asked. "They're bankrupt." The man moved away, annoyed at my ignorance. Here was a riddle: the hotel was closing! Yet so far as I knew, it did a good business. And how could you suddenly close a hotel with hundreds of guests? But in America I had decided it was better not to ask too many questions.

The air conditioning had already been shut off and the air in the lobby was musty. A long line of guests stood at the cashier's desk to pay their bills. Everywhere there was turmoil. People crushed out cigarettes on the marble floor. Children tore leaves and flowers off the potted tropical plants. Some South Americans, who only yesterday had pretended to be full-blooded Latins, were now talking loudly in Yiddish. I myself had very little to pack, only one valise. Taking it, I went in search of another hotel. Outside the burning sun reminded me of the Talmudic story of how, on the plains of Mamre, God had removed the sun from its case so that no strangers would bother Abraham. I felt a little giddy. The days of my bachelorhood came back when, carefree, I used to pack all my belongings in one valise, leave, and within five minutes find myself another room. Passing a small hotel, which looked somewhat run-down I read the sign: "Off-Season Rates from $2 a Day." What could be cheaper? I went inside. There was no air conditioning. A hunchbacked girl with black piercing eyes stood behind the desk. I asked her if I could have a room.

"The whole hotel," she answered.

"No one is here?"

"Nobody." The girl laughed, displaying a broken row of teeth with large gaps between. She spoke with a Spanish accent.

She had come from Cuba, she told me. I took a room. The hunchback led me into a narrow elevator, which took us up to the third floor. There we walked down a long, dark corridor meagerly lit by a single bulb. She opened a door and let me into my room, like a prisoner into his cell. The window, covered by mosquito netting, looked out over the Atlantic. On the walls the paint was peeling, and the rug on the floor was threadbare and colorless. The bathroom smelled of mildew, the closet of moth repellent. The bed linen, though clean, was damp. I unpacked my things and went downstairs. Everything was mine alone: the swimming pool, the beach, the ocean. In the patio stood a group of dilapidated canvas chairs. All around the sun beat down. The sea was yellow, the waves low and lazy, barely moving, as if they too were fatigued by the stifling heat. Only occasionally, out of duty, they tossed up a few specks of foam. A single seagull stood on the water trying to decide whether or not to catch a fish. Here before me, drenched in sunlight, was a summer melancholy—odd, since melancholy usually suggests autumn. Mankind, it seemed, had perished in some catastrophe, and I was left, like Noah—but in an empty ark, without sons, without a wife, without any animals. I could have swum naked, nevertheless I put on my bathing suit. The water was so warm, the ocean might have been a bathtub. Loose bunches of seaweed floated about. Shyness had held me back in the first hotel—here it was solitude. Who can play games in an empty world? I could swim a little, but who would rescue me if something went wrong? The Hidden Powers had provided me with an empty hotel—but they could just as easily provide me with an undertow, a deep hole, a shark, or a sea serpent. Those who toy with the unknown must be doubly careful.

After a while I came out of the water and lay down on one of the limp canvas beach chairs. My body was pale, my skull bare, and though my eyes were protected by tinted glasses, the sun's rays glared through. The light-blue sky was cloudless. The air smelled of salt, fish, and mangoes. There was no division, I felt, between the organic and the inorganic. Everything around me, each grain of sand, each pebble, was breathing, growing, lusting. Through the heavenly channels, which, says the Cabala, control the flow of Divine Mercy, came truths impossible to grasp in a northern climate. I had lost all ambition; I felt lazy; my few wants were petty and material—a glass of lemonade or orange juice. In my fancy a hot-eyed woman moved into the hotel for a few nights. I hadn't meant I wanted a hotel completely to myself. The imp had either misunderstood or was pretending to. Like all forms of life, I, too, wanted to be fruitful, wanted to multiply—or at least to go through the motions. I was prepared to forget any moral or aesthetic demands. I was ready to cover my guilt with a sheet and to give way wholly, like a blind man, to the sense of touch. At the same time the eternal questions tapped in my brain: Who is behind the world of appearance? Is it Substance with its Infinite Attributes? Is it the Monad of all Monads? Is it the Absolute, Blind Will, the Unconscious? Some kind of superior being has to be hidden in back of all these illusions.

On the sea, oily-yellow near the shore, glassy-green farther out, a sail walked over the water like a shrouded corpse. Bent forward, it looked as if it were trying to call something up from the depths. Overhead flew a small airplane trailing a sign: MARGOLIES' RESTAURANT—KOSHER, 7 COURSES, $1.75. So the Creation had not yet returned to primeval chaos. They still served soup with kasha and kneidlach, knishes and stuffed derma at Margolies' restaurant. In that case perhaps tomorrow I would receive a letter. I had been promised my mail would be forwarded. It was my only link, in Miami, with the outside world. I'm always amazed that someone has written me, taken the trouble to stamp and mail the envelope. I look for cryptic meanings, even on the blank side of the paper.

II

When you are alone, how long the day can be! I read a book and two newspapers, drank a cup of coffee in a cafeteria, worked a crossword puzzle. I stopped at a store that auctioned Oriental rugs, went into another where Wall Street stocks were sold. True, I was on Collins Avenue in Miami Beach, but I felt like a ghost, cut off from everything. I went into the library and asked a question—the librarian grew frightened. I was like a man who had died, whose space had already been filled. I passed many hotels, each with its special decorations and attractions. The palm trees were topped by half-wilted fans of leaves, and their coconuts hung like heavy testicles. Everything seemed motionless, even the shiny new automobiles gliding over the asphalt. Every object continued its existence with that effortless force which is, perhaps, the essence of all being.

I bought a magazine, but was unable to read past the first few lines. Getting on a bus, I let myself be taken aimlessly over causeways, islands with ponds, streets lined with villas. The inhabitants, building on a wasteland, had planted trees and flowering plants from all parts of the world; they had filled up shallow inlets along the shore; they had created architectural wonders and had worked out elaborate schemes for pleasure. A planned hedonism. But the boredom of the desert remained. No loud music could dispel it, no garishness wipe it out. We passed a cactus plant whose blades and dusty needles had brought forth a red flower. We rode near a lake surrounded by groups of flamingos airing their wings, and the water mirrored their long beaks and pink feathers. An assembly of birds. Wild ducks flew about, quacking—the swampland refused to give way.

I looked out the open window of the bus. All that I saw was new, yet it appeared old and weary: grandmothers with dyed hair and rouged cheeks, girls in bikinis barely covering their shame, tanned young men guzzling Coca-Cola on water skis.

An old man lay sprawled on the deck of a yacht, warming his rheumatic legs, his white-haired chest open to the sun. He smiled wanly. Nearby, the mistress to whom he had willed his fortune picked at her toes with red fingernails, as certain of her charms as that the sun would rise tomorrow. A dog stood at the stern, gazing haughtily at the yacht's wake, yawning.

It took a long time to reach the end of the line. Once there, I got on another bus. We rode past a pier where freshly caught fish were being weighed. Their bizarre colors, gory skin wounds, glassy eyes, mouths full of congealed blood, sharp-pointed teeth—all were evidence of a wickedness as deep as the abyss. Men gutted the fishes with an unholy joy. The bus passed a snake farm, a monkey colony. I saw houses eaten up by termites and a pond of brackish water in which the descendants of the primeval snake crawled and slithered. Parrots screeched with strident voices. At times, strange smells blew in through the bus window, stenches so dense they made my head throb.

Thank God the summer day is shorter in the South than in the North. Evening fell suddenly, without any dusk. Over the lagoons and highways, so thick no light could penetrate, hovered a jungle darkness. Automobiles, headlamps on, slid forward. The moon emerged extraordinarily large and red; it hung in the sky like a geographer's globe bearing a map not of this world. The night had an aura of miracle and cosmic change. A hope I had never forsaken awoke in me: Was I destined to witness an upheaval in the solar system? Perhaps the moon was about to fall down. Perhaps the earth, tearing itself out of its orbit around the sun, would wander into new constellations.

The bus meandered through unknown regions until it returned to Lincoln Road and the fancy stores, half-empty in summer but still stocked with whatever a rich tourist might desire—an ermine wrap, a chinchilla collar, a twelve-carat diamond, an original Picasso drawing. The dandified salesmen, sure in their knowledge that beyond nirvana pulses karma, conversed among themselves in their air-conditioned interiors. I wasn't hungry; nevertheless I went into a restaurant where a waitress with a newly bleached permanent served me a full meal, quietly and without fuss. I gave her a half-dollar. When I left, my stomach ached and my head was heavy. The late-evening air, baked by the sun, choked me as I came out. On a nearby building a neon sign flashed the temperature—it was ninety-six, and the humidity almost as much! I didn't need a weatherman. Already, lightning flared in the flowing sky, although I didn't hear thunder. A huge cloud was descending from above, thick as a mountain, full of fire and of water. Single drops of rain hit my bald head. The palm trees looked petrified, expecting the onslaught. I hurried back toward my empty hotel, wanting to get there before the rain; besides, I hoped some mail had come for me. But I had covered barely half the distance when the storm broke. One gush and I was drenched as if by a huge wave. A fiery rod lit up the sky and, the same moment, I heard the thunder crack—a sign the lightning was near me. I wanted to run inside somewhere, but chairs blown from nearby porches somersaulted in front of me, blocking my way. Signs were falling down. The top of a palm tree, torn off by the wind, careened past my feet. I saw a second palm tree sheathed in sackcloth, bent to the wind, ready to kneel. In my confusion I kept on running. Sinking into puddles so deep I almost drowned, I rushed forward with the lightness of boyhood. The danger had made me daring and I screamed and sang, shouting to the storm in its own key. By this time all traffic had stopped, even the automobiles had been abandoned. But I ran on, determined to escape such madness or else go under. I had to get that special delivery letter, which no one had written and I never received.

I still don't know how I recognized my hotel. I entered the lobby and stood motionless for a few moments, dripping water on the rug. In the mirror across the room, my half-dissolved image reflected itself like a figure in a cubist painting. I managed to get to the elevator and ride up to the third floor. The door of my room stood ajar: inside, mosquitoes, moths, fireflies, and gnats fluttered and buzzed about, sheltering from the storm. The wind had torn down the mosquito net and scattered the papers I had left on the table. The rug was soaked. I walked over to the window and looked at the ocean. The waves rose like mountains in the middle of seas—monstrous billows ready once and for all to overflow the shores and float the land away. The waters roared with spite and sprayed white foam into the darkness of the night. The waves were barking at the Creator like packs of hounds. With all the strength I had left, I pulled the window down and lowered the blind. I squatted to put my wet books and manuscripts in order. I was hot. Sweat poured from my body, mingling with rivulets of rain water. I peeled off my clothes and they lay near my feet like shells. I felt like a creature who has just emerged from a cocoon.

III

The storm had still not reached its climax. The howling wind knocked and banged as if with mighty hammers. The hotel seemed like a ship floating on the ocean. Something came off and crashed down—the roof, a balcony, part of the foundation. Iron bars broke. Metal groaned. Windows tore loose from their casements. The windowpanes rattled. The heavy blind on my window billowed up as easily as a curtain. The room was lit with the glare of a great conflagration. Then came a clap of thunder so strong I laughed in fear. A white figure materialized from the darkness. My heart plummeted, my brain trembled in its socket. I always knew that sooner or later one of that brood would show himself to me bodily, full of horrors that are never told because no one who has seen them has survived to tell the story. I lay there silently, ready for the end. Then I heard a voice:

"Excuse please, Señor, I am much afraid. You are asleep?" It was the Cuban hunchback.

"No, come in," I answered her.

"I shake. I think I die with fear," the woman said. "A hurricane like this never come before. You are the only one in this hotel. Please excuse that I disturb you."

"You aren't disturbing me. I would put on the light but I'm not dressed."

"No, no. It is not necessary . . . I am afraid to be alone. Please let me stay here until the storm is over."

"Certainly. You can lie down if you want. I'll sit on the chair."

"No, I will sit on the chair. Where is the chair, Señor? I do not see it."

I got up, found the woman in the darkness, and led her to the armchair. She dragged herself after me, trembling. I wanted to go to the closet and get some clothing. But I stumbled into the bed and fell on top of it. I covered myself quickly with the sheet so that the stranger would not see me naked when the lightning flashed. Soon after there was another bolt and I saw her sitting in the chair, a deformed creature in an overlarge nightgown, with a hunched back, disheveled hair, long hairy arms, and crooked legs, like a tubercular monkey. Her eyes were wide with an animal's fear.

"Don't be afraid," I said. "The storm will soon be over."

"Yes, yes."

I rested my head on the pillow and lay still with the

eerie feeling that the mocking imp was fulfilling my last wish. I had wanted a hotel to myself—and I had it. I had dreamed of a woman coming, like Ruth to Boaz, to my room—a woman had come. Each time the lightning flashed, my eyes met hers. She stared at me intently, as silent as a witch casting a spell. I feared the woman more than I did the hurricane. I had visited Havana once and, there, found the forces of darkness still in possession of their ancient powers. Not even the dead were left in peace—their bones were dug up. At night I had heard the screams of cannibals and the cries of maidens whose blood was sprinkled on the altars of idolaters. She came from there. I wanted to pronounce an incantation against the evil eye and pray to the spirits who have the final word not to let this hag overpower me. Something in me cried out: *Shaddai,* destroy Satan. Meanwhile, the thunder crashed, the seas roared and broke with watery laughter. The walls of my room turned scarlet. In the hellish glare the Cuban witch crouched low like an animal ready to seize its prey—mouth open, showing rotted teeth; matted hair, black on her arms and legs; and feet covered with carbuncles and bunions. Her nightgown had slipped down, and her wrinkled breasts sagged weightlessly. Only the snout and tail were missing.

I must have slept. In my dream I entered a town of steep, narrow streets and barred shutters, under the murky light of an eclipse, in the silence of a Black Sabbath. Catholic funeral processions followed one after the other endlessly, with crosses and coffins, halberds and burning torches. Not one but many corpses were being carried to the graveyard—a complete tribe annihilated. Incense burned. Moaning voices cried a song of utter grief. Swiftly, the coffins changed and took on the form of phylacteries, black and shiny, with knots and thongs. They divided into many compartments—coffins for twins, triplets, quadruplets, quintuplets . . .

. . .

I opened my eyes. Somebody was sitting on my bed—the Cuban woman. She began to talk thickly in her broken English.

"Do not fear. I won't hurt you. I am a human being, not a beast. My back is broken. But I was not born this way. I fell off a table when I was a child. My mother was too poor to take me to the doctor. My father, he no good, always drunk. He go with bad women, and my mother, she work in a tobacco factory. She cough out her lungs. Why do you shake? A hunchback is not contagious. You will not catch it from me. I have a soul like anyone else—men desire me. Even my boss. He trust me and leave me here in the hotel alone. You are a Jew, eh? He is also a Jew . . . from Turkey. He can speak—how do you say it?—Arabic. He marry a German Señora, but she is a Nazi. Her first husband was a Nazi. She curse the boss and try to poison him. He sue her but the judge is on her side. I think she bribe him—or give him something else. The boss, he has to pay her—how do you call it?—alimony."

"Why did he marry her in the first place?" I asked, just to say something.

"Well, he love her. He is very much a man, red blood, you know. You have been in love?"

"Yes."

"Where is the Señora? Did you marry her?"

"No. They shot her."

"Who?"

"Those same Nazis."

"Uh-huh . . . and you were left alone?"

"No, I have a wife."

"Where is your wife?"

"In New York."

"And you are true to her, eh?"

"Yes, I'm faithful."

"Always?"

"Always."

"One time to have fun is all right."

"No, my dear, I want to live out my life honestly."

"Who cares what you do? No one see."

"God sees."

"Well, if you speak of God, I go. But you are a liar. If I not a cripple, you no speak of God. He punish such lies, you pig!"

She spat on me, then got off the bed, and slammed the door behind her. I wiped myself off immediately, but her spittle burned me as if it were hot. I felt my forehead puffing up in the darkness, and my skin itched with a drawing sensation, as if leeches were sucking my blood. I went into the bathroom to wash myself. I wet a towel for a compress and wrapped it around my forehead. I had forgotten about the hurricane. It had stopped without my noticing. I went to sleep, and when I woke up again it was almost noon. My nose was stopped up, my throat was tight, my knees ached. My lower lip was swollen and had broken out in a large cold sore. My clothes were still on the floor, soaking in a huge puddle. The insects that had come in for refuge the night before were clamped to the wall, dead. I opened the window. The air blowing in was cool, though still humid. The sky was an autumn gray and the sea leaden, barely rocking under its own heaviness. I managed to dress and go downstairs. Behind the desk stood the hunchback, pale, thin, with her hair drawn back, and a glint in her black eyes. She wore an old-fashioned blouse edged with yellowed lace. She glanced at me mockingly. "You have to move out," she said. "The boss call and tell me to lock up the hotel."

"Isn't there a letter for me?"

"No letter."

"Please give me my bill."

"No bill."

The Cuban woman looked at me crookedly—a witch who had failed in her witchcraft, a silent partner of the demons surrounding me and of their cunning tricks.

Translated by Joel Blocker

Three Tales

I

There were three in the circle: Zalman the glazier, Meyer the eunuch, and Isaac Armshinover. Their meeting place was the Radzyminer study house where they visited daily to tell each other stories. Meyer was only present two weeks out of every month; being one of those whom the Talmud calls periodic madmen, he was out of his mind the other two. On nights when the full moon shone, Meyer paced up and down in the study house, rubbing his hands together, and muttering to himself. Though tall, his shoulders were so stooped he looked like a hunchback. His bony face was as smooth, or perhaps even smoother than a woman's. He had a long chin, high forehead, crooked nose. His eyes were those of a scholar. It was said that he knew the Talmud by heart. When he was not deranged, he peppered his talk with Hassidic proverbs and quotations from learned books. He had known the old rabbi of Kotsk and remembered him well. Both summer and winter, he dressed in an alpaca gabardine that reached to his ankles, wore mules and white stockings on his feet, and two skullcaps, one in the front and one in the back on his head; on top of them he put his silk hat. Though already an old man, Meyer had straight-hanging earlocks and a head of black hair. When he was in his sick periods, he apparently didn't eat, but the other half of the month fed on oatmeal porridge and chicken soup brought to the study house by pious women. He slept in a dark alcove at the house of a teacher.

It being the end of the month and a moonless night, Meyer the eunuch was rational. Opening a bone snuffbox, he took a pinch of tobacco mixed with ether and alcohol. He then offered pinches to Zalman the glazier and Isaac Amshinover, even though they had their own snuffboxes. So absorbed was he in his own thoughts that he scarcely heard what Zalman was saying. Wrinkling his brow, he pulled with his thumb and index finger at his beardless chin.

Isaac Amshinover's hair had not turned entirely gray; here and there traces of red were still to be seen in his eyebrows, earlocks and beard. Reb Isaac suffered from trachoma and wore dark glasses; he supported himself on a cane that had once belonged to Rabbi Chazkele of Kuzmir. Reb Isaac swore that he had been offered a large sum of money for the cane. But who would think of selling a stick that had known the hand of so saintly a rabbi? Reb Isaac earned his living with that cane. Women who were having difficult pregnancies borrowed it; it was also used to cure children suffering from scarlet fever, whooping cough, and croup, and was reputed to be helpful in exorcising dybbuks, stopping hiccups, and locating buried treasures. Reb Isaac did not lay the cane down even when praying. Saturdays and holidays, however, he locked it in the lectern. At the moment it was firmly clasped in his hairy, blue-veined hands. Reb Isaac had a weak heart, bad lungs, and defective kidneys. The Hasidim remarked that he would have been dead if he hadn't had Reb Chazkele's cane.

Zalman the glazier, a tall, broad-shouldered man, had a bushy beard the color of pepper and eyebrows as thick as brushes. Though eighty years old, he still drank two tumblers of vodka daily. For breakfast he had an onion, a radish, a two pound loaf of bread, and a pitcher of water. Zalman's wife, born crippled, was half mute, and could use neither her arms nor her legs. In her youth, Zalman had transported her to the ritual bath in a wheelbarrow. This broken shell of a woman had borne him eight sons and daughters. Zalman no longer worked at his craft because he received a pension of twelve rubles a month from his oldest son, a wealthy man. He and his wife lived in a small room which had a balcony that was reached by a ladder. Zalman did his own cooking and fed his wife like a baby. He even emptied the chamber pots.

Tonight he was telling of the time when he had lived in Radoshitz and traveled from village to village bearing a wooden frame loaded with glass on his back.

"Are there any real frosts today?" he inquired. "I wouldn't give you two kopeks for what they consider a freeze now. They think it's winter when there's ice on the Vistula. In my day the cold began just after the Feast of Tabernacles and at Passover you could still cross the river on foot. It was so cold then the trunks of oak trees burst. Wolves used to steal into Radoshitz at night and run off with chickens. Their eyes shone like candles. Their howling would drive you crazy. Once it hailed stones as big as goose eggs. They broke the shingles on the roofs. Some of the hail fell through the chimneys into the pots. I remember a storm when living fish and little animals fell from the sky. You could see them crawling in the gutters."

"How come there was fish in the sky?" Isaac Amshinover asked.

"Don't the clouds drink from the rivers? In one of the

villages near Radoshitz a snake dropped down. The fall killed it, but before it died it crawled into a well. The peasants were afraid to touch it; the rotting carcass made the most awful stink."

"There are many similar occurrences mentioned in the *Midrash Talpioth,*" interrupted Meyer the eunuch.

"What do I need the *Midrash Talpioth* for? I've seen it all with my own eyes. Nowadays there aren't many highwaymen. But in my time the forests were infested with them. They lived in caves. My father remembered seeing the king of them all, the notorious bandit Dobosh. Everyone was scared stiff of him. But he was only a figurehead; his mother was the power behind the throne. She was ninety years old, and she planned out everything, told them where and how to rob, how to hide the loot and where to get rid of it. She was also a witch and that's why everyone was frightened of her. She'd see someone, mumble a few words and down he fell with a burning fever. You probably never heard what happened between her and Rabbi Leib Saras. She was still young and lusty at the time, a shameless harlot. Well, the rabbi liked to go into the woods and immerse himself in a pool there before saying his prayers. One morning he looked up and saw the Dobosh woman standing naked before him with her unloosened hair falling down her back. When he cried out the Holy Name, a whirlwind caught hold of her and carried her to the top of a tree. 'Rabbi, marry me,' she called out from the branch from which she was sitting, 'and we'll rule the world together.' "

"What a brazen female," Isaac Amshinover said.

"There's no mention of the story in the *Community of the Hasidim,*" Meyer the eunuch remarked.

"*The Community of the Hasidim* doesn't contain everything. I had an encounter with a warlock myself. It happened in a forest just outside one of the villages near Radoshitz. It was a clear day and I'd been toting glass as usual. The night before I'd slept in a granary. But I always went home for the Sabbath. I was walking along deep in thought when suddenly I saw the tiniest man; he was even smaller than a dwarf. I swear he wasn't any bigger than my arm. I looked at him and I couldn't figure out what he was. He was dressed like the gentry in a green coat, feathered hat, and red boots. In his hand he carried a hunter's leather bag. It seems to me that he was also bearing a rifle—you know the small kind boys carry on the Feast of Omer. I just stood and gawked. Even if he was a midget or a freak what was he doing walking by himself? I stopped to let him pass by, but he stopped, too. When I started to walk, he walked beside me. How could he take such long steps with such short legs, I asked myself. Well, it was clear enough that he was one of the devil's people. I recited, 'Hear, O Israel,' and *'Shaddai,* destroy Satan,' but it didn't do any good. Laughing, he aimed his rifle at me. Things looked bad, and so when I caught sight of a stone, I picked it up and heaved it at him. The guffaw he let loose made me shiver. Then he stuck out his tongue. You know how long it was? Right down to his navel."

"Didn't he hurt you?"

"No, he ran away."

"Were you wearing a charm?"

"I had a bag around my neck in which there was the tooth of a wolf and a talisman blessed by the saintly rabbi of Kozhenitz. I started wearing it when I was a child."

"Well, that must have been helpful."

"How do you know that it was a warlock?" Meyer the eunuch asked. "It could have been an imp or a mock demon."

"I found out his story later. His father, a rich landowner, left him his manor, but the boy got interested in witchcraft. He knew how to make himself small or large, could change himself into a cat or dog or whatever he pleased. He lived with an old servant who was deaf as a wall and did his cooking for him. He had more money than he knew what to do with. It was his wife's death that drove him to magic. Sometimes he used his sorcery to help people. But not often. He preferred to make fun of the villagers and frighten them."

"What happened to him?" Isaac Amshinover asked.

"I don't know. He was still alive when I moved away from Radoshitz. You know what happens to such people. In the end they fall into the bottomless pit."

II

There was silence when Zalman the glazier finished speaking. Then Isaac Amshinover, having taken out his pipe and lit it, inquired: "What's so amazing about a Gentile sorcerer? There were sorcerers even in Egypt. Didn't the Egyptian magicians vie with Moses? But I knew of a Jewish one. Well, maybe not really a sorcerer, but someone who did business with the evil ones. His father-in-law was an acquaintance of mine, Mordecai Liskover. A very wealthy man and learned, too. He had five sons and a daughter. The girl was named Pesha and he was crazy about her. His sons all married well. Half the town belonged to them. He had a watermill that was always busy. The peasants came there for miles around to line up with their carts. They thought that flour ground in his mill was blessed. Mordecai wanted to find Pesha—she was his youngest—the finest possible husband. He gave her a large dowry and promised to support her husband and her for the rest of their lives. So he went to a yeshiva and asked the principal to show him his smartest student. 'That's him,' the principal said, indicating a not very large boy. 'His name is Zeinvele. He may look small but he has more brains than all the scholars of Poland put together.' What more could one want? The boy was an orphan and was supported by the town. He was taken to Reb Mordecai's house, dressed up like a king, and given the betrothal papers to sign. Then Zeinvele was put up at an inn because it is forbidden for a man to live in the same house as his fiancée. He fed on squabs and marzipan. When he came to the study house, all the other boys tried to engage him in learned conversation, but he didn't say much. He was the sort of person to whom a word is like a gold coin. But what he did say was worth hearing. I can still see him as he was then, small, light-skinned, and beardless; standing in the study house reeling off an entire page of the Commentaries from memory. Reb Mordecai gave him clothes a size too large for him expecting him to grow into them. His gabardine dragged along the floor. Actually he never did get any bigger, but that's another story. When he discussed learned matters, he spoke very softly; he didn't speak about worldly matters at all, merely said yes or no when he was asked something. Sometimes he just nodded his head. He always sat by himself in some remote corner of the study house. The boys complained that he wasn't friendly. When he prayed, he stood looking out the window and didn't turn his head until he was finished. The window faced Synagogue Street and overlooked the cemetery.

"Well, so he wasn't interested in the world. The town respected him. Why shouldn't they have? He was to be Reb Mordecai's son-in-law. Then an odd thing happened. One night a boy walked into the study house looking as white as chalk. 'What's happened to you?' the others asked. 'Who scared you?' At first the fellow refused to answer. Then he took three of his friends aside, and after swearing them to secrecy, told them the following: While he was walking in the synagogue yard, he'd caught sight of Zeinvele standing near the poorhouse making curious motions with his hands. He knew that Zeinvele never studied at night. And anyway what was he doing near the poorhouse? Everyone knew the poorhouse was a dangerous place; the cleansing board on which the corpses were washed was kept leaning against its door.

Two paths led to it; one from the town's outskirts and the other from the cemetery. The boy thought that perhaps Zeinvele being a stranger had lost his way, and called out, 'Zeinvele, what are you doing there?' No sooner did he say this than Zeinvele began to shrink until he became so small there was nothing left of him but a puff of smoke. Finally, even the smoke disappeared. The amazing thing was that the boy hadn't died of fright. 'Are you sure the tassels on your ritual garment are all there?' the other fellows asked. 'Maybe one of the letters in your mezuzah is missing?' It was clear to all of them that it was really one of the evil ones in disguise as Zeinvele. The incident was kept a secret. The town would have been saved a lot of trouble had it not been.

"The wedding was a noisy one. Musicians were brought from Lublin, Yukele the jester from far away Kovle. But Zeinvele didn't participate in the usual discussion of the Torah with his fellow students, nor pass around the cookies and drinks. He just sat at the head of the table as if he weren't there. He had such thick eyebrows it was difficult to tell whether he was meditating or asleep. There were those who even thought he was deaf. But all things pass away quickly. Zeinvele was married and moved in with his father-in-law. Now he sat in his corner of the study house reading the Tractate on Ablutions prescribed for newly married men. It wasn't very long, however, before Pesha started complaining that he didn't act like a young husband should. Though he did come to her bed after she had been to the ritual bath, he acted as cold as ice. Early one morning Pesha ran weeping into her mother's bedroom. 'What's happened, daughter?' Well, according to Pesha, she'd been to the ritual bath the evening before and Zeinvele had gotten in bed with her. But when she'd glanced over at his bed expecting to find it empty, she'd found a second Zeinvele lying there. She'd become so frightened that she'd crawled under the featherbed and refused to come out.

As soon as it was light, Zeinvele had gotten up and gone to his study. 'Daughter, you're imagining things,' her mother told her. But Pesha solemnly swore that she was telling the truth. 'Mother, I'm terrified,' she screamed. And her anxiety was so great that she fainted.

"How long can such matters be concealed? There really were two Zeinveles. Everybody realized it. Grabovitz did have a few sceptics who as usual with that sort made light of the matter. You know their sort of explanation: it was a hallucination, a fantasy, a morbid tendency, but for all of that, they were just as scared as everyone else. Zeinvele would be locked in his room lying asleep in his bed, but also he'd be wandering around the synagogue yard, or the market place. Sometimes he'd appear in the antechamber of the study house and stand there motionless near the wash basin until somebody realized that he was only the false Zeinvele. When that happened, he floated off and disintegrated like a cobweb.

"For some time no one said anything about this to Zeinvele. He may have had no idea himself of what was going on. But finally his wife Pesha refused to be quiet any longer. She announced that she would not sleep in the same room with him. They had to hire a night watchman. His father-in-law, thinking that Zeinvele would become alarmed and deny everything, confronted him with the facts, but he just stood there like a statue, not saying a word. So Reb Mordecai took him to the rabbi of Turisk who completely covered Zeinvele's body with talismans. But when Zeinvele returned home, nothing had changed. At night his mother-in-law locked the bedroom door from the outside and propped a heavy chair against it, but in spite of this Zeinvele continued to wander. At the sight of him dogs growled and horses reared in terror. The women didn't dare go out at night without putting on two aprons—one in the front and one in the rear. One evening a young townswoman went to the ritual bath and, after being washed down by the attendant in the anteroom, entered the bath chamber itself. As she descended the steps, she saw someone splashing around in the water. The candle in the room was flickering so badly she couldn't make out who it was. When she came closer and saw it was Zeinvele, she screamed and fainted. If the attendant hadn't been nearby, she would have drowned. The real Zeinvele happened to be in the study house at the moment. I was there myself and saw him. But actually it had become impossible to know which was the real Zeinvele and which the phantom. The townsboys now began to say that Zeinvele visited the ritual bath to peek at the naked women. Pesha said that she would no longer live with him. If he had had parents they would have shipped him home, but where can you send an orphan? His father-in-law took him to the rabbi and gave him a hundred gulden to divorce Pesha. I was one of the witnesses to the divorce papers. Pesha couldn't stop crying but Zeinvele sat quietly on the bench as if none of this concerned him. He seemed to be sleeping. The rabbi looked at the wall to make sure that Zeinvele was casting a shadow. Demons don't, you know. After the divorce Zeinvele was put in a cart Reb Mordecai had hired and taken to a yeshiva. The cart was driven by a Gentile, no Jew being willing to accept the job. When the coachman returned he claimed the Jews had bewitched him. His horses, though he had kept on whipping them, had refused to pull the wagon. He pointed to his team. They had left the marketplace healthy and had returned sick and wasted. Mordecai Liskover had to pay him damages. I was told that both horses died soon after.

"Even though Zeinvele was gone, people still continued to see him. They met him after dark at the flour mill, at the river where the women washed their linens, near the outhouse. Several times he was seen in the middle of the night standing like a chimney sweep on top of a roof. Students stopped studying in the evening knowing that Zeinvele liked to wander in the synagogue yard. Then when Pesha remarried, he disappeared. No one knows what happened to him. Somebody who visited the yeshiva he was supposed to have been taken to, said he never got there."

"Do you mean to imply by your story that the talismans of the rabbi of Turisk are ineffective?" Zalman the glazier asked.

"Not every talisman works."

"All of the rabbi of Kozhenitz's talismans do."

"How many such rabbis are there?"

III

Meyer the eunuch pulled at his naked chin. His left eye shut tightly and his right eye stared. Though he was now in his good period, he laughed insanely.

"What's so terribly novel about all that? We all know sorcerers exist. Maybe Zeinvele was innocent. He could have been bewitched. He might have been a mooncalf or a freak. Besides when a man sleeps, his spirit leaves him. Usually you can't see the spirit leaving the body, but sometimes it's visible. There was a woman in Krasnotstav who emitted a green light when she slept. When they put out the lamp, the wall near her bed lit up. I also know of a cat which after it had been drowned by a coachman came back to bite his nose. Everyone recognized the creature. It started to spit and mew and would have clawed out his eyes if he hadn't covered his face with his hands. The body dies but the spirit lives on. I speak of the spirit not the soul. Not everything has a soul. One has to have a certain merit to be worthy of having a soul. But even animals possess a spirit.

"Let me tell you about the Jenukah. You may not know it, Reb Zalman, but Jenukah means child in Aramaic. The Jenukah, as he was called, was the sixth child of Zekele, an ordinary water carrier. There didn't seem to be anything unusual about him when he was born. He was circumcised just like his brothers. His real name was Zaddock, after his grandfather. However his mother began to complain that the baby was growing too fast. But who listens to such talk from a woman? Every mother thinks her child is the most wonderful. But three months later, the whole town was gossiping about Zekele's amazing child. At five months the boy was talking; at six months he walked. When he was a year old, they wrapped him in a prayer shawl and took him to school. We have newspapers nowadays; in those times the Jews didn't. The boy was written up in one of the Gentile papers. The governor sent a delegation to interview him and make a report. The town doctor sent copies of his findings to Warsaw and Petersburg. All kinds of university professors and experts visited the town. They didn't believe that little Zaddock was only fifteen months old, but there were plenty of witnesses. The birth had been registered at the town hall and the midwife had kept her own record. The man who performed the circumcision, the rabbi who held the baby at the ceremony, and the woman who had handed the child to the latter, gave corroborating evidence. Zaddock had to be taken out of school. To begin with, all of the furor interrupted the classroom routine, and in the second place he was just too bright for the other children. He took one look at the alphabet and knew it by heart. When he was eighteen months old, he was deep in the study of the Pentateuch and the Commentaries of Rashi. At two, he began his study of the Gemara.

"I know it's hard to believe but I myself can attest to its truth. Zekele, who was our water carrier, used to bring the boy to our house to show him off. At three, Zaddock preached in the synagogue. He opened his mouth and out spouted the Torah. Anyone who wasn't present on that great Sabbath before Passover doesn't know what a miracle is. Even a blind man could see that the child must be the reincarnation of some ancient saint. At four he was as tall as an adolescent and began to sprout a beard. That was when they started calling him the Jenukah after the holy child in the *vohar*. But we'd sit here all night, if I told you everything about him. Why elaborate? At five Zaddock had a long beard. It was time for him to have a wife but who would marry his daughter to a five-year-old boy? Anyway, Zaddock was completely immersed in the Cabala. The community gave him a room and Zaddock spent his time there studying the *ohar,* the *Tree of Life,* the *Book of Creation,* and the *Book of the Esoterics.* People offered to give him money to pray for them, but he refused. There are unbelievers everywhere, but whoever looked at Zaddock no longer doubted. On the Sabbath he sat at the head of the table presiding like a rabbi, and only a few select people were allowed to be with him. Even these learned men found it difficult to understand his profound exegesis. He had a special genius for translating the alphabet into numbers and creating acrostics. Sometimes, when he was in a forgetful mood, he would speak entirely in Aramaic. His handwriting was such that what he wrote had to be read in a mirror.

"Then suddenly the news came that the Jenukah was engaged. It seemed that in the neighboring town there was a rich man, seven of whose children had died before they were three. His only surviving child was a girl whom he dressed in white linen and called Altele, Little Old One, to fool the Angel of Death. I don't remember the man's name but he was advised by some rabbi to marry his daughter to the Jenukah. The girl was fourteen. The Jenukah at five looked like a man of forty. They didn't think he would consent, but he did. I went to the engagement party myself. The girl looked as if she were marrying her father. They signed the contract and broke plates for good luck. Throughout the ceremony, the Jenukah kept mumbling to himself. He was probably receiving instructions from Heaven. I don't know why, but both sides were anxious to get the wedding over with quickly. The engagement took place on Chanukah and the wedding was set for the Sabbath after Pentecost. It took place not in the bride's town, as was the custom, but in the bridegroom's, because it was feared that the sight of the Jenukah would be too much for people not accustomed to him. Eighty rabbis, all specialists in miracles, were invited. They came not only from Poland proper, but also from Volhynia and Galicia. Many freethinkers, doctors, and philosophers also attended. Among the guests were the governor of Lublin and I think the vice governor, too. Barren women came, hoping that their presence there would cure them. Someone brought a girl whose hiccups sounded like the barking of a dog. She recited whole chapters from the Mishnah and when she sang from the prayer book, her voice was deep as a cantor's. The inns were packed, word having got about that whoever attended the wedding would never be condemned to the fires of Gehenna. Many visitors had to sleep in the streets. The stores were emptied so quickly of food that wagons had to be sent to Lublin for more provisions.

"Now listen to this. Three days before the wedding the Jenukah's mother entered his room to bring him a cup of tea. She took one look and saw that his beard was as white as snow. His face was yellow and as lined as parchment. She called the rest of the family. Though a child not yet six-years-old, he had turned into a hoary sage. A crowd gathered, but was not let into the house. Someone informed the bride's parents of what had happened. But they didn't dare break the engagement.

"The day of his wedding at the feast for the young men, the Jenukah divulged mystery upon mystery. When the time came to lift the veil from the bride, the crowd surged forward wildly. The groom's attendants did not escort, but carried him. He seemed to be completely debilitated. When the bride saw that the Jenukah was an old man, she began to weep and protest, but finally was quieted. I was there myself and saw everything. When the bride and groom were served the golden soup, they scarcely touched it, though both had fasted. The musicians were afraid to play. The jester didn't open his mouth. The Jenukah sat at the head of the table, holding his hands over his eyes. I don't remember whether he danced with the bride or not. He lived only three months more. Each day he became whiter and more shrunken. He drooped and melted like a wax candle. The last few days of his life no strangers were allowed in his room, not even the doctor. The Jenukah, dressed in a white robe, and wearing his prayer shawl and phylacteries, sat like an ancient saint not of this world. He stopped eating. When they gave him a spoonful of soup, he couldn't swallow it. I happened to be out of town when the Jenukah died, but I was told that at the moment of death his face shone like the sun. You couldn't pass near the house without feeling the heat of his saintly radiance. An apothecary who came to ridicule him became a believer and put peas in his boots as penance. A priest was converted. Those who were at the deathbed heard the beating of an angel's wings. The Jenukah had ordered that his shroud be made while he was still living. He died with the finishing of the last stitch.

"When the men from the Burial Society came, they found almost no body left to wash. With such saints, even matter turns into spirit. The pallbearers said that the corpse was lighter than a bird's. The eulogies took three days to complete. Afterwards, the community raised money to build a chapel on the grave in which was to burn an eternal light. Zekele was provided with a pension. One should receive something for being the father of such a son."

"What happened to the widow?" Zalman the glazier asked.

"She never remarried."

"Was there a child?"

"Ridiculous."

"Did she live long?"

"She's still alive."

"Who was the Jenukah really?" Isaac Amshinover wanted to know.

"How can you tell? Sometimes a soul is sent down from Heaven which has to fulfill its mission in a hurry. Why are some babies born who live only one day? Every soul descends to earth to correct some error. It's the same with souls as with manuscripts; there may be few or many errors. Everything that's wrong on this earth has to be corrected. The world of evil is the world of correction. This is the answer to all questions."

Translated by Ruth Whitman
and Cecil Hemley

Zeidlus the Pope

I

In ancient times there always lived a few men in every generation whom I, the Evil One, could not corrupt in the usual manner. It was impossible to tempt them to murder, lechery, robbery. I could not even get them to cease studying the Law. In one way only could the inner passions of these righteous souls be reached: through their vanity.

Zeidel Cohen was such a man. In the first place, he had the protection of noble ancestors: he was a descendant of Rashi whose genealogy reached back to King David. In the second place, he was the greatest scholar in the whole province of Lublin. At five he had studied the Gemara and Commentaries; at seven he had memorized the Laws of Marriage and Divorce; at nine, he had preached a sermon, quoting from so many books that even the oldest among the scholars were confounded. He was completely at home in the Bible; in Hebrew grammar he had no equal. What is more he studied constantly: summer and winter alike he rose with the morning star and began to read. As he seldom left his rooms for air and did no physical labor, he had little appetite and slept lightly. He had neither the desire nor the patience to converse with friends. Zeidel loved only one thing: books. The moment he entered the study house, or his own home for that matter, he ran straight to the shelves and began to leaf through volumes, sucking into his lungs the dust from ancient pages. So strong was his power of memory that one look at some passage in the Talmud, at some new interpretation in a Commentary and he could remember it forever.

Nor could I gain power over Zeidel through his body. His limbs were hairless; by seventeen his pointed skull was bald; only a few hairs grew on his chin. His face was long and stiff; three or four drops of perspiration always hung on the high forehead; his crooked nose was strangely naked, like that of a man who is accustomed to wearing glasses but has just taken them off. He had reddish eyelids behind which lay a pair of yellow, melancholy eyes. His hands and feet were small and white as a woman's, though as he never visited the ritual bath it was not known if he was a eunuch or an androgyne. But since his father, Reb Sander Cohen, was extremely rich, himself a scholar and a man of some note, he saw to it that his son made a match befitting the family. The bride came from a rich Warsaw family and was a beauty. Until the day of the wedding she had never seen the groom, and when she did set eyes upon him, just before he covered her face with the veil, it was already too late. She married him and was never able to conceive. She spent her time sitting in the rooms her father-in-law had allotted to her, knitting stockings, reading storybooks, listening to the large wall-clock with its gilded chains and weights ring out the half-hours—patiently waiting, it seemed, for the minutes to become days, the days years, until the time should come for her to go to sleep in the old Janov cemetery.

Zeidel possessed such intensity that all his surroundings acquired his character. Though a servant took care of his rooms, the furniture was always covered with dust; the windows, hung with heavy drapes, seemed never to have been opened; thick rugs covered the floors muffling his footsteps so that it sounded as if a spirit, not a man, were walking there. Zeidel received regularly an allowance from his father, but he never spent a penny on himself. He hardly knew what a coin looked like, yet he was a miser and never took a poor man home for a Sabbath meal. He never took the trouble to make friends, and since neither he nor his wife ever invited a guest, no one knew what the interior of their house looked like.

Untroubled by passions or the need to make a living, Zeidel studied diligently. He first devoted himself to the Talmud and the Commentaries. Then he delved into the Cabala and soon became an expert on the occult, even writing tracts on *The Angel Raziel* and *The Book of Creation*. Naturally he was well acquainted with *The Guide for the Perplexed,* the *Kuzari,* and other philosophical works. One day he happened to acquire a copy of the Vulgate. Soon he had learned Latin, and he began to read extensively in the forbidden literature, borrowing many books from a scholarly priest who lived in Janov. In short, just as his father had accumulated gold coins all his life, so Zeidel accumulated knowledge. By the time he was thirty-five no one in all Poland could equal him in learning. Just then I was ordered to tempt him to sin.

"Persuade Zeidel to sin?" I asked. "What kind of sin? He doesn't enjoy food, is indifferent to women, and never has anything to do with business." I had tried heresy before, without success. I remembered our last conversation:

"Let's assume that, God forbid, there is no God," he

had answered me. "So what? Then His non-being itself is divine. Only God, the Cause of all Causes, could have the power not to exist."

"If there is no Creator, why do you pray and study?" I continued.

"What else should I do?" he asked in return. "Drink vodka and dance with Gentile girls?"

To tell the truth I had no answer to that, so I left him in peace. His father had since died, and now I was ordered to devote myself to him again. With not the slightest idea of how to begin, I descended to Janov with a heavy heart.

II

I discovered after some time that Zeidel possessed one human weakness: haughtiness. He had much more than that sliver of vanity which the Law permits the scholar.

I laid my plans. In the middle of one night, I woke him from his slumber and said: "Do you know, Zeidel, that you are better versed than any rabbi in Poland in the fine print of the Commentaries?"

"Certainly I know it," he replied. "But who else does? Nobody."

"Do you know, Zeidel, that you outshine all other grammarians in your knowledge of Hebrew?" I continued. "Are you aware that you know more of the Cabala than was divulged to Reb Chaim Vital? Do you know that you are a greater philosopher than Maimonides?"

"Why are you telling me these things?" Zeidel asked, wondering.

"I'm telling you because it's not right that a great man such as you, a master of the Torah, an encyclopedia of knowledge, should be buried in a God-forsaken village such as this where no one pays the slightest attention to you, where the townspeople are coarse and the rabbi an ignoramus, with a wife who has no understanding of your true worth. You are a pearl lost in sand, Reb Zeidel."

"Well?" he asked. "What can I do? Should I go about singing my own praises?"

"No, Reb Zeidel. That wouldn't help you. The town would only call you a madman."

"What do you advise, then?"

"Promise me not to interrupt and I'll tell you. You know the Jews have never honored their leaders: They grumbled about Moses; rebelled against Samuel; threw Jeremiah into a ditch; and murdered Zacharias. The Chosen People hate greatness. In a great man, they sense a rival to Jehovah, so they love only the petty and mediocre. Their thirty-six saints are all shoemakers and water-carriers. The Jewish laws are concerned mainly with a drop of milk falling into a pot of meat or with an egg laid on a holiday. They have deliberately corrupted Hebrew, degraded the ancient texts. Their Talmud makes King David into a provincial rabbi advising women about menstruation. The way they reason, the smaller the greater, the uglier the prettier. Their rule is: The closer one is to dust, the nearer one is to God. So you can see, Reb Zeidel, why they find you a thumb in the eye—you with your erudition, wealth, fine breeding, brilliant perceptions, and extraordinary memory."

"Why do you tell me all these things?" Zeidel asked.

"Reb Zeidel, listen to me: what you must do is become a Christian. The Gentiles are the antithesis of the Jews. Since their God is a man, a man can be a God to them. Gentiles admire greatness of any kind and love the men who possess it: men of great pity or great cruelty, great builders or great destroyers, great virgins or great harlots, great sages or great fools, great rulers or great rebels, great believers or great infidels. They don't care what else a man is: if he is great, they idolize him. Therefore, Reb Zeidel, if you want honor, you must embrace their faith. And don't worry about God. To One so mighty and sublime the earth and its inhabitants are no more than a swarm of gnats. He doesn't care whether men pray to Him in a synagogue or a church, fast from Sabbath to Sabbath or bloat themselves with pork. He is too exalted to notice these puny creatures who delude themselves thinking that they are the crown of Creation."

"Does that mean God did not give the Torah to Moses at Sinai?" Zeidel asked.

"What? God open his heart to a man born of woman?"

"And Jesus was not His son?"

"Jesus was a bastard from Nazareth."

"Is there no reward or punishment?"

"No."

"Then what is there?" Zeidel asked me, fearful and confused.

"There is something that exists, but it has no existence," I answered in the manner of the philosophers.

"Is there no hope then ever to know the truth?" Zeidel asked in despair.

"The world is not knowable and there is no truth," I replied, turning his question around. "Just as you can't learn the taste of salt with your nose, the smell of balsam with your ear, or the sound of a violin with your tongue, it's impossible for you to grasp the world with your reason."

"With what can you grasp it?"

"With your passions—some small part of it. But you, Reb Zeidel, have only one passion: pride. If you destroy that too, you'll be hollow, a void."

"What should I do?" Zeidel asked, baffled.

"Tomorrow, go to the priest and tell him that you want to become one of them. Then sell your goods and property. Try to convince your wife to change her religion—if she's willing, good; if not, the loss is small. The Gentiles will make you a priest and a priest is not allowed to have a wife. You'll continue to study, to wear a long coat and skullcap. The only difference will be that instead of being stuck away in a remote village among Jews who hate you and your accomplishments, praying in a sunken hole of a study house where beggars scratch themselves behind the stove, you will live in a large city, preach in a luxurious church where an organ will play, and where your congregation will consist of men of stature whose wives will kiss your hand. If you excel and throw together some hodgepodge about Jesus and his mother the Virgin, they will make you a bishop, and later a cardinal—and God willing, if everything goes well, they'll make you Pope one day. Then the Gentiles will carry you on a gilded chair like an idol and burn incense around you; and they'll kneel before your image in Rome, Madrid, and Crackow."

"What will my name be?" asked Zeidel.

"Zeidlus the First."

So great an impression did my words make that Zeidel started violently and sat up in bed. His wife awoke and asked why he wasn't sleeping. With some hidden instinct, she knew he was possessed by a great desire, and thought: Who knows, perhaps a miracle has happened. But Zeidel had already made up his mind to divorce her, so he told her to keep still and not ask any more questions. Putting on his slippers and robe, he went to his study, where he lit a wax candle and sat until dawn re-reading the Vulgate.

III

Zeidel did as I advised. He went to the priest and let him know that he wished to speak about matters of faith. Of course the Gentile was more than willing. What better merchandise is there for a priest than a Jewish soul? Anyway, to cut a long story short, priests and noblemen from the entire province promised Zeidel a great career in the Church; he quickly sold all his possessions, divorced his wife, let himself be baptized with holy water, and became a Christian. For the first time in his life, Zeidel was honored: the ecclesiastics made a big fuss over him, the noblemen lavished praise on him, their wives smiled benignly at him, and he was invited to their estates. The Bishop of Zamosc was his godfather. His name was changed from Zeidel son of Sander to Benedictus Janovsky—the surname in honor of the village where he had been born. Although Zeidel was not yet a priest or even a deacon, he ordered a black cassock from a tailor and hung a rosary and cross around his neck. For the time being, he lived in the priest's rectory, seldom venturing out because when he did Jewish schoolboys ran after him in the streets shouting, "Convert! Apostate!"

His Gentile friends had many different plans for him. Some advised him to go to a seminary and study; others recommended that he enter the Dominican priory in Lublin. Still others suggested he marry a wealthy local woman and become a squire. But Zeidel had little inclination to travel the usual road. He wanted greatness immediately. He knew that in the past many Jewish converts to Christianity had become famous by writing polemics against the Talmud—Petrus Alfonzo, Fablo Christiani of Montpelier, Paul de Santa Maria, Johann Baptista, Johann Pfefferkorn, to mention only a few. Zeidel decided to follow in their footsteps. Now that he had converted and Jewish children abused him in the streets, he suddenly discovered that he had never loved the Talmud. Its Hebrew was debased by Aramaic; its pilpul was dull, its legends improbable, and its Biblical Commentaries were far-fetched and full of sophistries.

Zeidel traveled to the seminary libraries in Lublin and Crackow to study the treatises written by Jewish converts. He soon discovered they were all much alike. The authors were ignorant, plagiarized from one another liberally, and all cited the same few anti-Gentile passages from the Talmud. Some of them had not even used their own words, had copied the work of others and signed their names. The real *Apologia Contra Talmudum* had yet to be written, and no one was better prepared to do such a work than he with his knowledge of philosophy and the Cabalistic mysteries. At the same time, Zeidel undertook to find fresh proofs in the Bible that the prophets had foreseen Jesus' birth, martyrdom, and resurrection; and to discover corroborative evidence for the Christian religion in logic, astronomy, and natural science. Zeidel's treatise would be for Christianity what Maimonides' *The Strong Hand* was for Judaism—and it would carry its author from Janov directly to the Vatican.

Zeidel studied, thought, wrote, sitting all day and half the night in libraries. From time to time he met Christian scholars and conversed with them in Polish and Latin. With the same fervor that he had studied Jewish books, he now studied the Christian texts. Soon he could recite whole chapters of the New Testament. He became an expert Latinist. After a while he was so thoroughly versed in Christian theology that the priests and monks were afraid to talk to him for with his erudition he found mistakes everywhere. Many times he was promised a seminary appointment but somehow he never got one. A post as librarian in Crackow which was to be his went to a relative of the governor instead. Zeidel began to realize that even among the Gentiles things were far from perfect. The clergy cared more for gold than for their God. Their sermons were full of errors. Most of the priests did not know Latin, but even in Polish their quotations were incorrect.

For years Zeidel worked on his treatise, but still it was not finished. His standards were so high that he was continually finding flaws, yet the more changes he made, the more he found were necessary. He wrote, crossed out, rewrote, threw away. His drawers were stuffed with manuscript pages, notes, references, but he could not bring his work to a conclusion. After years of effort, he was so fatigued that he could no longer distinguish between right and wrong, sense and nonsense, between what would please and what displease the Church. Nor did he believe any more in what is called truth and falsehood. Nevertheless he continued to ponder, to come up occasionally with a few new ideas. He consulted the Talmud so often in his work that once more he delved into its depths, scribbling notes on the margins of the pages, comparing all the different texts, hardly knowing whether he did so to find new accusations or simply out of habit. At times, he read books about witch trials, accounts of young women possessed by the devil, documents of the Inquisitions, whatever manuscripts he could find that described such events in various countries and epochs.

Gradually, the bag of gold coins that hung around his neck became lighter. His face turned yellow as parchment. His eyes dimmed. His hands trembled like an old man's. His cassock was stained and torn. His hope to become famous among the nations vanished. He came to regret his conversion. But the way back was blocked: first because he doubted all faiths now; second because it was the law of the land that a Christian who returned to Judaism should be burned at the stake.

One day while Zeidel was sitting, studying a faded manuscript in the library in Crackow, everything went dark before his eyes. At first he thought dusk had fallen and asked why the candles had not been lit. But when a monk told him that the day was still bright, he realized he had gone blind. Unable to return home alone, Zeidel had to be led by the monk. From that time on Zeidel lived in darkness. Fearing that his money would soon run out and he would be left without a groschen as well as without eyes, Zeidel decided, after much hesitation, to become a beggar outside the church of Crackow. "I have lost both this world and the world to come," he reasoned, "so why be haughty? If there is no way up, one must go down." Thus Zeidel son of Sander, or Benedictus Janovsky, took his place among the beggars on the steps of the great cathedral of Crackow.

In the beginning the priests and canons tried to help him. They wanted to put him into a cloister. But Zeidel had no wish to become a monk. He wanted to sleep alone in his garret, and to continue to carry his money bag under his shirt. Nor was he inclined to kneel before an altar. Occasionally a seminary student would stop to talk with him for a few minutes on scholarly matters. But in a short while, everyone forgot him. Zeidel hired an old woman to lead him to the church in the morning and home at night. She also brought him a bowl of groats each day. Good-hearted Gentiles threw him alms. He was even able to save some money, and the bag around his neck became heavy again. The other mendicants mocked him, but Zeidel never replied. For hours he kneeled on the steps, his bald skull uncovered, his eyes closed, his black robe buttoned to the chin. His lips never ceased shaking and murmuring. Passers-by thought he was praying to the Christian saints, but actually he was reciting the Gemara, the Mishnah, and the Psalms. The Gentile theology he had forgotten as quickly as he had learned it; what remained was what he had acquired in his youth. The street was full of tumult: wagons rolled by on the cobblestones; horses neighed; coachmen screamed with hoarse voices and cracked their whips; girls laughed and screeched; children cried; women quarreled, called one another names, uttered obscenities. Every once in a while Zeidel stopped murmuring, but only to doze with his head sunken into his chest. He no longer had any earthly desire, but one yearning still plagued him: to know the truth. Was there a Creator or was the world nothing but atoms and their combinations? Did the soul exist or was all thought mere reverberations of the brain? Was there a final accounting with reward and punishment? Was there a Substance or was the whole of existence nothing but imagination? The sun burned down on him, the rains soaked him, pigeons soiled him with their droppings, but he was impervious to everything. Now that he had lost his only passion, pride, nothing material mattered to him. Sometimes he asked himself: Is it possible that I am Zeidel the prodigy? Was my father Reb Sander, the leader of the community? Did I really have a wife once? Are there still some who knew me? It seemed to Zeidel that none of these things could be true. Such events had never happened, and if they had not, reality itself was one great illusion.

One morning when the old woman came to Zeidel's attic room to take him to the church, she found him ill. Waiting until he dozed off, she stealthily cut the bag of money from around his neck and left. In his stupor Zeidel knew he was being robbed, but he didn't care. His head lay as heavy as a stone on the straw pillow. His feet ached. His joints were filled with pain. His emaciated body was hot and hollow. Zeidel fell asleep, awoke, dozed off; then he awoke again with a start, unable to tell whether it was night or day. Out in the streets he heard voices, screams, stamping hoofs, ringing bells. It seemed to him some pagan multitude was celebrating a holiday with trumpets and drums, torches and wild beasts, lascivious dances, idolatrous sacrifices. "Where am I?" he asked himself. He could not remember the name of the city; he had even forgotten he was in Poland. He thought he might be in Athens, or Rome, or perhaps he was in Carthage. "In what age do I live?" he wondered. His fevered brain made him think it was hundreds of years before the Christian era. Soon he tired from too much thought. Only one question remained to perplex him: Are the Epicureans right? Am I really dying without any revelation? Am I about to be extinguished forever?

Suddenly I, the Tempter, materialized. Although blind, he saw me. "Zeidel," I said, "prepare yourself. The last hour has come."

"Is it you, Satan, Angel of Death?" Zeidel exclaimed joyously.

"Yes, Zeidel," I replied, "I have come for you. And it won't help you to repent or confess, so don't try."

"Where are you taking me?" he asked.

"Straight to Gehenna."

"If there is a Gehenna, there is also a God," Zeidel said, his lips trembling.

"This proves nothing," I retorted.

"Yes it does," he said. "If Hell exists, everything exists. If you are real, He is real. Now take me to where I belong. I am ready."

Drawing my sword I finished him off, took hold of his soul in my claws and, accompanied by a band of demons, flew to the nether world. In Gehenna the Angels of Destruction were raking up the coals. Two mocking imps stood at the threshold, half-fire and half-pitch, each with a three-cornered hat on his head, a whipping rod on his loins. They burst out laughing.

"Here comes Zeidlus the First," one said to the other, "the yeshiva boy who wanted to become Pope."

Translated by Joel Blocker
and Elizabeth Pollet

I Place My Reliance on No Man

I

From the day people began to talk about his becoming the rabbi at Yavrov, Rabbi Jonathan Danziger of Yampol didn't have a minute's peace. His Yampol enemies begrudged his going to the bigger city, though they couldn't wait for him to leave Yampol because they already had someone to take his place. The Yampol elders wanted the rabbi to leave Yampol without being able to go to Yavrov. They tried to ruin his chances for the Yavrov appointment by spreading rumors about him. They intended to treat him the way they had treated the previous rabbi: he was to leave town in disgrace riding in an ox-drawn cart. But why? What evil had he done? He had hurt no one's honor; he was invariably friendly to everyone. Yet they all had private grudges against him. One claimed that the rabbi gave a wrong interpretation of the Talmud; another had a son-in-law who wanted to take over the rabbi's position; a third thought Rabbi Jonathan should follow a Hasidic leader. The butchers whined that the rabbi found too many cows unkosher, the ritual slaughterer that the rabbi asked to check his knife twice a week. The bathhouse attendant complained because once, on the eve of a holy day, the rabbi had declared the ritual bath impure, and thus the women could not copulate with their husbands.

On Bridge Street the mob insisted that the rabbi spent too much time at his books, that he didn't pay attention to the common people. In taverns ruffians made fun of the way the rabbi shouted when reciting "Hear, O Israel," and how he spat when he mentioned the idols. The enlightened proved that the rabbi made mistakes in Hebrew grammar. The rabbi's wife was mocked by the ladies because she spoke in the accent of Great Poland and because she drank her chicory and coffee without sugar. There was nothing they didn't make fun of. They didn't like it when the rabbi's wife baked bread every Thursday rather than once every three weeks. They looked askance at the rabbi's daughter, Yentl the widow, who, they said, spent too much time knitting and embroidering. Before each Passover there was a row because of the Passover matzohs, and the rabbi's enemies ran to his house to break his windows. After Succoth, when many children fell ill, the pious matrons screamed that the rabbi hadn't cleansed the town of sins, that he had allowed the young women to go about with uncovered hair, and that the Angel of Death was thus punishing innocent infants with his sword. One way or another, every faction carped and found fault. With all this, the rabbi received the lowly salary of five gulden a week; he lived in the direst need.

As if he wasn't burdened enough with enemies, even his friends behaved like enemies. They relayed every petty accusation to him. The rabbi told them that this was a sin, quoting from the Talmud that gossip hurts all three parties: the gossiper, the one who receives the gossip, and the one gossiped about. It breeds anger, hatred, desecration of the Holy Name. The rabbi begged his followers not to trouble him with slander; but every word his enemies uttered was reported to him. If the rabbi expressed disapproval of the messenger of evil, then that person would immediately defect to the hostile camp. The rabbi could no longer pray and study in peace. He would plead with God: How long can I endure this Gehenna? Even condemned men don't suffer more than twelve months. . . .

Now that Rabbi Jonathan was about to take over the office in Yavrov, he could see that it was very much like Yampol. There was already an opposition in Yavrov, too. There, as well, was a rich man whose son-in-law coveted the rabbi's post. Besides, though the Yavrov rabbi made his living by selling candles and yeast, a few merchants had taken the forbidden merchandise into their stores, even after being threatened with excommunication.

The rabbi was barely fifty, but he was already gray. His tall figure was bent. The beard which once had been the color of straw had become white and sparse like that of an old man. His eyebrows were bushy, and below his eyes hung mossy, brownish-blue bags. He suffered from all sorts of ailments. He coughed, winter and summer. His body was mere skin and bone; he was so light that when he walked in the wind, his coattails almost lifted him into the air. His wife lamented that he didn't eat enough, drink enough, sleep enough. Racked by nightmares he would wake from sleep with a start. He dreamed of persecutions and pogroms, and because of these he often had to fast. The rabbi believed that he was being punished for his sins. Sometimes he would say harsh words against his tormentors; he would question the ways of God and even doubt His mercy. He would put on his prayer shawl and phylacteries and the thought would suddenly flash through his mind: Suppose there is no Creator? After such blasphemy, the rabbi would not allow himself to taste food all day, until the stars came out. "Woe is me, where shall I run?" the rabbi sighed, "I'm a lost man."

In the kitchen sat mother and daughter and each one kept her own counsel. Ziporah, the rabbi's wife, came from a wealthy family. As a girl she had been considered beautiful, but the years of poverty had ruined her looks. In her unbecoming old-fashioned bonnet and dress from the time of King Sobieski, she seemed stooped and emaciated; her face was wrinkled and had taken on the rustiness of an unripe pear. Her hands had grown large and full of veins like those of a man. But Ziporah found one consolation in all her misery: work. She washed, chopped wood, carried water from the well, scoured the floors. People in Yampol joked that she scrubbed the dishes so hard that she made holes in them. She darned the table cloths and sheets so thickly that not a thread remained of the original weave. She even repaired the rabbi's slippers. Of the six children to which she had given birth, only Yentl had survived.

Yentl took after her father: her hair was yellowish, she was tall, fair-skinned, freckled, flat-chested. Yentl was no less diligent than her mother, but her mother would not allow her to touch any housework. Yentl's husband Ozer, a yeshiva student, had died of consumption. Yentl now sewed, knitted, read books which she borrowed from peddlers. At first she had received many marriage offers, but she managed to discourage the matchmakers. She never stopped mourning her husband. As soon as someone began arranging a match for her, she suddenly began to suffer from cramps. People in Yampol spread the rumor that she had given Ozer an oath on his deathbed that she would never marry again. She didn't have a single girl friend in Yampol. Summers she would take a basket, a rope, and go off into the woods to pick berries and mushrooms. Such behavior was considered highly improper for a rabbi's daughter.

The move to Yavrov seemed a good prospect, but the rabbi's wife and Yentl worried more than they rejoiced. Neither mother nor daughter had a decent stitch of clothing or piece of jewelry. During the years at Yampol, they had become so destitute that the rabbi's wife wailed to her husband that she had forgotten to speak to people. She prayed at home, avoided escorting brides to the synagogue or taking part in a circumcision ceremony. But Yavrov was a different matter. There, ladies decked themselves out in fashionable dresses, costly furs, silken wigs, shoes with high heels and pointed toes. The young married women went to the synagogue in feathered hats. Each had a golden chain or brooch. How could one come to such a place in rags, with broken-down furniture and patched linen? Yentl simply refused to move. What would she do in Yavrov? She was neither a girl nor a married woman; at least in Yampol she had a mound of earth and a gravestone.

Rabbi Jonathan listened and shook his head. He had been sent a contract from Yavrov, but had not as yet received any advance. Was that the custom, or were they treating him this way because they considered him naive? He was ashamed to ask for money. It went against his nature to use the Torah for profit. The rabbi paced back and forth in his study; "Father in heaven, save me. 'I am come into deep waters, where the floods overflow me!' "

II

It was the rabbi's custom to pray in the synagogue rather than in the study house, for among the poor Jews he had fewer enemies. He prayed at sunrise with the first quorum. It was after Pentecost. At three-thirty the morning star rose. At four the sun was already shining. The rabbi loved the stillness of the morning when most of the townfolk were still sleeping behind closed shutters. He never tired of watching the sun come up: purple, golden, washed in the waters of the Great Sea. The rising sun always brought the same thought to his mind: unlike the sun, the son of man never renews himself; that is why he is doomed to death. Man has memories, regrets, resentments. They collect like dust, they block him up so he can't receive the light and life that descends from heaven. But God's creation is constantly renewing itself. If the sky becomes cloudy, it clears up again. The sun sets, but is reborn every morning. There is no blemish of the past on the moon or stars. The ceaselessness of nature's creation is never so obvious as at dawn. Dew is falling, the birds twitter, the river catches fire, the grass is moist and fresh. Happy is the man who can renew himself together with creation "when all the stars of the morning sing together."

This morning was like any other morning. The rabbi rose early in order to be first in the synagogue. He knocked on the oak door to warn the spirits who pray there of his arrival. Then he went into the dark antechamber. The synagogue was hundreds of years old, but it remained almost as it was on the day it was built. Everything exuded eternity: the gray walls, the high ceiling, the brass candelabras, the copper wash basin, the lectern with the four pillars, the carved high Ark with the tables of the Commandments and the two gilded lions. Streams of sun moats passed through the oval, stained-glass windows. Even though the ghosts who pray there usually leave it at cockcrow to make room for the living, there remained behind them a breathlessness and stillness. The rabbi began to pace up and down and to recite the "Lord of the Universe." The rabbi repeated the words, "And after all things shall have had an end, He alone shall reign," several times. The rabbi imagined the family of man perishing, houses crumbling, everything evil melting away and God's light again inhabiting all space. The shrinking of His power, the unholy forces, everything mean and filthy would cease. Time, accidents, passions, struggles would vanish, for these were but illusion and deception. The real truth was sheer goodness.

The rabbi said his prayers, contemplating the inner

meaning of the words. Little by little the worshipers began to arrive: the first quorum was of hardworking men who rise at the rooster's crow—Leibush the carter, Chaim Jonah the fish merchant, Avrom the saddlemaker, Shloime Meyer who grows orchards outside Yampol. They greeted the rabbi, then put on their phylacteries and prayer shawls. It occurred to the rabbi that his enemies in the town were either the rich or the lazy idlers. The poor and hardworking, all those who made an honest living, were on his side. "Why didn't it ever occur to me?" the rabbi wondered. "Why didn't I realize it?" He felt a sudden love for these Jews who deceived no one, who knew nothing of swindling and grabbing, but followed God's sentence: "From the sweat of thy brow thou shalt eat bread . . ." Now they thoughtfully wrapped the phylactery thongs around their arms, kissed the fringes of the prayer shawls, and assumed the heavy yoke of the Kingdom of Heaven. A morning tranquillity rested on their faces and beards. Their eyes shone with the mildness of those who have been burdened from childhood on.

It was Monday. After confession the scroll was taken from the Ark while the rabbi recited "Blessed be Thy Name." The opening of the Holy Ark always moved him. Here they stood, the pure scrolls, the Torah of Moses, silken-skirted and decorated with chains, crowns, silver plates—all similar, but each with its separate destiny. Some scrolls were read on weekdays, others on the Sabbath, still others were taken out only on the Day of the Rejoicing of the Law. There were also several worn books of the Law with faded letters and mouldering parchment. Every time the rabbi thought about these holy ruins, he felt a pain in his heart. He swayed back and forth, mumbling the Aramaic words, "Thou rulest over all . . . I, the servant of the Holy One, blessed be He, bow down before Him and the splendor of His law . . ." When the rabbi came to the words, "I place my reliance on no man," he stopped. The words stuck in his throat.

For the first time he realized that he was lying. No one relied on people more than he. The whole town gave him orders, he depended on everyone. Anyone could do him harm. Today it happened in Yampol, tomorrow it would happen in Yavrov. He, the rabbi, was a slave to every powerful man in the community. He must hope for gifts, for favors, and must always seek supporters. The rabbi began to examine the other worshipers. Not one of them needed allies. No one else worried about who might be for or against him. No one cared a penny for the tales of rumor-mongers. "Then what's the use of lying?" the rabbi thought. "Whom am I cheating? The Almighty?" The rabbi shuddered and covered his face in shame. His knees buckled. They had already put the scroll on the reading table, but the rabbi had not noticed this. Suddenly something inside the rabbi laughed. He lifted his hand as if swearing an oath. A long forgotten joy came over him, and he felt an unexpected determination. In one moment everything became clear to him . . .

They called the rabbi to the reading and he mounted the steps to the lectern. He placed a fringe on the parchment, touched it to his brow and kissed it. He recited the benediction in a loud voice. Then he listened to the reader. It was the chapter, "Send thou men . . ." It told of the spies who went to search the land of Canaan and who returned frightened by the sons of Anak. Cowardice had destroyed the generation of the desert, Rabbi Jonathan said to himself. And if they were not supposed to fear giants, why should I tremble before midgets? It's worse than cowardice; it's nothing but pride. I'm afraid to lose my rabbinical vestments. The co-worshipers gaped at the rabbi. He seemed transformed. A mysterious strength emanated from him. It's probably because he's moving to Yavrov, they explained to themselves.

After praying, the men began to disperse. Shloime Meyer took his prayer shawl, ready to leave. He was a small man, wide-boned, with a yellow beard, yellow eyes, yellow freckles. His canvas cap, his gabardine coat and his coarse boots were parched yellow by the sun. The rabbi made a sign to him. "Shloime Meyer, please wait a minute."

"Yes, Rabbi."

"How are the orchards?" the rabbi asked. "Is the harvest good?"

"Thank God. If there are no winds, then it will be good."

"Do you have men to do the picking?"

Shloime Meyer thought it over for a moment. "They're hard to get, but we manage."

"Why are they hard to get?"

"The work isn't easy. They have to stand on ladders all day and sleep in the barn at night."

"How much do you pay?"

"Not much."

"Enough to live on?"

"I feed them."

"Shloime Meyer, take me on. I'll pick fruit for you." Shloime Meyer's yellow eyes filled with laughter. "Why not?"

"I'm not joking."

Shloime Meyer's eyes saddened. "I don't know what the Rabbi means."

"I'm not a rabbi any more."

"What? Why is that?"

"If you have a minute, I'll tell you."

Shloime Meyer listened while the rabbi spoke. The quorum had left and the two men remained alone. They stood near the pulpit. Although the rabbi spoke quietly, each word echoed back as though someone unseen were repeating it after him.

"What do you say, Shloime Meyer?" the rabbi finally asked.

Shloime Meyer made a face as though he had swallowed something sour. He shook his head from side to side.

"What can I say? I'm afraid I'll be excommunicated."

"You must not fear anyone. 'Ye shall not fear the face of man.' That's the essence of Jewishness."

"What will your wife say?"

"She'll help me with my work."

"It's not for the likes of you."

"They that wait on the Lord shall renew their strength."

"Well, well . . ."

"You agree, then?"

"If the Rabbi wants . . ."

"Don't call me Rabbi anymore. From now on I'm your employee. And I'll be an honest worker."

"I'm not worried about that."

"When do you leave for the orchards?"

"In a couple of hours."

"Come by with your cart. I'll be waiting."

"Yes, Rabbi."

Shloime Meyer waited a while longer and then left. Near the door to the antechamber he glanced back. The rabbi stood alone, his hands clasped, his gaze wandering from wall to wall. He would make his departure from the synagogue where he had prayed for so many years. It was all so familiar: the twelve signs of the zodiac, the seven stars, the figures of the lion, the stag, the leopard and the eagle, the unutterable Name of God, painted in red. The gilded lions on the top of the Ark stared at the rabbi with their amber eyes while their curved tongues supported the tables with the Ten Commandments. It seemed to the rabbi that these sacred beasts were asking: Why did you wait so long? Couldn't you see from the start that one cannot serve God and man at the same time? Their open mouths seemed to laugh with benign ferocity. The rabbi clutched at his beard. "Well, it is never too late. Eternity is still before one . . ." He walked backwards until he reached the threshold. There is no mezuzah in a synagogue, but the rabbi touched the jamb with his index finger and then his lips.

In Yampol, in Yavrov, the strange news soon spread. Rabbi Jonathan, his wife, and Yentl his daughter, had gone off to pick fruit in Shloime Meyer's orchards.

Translated by Ruth Whitman

Short Friday

I

In the village of Lapschitz lived a tailor named Shmul-Leibele with his wife, Shoshe. Shmul-Leibele was half tailor, half furrier, and a complete pauper. He had never mastered his trade. When filling an order for a jacket or a gabardine, he inevitably made the garment either too short or too tight. The belt in the back would hang either too high or too low, the lapels never matched, the vent was off center. It was said that he had once sewn a pair of trousers with the fly off to one side. Shmul-Leibele could not count the wealthy citizens among his customers. Common people brought him their shabby garments to have patched and turned, and the peasants gave him their old pelts to reverse. As is usual with bunglers, he was also slow. He would dawdle over a garment for weeks at a time. Yet despite his shortcomings, it must be said that Shmul-Leibele was an honorable man. He used only strong thread and none of his seams ever gave. If one ordered a lining from Shmul-Leibele, even one of common sackcloth or cotton, he bought only the very best material, and thus lost most of his profit. Unlike other tailors who hoarded every last bit of remaining cloth, he returned all scraps to his customers.

Had it not been for his competent wife, Shmul-Leibele would certainly have starved to death. Shoshe helped him in whatever way she could. On Thursday she hired herself out to wealthy families to knead dough, and on summer days went off to the forest to gather berries and mushrooms, as well as pinecones and twigs for the stove. In winter she plucked down for brides' featherbeds. She was also a better tailor than her husband, and when he began to sigh, or dally and mumble to himself, an indication that he could no longer muddle through, she would take the chalk from his hand and show him how to continue. Shoshe had no children, but it was common knowledge that it wasn't she who was barren, but rather her husband who was sterile, since all of her sisters had borne children, while his only brother was likewise childless. The townswomen repeatedly urged Shoshe to divorce him, but she turned a deaf ear, for the couple loved one another with a great love.

Shmul-Leibele was small and clumsy. His hands and feet were too large for his body, and his forehead bulged on either side as is common in simpletons. His cheeks, red as apples, were bare of whiskers, and but a few hairs sprouted from his chin. He had scarcely any neck at all; his head sat upon his shoulders like a snowman's. When he walked, he scraped his shoes along the ground so that every step could be heard far away. He hummed continuously and there was always an amiable smile on his face. Both winter and summer he wore the same caftan and sheepskin cap with earlaps. Whenever there was any need for a messenger, it was always Shmul-Leibele who was pressed into service, and however far away he was sent, he always went willingly. The wags saddled him with a variety of nicknames and made him the butt of all sorts of pranks, but he never took offense. When others scolded his tormentors, he would merely observe: "What do I care? Let them have their fun. They're only children, after all. . . ."

Sometimes he would present one or another of the mischief makers with a piece of candy or a nut. This he did without any ulterior motive, but simply out of goodheartedness.

Shoshe towered over him by a head. In her younger days she had been considered a beauty, and in the households where she worked as a servant they spoke highly of her honesty and diligence. Many young men had vied for her hand, but she had selected Shmul-Leibele because he was quiet and because he never joined the other town boys who gathered on the Lublin road at noon Saturdays to flirt with the girls. His piety and retiring nature pleased her. Even as a girl Shoshe had taken pleasure in studying the Pentateuch, in nursing the infirm at the almshouse, in listening to the tales of the old women who sat before their houses darning stockings. She would fast on the last day of each month, the Minor Day of Atonement, and often attended the services at the women's synagogue. The other servant girls mocked her and thought her old-fashioned. Immediately following her wedding she shaved her head and fastened a kerchief firmly over her ears, never permitting a stray strand of hair from her matron's wig to show as did some of the other young women. The bath attendant praised her because she never frolicked at the ritual bath, but performed her ablutions according to the laws. She purchased only indisputably kosher meat, though it was a half-cent more per pound, and when she was in doubt about the dietary laws she sought out the rabbi's advice. More than once she had not hesitated to throw out all the food and even to smash the earthen crockery. In short, she was a capable, God-fearing woman, and more than one man envied Shmul-Leibele his jewel of a wife.

Above all of life's blessings the couple revered the Sabbath. Every Friday noon Shmul-Leibele would lay aside his tools and cease all work. He was always among the first at the ritual bath, and he immersed himself in the water four times for the four letters of the Holy Name. He also helped the beadle set the candles in the chandeliers and the candelabra. Shoshe scrimped throughout the week, but on the Sabbath she was lavish. Into the heated oven went cakes, cookies and the Sabbath loaf. In winter, she prepared puddings made of chicken's neck stuffed with dough and rendered fat. In summer she made puddings with rice or noodles, greased with chicken fat and sprinkled with sugar or cinnamon. The main dish consisted of potatoes and buckwheat, or pearl barley with beans, in the midst of which she never failed to set a marrowbone. To insure that the dish would be well cooked, she sealed the oven with loose dough. Shmul-Leibele treasured every mouthful, and at every Sabbath meal he would remark: "Ah, Shoshe love, it's food fit for a king! Nothing less than a taste of Paradise!" to which Shoshe replied, "Eat hearty. May it bring you good health."

Although Shmul-Leibele was a poor scholar, unable to memorize a chapter of the Mishnah, he was well versed in all the laws. He and his wife frequently studied *The Good Heart* in Yiddish. On half-holidays, holidays, and on each free day, he studied the Bible in Yiddish. He never missed a sermon, and though a pauper, he bought from peddlers all sorts of books of moral instructions and religious tales, which he then read together with his wife. He never wearied of reciting sacred phrases. As soon as he arose in the morning he washed his hands and began to mouth the preamble to the prayers. Then he would walk over to the study house and worship as one of the quorum. Every day he recited a few chapters of the Psalms, as well as those prayers which the less serious tended to skip over. From his father he had inherited a thick prayer book with wooden covers, which contained the rites and laws pertaining to each day of the year. Shmul-Leibele and his wife heeded each and every one of these. Often he would observe to his wife: "I shall surely end up in Gehenna, since there'll be no one on earth to say Kaddish over me." "Bite your tongue, Shmul-Leibele," she would counter, "For one, everything is possible under God. Secondly, you'll live until the Messiah comes. Thirdly, it's just possible that I will die before you and you will marry a young woman who'll bear you a dozen children." When Shoshe said this, Shmul-Leibele would shout: "God forbid! You must remain in good health. I'd rather rot in Gehenna!"

Although Shmul-Leibele and Shoshe relished every Sabbath, their greatest satisfaction came from the Sabbaths in wintertime. Since the day before the Sabbath evening was a short one, and since Shoshe was busy until late Thursday at her work, the couple usually stayed up all of Thursday night. Shoshe kneaded dough in the trough, covering it with cloth and a pillow so that it might ferment. She heated the oven with kindling-wood and dry twigs. The shutters in the room were kept closed, the door shut. The bed and bench-bed remained unmade, for at daybreak the couple would take a nap. As long as it was dark Shoshe prepared the Sabbath meal by the light of a candle. She plucked a chicken or a goose (if she had managed to come by one cheaply), soaked it, salted it and scraped the fat from it. She roasted a liver for Shmul-Leibele over the glowing coals and baked a small Sabbath loaf for him. Occasionally she would inscribe her name upon the loaf with letters of dough, and then Shmul-Leibele would tease her: "Shoshe, I am eating you up. Shoshe, I have already swallowed you." Shmul-Leibele loved warmth, and he would climb up on the oven and from there look down as his spouse cooked, baked, washed, rinsed, pounded and carved. The Sabbath loaf would turn out round and brown. Shoshe braided the loaf so swiftly that it seemed to dance before

Shmul-Leibele's eyes. She bustled about efficiently with spatulas, pokers, ladles and goosewing dusters, and at times even snatched up a live coal with her bare fingers. The pots perked and bubbled. Occasionally a drop of soup would spill and the hot tin would hiss and squeal. And all the while the cricket continued its chirping. Although Shmul-Leibele had finished his supper by this time, his appetite would be whetted afresh, and Shoshe would throw him a knish, a chicken gizzard, a cookie, a plum from the plum stew or a chunk of the pot-roast. At the same time she would chide him, saying that he was a glutton. When he attempted to defend himself she would cry: "Oh, the sin is upon me, I have allowed you to starve . . ."

At dawn they would both lie down in utter exhaustion. But because of their efforts Shoshe would not have to run herself ragged the following day, and she could make the benediction over the candles a quarter of an hour before sunset.

The Friday on which this story took place was the shortest Friday of the year. Outside, the snow had been falling all night and had blanketed the house up to the windows and barricaded the door. As usual, the couple had stayed up until morning, then had lain down to sleep. They had arisen later than usual, for they hadn't heard the rooster's crow, and since the windows were covered with snow and frost, the day seemed as dark as night. After whispering, "I thank Thee," Shmul-Leibele went outside with a broom and shovel to clear a path, after which he took a bucket and fetched water from the well. Then, as he had no pressing work, he decided to lay off for the whole day. He went to the study house for the morning prayers, and after breakfast wended his way to the bathhouse. Because of the cold outside, the patrons kept up an eternal plaint: "A bucket! A bucket!" and the bath attendant poured more and more water over the glowing stones so that the steam grew constantly denser. Shmul-Leibele located a scraggly willow-broom, mounted to the highest bench and whipped himself until his skin glowed red. From the bathhouse, he hurried over to the study house where the beadle had already swept and sprinkled the floor with sand. Shmul-Leibele set the candles and helped spread the tablecloths over the tables. Then he went home again and changed into his Sabbath clothes. His boots, resoled but a few days before, no longer let the wet through. Shoshe had done her washing for the week, and had given him a fresh shirt, underdrawers, a fringed garment, even a clean pair of stockings. She had already performed the benediction over the candles, and the spirit of the Sabbath emanated from every corner of the room. She was wearing her silk kerchief with the silver spangles, a yellow and gray dress, and shoes with gleaming, pointed tips. On her throat hung the chain that Shmul-Leibele's mother, peace be with her, had given her to celebrate the signing of the wedding contract. The marriage band sparkled on her index finger. The candlelight reflected in the window panes, and Shmul-Leibele fancied that there was a duplicate of this room outside and that another Shoshe was out there lighting the Sabbath candles. He yearned to tell his wife how full of grace she was, but there was no time for it, since it is specifically stated in the prayer book that it is fitting and proper to be amongst the first ten worshipers at the synagogue; as it so happened, going off to prayers he was the tenth man to arrive. After the congregation had intoned the Song of Songs, the cantor sang, "Give thanks," and "O come, let us exult." Shmul-Leibele prayed with fervor. The words were sweet upon his tongue, they seemed to fall from his lips with a life of their own, and he felt that they soared to the eastern wall, rose above the embroidered curtain of the Holy Ark, the gilded lions, and the tablets, and floated up to the ceiling with its painting of the twelve constellations. From there, the prayers surely ascended to the Throne of Glory.

II

The cantor chanted, "Come, my beloved," and Shmul-Leibele trumpeted along in accompaniment. Then came the prayers, and the men recited, "It is our duty to praise . . ." to which Shmul-Leibele added a "Lord of the Universe." Afterwards, he wished everyone a good Sabbath: the rabbi, the ritual slaughterer, the head of the community, the assistant rabbi, everyone present. The *cheder* lads shouted, "Good Sabbath, Smul-Leibele," while they mocked him with gestures and grimaces, but Shmul-Leibele answered them all with a smile, even occasionally pinched a boy's cheek affectionately. Then he was off for home. The snow was piled high so that one could barely make out the contours of the roofs, as if the entire settlement had been immersed in white. The sky, which had hung low and overcast all day, now grew clear. From among white clouds a full moon peered down, casting a day-like brilliance over the snow. In the west, the edge of a cloud still held the glint of sunset. The stars on this Friday seemed larger and sharper, and through some miracle Lapschitz seemed to have blended with the sky. Shmul-Leibele's hut, which was situated not far from the synagogue, now hung suspended in space, as it is written: "He suspendeth the earth on nothingness." Shmul-Leibele walked slowly since, according to law, one must not hurry when coming from a holy place. Yet he longed to be home. "Who knows?" he thought. "Perhaps Shoshe has become ill? Maybe she's gone to fetch water and, God forbid, has fallen into the well? Heaven save us, what a lot of troubles can befall a man."

On the threshold he stamped his feet to shake off the snow, then opened the door and saw Shoshe. The room made him think of Paradise. The oven had been freshly whitewashed, the candles in the brass candelabras cast a Sabbath glow. The aromas coming from the sealed oven blended with the scents of the Sabbath supper. Shoshe sat on the bench-bed apparently awaiting him, her cheeks shining with the freshness of a young girl's. Shmul-Leibele wished her a happy Sabbath and she in turn wished him a good year. He began to hum, "Peace upon ye ministering angels . . ." and after he had said his farewells to the invisible angels that accompany each Jew leaving the synagogue, he recited: "The worthy woman." How well he understood the meaning of these words, for he had read them often in Yiddish, and each time reflected anew on how aptly they seemed to fit Shoshe.

Shoshe was aware that these holy sentences were being said in her honor, and thought to herself, "Here am I, a simple woman, an orphan, and yet God has chosen to bless me with a devoted husband who praises me in the holy tongue."

Both of them had eaten sparingly during the day so that they would have an appetite for the Sabbath meal. Shmul-Leibele said the benediction over the raisin wine and gave Shoshe the cup so that she might drink. Afterwards, he rinsed his fingers from a tin dipper, then she washed hers, and they both dried their hands with a single towel, each at either end. Shmul-Leibele lifted the Sabbath loaf and cut it with the bread knife, a slice for himself and one for his wife.

He immediately informed her that the loaf was just right, and she countered: "Go on, you say that every Sabbath."

"But it happens to be the truth," he replied.

Although it was hard to obtain fish during the cold weather, Shoshe had purchased three-fourths of a pound of pike from the fishmonger. She had chopped it with onions, added an egg, salt and pepper, and cooked it with carrots and parsley. It took Shmul-Leibele's breath away, and after it he had to drink a tumbler of whiskey. When he began the table chants, Shoshe accompanied him quietly. Then came the chicken soup with noodles and tiny circles of fat which glowed on the surface like golden ducats. Between the soup and the main course, Shmul-Leibele again sang Sabbath hymns. Since goose was cheap at this time of year, Shoshe gave Shmul-Leibele an extra leg for good measure. After the dessert, Shmul-Leibele washed for the last time and made a benediction. When he came to the words: "Let us not be in need either of the gifts of flesh and blood nor of their loans," he rolled his eyes upward and brandished his fists. He never stopped praying that he be allowed to continue to earn his own livelihood and not, God forbid, become an object of charity.

After grace, he said yet another chapter of the Mishnah, and all sorts of other prayers which were found in his large prayer book. Then he sat down to read the weekly portion of the Pentateuch twice in Hebrew and once in Aramaic. He enunciated every word and took care to make no mistake in the difficult Aramaic paragraphs of the Onkelos. When he reached the last section, he began to yawn and tears gathered in his eyes. Utter exhaustion overcame him. He could barely keep his eyes open and between one passage and the next he dozed off for a second or two. When Shoshe noticed this, she made up the bench-bed for him and prepared her own featherbed with clean sheets. Shmul-Leibele barely managed to say the retiring prayers and began to undress. When he was already lying on his bench-bed he said: "A good Sabbath, my pious wife. I am very tired . . ." and turning to the wall, he promptly began to snore.

Shoshe sat a while longer gazing at the Sabbath candles which had already begun to smoke and flicker. Before getting into bed, she placed a pitcher of water and a basin at Shmul-Leibele's bedstead so that he would not rise the following morning without water to wash with. Then she, too, lay down and fell asleep.

They had slept an hour or two or possibly three—what does it matter, actually?—when suddenly Shoshe heard Shmul-Leibel's voice. He waked her and whispered her name. She opened one eye and asked, "What is it?"

"Are you clean?" he mumbled.

She thought for a moment and replied, "Yes."

He rose and came to her. Presently he was in bed with her. A desire for her flesh had roused him. His heart pounded rapidly, the blood coursed in his veins. He felt a pressure in his loins. His urge was to mate with her immediately, but he remembered the law which admonished a man not to copulate with a woman until he had first spoken affectionately to her, and he now began to speak of his love for her and how this mating could possibly result in a male-child.

"And a girl you wouldn't accept?" Shoshe chided him, and he replied, "Whatever God deigns to bestow would be welcome."

"I fear this privilege isn't mine anymore," she said with a sigh.

"Why not?" he demanded. "Our mother Sarah was far older than you."

"How can one compare oneself to Sarah? Far better you divorce me and marry another."

He interrupted her, stopping her mouth with his hand. "Were I sure that I could sire the twelve tribes of Israel with another, I still would not leave you. I cannot even imagine myself with another woman. You are the jewel of my crown."

"And what if I were to die?" she asked.

"God forbid! I would simply perish from sorrow. They would bury us both on the same day."

"Don't speak blasphemy. May you outlive my bones. You are a man. You would find somebody else. But what would I do without you?"

He wanted to answer her, but she sealed his lips with a kiss. He went to her then. He loved her body. Each time she gave herself to him, the wonder of it astonished him anew. How was it possible, he would think, that he, Shmul-Leibele, should have such a treasure all to himself? He knew the law, one dared not surrender to lust for pleasure. But somewhere in a sacred book he had read that it was permissible to kiss and embrace a wife to whom one had been wed according to the laws of Moses and Israel, and he now caressed her face, her throat and her breasts. She warned him that this was frivolity. He replied, "So I'll lie on the torture rack. The great saints also loved their wives." Nevertheless, he promised himself to attend the ritual bath the following morning, to intone psalms and to pledge a sum to charity. Since she loved him also and enjoyed his caresses, she let him do his will.

After he had satiated his desire, he wanted to return to his own bed, but a heavy sleepiness came over him. He felt a pain in his temples. Shoshe's head ached as well. She suddenly said, "I'm afraid something is burning in the oven. Maybe I should open the flue?"

"Go on, you're imagining it," he replied. "It'll become too cold in here."

And so complete was his weariness that he fell asleep, as did she.

That night Shmul-Leibele suffered an eerie dream. He imagined that he had passed away. The Burial-Society brethren came by, picked him up, lit candles by his head, opened the windows, intoned the prayer to justify God's ordainment. Afterwards, they washed him on the ablution board, carried him on a stretcher to the cemetery. There they buried him as the gravedigger said Kaddish over his body.

"That's odd," he thought, "I hear nothing of Shoshe lamenting or begging forgiveness. Is it possible that she would so quickly grow unfaithful? Or has she, God forbid, been overcome by grief?"

He wanted to call her name, but he was unable to. He tried to tear free of the grave, but his limbs were powerless. All of a sudden he awoke.

"What a horrible nightmare!" he thought. "I hope I come out of it all right."

At that moment Shoshe also awoke. When he related his dream to her, she did not speak for a while. Then she said, "Woe is me. I had the very same dream."

"Really? You too?" asked Shmul-Leibele, now frightened. "This I don't like."

He tried to sit up, but he could not. It was as if he had been shorn of all his strength. He looked towards the window to see if it were day already, but there was no window visible, nor any windowpane. Darkness loomed everywhere. He cocked his ears. Usually he would be able to hear the chirping of a cricket, the scurrying of a mouse, but this time only a dead silence prevailed. He wanted to reach out to Shoshe, but his hand seemed lifeless.

"Shoshe," he said quietly, "I've grown paralyzed."

"Woe is me, so have I," she said. "I cannot move a limb."

They lay there for a long while, silently, feeling their numbness. Then Shoshe spoke: "I fear that we are already in our graves for good."

"I'm afraid you're right," Shmul-Leibele replied in a voice that was not of the living.

"Pity me, when did it happen? How?" Shoshe asked. "After all, we went to sleep hale and hearty."

"We must have been asphyxiated by the fumes from the stove," Shmul-Leibele said.

"But I said I wanted to open the flue."

"Well, it's too late for that now."

"God have mercy upon us, what do we do now? We were still young people . . ."

"It's no use. Apparently it was fated."

"Why? We arranged a proper Sabbath. I prepared such a tasty meal. An entire chicken neck and tripe."

"We have no further need of food."

Shoshe did not immediately reply. She was trying to sense her own entrails. No, she felt no appetite. Not even for a chicken neck and tripe. She wanted to weep, but she could not.

"Shmul-Leibele, they've buried us already. It's all over."

"Yes, Shoshe, praised be the true Judge! We are in God's hands."

"Will you be able to recite the passage attributed to your name before the Angel Dumah?"

"Yes."

"It's good that we are lying side by side," she muttered.

"Yes, Shoshe," he said, recalling a verse: *Lovely and pleasant in their lives, and in their death they were not divided.*

"And what will become of our hut? You did not even leave a will."

"It will undoubtedly go to your sister."

Shoshe wished to ask something else, but she was ashamed. She was curious about the Sabbath meal. Had it been removed from the oven? Who had eaten it? But she felt that such a query would not be fitting of a corpse. She was no longer Shoshe the dough-kneader, but a pure, shrouded corpse with shards covering her eyes, a cowl over her head, and myrtle twigs between her fingers. The Angel Dumah would appear at any moment with his fiery staff, and she would have to be ready to give an account of herself.

Yes, the brief years of turmoil and temptation had come to an end. Shmul-Leibele and Shoshe had reached the true world. Man and wife grew silent. In the stillness they heard the flapping of wings, a quiet singing. An angel of God had come to guide Shmul-Leibele the tailor and his wife, Shoshe, into Paradise.

Translated by Joseph Singer
and Roger Klein

249 CALDWELL, ERSKINE: *Tobacco Road*
352 CAMUS, ALBERT: *The Fall & Exile and the Kingdom*
109 CAMUS, ALBERT: *The Plague*
349 CAMUS, ALBERT: *Notebooks 1935–1942*
353 CAPOTE, TRUMAN: *Selected Writings*
339 CAMUS, ALBERT: *Resistance, Rebellion and Death*
79 CARROLL, LEWIS: *Alice in Wonderland*, etc.
165 CASANOVA, JACQUES: *Memoirs of Casanova*
150 CELLINI, BENVENUTO: *Autobiography of Cellini*
174 CERVANTES: *Don Quixote*
161 CHAUCER: *The Canterbury Tales*
171 CHEKHOV, ANTON: *Best Plays*
50 CHEKHOV, ANTON: *Short Stories*
272 CICERO: *Basic Works*
279 COLERIDGE: *Selected Poetry and Prose*
251 COLETTE: *Six Novels*
235 COMMAGER, HENRY STEELE & NEVINS, ALLAN: *A Short History of the United States*
306 CONFUCIUS: *The Wisdom of Confucius*
186 CONRAD, JOSEPH: *Lord Jim*
275 CONRAD, JOSEPH: *Nostromo*
34 CONRAD, JOSEPH: *Victory*
105 COOPER, JAMES FENIMORE: *The Pathfinder*
194 CORNEILLE & RACINE: *Six Plays by Corneille and Racine*
130 CRANE, STEPHEN: *The Red Badge of Courage*
214 CUMMINGS, E. E.: *The Enormous Room*

236 DANA, RICHARD HENRY: *Two Years Before the Mast*
208 DANTE: *The Divine Comedy*
122 DEFOE, DANIEL: *Moll Flanders*
92 DEFOE, DANIEL: *Robinson Crusoe* and *A Journal of the Plague Year*
43 DESCARTES, RENÉ: *Philosophical Writings*
173 DEWEY, JOHN: *Human Nature and Conduct*
348 DEWEY, JOHN: *John Dewey on Education*
110 DICKENS, CHARLES: *David Copperfield*
204 DICKENS, CHARLES: *Pickwick Papers*
308 DICKENS, CHARLES: *Our Mutual Friend*
189 DICKENS, CHARLES: *A Tale of Two Cities*
25 DICKINSON, EMILY: *Selected Poems*
23 DINESEN, ISAK: *Out of Africa*
54 DINESEN, ISAK: *Seven Gothic Tales*
12 DONNE, JOHN: *Complete Poetry and Selected Prose*
205 DOS PASSOS, JOHN: *Three Soldiers*
293 DOSTOYEVSKY, FYODOR: *Best Short Stories*
151 DOSTOYEVSKY, FYODOR: *The Brothers Karamazov*
199 DOSTOYEVSKY, FYODOR: *Crime and Punishment*
55 DOSTOYEVSKY, FYODOR: *The Possessed*
5 DOUGLAS, NORMAN: *South Wind*
206 DOYLE, SIR ARTHUR CONAN: *The Adventure and Memoirs of Sherlock Holmes*
8 DREISER, THEODORE: *Sister Carrie*
69 DUMAS, ALEXANDRE: *Camille*
143 DUMAS, ALEXANDRE: *The Three Musketeers*
227 DU MAURIER, DAPHNE: *Rebecca*

338 Ellison, Ralph: *Invisible Man*
192 Emerson, Ralph Waldo: *The Journals*
91 Emerson, Ralph Waldo: *Essays and Other Writings*
331 Erasmus, Desiderius: *The Praise of Folly*
314 Euripides: *The Complete Greek Tragedies,* vol. v
315 Euripides: *The Complete Greek Tragedies,* vol. vi
316 Euripides: *The Complete Greek Tragedies,* vol. vii

271 Faulkner, William: *Absalom, Absalom!*
175 Faulkner, William: *Go Down, Moses*
351 Faulkner, William: *Intruder in the Dust*
88 Faulkner, William: *Light in August*
61 Faulkner, William: *Sanctuary* *[Dying*
187 Faulkner, William: *The Sound and the Fury* and *As I Lay*
324 Faulkner, William: *Selected Short Stories*
117 Fielding, Henry: *Joseph Andrews*
185 Fielding, Henry: *Tom Jones*
28 Flaubert, Gustave: *Madame Bovary*
102 Forester, C. S.: *The African Queen*
210 France, Anatole: *Penguin Island*
298 Frank, Anne: *Diary of a Young Girl*
39 Franklin, Benjamin: *Autobiography,* etc.
96 Freud, Sigmund: *The Interpretation of Dreams*

358 Genet, Jean: *Our Lady of the Flowers*
36 George, Henry: *Progress and Poverty*
327 Gide, André: *The Counterfeiters*
177 Goethe: *Faust*
40 Gogol, Nicholai: *Dead Souls* *[Writings*
291 Goldsmith, Oliver: *The Vicar of Wakefield and Other*
20 Graves, Robert: *I, Claudius*
286 Gunther, John: *Death Be Not Proud*

265 Hackett, Francis: *The Personal History of Henry the Eighth*
163 Haggard, H. Rider: *She* and *King Solomon's Mines*
320 Hamilton, Edith: *The Greek Way*
135 Hardy, Thomas: *Jude the Obscure*
17 Hardy, Thomas: *The Mayor of Casterbridge*
121 Hardy, Thomas: *The Return of the Native*
72 Hardy, Thomas: *Tess of the D'Urbervilles*
233 Hart & Kaufman: *Six Plays*
329 Hart, Moss: *Act One*
250 Harte, Bret: *Best Stories*
93 Hawthorne, Nathaniel: *The Scarlet Letter*
239 Hegel: *The Philosophy of Hegel*
223 Hellman, Lillian: *Six Plays*
26 Henry, O.: *Best Short Stories*
255 Herodotus: *The Persian Wars*
328 Hersey, John: *Hiroshima*
334 Hesse, Herman: *Steppenwolf*
166 Homer: *The Iliad*
167 Homer: *The Odyssey*
141 Horace: *Complete Works*
302 Howard, John Tasker: *World's Great Operas*
277 Howells, William Dean: *The Rise of Silas Lapham*

89 HUDSON, W. H.: *Green Mansions*
35 HUGO, VICTOR: *The Hunchback of Notre Dame*
340 HUME, DAVID: *Philosophy*
209 HUXLEY, ALDOUS: *Antic Hay*
48 HUXLEY, ALDOUS: *Brave New World*
180 HUXLEY, ALDOUS: *Point Counter Point*

305 IBSEN, HENRIK: *Six Plays*
307 IBSEN, HENRIK: *The Wild Duck and Other Plays*
240 IRVING, WASHINGTON: *Selected Writings*

16 JAMES, HENRY: *The Bostonians*
107 JAMES, HENRY: *The Portrait of a Lady*
169 JAMES, HENRY: *The Turn of the Screw*
269 JAMES, HENRY: *Washington Square*
244 JAMES, HENRY: *The Wings of the Dove*
114 JAMES, WILLIAM: *The Philosophy of William James*
70 JAMES, WILLIAM: *The Varieties of Religious Experience*
234 JEFFERSON, THOMAS: *The Life* and *Selected Writings*
355 JOHNSON, SAMUEL: *Johnson's Dictionary: A Modern Selection*
124 JOYCE, JAMES: *Dubliners*
300 JUNG, C. G.: *Basic Writings*

318 KAFKA, FRANZ: *The Trial*
283 KAFKA, FRANZ: *Selected Stories*
297 KANT: *Critique of Pure Reason*
266 KANT: *The Philosophy of Kant*
233 KAUFMAN & HART: *Six Plays*
273 KEATS: *Complete Poetry and Selected Prose*
303 KIERKEGAARD, SØREN: *A Kierkegaard Anthology*
99 KIPLING, RUDYARD: *Kim*
74 KOESTLER, ARTHUR: *Darkness at Noon*

262 LAOTSE: *The Wisdom of Laotse*
148 LAWRENCE, D. H.: *Lady Chatterley's Lover*
128 LAWRENCE, D. H.: *The Rainbow*
333 LAWRENCE, D. H.: *Sons and Lovers*
68 LAWRENCE, D. H.: *Women in Love*
252 LEWIS, SINCLAIR: *Dodsworth*
221 LEWIS, SINCLAIR: *Cass Timberlane*
325 LIVY: *A History of Rome*
56 LONGFELLOW, HENRY W.: *Poems*
77 LOUYS, PIERRE: *Aphrodite*
95 LUDWIG, EMIL: *Napoleon*

65 MACHIAVELLI: *The Prince* and *The Discourses*
321 MAILER, NORMAN: *The Naked and the Dead*
317 MALAMUD, BERNARD: *Two Novels*
33 MALRAUX, ANDRÉ: *Man's Fate*
309 MALTHUS, THOMAS ROBERT: *On Population*
360 MANN, THOMAS: *Confessions of Felix Krull*
182 MARQUAND, JOHN P.: *The Late George Apley*
202 MARX, KARL: *Capital and Other Writings*
14 MAUGHAM, W. SOMERSET: *Best Short Stories*
270 MAUGHAM, W. SOMERSET: *Cakes and Ale*

27 Maugham, W. Somerset: *The Moon and Sixpence*
176 Maugham, W. Somerset: *Of Human Bondage*
98 Maupassant, Guy de: *Best Short Stories*
46 Maurois, André: *Disraeli*
119 Melville, Herman: *Moby Dick*
253 Meredith, George: *The Egoist*
134 Meredith, George: *The Ordeal of Richard Feverel*
138 Merejkowski, Dmitri: *The Romance of Leonardo da Vinci*
296 Michener, James A.: *Selected Writings*
322 Mill, John Stuart: *Selections*
132 Milton, John: *Complete Poetry and Selected Prose*
78 Molière: *Eight Plays*
218 Montaigne: *Selected Essays*

343 Nash, Ogden: *Verses From 1929 On*
235 Nevins, Allan & Commager, Henry Steele: *A Short History of the United States*
113 Newman, Cardinal John H.: *Apologia Pro Vita Sua*
9 Nietzsche, Friedrich: *Thus Spake Zarathustra*
81 Nostradamus: *Oracles*

67 Odets, Clifford: *Six Plays*
42 O'Hara, John: *Appointment in Samarra*
211 O'Hara, John: *Selected Short Stories*
323 O'Hara, John: *Butterfield 8*
342 O'Neill, Eugene: *Ah, Wilderness! and Two Other Plays*
146 O'Neill, Eugene: *The Emperor Jones, Anna Christie* and *The Hairy Ape*
111 O'Neill, Eugene: *The Long Voyage Home: Seven Plays of [the Sea*

232 Palgrave, Francis (editor): *The Golden Treasury*
123 Parker, Dorothy: *Collected Short Stories*
237 Parker, Dorothy: *Collected Poetry*
267 Parkman, Francis: *The Oregon Trail*
164 Pascal, Blaise: *Penseés* and *The Provincial Letters*
86 Pater, Walter: *The Renaissance*
103 Pepys, Samuel: *Passages from the Diary*
247 Perelman, S. J.: *The Best of S. J. Perelman*
153 Plato: *The Republic*
181 Plato: *The Works of Plato*
82 Poe, Edgar Allan: *Selected Poetry and Prose*
196 Polo, Marco: *The Travels of Marco Polo*
257 Pope, Alexander: *Selected Works*
284 Porter, Katherine Anne: *Flowering Judas*
45 Porter, Katherine Anne: *Pale Horse, Pale Rider*
120 Proust, Marcel: *The Captive*
220 Proust, Marcel: *Cities of the Plain*
213 Proust, Marcel: *The Guermantes Way*
278 Proust, Marcel: *The Past Recaptured*
59 Proust, Marcel: *Swann's Way*
260 Proust, Marcel: *The Sweet Cheat Gone*
172 Proust, Marcel: *Within a Budding Grove*

194 Racine & Corneille: *Six Plays by Corneille and Racine*
62 Reade, Charles: *The Cloister and the Hearth*

215 Reed, John: *Ten Days That Shook the World*
140 Renan, Ernest: *The Life of Jesus*
336 Renault, Mary: *The Last of the Wine*
10 Richardson, Samuel: *Clarissa*
200 Rodgers & Hammerstein: *Six Plays*
154 Rostand, Edmond: *Cyrano de Bergerac*
243 Rousseau, Jean Jacques: *The Confessions*
53 Runyon, Damon: *Famous Stories*
137 Russell, Bertrand: *Selected Papers of Betrand Russell*

280 Saki: *Short Stories*
301 Salinger, J. D.: *Nine Stories*
90 Salinger, J. D.: *The Catcher in the Rye*
292 Santayana, George: *The Sense of Beauty*
335 Sartre, Jean-Paul: *The Age of Reason*
52 Schopenhauer: *The Philosophy of Schopenhauer*
281 Schulberg, Budd: *What Makes Sammy Run?*
2,3 Shakespeare, William: *Tragedies*—complete, 2 vols.
4,5 Shakespeare, William: *Comedies*—complete, 2 vols.
6 Shakespeare, William: *Histories* } complete, 2 vols.
7 Shakespeare, William: *Histories, Poems* }
19 Shaw, Bernard: *Four Plays*
294 Shaw, Bernard: *Saint Joan, Major Barbara,* and *Androcles and the Lion*
112 Shaw, Irwin: *The Young Lions*
319 Shaw, Irwin: *Selected Short Stories*
274 Shelley: *Selected Poetry and Prose*
159 Smollett, Tobias: *Humphry Clinker*
312 Sophocles I: *Complete Greek Tragedies,* vol. iii
313 Sophocles II: *Complete Greek Tragedies,* vol. iv
60 Spinoza: *The Philosophy of Spinoza*
332 Stein, Gertrude: *Selected Writings*
115 Steinbeck, John: *In Dubious Battle*
29 Steinbeck, John: *Of Mice and Men*
216 Steinbeck, John: *Tortilla Flat*
157 Stendhal: *The Red and the Black*
147 Sterne, Laurence: *Tristram Shandy*
254 Stewart, George R.: *Storm*
31 Stoker, Bram: *Dracula*
11 Stone, Irving: *Lust for Life*
261 Stowe, Harriet Beecher: *Uncle Tom's Cabin*
212 Strachey, Lytton: *Eminent Victorians*
351 Styron, William: *Lie Down in Darkness*
188 Suetonius: *Lives of the Twelve Caesars*
100 Swift, Jonathan: *Gulliver's Travels and Other Writings*
49 Symonds, John A.: *The Life of Michelangelo*

222 Tacitus: *Complete Works*
230 Tennyson: *Selected Poetry*
80 Thackeray, William: *Henry Esmond*
131 Thackeray, William: *Vanity Fair*
38 Thompson, Francis: *Complete Poems*
155 Thoreau, Henry David: *Walden and Other Writings*
58 Thucydides: *Complete Writings*
85 Thurber, James: *The Thurber Carnival*
37 Tolstoy, Leo: *Anna Karenina*—tr. revised

347 TOLSTOY, LEO: *Selected Essays*
354 TOLSTOY, LEO: *Short Novels*
346 TOLSTOY, LEO: *Short Stories*
361 TOLSTOY, LEO: *Short Stories,* VOL. II
41 TROLLOPE, ANTHONY: *Barchester Towers* and *The Warden*
21 TURGENEV, IVAN: *Fathers and Sons*
162 TWAIN, MARK: *A Connecticut Yankee in King Arthur's Court*

357 UPDIKE, JOHN: *The Poorhouse Fair* and *Rabbit, Run*

190 VASARI, GIORGIO: *Lives of the Most Eminent Painters, Sculptors and Architects*
63 VEBLEN, THORSTEIN: *The Theory of the Leisure Class*
156 VINCI, LEONARDO DA: *The Notebooks*
75 VIRGIL: *The Aeneid, Eclogues* and *Georgics*
47 VOLTAIRE: *Candide and Other Writings*

178 WALPOLE, HUGH: *Fortitude*
170 WARREN, ROBERT PENN: *All The King's Men*
219 WEBB, MARY: *Precious Bane*
225 WEIDMAN, JEROME: *I Can Get It for You Wholesale*
197 WELLS, H. G.: *Tono Bungay*
290 WELTY, EUDORA: *Selected Stories*
299 WHARTON, EDITH: *The Age of Innocence*
97 WHITMAN, WALT: *Leaves of Grass*
125 WILDE, OSCAR: *Dorian Gray* and *De Profundis*
83 WILDE, OSCAR: *The Plays of Oscar Wilde*
84 WILDE, OSCAR: *Poems* and *Fairy Tales*
126 WODEHOUSE, P. J.: *Selected Stories*
268 WORDSWORTH: *Selected Poetry*

44 YEATS, W. B. (editor): *Irish Fairy and Folk Tales*
179 YOUNG, G. F.: *The Medici*

207 ZIMMERN, ALFRED: *The Greek Commonwealth*
142 ZOLA, ÉMILE: *Nana*

MISCELLANEOUS

288 *An Anthology of Irish Literature*
330 *Anthology of Medieval Lyrics*
326 *The Apocrypha*
201 *The Arabian Nights' Entertainments*
87 *Best American Humorous Short Stories*
18 *Best Russian Short Stories*
129 *Best Spanish Stories*
Complete Greek Tragedies
310 VOL. I (Aeschylus I); 311 VOL. II (Aeschylus II); 312 VOL. III (Sophocles I); 313 VOL. IV (Sophocles II); 314 VOL. V (Euripides I); 315 VOL. VI (Euripides II)
359 *Complete Poems and Selected Letters of Michelangelo*
101 *A Comprehensive Anthology of American Poetry*
226 *The Consolation of Philosophy*
94 *Eight Famous Elizabethan Plays*
345 *Eight Spanish Plays of the Golden Age*
224 *Eighteenth-Century Plays*
73 *Famous Ghost Stories*
139 *The Federalist*
30 *Five Great Modern Irish Plays*
144 *Fourteen Great Detective Stories*
108 *Great German Short Novels and Stories*
168 *Great Modern Short Stories*
238 *Great Tales of the American West*
203 *The Greek Poets*
356 *Hellenistic Philosophy*
217 *The Latin Poets*
149 *The Making of Man: An Outline of Anthropology*
183 *Making of Society*
344 *Medieval Philosophy*
133 *Medieval Romances*
1 *The Modern Library Dictionary*
258 *New Voices in the American Theatre*
152 *Outline of Abnormal Psychology*
66 *Outline of Psychoanalysis*
287 *Restoration Plays*
337 *Roman Comedies*
158 *Seven Famous Greek Plays*
57 *The Short Bible*
276 *Six Modern American Plays*
38 *Six American Plays for Today*
118 *Stories of Modern Italy*
127 *Twentieth-Century American Poetry*—revised
341 *Twenty German Poets*

MODERN LIBRARY GIANTS

A series of sturdily bound and handsomely printed, full-sized library editions of books formerly available only in expensive sets. These volumes contain from 600 to 1,400 pages each.

THE MODERN LIBRARY GIANTS REPRESENT A SELECTION OF THE WORLD'S GREATEST BOOKS

G76 ANDERSEN & GRIMM: *Tales*
G74 AUGUSTINE, ST.: *The City of God*
G58 AUSTEN, JANE: *Complete Novels*
G70 BLAKE, WILLIAM & DONNE, JOHN: *Complete Poetry*
G2 BOSWELL, JAMES: *Life of Samuel Johnson*
G17 BROWNING, ROBERT: *Poems and Plays*
G14 BULFINCH: *Mythology* (ILLUSTRATED)
G35 BURY, J. B.: *A History of Greece*
G13 CARLYLE, THOMAS: *The French Revolution*
G28 CARROLL, LEWIS: *Complete Works*
G15 CERVANTES: *Don Quixote*
G33 COLLINS, WILKIE: *The Moonstone* and *The Woman in White*
G27 DARWIN, CHARLES: *Origin of Species* and *The Descent of Man*
G43 DEWEY, JOHN: *Intelligence in the Modern World: John Dewey's Philosophy*
G70 DONNE, JOHN & BLAKE, WILLIAM: *Complete Poetry*
G36 DOSTOYEVSKY, FYODOR: *The Brothers Karamazov*
G60 DOSTOYEVSKY, FYODOR: *The Idiot*
G51 ELIOT, GEORGE: *Best-Known Novels*
G41 FARRELL, JAMES T.: *Studs Lonigan*
G82 FAULKNER, WILLIAM: *The Faulkner Reader*
G39 FREUD, SIGMUND: *The Basic Writings*
G6, G7, G8 GIBBON, EDWARD: *The Decline and Fall of the Roman Empire* (COMPLETE IN THREE VOLUMES)
G25 GILBERT & SULLIVAN: *Complete Plays*
G76 GRIMM & ANDERSEN: *Tales*
G37 HAWTHORNE, NATHANIEL: *Compl. Novels & Selected Tales*
G78 HOLMES, OLIVER WENDELL: *The Mind and Faith of Justice Holmes*
G19 HOMER: *Complete Works*
G3 HUGO, VICTOR: *Les Miserables*
G18 IBSEN, HENRIK: *Eleven Plays*
G11 JAMES, HENRY: *Short Stories*
G52 JOYCE, JAMES: *Ulysses*
G4 KEATS & SHELLEY: *Complete Poems*
G24 LAMB, CHARLES: *The Complete Works and Letters*
G20 LINCOLN, ABRAHAM: *The Life and Writings of Abraham Lincoln*
G84 MANN, THOMAS: *Stories of Three Decades*
G26 MARX, KARL: *Capital*
G57 MELVILLE, HERMAN: *Selected Writings*
G38 MURASAKA, LADY: *The Tale of Genji*
G30 MYERS, GUSTAVUS: *History of the Great American Fortunes*
G34 NIETZSCHE, FRIEDRICH: *The Philosophy of Nietzsche*
G88 O'HARA, JOHN: *49 Stories*

G55 O'NEILL, EUGENE: *Nine Plays*
G68 PAINE, TOM: *Selected Work*
G86 PASTERNAK, BORIS: *Doctor Zhivago*
G5 PLUTARCH: *Lives* (The Dryden Translation)
G40 POE, EDGAR ALLAN: *Complete Tales and Poems*
G29 PRESCOTT, WILLIAM H.: *The Conquest of Mexico* and *The Conquest of Peru*
G62 PUSHKIN: *Poems, Prose and Plays*
G65 RABELAIS: *Complete Works*
G12 SCOTT, SIR WALTER: *The Most Popular Novels* (Quentin Durward, Ivanhoe & Kenilworth)
G4 SHELLEY & KEATS: *Complete Poems*
G32 SMITH, ADAM: *The Wealth of Nations*
G61 SPAETH, SIGMUND: *A Guide to Great Orchestral Music*
G92 SPENGLER, OSWALD: *The Decline of the West* (one volume)
G91 SPENSER, EDMUND: *Selected Poetry*
G75 STEVENSON, ROBERT LOUIS: *Selected Writings*
G53 SUE, EUGENE: *The Wandering Jew*
G42 TENNYSON: *The Poems and Plays*
G23 TOLSTOY, LEO: *Anna Karenina*—tr. revised
G1 TOLSTOY, LEO: *War and Peace*
G49 TWAIN, MARK: *Tom Sawyer* and *Huckleberry Finn*
G50 WHITMAN, WALT: *Leaves of Grass*
G83 WILSON, EDMUND: *The Shock of Recognition*

MISCELLANEOUS

G77 *An Anthology of Famous American Stories*
G54 *An Anthology of Famous British Stories*
G67 *Anthology of Famous English and American Poetry*
G81 *An Encyclopedia of Modern American Humor*
G47 *The English Philosophers from Bacon to Mill*
G16 *The European Philosophers from Descartes to Nietzsche*
G31 *Famous Science-Fiction Stories*
G85 *Great Ages and Ideas of the Jewish People*
G89 *Great Classical Myths*
G72 *Great Tales of Terror and the Supernatural*
G9 *Great Voices of the Reformation*
G87 *Medieval Epics*
G48 *The Metropolitan Opera Guide*
G46 *A New Anthology of Modern Poetry*
G69 *One Hundred and One Years' Entertainment*
G93 *Parodies: An Anthology from Chaucer to Beerbohm and After*
G90 *Philosophies of Art and Beauty: Readings in Aesthetics from Plato to Heidegger*
G21 *Sixteen Famous American Plays*
G63 *Sixteen Famous British Plays*
G71 *Sixteen Famous European Plays*
G45 *Stoic and Epicurean Philosophers*
G22 *Thirty Famous One-Act Plays*
G66 *Three Famous Murder Novels, Before the Fact,* FRANCIS ILES, *Trent's Last Case,* E. C. BENTLEY, *The House of the Arrow,* A. E. W. MASON
G10 *Twelve Famous Plays of the Restoration and Eighteenth Century* (1660–1820): Dryden, Congreve, Wycherley, Gay, etc.
G56 *The Wisdom of Catholicism*
G59 *The Wisdom of China and India*
G79 *The Wisdom of Israel*